The Secret of Stardust

The Tethered World Chronicles

Book one—The Tethered World
Book two—The Flaming Sword
Book three—The Genesis Tree
Book four—The Secret of Stardust

The Secret of Stardust

Book Four of
The Tethered World Chronicles

Heather L.L. FitzGerald

The Secret of Stardust
Published by Mountain Brook Ink
White Salmon, WA U.S.A.

The website addresses recommended throughout this book are offered as a resource. These websites are not intended in any way to be or imply an endorsement on the part of Mountain Brook Ink, nor do we vouch for their content.

This story is a work of fiction. All characters and events are the product of the author's imagination. Any resemblance to any person, living or dead, is coincidental.

ESV Study Bible. (2008). Crossway Books

ISBN 9781953957-40-5

The Team: Miralee Ferrell, Jenny Gibbs, Tim Pietz, Kristen Johnson, Cindy Jackson

Cover Design: Indie Cover Design, Lynnette Bonner, Designer

Mountain Brook Ink is an inspirational publisher offering fiction you can believe in.

Map illustration by William Love@sevenoversix.com

Printed in the U.S.A. 2023

Dedication

This one is for the Littles.
Mimi loves you!

*"Then I heard every creature in heaven and on earth and **under the earth**...saying: To him who sits on the throne and to the Lamb be praise and honor and glory and power, for ever and ever!" Revelation 5:13*

*This book is a work of fiction from a Christian worldview. The ideas are strictly from the author's imagination, portraying what might be possible in places that Scripture is silent.

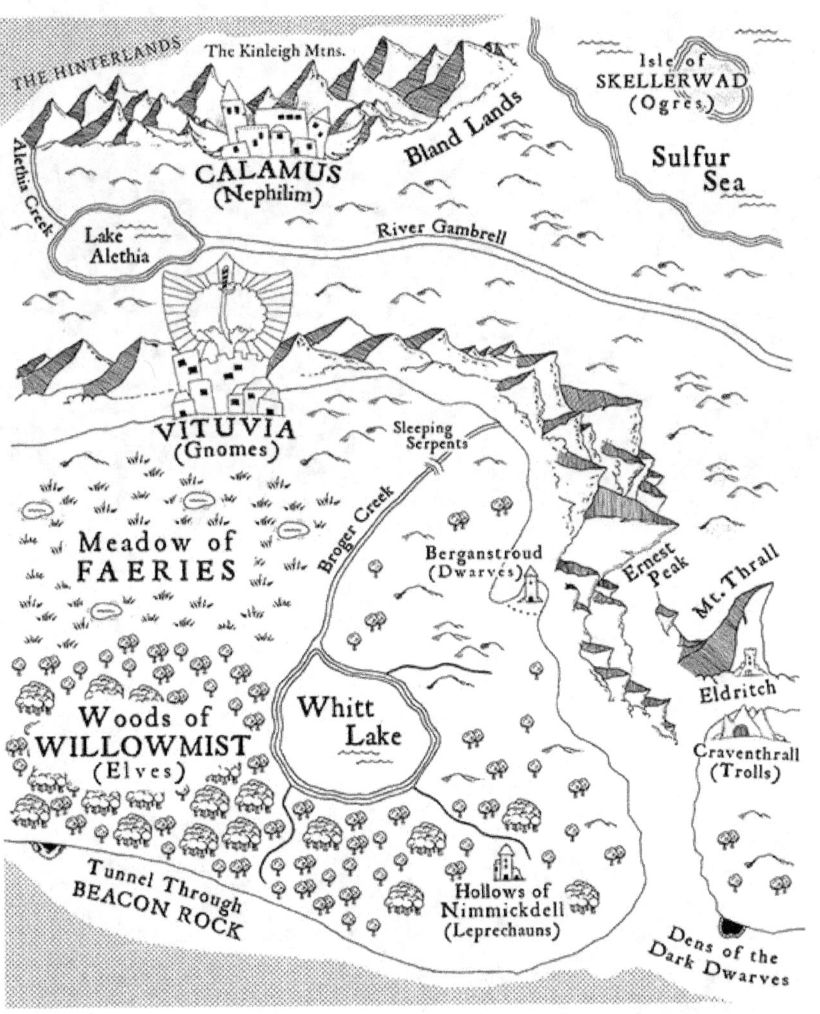

THE HINTERLANDS
The Kinleigh Mtns.
Isle of
SKELLERWAD
(Ogres)
Bland Lands
Sulfur
Sea
CALAMUS
(Nephilim)
Alethia Creek
Lake
Alethia
River Gambrell
VITUVIA
(Gnomes)
Sleeping
Serpents
Ernest
Peak
Mt. Thrall
Meadow of
FAERIES
Broger Creek
Berganstroud
(Dwarves)
Eldritch
Whitt
Lake
Craventhrall
(Trolls)
Woods of
WILLOWMIST
(Elves)
Tunnel Through
BEACON ROCK
Hollows of
Nimmickdell
(Leprechauns)
Dens of the
Dark Dwarves

CHAPTER ONE

Alex

THE ACRID ODOR OF INCENSE WAS a harbinger of death. Alex detested the smell only slightly less than he hated the inevitable loss to follow. From the shadow of the king's bedchamber, he watched the muted display of prayers and tears being offered on King Aviel's behalf. The emotions and the rituals somehow clung to the pungent incense, awakening memories of other deaths and the swell of prayers on his lips and tears in his eyes—neither providing satisfaction. Alex now shunned such insufficient endeavors. They belonged to the hopeful hearts of others.

Though King Aviel was also Alex's grandfather, Alex could only mourn the man distantly—as much from the king's coolness toward Alex as from the callousness born of repeated loss in Alex's own life. If anything, Alex ached more for his father, Xander, and how hard he was taking the impending death of his own father.

Summoned to the bedchamber hours earlier, Alex had claimed a shadowy corner, beyond the reach of candlelight and out of the ceaseless ebb and flow of bodies. The king's spacious quarters had become a press of attendants jostling alongside Gouldor the physician, Father Juniper the presbyter, Grandmama Lucia, and Alex's parents. From his self-imposed exile on a tufted chair, Alex dozed and woke and waited for something—anything—to happen.

It was his unfortunate, princely duty to be present as his grandfather passed from life as the ruler of Calamus, Realm of the Nephilim, in the order of Tuatha Dé, into life everlasting. Death was taking its sweet time. Today marked day three of "any moment now."

"Earth to Alex."

Alex blinked at his sister Ellynn, perched on the arm of

his chair. "You say something?" He took in her unruly curls and wrinkled linen pajamas. Frosty blue eyes—a hand-me-down from grandfather, to father, to little sister—glistened with sadness.

"Can I sit with you?" Her voice sounded strong, despite the tear that slipped down her olive-skinned cheek.

Alex scooted his seven-foot-plus frame, knowing this would never work if the two of them weren't narrow as a couple of sword blades. Thirteen-year-old Ellynn wiggled into the space beside him, and he pulled her snugly beneath his arm.

"How's my Elly-belly?" He kissed the top of her messy sepia curls.

She nudged his ribcage with her shoulder. "Don't. I'm in no mood, and I'm too old for that nickname."

"Sorry." He gave her a squeeze, biting back another tease that she considered thirteen to be *old*. "Seriously, you okay? Not sure how much you remember from when Aunt Jules passed away. It's all pretty depressing."

She released a tired, protracted sigh. "Is it ever. I keep thinking I ought to run out of tears...but every time Grandfather has one of those fever-dreams, it scares me so bad I start crying all over again." She grasped the tiny book charm that glinted on a silver chain around her neck. It had once been their mother's necklace, and Ellynn unconsciously reached for it whenever she was distressed.

"Didn't Mom tell you to leave when the dreams come?" Alex whispered. He could hear the familiar *zip-zip-zip* of Ellynn toggling the charm on its chain.

Her shoulder shrugged against his ribs. "I did, several times. But, I mean, I watched a couple of episodes before Mom decided to send me out of the room. It's not like I can *unsee* it now. Anyway, everyone's too wrapped up in calming him down to notice that I'm still here."

Alex's gaze drifted to their parents, Sadie and Xander. The two shared a bearskin-covered bench on one side of the king's extravagantly carved four-poster bed. The stone fireplace at their backs was alternately stoked and doused, depending on Aviel's temperature. They sat close, fingers entwined, their contrasting skin tones reminding Alex of the black and white keys of a piano. His father's silvery wings looked limp, drooping off the bench and onto the floor like flower petals in need of water. His mother, so petite in comparison, leaned into him, as if she hadn't the strength to support herself. Though the two were a study in opposites, Alex noticed matching purple crescents beneath their eyes and the way one would yawn right after the other.

His mother was not especially close to King Aviel—or hadn't been, anyway, until her father-in-law's health took a downward plunge. She was a Topsider—as in, from the *topside* of the earth. He was a Nephilim descendant from one of the pockets *within* the earth, where his realm of Calamus resided. Thus, the king had never fully embraced Sadie as his daughter-in-law.

Frequent fever-dreams had worn down his stoic exterior, however, and he began to appreciate her presence once his condition required round-the-clock care. Didn't hurt that Sadie's mother was a former nurse who had taught her daughter much about keeping a patient comfortable.

Now, Sadie stayed close for Xander's sake, as there appeared little comfort to offer Aviel in his final hours. The king's health may have taken a turn for the worse this past year, but Alex noticed it also had the positive side effect of strengthening his parents' relationship. The crisis had helped their separate orbits to be drawn back together, becoming more centered.

His mother slipped an arm around his father, whose head bowed with grief, and Alex sensed her inner strength. She might be an average-sized Topsider, but her fortitude rivaled her husband's hulking Nephilim body. Alex watched as she pulled the curtain of slender, lengthy braids away from Xander's face, smoothing them across his winged back before kissing his cheek. Reflecting on the many relatives his mother had lost in her lifetime made Alex ashamed to feel as hard-bitten as he did toward the few losses he had experienced in his seventeen years.

"Death is as much a part of life as birth," Sadie had explained when he had cried inconsolably at the passing of Aunt Jules. He remembered wondering why—if what his mother said was true—everyone rejoiced about birth but cried over death.

Ellynn sniffled, and Alex rubbed her arm reassuringly. "This is the hardest part. Watching and waiting. Feels endless."

"Grandfather looks so frail and unlike himself since they shaved his dreadlocks. I don't want to remember him like this. Though I mostly hate it when the dreams take over," she said with a shudder, "I hate how he wakes up calling for Uncle Magnum, too. He gets so upset! I'm afraid his heart is going to give out on him."

Alex felt a flash of anger at the mention of Uncle Magnum. If that impulsive imbecile hadn't run off a few months earlier, it would have made the king's final days much more peaceable. Instead, the king dreamt of his son in fever-dreams, and hallucinated conversations with him when he awoke.

Not that things were wrinkle-free when Magnum was about. As Xander's much younger half-brother, Magnum was jealous of Xander's heir-to-the-throne status. Unable to do anything about it, he turned his impotent anger on Alex, making it his mission to belittle everything about his nephew, despite Alex being only two years younger. Aided and excused by Magnum's equally awful mother—King Aviel's second wife, Lucia—Uncle Magnum had few fans among royals or servants alike. Alex was thrilled to be Magnum-free the past months, but he could understand his grandfather's wish to have his entire family together in his final hours.

"Where's Grandmama Lucia?" Ellynn asked. "I haven't seen her since last night at dinner. Shouldn't she be here?"

"She stayed by his side most of the night." Alex stretched his legs straight and crossed them at the ankles. "Gouldor told her to get some sleep. He'd wake her when, y'know, things moved to the final stages."

"I feel like Grandfather has been in his 'final stage' all week," she said.

Alex grunted. "Same here."

A soft tap on the door to the outer chamber signaled Merrik, the king's bodyguard, to step aside. Two female servants entered the room—a Dwarf carrying a tray laden with food and a Nephilim toting a basket of medication.

The Dwarf headed for Sadie and Xander, offering them tea and scones. The other wound her way to Gouldor the physician.

If Alex had to choose his least favorite person in Calamus, it would be a toss-up between Uncle Magnum and Gouldor. He found the stooped-over, bug-eyed Nephilim physician intensely disturbing. Sallow skin clung to his emaciated frame, giving him a cadaverous quality. He also had the longest, scrawniest beard that Alex had ever seen—more of a dangling grey cobweb than whiskers. Thick wool robes transformed him into a medieval monk, and he always smelled of herbs and incense—which only added to the reasons Alex disliked both Gouldor and, of course, incense.

"*Noooo.* I will not condone that. I've had enough of your underhanded—*ugh!*" King Aviel's body arched beneath his quilt. Candlelight glinted from his shaved scalp, glossed with perspiration.

The Dwarf jumped at the outburst, spilling hot tea, mid-pour. It sloshed across Sadie's hand and the bearskin bench.

Sadie yelped in pain, even as Xander leapt up and thrust his flailing father against the bed.

"Release me, Magnum. When will you learn?" King Aviel ground his teeth as he tried to press Xander away. "*Noooo.*"

Alex hugged his sister to himself, her head buried into his chest.

"Wake up, Father! It's okay. You're okay," Xander commanded, his hands clamped against her father's shoulders. "C'mon, now. Wake up. You'll see. Everything's fine."

Standing on the opposite side of the bed, Gouldor attempted to apply a cool cloth to Aviel's forehead. He only succeeded in chasing the king's writhing dome across the pillow. Sadie stepped away, holding her hand as the Dwarf buzzed about, apologizing over the din. The stout woman grabbed a clean cloth from Gouldor's supply, dunking it into the basin of water, and returning to Sadie's side.

A booming "No!" from King Aviel instantly quieted the room. The shock of it made Xander relax his grip enough for the king to sit up, shoving Xander so that he stumbled to avoid landing on his father's legs.

The king's eyes were round and bright as frosty marbles, which somehow emphasized the roundness of his head sans dreadlocks. "Murrg," he wheezed, almost as if he were breathing more than speaking. "*Muhhrky.*"

"What was that?" Xander asked, tossing a quick glance at Sadie.

She gave him a small, uncomprehending shrug.

The king looked at the contingent of faces who stared back at him. With deep, gasping breaths he blinked, seeming to come to his senses. A filmy froth encircled his full lips. Sweat-slicked mahogany skin pressed dark, damp patches against his white linen dressing gown. Salt and pepper feathers jutted at odd angles from the wings at his back, after days spent thrashing about in bed.

"Xahhn-der." King Aviel rasped his son's name between labored breaths. He patted the bed, indicating that Xander should sit. "I have...something to say."

Xander sat on the edge of the bed, near his father's legs. The king immediately seized his son's collar and awkwardly hauled him across the bed so they were inches apart. No one moved or spoke.

"Listen to me, Xander." King Aviel gave Xander a rough shake. "Listen!" He pulled his son so close they were cheek to cheek, and his voice dropped to an inaudible whisper.

Xander pushed away enough to search his father's face, then gave a subtle nod.

"I want you to promise me, Xander. In the presence of these witnesses," King Aviel said, his voice authoritative despite the weak volume.

Xander swallowed. Nodded.

"You must promise to watch over Magnum. When you become king, deal gently with him. He—he is troubled. I know he is—but he looks up to you. More—" he gave an asthmatic wheeze, then cleared his throat—"He looks to you more as an uncle than a brother. Deep down, I know he respects you. But he needs help. Give him that."

A fit of coughing interrupted his diatribe. Hard, gut-deep coughs that made Ellynn renew her efforts to burrow into her Alex's embrace.

Despite the spasmodic outburst the king kept his grip on Xander, who could only look away to avoid the hacking spray expelled from his father's throat.

"*Promise* me," Aviel said at last. He paused to take a few more breaths. "Promise me, Xander. Magnum needs mercy."

Xander dipped his head. "Yes. I promise, Father."

King Aviel leaned closer still, the tip of his nose touching Xander's. He lowered his voice. "We *all* need mercy."

The king released his son with a sorrowful cry and flopped back onto the bed, as limp and spent as an empty cornhusk.

Xander reflexively stood, eyes wide, fingers knotted. Alex watched his father's broad chest heaving greedy lungsful of air while everyone else, it seemed, held their breath.

But no. Xander wasn't catching his breath. He was crying.

His mountainous body began to quake. He slipped to his knees, burying his face against his father's shoulder. "*Nooo,*" he cried, his voice a weak but eerie echo of the king's. In an instant, Sadie was behind him, arms stretched across his wings, fingers grasping the span of his shoulders.

Alex had rarely seen his father cry. The sight elicited an unsettling concoction of pain and embarrassment. He didn't recognize this broken version of his stalwart father. It left him unsettled, despite its brevity. Within a couple of minutes, Xander was on his feet, nodding at the attendants to perform their duties.

Gouldor grasped the king's wrist and felt for a pulse, then shook his head. He reached his fingertips to close King Aviel's eyes for the final time. Looking defeated, he busied himself arranging the king's body beneath the bedsheet.

Father Juniper stepped forward. From the folds of his embroidered cassock, the portly minister produced an amber bottle of oil. He uncorked it, tilting its contents onto blunt fingertips before dabbing it onto King Aviel's forehead, chin, and earlobes. The woody, astringent scent of myrrh commingled with the smoky incense, making Alex long for fresh air and to be anywhere else.

With soft spatters, like rain, onlookers began to cry. Even the king's unflappable bodyguard, Merrik, pressed a fist to his mouth and closed his eyes. Courtiers and servants alike placed their palms together in prayer, foreheads pressed against thumbs, heads lowered.

"Is he...dead?" asked Ellynn, still muffled against Alex's chest.

"Yes." Alex looked about, feeling strangely disconnected— more shocked than anything. One moment, the room had resonated with his grandfather's hoarse baritone. Swollen with words that were pointed, impassioned, and pleading. The next, all that life and energy had been sucked dry, like some hungry, invisible beast had consumed it—and consumed the king.

Behind Merrik, the bedroom door opened. The bodyguard stepped aside as Lucia, the king's wife, swept in with her lady-in-waiting in tow. She stopped in the middle of the room and stared at her prone, inanimate husband.

Alex heard her exclaim. Saw her hands fly to her face even as her wings unfurled, their turquoise-dyed feathers slipping from beneath her black cloak.

"What is this?" Her voice accused more than questioned. She strode toward the foot of the bed and let out a strangled gasp. With quavering hands she reached for King Aviel's blanketed feet, bowing her head, then taking a knee.

Alex felt time suspend, as if everyone except Lucia had turned to stone. His step-grandmother's trembling shoulders the only movement in the room. Not even the candlelight dared to flicker, or so it appeared.

She stood, breaking the chilling enchantment. Her fingers swiped her damp cheeks, then curled into fists.

Alex could see her profile from where he sat. Her pale skin waxed paler still, despite the golden candlelight. Her almond-shaped eyes narrowed to slits, and she inhaled sharply, nostrils flared. Lucia had always reminded Alex of a sleek, amber-eyed cat, and now he half-expected her to hiss and bare a set of fangs.

"I told you people to send for me! I was *supposed* to be by his side in the end." She pivoted in a slow circle, so slow that the curtain of glossy black hair around her shoulders didn't shift. Her fiery gaze scorched any individual bold enough to look her in the eye. "How dare you let this happen without me. I...am...the *queen*. I...gave...an *order*." She continued her penetrating pirouette until she faced the physician. Her long, pointy-nailed finger jabbed in Gouldor's direction. "*You* are dismissed."

Gouldor blinked his bug-eyes while his mouth mimed a fish-out-of-water. "What? Your Majesty, please! It happened so quickly. So unexpectedly. There was no time—"

"I'll hear none of your excuses," Lucia hissed. "Leave." She pointed to the door.

"But—"

"*Leave.*" Her finger shook as she continued to point.

"Fine! Fine." Gouldor lifted his hands in surrender, then grasped his robe and made a beeline for the door, scrawny beard trailing like a weak wisp of smoke.

Lucia strode to where Xander stood, arms folded across his chest, watching her outburst. The queen tossed Sadie a sidelong glance of disdain. Sadie stared back, unmoved. Xander and Lucia stood eye-to-eye—both approaching seven feet tall—the tension between them taut as a bowstring.

As was her haughty habit, Lucia raised her chin and looked down her arrow-straight nose at him. "Are you happy, Xander? Pleased with yourself?"

Xander's heavy jaw flexed, clearly chomping back words. He shook his head with tight little jerks, setting his long braids shifting like restless, black snakes.

"Well?"

"My father just died. *Suddenly*, I might add. Why would I be pleased?"

Ellynn slipped from the chair. "I can't see," she whispered, moving to an empty space a few yards away.

Alex followed, placing an arm around her shoulders to keep her at a safe distance from any potential fireworks.

"Because you succeeded in keeping me from him." She placed that same pointy-nailed finger on his chest. "You had your father *all* to yourself, which is how you like it. You and your greedy little family all alone with daddy-dearest. You ran Magnum off months ago, which no doubt made that—that wingless, blighted son of yours"—she gestured in Alex's general direction without looking at him—"as happy as a meat maggot. And now, in Aviel's final hours, you were able to keep us apart as well."

"Look, Lucia." Xander knocked her wrist away. He paused, huffing loudly as if he didn't trust himself to speak. "I've been *very* considerate of your feelings in all of this. I've tried to be sensitive to your needs, giving you space. Offering relief when you've been up all night. Keeping you updated. You have no right to barge in here vomiting accusations at people. No right to dismiss Gouldor. No right to look at my wife like you did, and no right to stoop to calling Alex insulting names— let alone speak to *me* like this. However, I will *choose* to overlook your indiscretion, considering the circumstances."

She opened her mouth to reply, but Xander cut in. "I won't deign to comment on your *ridiculous* allegation concerning your uncontrollable offspring. I had nothing to do with Magnum running away from home like some spoiled, overgrown child."

Lucia tensed, arms like pistons, long neck rigid and unyielding.

Ellynn looked at her brother, suppressing a grin. He gave a subtle shake of his head, discouraging the triumph he saw on her face. His own face felt hot from Lucia's lowbrow comment about his lack of wings and his "blight"—the large, brownish birthmark that encircled his right eye.

"I have no right?" Lucia gave a mocking laugh. "I am queen, which gives me *every* right. End of story."

Xander offered a sardonic smile. "Indeed, this is the end of *your* story." He took a step closer. "The end of *your* quasi-reign. *I* am heir to the throne. As of five minutes ago, you are naught but the dowager queen."

"A dowager whose husband entrusted her with his final wishes." She matched his smile in insincerity. "Aviel asked *me* to oversee certain, particular affairs of his house. There are things—impactful, important plans—to which only *I* have been privy. Plans set in motion which you know nothing about."

"Don't be ridiculous."

"Me, ridiculous?" Lucia asked, fingertips pressed to her throat in mock indignation. "I would never make light of such weighty matters. Your father—*my* late husband—made some decisions the past few months. Decisions he asked me to carry out when his illness progressed to the point that he was unable to do so himself." She swept a hand toward King Aviel's prone body. "Case in point."

"I'm fully versed on the business of the realm, Lucia." Xander shifted away, his anger thinly veiled. "We've had a plethora of meetings, both alone and with his advisors. I'm also aware of the transfer of power. I became king the moment Father..." He trailed off and tilted his head at the still form. "The moment he left us for good. He has never mentioned special plans, nor did he ask me to grant you any favors."

"I'll let you and the palace gossips here in on a secret." Lucia stepped closer, an imperious sneer lending a chill to her words. "King Aviel signed a royal edict granting me power to enforce his will—and I'm *not* referring to his last will and testament. And, yes, I do, in fact, have this in writing and set with his seal. The king has some delicate business that requires *my* attention. Business that secures a fitting legacy to his name and a future for me, of which you know nothing." Her iciness melted a bit, she took a half step back and her voice was subdued when she added, "Really, Xander, what your father has set in motion, what I need to see through...it's a good thing. A *noble* thing. It's all I have left of Aviel's and my future."

Xander only stared, skepticism etched in his frown.

Lucia clasped her hands together, her fierceness in full retreat. "Look, I didn't intend to bring this up the moment Aviel...passed. I was only shocked that his death happened without me. That hurts. I—I was lashing out, using something Aviel and I had that excluded you. This wasn't the ideal time to bring it up."

"I see." Xander nodded. "Well, we're all exhausted, which isn't conducive to patience or good judgment. We must give ourselves time to grieve and, if possible, to rest. We will discuss this tomorrow, however—I assure you.”

Lucia bristled again. “Very well.”

She turned to leave, and the room seemed to collectively exhale into murmurs and movement.

Ellynn broke away from Alex and flew to their mother, arms encircling Sadie’s waist. Lucia neared Alex on her way to the door. She paused and placed her hand on his arm in a comforting way.

He looked into her unblinking cat-eyes and found nothing but contempt in their smoldering caramel depths.

“I’m sorry for your loss,” she said, clearly for the benefit of anyone within earshot. Neither her tone nor her smile girded her words with sincerity. She leaned close and lowered her voice, squeezing his arm so that her nails made as much of a point as her words. “You have caused me much pain in your short, miserable life. Prepare for payback.”

Alex stiffened, taking full advantage of the three inches he had on her. With a forceful tug, he pulled free of her grasp. “Nice to know you’ve spent the last eight years plotting your revenge, Grandmama. Didn’t know my childhood mistakes still factored into your schemes. Big of you.”

At this, Lucia flushed, but her glacial glare remained fixed. “No, no. Not a scheme, Brady Alexander. Not a scheme. A *wedding*.”

Wedding? Was she planning to wed, before King Aviel’s body grew cold? This seemed unconscionable, even for her.

“*Your* wedding, specifically.” The corners of her mouth curled into a self-satisfied smirk. “Allow me to be the first to congratulate you. Your grandfather and I have arranged for you to be married.”

CHAPTER TWO

Alex

ALEX FELT AS COLD AND IMPASSIVE as the stone wall at his back. Sitting on the expansive window sill in his bedroom, he attempted to disconnect from the fuss and formality of a day spent mourning the king of Calamus. The royal family had become the churning eye of a hurricane whose arms of grief encompassed dozens of dignitaries, hundreds of lamenting denizens, and curious onlookers.

Many Gnomes from the realm of Vituvia were present, part of the entourage traveling with Alex's Uncle Brock and Aunt Sophie—High King and King's Advisor, respectively—along with his Topsider grandparents, who split time between Vituvia and Calamus. Quite a contingency of Dwarves came as well, making the two-day journey from Berganstroud. Several were close friends of the royals, a number of whom held important posts in Calamus. Unfortunately, there wasn't time to send word to Alex's topside family before the funeral—not that Alex wished for any further reason to politely socialize. He had nearly scaled the palace walls to exchange the crowd and commotion for the solace of his room.

Beyond his window opening, vineyards stitched neat rows between the back pasture and the foothills of the Kinleigh mountain range. The soaring crystal skydome above had dimmed to its dusktime hue of burnt honey, casting the far-flung, craggy peaks into violet relief.

With eyelids shuttered, Alex saw none of the familiar scene below. Instead he bobbed his head to an alternative band, piping unrealistic ideas into his earbuds. Their lyrics promised that speeding down the highway in a convertible was the tonic to any problem. A breezy, summer day with the top down and volume up, the simple solution to life's complexities.

A bittersweet message. Alex knew he had plenty of

complexities, but his station in life left him lacking both a motorized vehicle and a license to drive it—let alone a convertible. A paved road didn't exist in Calamus—let alone endless miles of highway. He lived in a land with an appalling lack of breezes or sunshine. The golden geode skydome might be a suitable substitute for daylight, but sweeping blue skies and cottony clouds were treats as fanciful as ice cream and airplanes in this world beneath the world.

In his palm, Alex cradled an antiquated smartphone. It had been his mother's back in the day. Though it was completely incompatible—nearly unrecognizable—with current topside tech, he loved having a selection of music at his fingertips, even if every song was older than he was.

Wasn't as if he needed to call or text anyone. Among the list of missing marvels, he also lived in a land without electricity, cell towers, or Wi-Fi. Technology newer than the 19th century didn't exist until Sadie's Uncle Brent transported a generator to Calamus—along with a small supply of gasoline that he replenished with each visit. This allowed the family the convenience of a few topside necessities such as charging the old smartphone. Arguably more of a luxury, but it was originally his mother's habit—one gifted to Alex on his twelfth birthday.

He treasured this rectangular dinosaur with its cracked screen more than any of his other things. It made him feel like an actual Topsider—and he *longed* to be just that. To live topside and be a person of no consequence. Not the grandson of the king. Not the namesake of a legend. And *definitely* not a prince expected to marry at the whim of his step-grandmother.

Nope. Sitting here with his earbuds and phone, he was merely another seven-foot-two guy.

Since Alex had been old enough to understand the concept of moving, he had plotted to relocate to the land of breezes and sunshine and convertible automobiles. Yearly jaunts with his mother's topside family left him yearning to go back permanently, although he couldn't simply relocate and hope for a job and home to fall out of that brilliant blue sky.

But this year Alex had turned seventeen—recognized as an adult in Calamus—and he had concrete plans at last. Despite the delay from King Aviel's decline and death, Alex felt certain he could still pull everything together in time to head topside within a month. Though he would meet resistance from his family, they ultimately couldn't prevent him from going, now that he was an adult.

There was the pesky matter of his being heir to the throne, but that was a far-future event that should not dictate his near-future objective, right? The nonsense about marriage that Grandmama Lucia had flung at him was not worth taking seriously. He'd mentioned it to his parents, who assured him that the subject of marriage had never come up with the king before he passed. "We spoke of everything from affairs of state to what type of flowers he preferred at his funeral," his father had said. Queen Lucia was also queen of theatrics, so Alex chose to shut out the memory of her menacing words and prodding fingernails.

Since the funeral prep, royal protocol, and bureaucratic blah-blah-blah had droned on, occupying every nook and cranny of the past seventy-two hours, there had not been time to ponder topside freedoms or arranged marriages.

Though he hadn't lingered before the open casket, the image of his grandfather's sunken cheeks and deep-set eyes presented themselves now, despite the music surging through Alex's earbuds. And, oh, the wig! His grandfather's awful wig caused many a mourner to cringe. Created from Aviel's shorn dreadlocks, it had been woven into a parody of his hairstyle. Looking at his grandfather lying in state was like looking at a caricature of the king rather than the man himself.

Not real. Or maybe *surreal*. One of those words that meant it felt like life was playing on a topside movie screen, disconnected. The parts everyone played didn't fit, weren't quite recognizable, not even his own.

Things had felt this way for the past month, Alex realized. He had barely gotten to enjoy his Feast of Ascension—the big bash signifying his stride into adulthood at seventeen. Alex had used the celebration to make an important announcement. An announcement that he'd been rehearsing for months.

His first act of independence was to ask for—no, *demand*—a name change.

Born Brady Alexander Aviel Tuatha Dé, he had been named after his mother's heroic late brother Brady, followed by the names of his father and grandfather, along with the royal Gaelic designation of *Tuatha Dé*—literally: the people of God, per royal tradition. The first Nephilim rulers of ancient Ireland were the Tuatha Dé Danann, meaning "people of the Goddess Danu, but the pagan name and his name continued to be honored in this way among the God-fearing families.

During his Feast of Ascension, Brady had made the scandalous pronouncement that he wished to be called by his middle name, Alexander. Shedding his deceased uncle's moniker felt like a symbolic way to also shed the expectations everyone placed on him to live up to his late uncle's stellar, sacrificial, superhero character. An awe-inspiring trifecta that Alex always fell short of achieving. He'd overheard as much on many occasions, not to mention his own condemning voice when he looked in the mirror.

As expected, the partygoers had been aghast at his blasphemy. Why wouldn't *Brady* want to use his uncle's near-sacred name?

Alex's planned speech was cut short when King Aviel fainted, leaving the feast on a stretcher. The partygoers insinuated that Brady—or, *ahem*, "Alexander"—may have been the cause of the king's condition. They left the gathering in clusters of scowls and dubious glances.

So much for celebratory milestones.

Alex should've been strutting about the palace as a freshly minted man with a new name, enjoying leftover birthday cake. Instead, it had been a four-week endurance test for both his grandfather and the family as they kept a bedside vigil. And now that the funeral was over, plans for Xander's coronation would commence.

Beyond these plot twists, Grandmama Lucia's insidious threat to Alex churned up dark memories and an uneasy portend. He knew the unforgiving woman disdained him, but could she be that vindictive? Thankfully, she'd virtually ignored him after the night of King Aviel's death.

Since then, Lucia had behaved like the perfectly sorrowful widow she probably was not. No doubt she recognized that her usual temper tantrums would serve only to complicate the series of rites and mourning, rather than bring it all to a swift conclusion. Whatever her motivation, at least the family didn't have to deal with her drama on top of all the other demands and emotions.

Her cattiness would emerge soon enough, Alex knew. He groaned, pressing the heels of his hands against his eyelids. Hadn't he escaped to his room to distract from the craziness of the past few days? The music wasn't doing its job.

A touch on Alex's arm startled him. He turned to find his mother at his side, eyes red-rimmed and tired, mouth pressed into a grim line—an all-too familiar sight these days.

Popping out his earbuds he said, "Sorry. Didn't hear you knock."

She shrugged. "The door was open a crack, so I peeked in."

"What's up?" He swung his legs off the window ledge.

His mother still wore her funeral attire. Her full-skirted charcoal and silver dress sporting a chalky ring of dust along the bottom, while her shoulder-length brunette hair retained the impression from where her veiled hat had perched.

Alex hoped there wasn't some forgotten function he had to dress up for again. He'd experienced a small thrill when he finally shed his royal raiment for basketball shorts and a muscle shirt.

Sadie's eyes crinkled in concern, tiny crow's feet beginning to map their journey upon her face. Her focus shifted about the room.

"Mom?" Alex felt a scratch of frustration. What now?

"Brady, I—"

"It's *Alex*, Mom."

She gave her head a little shake, her gaze flitting to his as if waking from a stupor. "Sorry. It's a seventeen-year habit."

He nodded, knowing it wasn't the best time to show irritation.

"Can we sit?" She nodded toward the tufted wingback chairs flanking the fireplace.

Alex followed her over, kicking an inside-out pair of jeans to the side while avoiding his mother's reproving eye. Despite all the worker-bees in the castle, his mom insisted on Alex and Ellynn keeping their own quarters tidy. Though Alex wasn't great at staying on top of his clutter in calmer times, the past few days had brought out his inner slob. A mound of clothes at the foot of his bed looked like it could provide shelter for small woodland creatures.

But his mother seemed oblivious, lost in thought. She arranged her full skirt and took a seat, dwarfed by the Nephilim-sized chair. Alex noticed she gripped a rolled-up piece of paper in her left hand, the palm of which was still wrapped in gauze from the burning tea sloshed by the Dwarf.

Not just paper, he realized, but a scroll. He spied an emerald wax seal between her fingers.

She followed his gaze and shifted the small cylinder between her thumb and forefinger, twisting it back and forth.

"How are you doing, Br—Alex?"

He cocked an assessing eyebrow from her face to the scroll and back. "I'm going to guess that you're not actually here to check on my wellbeing. Where's that from?" Since Calamus's official seal was deep purple, he knew the scroll must've come from elsewhere.

Her gaze ran across his features, as if looking for an answer to her question. "No, really. I want to check in. Things have been plowing ahead and there's been little time to reflect. I'm...I'm glad you were able to unwind for a bit here in your room."

The last thing he wanted was to talk about his feelings. "I'm fine. Ready for all of the pomp and ceremony to be over, that's all."

She nodded, but the set of her mouth revealed she wasn't convinced. "I'm sorry you've been rather lost in the mayhem of your grandfather's sickness. What a way to bring in your Ascension, right? You should be—"

"*Mom*," Alex cut in. "I said I'm okay. Can we please leave it at that?"

Sadie swallowed and gave a curt nod. "Very well." She glanced at the scroll, then back to Alex. "I'm sure I don't need to remind you about Grandmama Lucia's mysterious claims the night King Aviel passed."

Aaand here it is. Grandmama's plot exposed.

"Last year—-that is, when your grandfather grasped his terminal condition—he spoke to your grandmother about what lies ahead for Calamus. He..." She trailed off and looked at the ash-strewn fireplace as if the rest of her thoughts might be crouching inside the charred compartment.

Alex leaned his forearms on his knees and tried not to look impatient.

"They—they made some decisions together," Mom said without looking at him. "About her future. About you."

Alex frowned. "Me? Why me? They barely acknowledge my existence. Grandfather doesn't even like me," he added, realizing too late that he was speaking about his grandfather in present tense.

"That's not true." She shook her head. "They... He—"

"Fine. I can pretend. You were saying..." Alex knew he was treading on thin ice, speaking so curtly.

His mother gave him an exasperated huff. "Fine," she echoed, leveling her gaze on him. "Have it your way. Your grandfather, assuming his time was short, was thinking about the long-term future of the realm. Obviously, you're to be king one day. Until then, your grandfather understood there might be a challenge to Xander or," she gestured at him, "yourself. From Uncle Magnum."

"So, what are you saying? Magnum is going to, like, *off* Dad and me and proclaim himself king?"

Her eyebrows shot up. "That's a bit blunt. Although it's not out of the realm of possibility. Even Lucia, much to my surprise, agrees that Magnum is unpredictable and may not have the best interest of the realm at heart."

Big of her—and very suspicious. Alex had never gotten the impression that his grandmother had more than her own best interests in her sights.

"What does this have to do with me?" He pointed at the scroll. "Or that?" *Please, please, please don't let it have anything to do with marriage.*

Mom pinched the bridge of her nose and squeezed her eyes shut. Alex could see stress rising like mercury, and he wondered how it had fallen on his mother to be the bearer of this mysterious message.

"Your dad wanted to have this conversation with you," she said, as if reading his thoughts. "But there are still a few dignitaries bending his ear, and time is of the essence in this matter."

"O-*kay*." Alex drew the word out, annoyance seeping into his tone. "Still not clear on what, in fact, *is* the matter."

"Well, *Alex*, it's complicated. Even though, we, uh. That is, your father and I...we happen to agree with your grandfather in this instance." She fiddled with the scroll and kept her eyes averted.

Alex's pulse gave a warning spike. "Say it." He made a swiping motion with his hand. "Like ripping off a bandage."

His mother nodded. "All right. Here goes." She took a deep breath and leaned forward, her gaze tired but intentional. "Before King Aviel died, he and Grandmama Lucia did, in fact, arrange for you to be married. Wedding plans have been set in motion."

CHAPTER THREE

Alex

"I'M AN OVERGROWN CHILD—OR so Grandfather was fond of saying—and now he expects me to *marry*? Surely this is some sick joke." Alex gaped at his mother, waiting for the punchline. Despite the vindictive heads-up from his grandmother, Alex still felt the sadistic slap of the announcement.

His mom's complexion looked as grey as the fireplace ashes. "It's—it's actually the best way to ensure that you're next in line for the throne. If something happened to your father, God forbid, your ridiculous uncle would have grounds to challenge you since—since you're both second-born sons. Unless..." She dropped her gaze as well as her voice. "Unless you marry and produce an heir."

"Mother. Do you *hear* yourself?" Alex gripped the armrests to keep from pulling his hair in frustration. "I'm seventeen—"

"Officially an adult." She held up her hand as if to halt his line of reasoning.

"Yeah. An adult who was *officially* a kid only a month ago. I definitely don't want a kid of my own anytime soon. Let alone 'produce an heir.'" Alex air-quoted between wild, uncomprehending gestures. Were they really having this conversation? "You and Dad married for love, but now I have to marry because my deceased grandfather and his spiteful wife say so? No. No way. I've never wanted to be king. I'm—I *shouldn't* even be the next in line, as you so helpfully pointed out. How would my offspring change anything?" Alex looked away, feeling his blotchy birthmark flush.

"You *are* next in line. Regardless of"—she gave a half-hearted swipe with her hand—"what happened when you were born. Mere minutes separated you from your twin brother. You were the firstborn *living* son. That's what matters. You are the one Calamus needs after your father's reign. Xander is King Aviel's firstborn, and it is the natural and historical progression for *his* descendants to rule."

"What if I don't want that responsibility now? Or maybe ever? Magnum can have it, for all I care. Or Ellynn. Why not Ellynn?"

"Don't say that." Her dark eyes flashed. "Magnum would ruin Calamus. His own mother knows that, which is why she helped your grandfather set this union up by contacting her uncle, King Odhran. As far as your sister goes, there's an old, rather misogynistic law stating that females only rule in the absence of male heirs—that goes for sisters as well as widows. It's the very reason Lucia's Uncle Odhran was installed as king when her father died in the Siege of Brihndle Castle. She hadn't yet married and begun a family, which meant Odhran was crowned King of Éire House. It was he, in fact, who arranged Lucia's marriage to your grandfather."

"Sounds like the law is backward and needs to be changed. Doesn't Dad have the power to alter dumb things like that, now that he's king? Plus, aren't you suspicious of Grandmama Lucia's intentions?"

His mother ignored his questions. "Alex, the fact is you have a responsibility to both the throne and to Calamus itself. Don't you care about the condition of your country? Besides, you haven't met the young lady. Have an open mind! Her name is Larkin. Isn't that pretty?"

"I don't care about her name and I don't care if she's beautiful or as ugly as a potato. I'm not looking for an instant, sight-unseen relationship—let alone *marriage*." His eyes widened as he suddenly comprehended the *real* agenda. "*Ohhh*. I get it. If some foreign princess agrees to marry *me* sight unseen, there's no chance of my getting rejected for this monstrosity on my face." He pointed emphatically at his right eye, indicating his darkly stained birthmark. "I might've guessed that grandfather could be so heartless, but not you, Mom. That's a low blow."

"No!" His mother dropped the scroll and sprang from her chair, kneeling before him. "No, Brady."

"It's *Alex*."

"Sorry. Alex. Absolutely not. Never." She grasped his forearms and blinked brown eyes at him. "That did *not* occur to me. I don't see your birthmark, son. I've told you as much. If anything, I think it gives you a bit of...mysterious charm."

Alex leaned back, pulling from her grasp. "Oh, please. That's such a—a motherly thing to say. Fine. Forget it. Maybe you didn't mean to keep my flawed face a secret. But your total obliviousness to how this thing affects *me* is nearly as bad. What will this girl say when she meets a Nephilim with a giant birthmark and no wings?" He shook his head in frustration.

"Not all Nephilim have wings."

"Yeah, if they're commoners. But, whatever." He waved the subject away. "There's no good scenario here. No matter how it plays out, I'm absolutely not interested. Period."

"Preserving your father's line is the *best* scenario." Mom gathered her skirt as she fumbled to her feet.

"No. It's not! Not if I don't want to be king. Magnum is the one who likes to be the center of attention and to order people around. I only want to live a normal life."

She leveled him with her gaze. "No! A thousand times *no*. He would be a tyrant. Besides, Xander is the rightful heir, which means his heir—you—should naturally follow. Not some—some spawn of your grandfather's midlife crisis." Sadie's forehead creased, pulled tight to match the frown on her lips.

"Spawn?" Alex barked a laugh. "I guess that's a nicer word than I had in mind. But marriage? How can *that* be the answer? Besides, Dad's got years to rule before we need to have this discussion. By then, maybe I'll have fallen in love and, uh, *produced an heir*." The implication made him blush again, sparking a fresh round of resentment at the heat that flushed his birthmark.

His mother's face stilled at this, inscrutable as stone. She stared past Alex and swallowed.

"Mom?" Alex stood. "What is it?"

She fixed her tear-filled gaze on a point above his head. "It's...it's your father. He didn't want me to tell you. Not yet. You see, there's a—a good reason he supports your getting married soon."

"What do you mean?" Alex stepped forward and grabbed his mother's shoulders, forcing her to look at him. "What's wrong?"

She blinked, releasing a fat, wet tear. "He...he has had fever-dreams for the past several months. Whatever killed your grandfather seems to have infected your father too. Unless a cure can be found, he may not rule for long."

CHAPTER FOUR

Alex

"MOM. OH, MOM!" HE REACHED TO hug her, but her hands flew up between them, the bandage gaping to reveal tender, red skin.

"No. I can't." Eyes squeezed shut, she shook her head. Tears plunged down her spray of freckles. "I really can't let myself entertain the possibilities right now." She sniffed and took a deep breath, looking up with bloodshot eyes and a pink-tipped nose. "There's too much to do. And I have to stay positive for your father's sake."

Alex nodded, processing these revelations. Why had he been such a jerk? "Mom...I'm so sorry. I—"

"Please. Forget it. Let's move forward as best we can." She smoothed her hair and tugged at her stiff bodice. "I've asked Prilla, the Vituvian Healer, to come at once. In the meantime, I have to constantly shoo that vulture Gouldor away. The quack couldn't help a snake recover from biting its own tongue, let alone help King Aviel. After all that charlatan put you through a few years ago, you'd think Aviel would've seen the man's ineptitude and dismissed him."

Alex gave her a wry grin. "You'd think."

He never understood what use his grandfather had for the gnarly, snarly old hunchback. Gouldor gave everyone in the palace a case of the full-blown creeps. But none more than Alex. The old quack made ongoing efforts to befriend him, thanks to their unfortunate shared physical trait—both were wingless Nephilim.

An absence of wings was a rarity among royals, which generally made it easy to distinguish royals from commoners. The odd citizen born with wingbuds would be culled out, schooled within the palace, and given a special opportunity to join the Nephilim army or work in the royal household. History even recorded a few love stories between nobles who had fallen in love with winged commoners who came to work in the palace.

This shared, regrettable attribute only added to Alex's vexation over his own flightlessness. Would he end up hunched and decrepit like the physician? Maybe wings provided a counterbalance to gravity as one's tall, spindly body grew weak and feeble.

The worst part of winglessness, for Alex, was that he did, indeed, have wingbuds on his shoulder blades. By puberty, Gouldor had diagnosed Alex as having "false wingbuds," a term for a rare genetic joke that left Alex with undersized bumps the size of walnuts rather than lemons on his upper back. Which meant no hope of joining the ranks of the flying Nephilim warriors of the Tuatha Dé line of royals.

Somehow his topside mother's DNA in combination with his Nephilim father—and his "dash of extraordinary" DNA—resulted in an inordinately tall yet flightless Alex, birthmark and all. Yet his little sister had recently complained about tenderness in *her* wingbuds. It seemed that Ellynn was emerging the clear winner of the family's genetic jackpot, though Alex inwardly worried about the agony she would endure.

He still recalled watching his friends Josiah and Finnegan go through the painful plumage process. The full-blown metamorphosis was rough. At the time—seeing them writhe and sweat and scream for the weeks it took the wings to expand and burst from their confines—Alex had thanked the Maker he was spared such torture.

Those false-buds had been a frequent topic of discussion between his father and grandfather, however. Though Prince Xander accepted the difference in his son's body, King Aviel had ordered Gouldor to examine and "treat" Alex, thinking to encourage the buds to develop. After Alex's thirteenth birthday, he had been subjected to herbal poultices, mud baths, bitter teas, and painful probings with needles.

When a month of creative torture yielded nothing except scabs and bruises, Sadie begged Xander to call off Gouldor and his half-baked treatments. In the past, she had allowed the old man to occasionally treat her family's illnesses, but after this fiasco, she refused to let the healer touch her or her children again.

Alex paced between the fireplace and bed as his mother

looked on from swollen, weary eyes. The news that his father had been suffering with fever dreams was indeed problematic. Hopefully Prilla would have some antidote to this bizarre disorder. But how could a rushed, arranged marriage be part of the solution? Alex didn't want to disappoint his parents—though he seemed to have a flare for doing so—however, this was *his* life. Not theirs. *His* future. Not theirs. There must be a way to help the family that didn't involve wedding and bedding a total stranger.

"When will Uncle Brent return for a visit? I bet he could help," Alex asked, stopping himself mid-stride to grasp the fingers of his mother's non-bandaged hand.

She shrugged, giving his fingers a half-hearted squeeze. "Not for a while. When he left after your Feast of Ascension, he said he'd see us in autumn. I begged your father to speak to Brent at the time, but he refused. The dreams were rare. He merely excused each incident as a nightmare. The frequency has increased this past month, though. Likely thanks to the stress of your grandfather growing worse."

"Then let me fetch him. Surely Uncle Brent will know what to do." His great uncle was a pharmacist-turned-botanist. He still lived topside but made regular visits to the Tethered World, bearing the gift of topside luxuries unavailable in Calamus.

Mom gave a slow, exhausted shake of her head. "Let's allow Prilla to treat him before we go to those lengths. Besides, I won't let you travel topside alone."

Alex crossed his arms and glanced away from his mother's stare. She had no clue of the many excursions he and his friends had taken topside while "camping" in the nearby Kinleigh mountains. The gang of friends often summoned the Meadow Faeries to whisk them topside for a few stolen hours.

Granted, they usually headed to a certain secluded stone family farmhouse on the sparsely populated *Inis Chléire*—that is, Cape Clear Island—in Ireland, but there had been a few daring jaunts to places near his family's former home in Orchards, Washington. They never stayed long or ventured far for fear of getting caught. Still, a few hours under the stars was always a worthwhile risk. The friends held a collective fascination with the vastness of outer space and its contrast to the finite boundary of their skydome. They avoided daytime visits to steer clear of being seen by Topsiders, but also for the sake of their buddy Spock, since Gnomes and sunlight were a dangerous combination.

"So, I'm mature enough to get married but *not* mature enough to retrieve my uncle. Got it." Bitterness spiced his words.

His mother had the decency to look chagrined. "You're right." She lifted her hands in a helpless shrug. "I'm sorry. Yes, of course you can manage a trip topside. Let's first give Prilla an opportunity to assess your father. She's a very old Gnome who has experience with viruses and illnesses unique to the Tethered World."

Alex gave a begrudging grunt of agreement.

His mom stepped to the tufted chair and scooped up the scroll. "I've asked Prilla to keep her reasons for travel private for now. No sense worrying your Aunt Sophie or Uncle Brock—and, by the way, they're both returning to Vituvia in the morning, along with your grandparents, so don't miss dinner tonight."

Alex merely blinked, his brain scrambling to find answers to these newfound problems that did *not* include marriage.

"Look." His mother stepped forward and placed a hand on his forearm. "We don't know what to expect. Your grandfather suffered for nearly two years before..." She left the sentence unfinished. "It would be foolish not to be proactive, that's all. Which reminds me. Your sister need not worry about her daddy, either. Let's keep this between us."

Alex dipped his head. "Of course."

Ellynn was a daddy's girl and would be devastated if she thought her hero was ill. For her sake alone, they needed to find a cure. A cure to ensure long life. Not Alex's marriage to a stranger—and an heir—to give his father peace of mind before he died. *Negative.*

Mom tapped the scroll against her lower lip and turned to walk toward the fireplace, exhaling loudly. "There's something else."

Alex stiffened. "Yeah?"

"The messenger from Éire House arrived this morning." She faced him, gaze steady despite her unsteady voice. "With the day's events and the funeral, your father didn't receive this scroll until about an hour ago." She extended it to Alex, who only eyed it warily. "It seems the messenger was delayed by topside weather and then an injured horse. He had to put the poor animal down and walk the remaining distance to Calamus."

Alex was unmoved. "So?"

"So..." Mom bit her lower lip and dropped her proffered hand. "So, he should've arrived with this letter about two weeks ago, giving us time to prepare a proper welcome and, naturally, to give us—and most importantly *you*—time to come to grips with this situation your grandfather has negotiated. Instead"—her gaze was desperate and pleading—"the entourage from Éire House is due to arrive tomorrow. This is happening, Alex, whether you want it to or not."

What Alex *wanted* was to lash out. Throw something across the room. Burn the scroll. Anything but face such an abrupt and distasteful fate.

He stomped over to his window and gripped the sill, head slumped. "This can't be happening," he hissed through his teeth.

"I'm sorry. I know it's sudden." Her voice was small, almost timid. "Your grandfather truly believed this was the best way to protect the interests and future of Calamus. Lucia showed Xander the papers that Aviel had drawn up without consulting us. With your father's new...condition...this arrangement does provide some peace of mind. Please. Just, please, pray about it."

Yeah, nothing says peace of mind like marriage to a total stranger. Alex didn't reply.

His mother came to his side and set the scroll on the windowsill, her other hand on the small of his back. With a soft sob, she hurried from the room.

Alex tried to recall the last time he'd even attempted to pray.

CHAPTER FIVE

Alex

"Dude, you're gettin' married?"

Alex jumped and gave a yelp of surprise. He turned toward the voice, knowing full well who it was.

The mound of clothes at the foot of Alex's bed erupted with the wriggling figure of Spock, his Gnome friend from Vituvia. As often as he snuck into Alex's room, the eighteen-inch twerp still managed to scare the salsa out of Alex on a regular basis. The diminutive Gnome liked the challenge of slipping past gargantuan Nephilim guards, shimmying up vines that clung to the stone castle, and slipping in through Alex's window—though he was perfectly welcome to walk through the front gate like Alex's other friends.

Spock was, after all, the son of the legendary Commander Reiko of Vituvia, one of the greatest Gnome warriors of all time. Not to mention a hero from the early visits made by Alex's mother and her family to the Tethered World. Feisty Reiko had once been head of the Vituvian Special Forces.

"Sheesh, Spock. Quit doing that." Alex dragged a hand across his face as if to reset his startled features. "I'm going to special-order topside glass for my window opening to keep you from inviting yourself in whenever you feel like it."

Spock snatched his slouched beanie from his bristly black hair, revealing his peculiarly pointed ears. He slapped his hat against his leg, laughing. "Bro, you scared *me*, yelping like that. You sounded like your little sister."

Alex glared and plopped down on his four-poster bed. "Why are you hiding inside my dirty clothes? You're disgusting."

"I was waiting for you. Skipped out on the graveside ceremony. Such a yawn." Like a mountain climber, the Gnome scaled the sheets up onto Alex's unmade bed. "So, I grabbed some grub and headed here to wait. Then Ellynn came looking for you so I dove into the discards here. Guess I zonked out. You know how sleepy I get after I eat."

Spock replaced his hat, arranging it over the ears that had earned him his nickname years ago after Alex and friends binge-watched the original Star Trek DVDs—a family favorite that had once belonged to Alex's grandfather Liam. Occasionally Alex would hear someone refer to Spock by his actual name—Lucas—and it would take him a moment to realize who they were talking about. Like Alex, the Gnome loved all things topside and had even accompanied the family on vacation twice. Well, more like stowed away in the luggage. He quickly picked up all manner of topside slang, along with a taste for non-Gnome clothing.

Unless he was wearing body armor for a mission, Spock refused the typical tunic of his Gnome compatriots. He opted for Converse high tops, jeans, T-shirts, and hoodies. And forget the standard issue pointed, conical hat. Spock was all about the beanie. Alex never had the heart to explain to his friend that they bought the Gnome's clothing in the infant section of department stores and thrift shops. His mother gladly purchased the items, since she "missed buying these itty-bitty clothes for my babies."

Flopping back onto the bed, Alex puffed his cheeks and exhaled. "Guess you heard my grandfather's crazy plan, then. Dumbest thing ever."

Spock crisscrossed his legs, looking extra compact. "I'd say! And, dude, like, *tomorrow*? Tomorrow you're gonna meet the girl you're supposed to spend the rest of your life with? Uh, no thanks. I'm never getting married. *Ne-ver*. Can't believe your parents are okay with this."

"Ugh!" Alex gave a frustrated groan and pushed himself upright again. "Me neither. Maybe they're *both* sick."

"Maybe." Spock chewed on his lip then added, "Sure stinks about your dad."

"I know. What am I gonna do?" Alex leaned his elbows

onto his knees and bent his head, his short crop of dreadlocks falling forward like a lion's mane. "There's no way they can force me to marry right now. And my dad cannot—and I mean *cannot*—die. That's ridiculous. He's the strongest, fiercest man I know." Alex felt the prick of tears.

Spock gave an agreeable grunt. "For sure. So, now what?"

"Listen." Alex tried to keep his tone neutral. "I'm not sure what the answer is, but I'll figure it out a whole lot faster on my own. Nothing personal, but you need to scram."

"Yeah. Okay. I understand." Spock unfolded his legs and slowly slid off the side of the bed. "I'll, uh…" He nodded toward the window and stuffed his hands into his pockets. "I'll just—"

"Leave," Alex supplied.

"Yeah. That." Spock turned and shimmied up the wingback chair closest to the window. He leapt to the wide stone windowsill, hopped over the discarded scroll, and disappeared through the opening with the stealth of a well-trained Gnome.

Alex collapsed back onto his lumpy, unmade bed wishing he could fall asleep as easily as Spock. What a perfect escape *that* would make. Then again, the last thing he needed was to doze off and wake the next day—The Day—to meet a stranger who wanted to marry him.

Yikes! No. He needed to figure something out, and quick.

Back on his feet, he snatched the scroll from the windowsill. Returning to the bed, he brought it close to his face, studying the imprinted wax seal. What kind of symbol was it? Looked like an oddly shaped X, not that he cared. The only thing he knew about Éire house was that *Éire* is the Irish word for Ireland. And he didn't care about that either.

The seal had been broken, and the weight of it allowed the thick paper to relax its coil like a nautilus shell. Alex stared with dread. Did he want to read what was in it? How could his parents do this to him? Then again, why was he surprised? His entire life was defined by others' expectations—or how he'd failed to live up to them, anyway. The pattern began at birth, after all.

The *true* heir to the throne had lived only a few moments

because Alex's umbilical cord had been wrapped around his brother's neck, squeezing off his oxygen. The first-born son of the first-born son of Calamus didn't make it through labor. It was Benjamin who should have been marrying this perfect stranger. Not Alex.

As if snatching the life and royal title from one's twin wasn't bad enough, Alex went on to inherit the name of his mother's heroic brother Brady. Maybe his parents had hoped his uncle's legacy would help redeem their new son from such an ominous entrance into the world. Except growing up as *Brady* only meant that everyone compared the namesake to the original—would *this* Brady act in much the same way as *that* one?

Most of the time *this* Brady had not.

Then there was the pressure of being grandson of the king, in line for the throne—*by default*, Alex silently added whenever someone mentioned it. The protocol and training, the constant reminders of conduct and tradition, each expectation only frustrated Alex and highlighted his utter inability to get it right. He also had the distinction of being the "first flightless royal in over a century". Not to mention the brownish brand around his eye, making him a target of teasing both inside the palace and out.

Falling short of everyone's expectations was exhausting. Left him brooding at a slow simmer that eventually boiled over into runaway anger. Thankfully, he had a few close friends who knew how to talk him down from the proverbial ledge.

But this...this insta-marriage felt like a punch to his gut from his grandfather's grave. Surely his parents had lost their collective minds. In light of the love story *they* shared, their arranging Alex's marriage was the definition of hypocrisy.

His father and mother had made quite the dynamic duo back in the day. The resourceful princess and the wise and powerful prince. They had a love story worthy of a movie. No arranged marriages for them, no sir. His father had taken the Prince Charming thing to another level entirely.

Alex had grown up listening to their daring feats—his mother had even taken the time to record them in a series of books, under a pen name, which she'd read to him as a child.

He'd easily imagined himself in the roll of guardian angel and hero, exactly like his father. That is, until Alex realized he had no wings and would remain flightless for life.

Yet another way in which Alex could never, would never, measure up.

He lurched from his bed, certain of one thing—it was time to start writing his own story and to stop being a mere character in someone else's production. Alex would be neither scapegoat nor savior in the plot to rescue Calamus.

He looked at the scrolled letter, then glanced at the yawning, empty fireplace and lobbed the parchment inside. Before he could let curiosity get the best of him, he knelt at the hearth, opened the tinderbox, and struck flint to steel, igniting the charcloth. He encouraged the flame by blowing on it, then touched it to the scroll and watched as the paper contorted, blackening in contrast to the hungry, hot blaze.

It was quick. It was irreversible. It was freeing. His obligatory bride was due to arrive tomorrow, and he could only think of one fitting response. One that he had been dreaming about for years and planning to do soon, anyway:

Run.

CHAPTER SIX

Alex

THE TIMELINE WAS TIGHT.

If Alex wanted to slip out of a heavily guarded palace without notice, he needed to construct a hasty getaway. Hasty—but not sloppy. Though his best thinking happened on the basketball court, there wouldn't be time for that tonight. Certainly, no time for dinner and bidding his Vituvian family goodbye, either.

He settled for snatching up one of two basketballs from his dwindling topside-dependent supply and dribbling the length of his room. Alex had discovered the sport on one of his family's topside getaways, when he was ten. Living below ground without electricity, let alone television, meant he was perpetually fascinated by all things electronic. He happened upon a Portland Trailblazers basketball game on TV while at Uncle Brent's house. The sight had galvanized him. There, on the screen, were other freakishly tall and rangy guys, many with his coffee-and-cream skin tone.

These are my people! Alex had thought.

At the time, he believed pro basketball players to be flightless Nephilim commoners. He fell in love with the sport and hoped they would one day allow him to play, despite the wings he assumed would eventually sprout. When puberty hit and Alex failed to develop said plumage, it only solidified his desire to find a place to fit in among his topside heroes.

Thankfully, his mother was delighted with his newfound hobby. For his eleventh birthday, she surprised him with several basketballs, a hand pump, and a metal hoop with a net, all of which she'd somehow smuggled back to Calamus without his noticing. Despite King Aviel's protests, Xander had secured a small patch of land at the back of the palace grounds for a half-court.

And moody, hostile Alex had flourished. The ball became a therapeutic extension of himself. A part of his life over which he had absolute control while freeing him from protocol and presumptions. When he soared toward the net, he didn't need wings. He could fly with his feet.

Sadly, there would be no on-court therapy tonight. For the first time in a long time, Alex wished he had wings. He needed to fly far, far from here. Needed to escape.

Instead, his indignation slammed the ball against the stone floor like hammer blows. Each *whack* a resentful, resounding complaint against his parents, against his grandfather and grandmother, and against God Himself for doling out an unfair amount of hardship in Alex's life.

No one would point to Alex and think "marriage material." He wasn't even much of an older brother to Ellynn. She always wanted to tag along, but he basically tricked her into running an errand or fetching a snack so he could slip away without her.

And now…marriage? Hilarious! So far, adulthood fit about as comfortably as comparisons to the original Brady— Brady Larcen. That Brady had been everything Brady Alexander was not. And no one let him forget that for long. Comparisons were rampant, often disguised as a fond memory. It's a wonder they hadn't granted the guy sainthood.

With his new moniker in place, Alex hoped to shift away from Brady Larcen's shadow—along with other dark places that lurked in his past. Alex wanted to discover who he really was. Or, at least, who he could become.

He certainly didn't need the burden of getting to know a strange girl with strange customs from a strange land. Alex was a stranger to *himself.*

He gripped the ball, silencing the room while the angry throb of his pulse carried on. Uncle Magnum might be a jerk, but at least no one expected anything different from him. Whereas, Alex's life had been one constant contrast to his late uncle, to the Nephilim heroes, and to the royal line of Tuatha

Dé.

And he had been found lacking.

He was too different. A Brady-fail. A blazing birthmark. A half-breed. A Nephilim without wings. An awkwardly tall human. He wasn't black. He wasn't white. He wasn't wise or smart or handsome.

He was the one thing that no one—*no one*—ever mentioned, although the truth of it throbbed beneath every interaction like an unseen artery.

Alex was a murderer.

CHAPTER SEVEN

Alex

WHAT ALEX LACKED IN PLUMAGE HE had learned to make up for in stealth. Unlike Finnegan and Josiah, who could simply loft themselves from their bedroom windows for late night excursions, Alex had to maneuver through the echoing stone hallways of the palace on foot. True, his younger self had managed to climb out his bedroom window many a night, clinging to nearby vines or trellises, and fingering the slight contrast in mortar seams. Unfortunately, his fingertips and size-fifteens could no longer support his expansive body on less than a quarter inch of ledge. Which meant he had to teach himself to traverse halls, dash across corridors, or slip into hidden passageways with silent ease.

So why was his heart hammering like a trapped jackrabbit inside the cage of his chest? If he didn't know better, its pounding might wake his parents as he crept past their bedchamber.

Getting caught wasn't an option. Thankfully, no one had insisted Alex join the family for dinner earlier in the evening. No doubt his mother found it wise to let him sulk about the bad news rather than foist him into polite chitchat. Although his instinct was to immediately distance himself from Calamus, he waited for the household to get to sleep.

It had been torturous. He paced and planned and tossed most ideas aside. The only thing that promised enough space between himself and his parents's expectations was getting topside—Oregon or Washington the only realistic options under the circumstances.

Alex knew his disappearance would be considered an extreme act of disrespect. One that would bring down the wrath of his father like Thor's hammer. But since the alternative meant *marriage*, Alex had to do what he had to do.

When enough time passed for his parents to miss him—more than they wished to throttle him—he would return for a visit.

In the meantime, Alex hoped he could convince his pharmaceutically savvy Uncle Brent to concoct a treatment or two that Alex's father could use to fend off the cursed fever-dreams. If Alex returned with a possible cure, surely his parents would forgive him.

Whatever their eventual feelings or reactions might be, Alex would take it like a man...despite currently running away like a coward.

After a few detours to avoid being spotted, Alex made it through the maze of dimly lit corridors with the rehearsed ease of a lab rat. Finally, he spied the scullery and tiptoed inside, snatching a leftover dinner roll from the cloth-wrapped bundle on the weathered table that doubled as a work station. He clamped the crusty bread between his teeth while he carefully unlatched the door, relieved that it swung open in silence.

Stepping into the walled kitchen garden, he weaved around the fragrant herb bed and hunkered into the far corner to monitor the guards pacing the palace rooftop. Alex scarfed the yeasty bread as he noted the unhurried pace of a soldier silhouetted against the dim pseudo-sky. Tonight more than ever, Alex disliked the lack of true nighttime in the Tethered World. The crystalline skydome only dimmed to the glow of an ember, like one continuous, expansive nightlight.

Though he harbored no love for the Leprechauns who lived in the Hallows of Nimmickdell, it would be stellar to have their ability to become invisible about now. Still, he managed to dash through the garden egress and sidestep along the courtyard wall, keeping to the shadows. Someone had left the gate open—a huge security oversight for which Alex was currently grateful—and he slipped out, hoofing it across the lane to the stables, hoping he hadn't misjudged the timing of the rooftop patrols.

With a silent huff he leaned against the wall of the barn, weighing his next move. Though it seemed impossible to ride out of the stables on horseback, sight unseen, he hadn't completely ruled out the risk. Horseback would take him much farther than walking and get him across the Berganstroud mountains and headed toward the closest tunnel topside. It didn't escape him, once again, that his quandary could easily be solved with a set of wings.

A nearby *creak* made him straighten with a quick intake

of breath. Was that the squeak of a rusty door hinge? Doors didn't sway in a static land that had no wind. A squeaking door could only be moved by man or beast.

Alex stepped to the corner and peeked. The barn door stood ajar, but all was quiet. Maybe one of the horses had pressed its considerable bulk against a wall, shifting the structure in some way. This barn was the family stable and featured many a raspy metal hinge.

Looking at the quiet nighttime landscape, Alex felt silly about his sudden paranoia. He shrugged, as if to physically shed his anxiety. In order to keep out of view while weighing his options, he slipped into the open door of the barn.

"'Bout time."

Alex jumped.

In the dusky, shadowed barn, somewhat lit by the dimmed skydome outside, his four friends stepped from behind thick support beams and empty stalls. A horse whickered and gave an impatient stamp of its hoof, as if it, too, had grown tired of waiting.

Alex blinked at his impromptu surprise party. "What in the...what are you guys doing here?"

Finn, Josiah, Spock, and Dempsey—a Dwarf whose diplomatic father worked out of Calamus—stood half-submerged in shadows that couldn't quite hide their mischievous grins.

Spock swiped his beanie from his head and swooped into a bow. "Dude. You didn't think we'd let you run away by yourself, did ya?"

Alex stiffened. How did they know? "What makes you losers think I'm running away?"

Josiah chuckled. "Asks the guy wearing a backpack in a barn in the middle of the night."

Alex gave a sheepish grin and shrugged out of said backpack. "Am I that predictable?"

"Apparently." Finn drew closer, a thick strand of straw clenched between his teeth. "Spock told us your, uh, *exciting* prenuptial news. Figured you needed either a bachelor party or an escape plan."

Alex hid a grin behind his fist and nodded. "Yeah, guess those are my choices at this point."

Josiah leaned close as everyone clustered together. "You know your dad is going to send the huffing lungs of the militia to breathe down your neck. He's not going to like the idea of your making him look bad to these guests and your"—he barked a laugh—"*fiancée.*"

"Shh!" Alex made a slicing motion across his neck. "Keep it down or they'll find me before I can even leave."

"So what's your plan, laddie?" Dempsey asked in his heavy, dwarfish brogue. "We're guessin' ya haven't had time to make much of one yet."

Alex pressed his lips together, gazing at his four compadres. "I can guarantee it doesn't include trying to smuggle the likes of you guys out of here with me. If you misfits think the five of us can manage such a miracle, maybe I've got a shot at sprouting some wings real quick, too."

"Ah, c'mon," Spock piped. "We've had our share of escapes together. This is no different."

"Actually, it's way different," Alex said. "We've always had time to make plans we knew would work. Not to mention the stakes usually aren't so high. If we get caught, *I'm* the one standing at the altar with Princess Buttercup. Not any of you."

"Nah, we'll be standing at the altar right beside ya," said Dempsey, nudging Alex. "You'll need us to be yer groomsmen, aye?"

"Buttercup? Is that really her name?" Finn snickered.

Alex crossed his arms and glared in Dempsey's direction. "If I end up at the altar, it's because the lot of you made it impossible for me to get away. You can forget an invitation to the wedding, if there is one, let alone a place of honor." He looked at Finn. "No. Her name isn't Buttercup. That's from— forget it. Her name is Larkin, not that it matters."

"Larkin..." Finn mused, eyebrows bouncing.

"I'm only japin' with ya." Dempsey lifted his palms in innocence. "We can't let ya run off alone. Ya wouldn't have any fun without us."

"I didn't come here looking for fun. I came to get as far away as possible, as fast as possible. We usually leave in shifts, not all at once like some giant amoeba. I appreciate the offer, but I've only got a general idea of what to do with *myself.*"

Finn pointed the flattened, gnawed end of his straw at Alex. "Except you've got *us*, you lucky dog. While you've been waiting for the palace to snooze, we've been problem-solving." He tapped his auburn hair with the straw. "Using our collective wisdom."

Alex gave a dubious smirk. "So, what, that makes one whole brain cell between the four of you?"

Finn grinned, eyes narrowed. "Ha ha. *No.* It means you have four times the brilliant plan ready to be set in motion." He prodded Spock with his foot. "Tell him what you did."

Spock cleared his throat. "Mind if I...?"

"Fine." Finn reached down and swiped the Gnome off the ground, plunking him onto his broad shoulder.

"Oh, I see." Alex frowned. "You guys aren't really interested in my plan—or maybe you assumed I didn't actually have one—because you've made your own."

"Hey, we're on *your* side here," Spock said. "I'd personally be running like my pants were on fire if I were you. Why do you think I hang out with you guys instead of my family? They're always dropping hints about the 'ladies' and my needing to 'settle down.'" Spock leaned an elbow onto Finn's head, which prompted a nudge from the Nephilim, nearly knocking Spock from his perch. He grabbed Finn's coppery hair to steady himself. "Sheesh, you trying to kill me?"

"I'm neither a stool nor a table, thank you. Can you manage to sit and speak, like a good Gnome?" Finn gave him a sideways glance.

Spock mumbled under his breath, then said, "Josiah and I came to the stables after the stable hands made their rounds. I chatted with the family equines and told them about your plight. Though they found your impending nuptials humorous—as you know, horses don't mate for life—they agreed to help. Josiah outfitted them in their bridles and reins, skipping the saddles to keep a low profile. Since a late-night trail ride for five would draw too much attention, I unlatched the stalls and the barn door so they could wander out at their own discretion. Assuming it all went well, they're waiting for your Royal Highness"—he swept a tiny hand to indicate the group—"and his royal dudes, in the woodlands of the Kinleigh foothills."

Alex looked about, suddenly aware that the barn was indeed void of the normal sounds of horses huffing, snuffling, and settling in. Only one stall currently housed a horse, an old, achy steed that wouldn't get Alex over the Berganstroud mountains much faster than his own two feet. Still, he wasn't sure how he felt about his friend's so-called plan. Too many moving parts. "How on earth did the *horses* slip out unnoticed? That's as risky as riding them ourselves."

Spock shrugged. "Used their horse sense, obviously. They're gone, aren't they? All except for Old Ethan there."

The bewhiskered stallion snorted at the five-some, as if he understood they were talking about him. Maybe he did.

"Said his arthritis is really flaring up these days," Spock added.

Alex couldn't help but be impressed by Spock's problem-solving skills. A Gnome's ability to speak to animals sure came in handy. The Kinleigh mountain range might be in the opposite direction from the Berganstroud mountains, but it was still far from Calamus. And though he wasn't aware of any direct routes topside, it might throw off his father's men. Berganstroud and the tunnel up through Beacon Rock was the most obvious direction to search. Maybe heading the other way, at least temporarily, would be best.

"All right." Alex felt the adventurous side of his brain approving of the plan. He debated sharing his final topside destination, deciding he would have time to explain once they were safely elsewhere. "That's quite the skillset you have, Spock. Good work. But how about us? We still have to get from point A to point B."

"We've got it handled. Trust us." Spock gave Alex a thumbs-up.

"That's what worries me," Alex said.

Finn waved him off. "Hey, would we jeopardize our own backsides, let alone your bachelorhood, on a whim? It's a pretty solid spur-of-the-moment plan."

Alex winced at the dichotomy. "Obviously, *I* get no say in the matter. Lead on." He reached for his backpack and hefted it into place beneath his cape. Further argument only meant further delay. "Putting some distance between myself and the palace is my immediate concern." He paused with a fistful of cape, ready to smooth it over his shoulders. "Actually, I also care about one other thing. My dad. I'm not sure where to begin searching for answers, but if I can bring back something helpful...maybe he'll forgive me in the end."

Everyone grew still, eyes downcast, evasive.

"Look," Alex said. "If I know Spock at all, he told you about the other negative news my mother dumped on me."

They nodded one by one.

"'Tis a shame." Dempsey shifted his feet, kicking at the straw. "Real sorry t'hear it, Alex."

"Thanks." Alex cleared his throat and forced a lighthearted tone. "Now then, on with the shenanigans."

"Right. Let's do this." Josiah clapped Alex on the shoulder

and nodded at the others, snatching his leather duffle from where it leaned against a busted crate.

"Anyone care to enlighten me on how we're all getting out of here, sight unseen?" Alex stepped around two stacked, rectangular hay bales that someone had placed squarely in the walkway. Old straw littered the floor in greying drifts, hiding a discarded pitchfork pinned beneath the bales. Tines and toes collided, launching him onto a mound of saddle blankets heaped in the corner.

"*Ugh!*"

"Ouch!"

The first word came from Alex as he landed hard on his shoulder.

The second came from beneath the pile of blankets.

CHAPTER EIGHT

Alex

ALEX SPRANG BACK LIKE HE'D LANDED on a smoldering campfire. "What—?"

"Bleeding barnacles." The lump of blankets expanded and moved, seemingly on its own. "That *hurt.*"

"Watch it!" Finn grabbed Alex, yanking him back. With dagger extended, he approached the moving mound, blocking Alex's view.

Josiah followed, thrusting Alex behind his own bulk, withdrawing his dagger.

"Hey!" Alex couldn't see around his broad, winged friends and hated it when they morphed into protect-our-royal-bff mode. "I can handle—"

"Come out slowly, you lowlife, stable-slinking snake," Finn hissed.

Alex slung the backpack to the ground behind him, smacking it into Dempsey, who was scaling the stacked hay bales on the heels of Spock.

"All right, all right! I'm coming," said the disembodied voice. It sounded young and more indignant than afraid.

Alex closed the gap behind Josiah and Finn. He withdrew his own blade from its belted sheath, thankful he'd decided on Calamus-style clothing for this leg of the journey. It provided easy access to his steel. He'd stuffed his topside clothing into his backpack for later.

A scrawny, filthy figure hatched from its heavy woolen egg. Fingers splayed from black, fingerless gloves emerged, spider-like. Then a pale arm, so thin and hash-marked it looked like a cat had used it for a scratching post. A knee poked out, followed by an entire body slipping to the floor with a regurgitated *plunk.*

Though Josiah and Finn still pointed their daggers in the

intruder's direction, this scrap of a person obviously posed no threat to the looming giants.

The stowaway rolled onto his back, white-blond hair full of straw, resembling a dismembered bird's nest. Impossibly large eyes blinked up disapprovingly, as if *they* were the intruders. "You can put your little knives away. You guys can obviously take me." His raspy voice had a lilt of brogue.

"Not until you tell us who you are and what in the name of Whitt Lake you're doing here." Finn stepped closer, his mass as much a threat as his weapon.

The boy—for that is what he was, a pubescent Topsider of maybe fourteen, much too short to be a teenage Nephilim— flared his nostrils, mustering a fearless expression. With chin held high, he whispered, "You'll treat me with civility, or I'll not cooperate."

Alex gave a wry chuckle and shouldered his friends aside. He didn't have time for a war of words. In one quick swipe, his left hand grasped the boy's crinkled, dirt-smudged tunic.

"Is that how you talk to your betters?" He hauled the boy eye level, legs flailing, and flashed the tip of the dagger between them. In close proximity, Alex noticed the boy had two different-colored eyes. One dark as burnt wood, the other a coppery-green. Or was that a trick of the paltry light?

Tall leather boots laced up his scrawny calves. His legs dangled for purchase, then attempted to kick Alex with awkward blows like an unhinged marionette.

Alex gave a quiet, sarcastic laugh. "You're either stupidly brave or perfectly stupid." He heaved the boy onto the blankets again, keeping the blade between them.

The boy plopped, starfish-like, then scrambled to his feet. "Looks like your brawn outweighs anything resembling brains." Hands on hips, his scowl scraped across the three warriors who now walled him in. If gazes could gouge, his would have drawn blood.

"Dude, do you realize who you're talking to?" Spock dropped from an overhead rafter landing on Alex's shoulder with practiced ease. "This here is—*umph.*"

"Shut it, shrimp." Josiah had shoved the Gnome so hard he flew backward into Dempsey's arms like a missile.

The Dwarf clamped a hand over Spock's gaping mouth.

Finn jabbed his dagger at the airspace. "Who are you and what're you doing hiding in the palace stables? *Speak* before I take away your ability to do so," he whisper-shouted.

The boy drew himself up. Alex had to admire the kid's pluck. Such self-possession wasn't found in many commoners, whether in the Tethered World or topside.

"My name is Colin. And I..." he looked defiantly from Josiah to Alex to Finn. "I've run away."

Alex shook his head. "That much is obvious. Where'd you come from and how'd you get here?" He leaned in. "And you best lower your voice if you want future use of your vocal chords."

Colin's lips pressed together for a moment as if weighing his answer. "My presence here is none of your business," he growled.

"I beg to differ." Finn cocked his head. "Actually, I never resort to begging."

Alex lowered his blade a fraction. The twiggy kid was no match for any of them, not even Spock.

Colin crossed his arms and looked at Alex. "No sense trying to keep the little Gnome from talking. I know who you are." The corner of his mouth lifted. "Your *Highness*. And I know what you're doing."

"Do you now?" Alex feigned a look of boredom. "Well, enlighten me."

The young man squinted his mismatched eyes at Alex. "Same as me. Running. And unless you want me to sound the alarm, you're gonna take me with you."

Alex and Finn exchanged exaggerated looks of incredulity.

"Good one. Got ourselves a real dreamer here." In a blink, Alex gripped Colin beneath his collar again, poking the blade at his bony jaw. "I'm through taking it easy on you. Now, where did you come from and what *precisely* are you doing here?"

"Alex. He's just a kid." Josiah, a gentle giant like his grandfather Gage, placed a warning hand on Alex's shoulder.

"A smart-mouthed sneaky kid who needs to be taught a lesson," Alex grumbled, holding his ground. Truthfully, he was more annoyed by the delay of plans than the insolence of the boy. He shoved Colin away. "Fine. I don't have time for an inquisition anyway. I need to *leave*. He comes with us until we're far enough away to leave him to the wild animals and Trolls."

The boy widened his eyes in a look that was somehow both hopeful and afraid.

"Gag him. And tie him up." Alex commanded no one in

particular, turning to retrieve his pack. "I don't want to hear his smart mouth and I don't want to risk him running off and yammering to someone about us. Let's move."

Dempsey leaped from the hay, Spock riding piggyback.

"G-gag me?" the kid stammered. "You don't need to resort to that. I'm not gonna say anything to anyone. I *asked* you to take me with you. I want as far away from here as possible."

In three long strides, Alex closed the gap between them again. "I don't know you, and I don't trust you, Topsider. You will be gagged and tied until I say otherwise."

"I've got him." Josiah grasped Colin's arm. "Finn, find me a short bit of rope and a clean rag, will ya?"

Finn nodded but didn't move. He held the boy's gaze as he made a deliberate show of replacing his dagger in its sheath. "Watch yourself, kid, because we will be watching you."

Josiah pulled the boy closer. "Enough. Let's take care of business." As the oldest of the three Nephilim friends, he often played big brother.

"Thanks," Colin mumbled.

"Don't thank me." Josiah shoved the boy's chin up and bent over him threateningly. "I can be as ruthless as either of these hotheads, if you push me. Sounds like you know when you're outsized and outnumbered. Yes?"

Colin met the warrior's gaze and gave a curt nod.

Between wary glances and the snorts and sniffles of Old Ethan, the group gathered their packs and gear. Dempsey slung his quiver and bow across his back, Finn and Josiah grabbed their rucksacks, and Alex placed a handful of dried molasses in one of the pockets of his backpack for the horses. The friends coalesced beneath the dim glow provided by a skylight in the center of the barn, with Colin harnessed like the prisoner he was.

Alex arched his back, stretching. "Looks like a good time to reveal the rest of your genius plan, Spock. Are we making a run for it to the woods, or what? You guys have greatly complicated things, you know." He grimaced at the newcomer. "And *you* are dead weight that I plan to cut loose the first chance I get."

Colin gave a snarl of mutual loathing through the gag.

"No," Spock said. "We're not going to risk being seen leaving together. I thought a little insta-travel might be best." Spock swaggered into the center of the group and removed a

Faery whistle from his pocket, raising it in his fist. "What would you do without me?"

Relief washed over Alex at the sight. Of course! The Faeries were definitely the upside to traveling together. Along with speaking to animals, Gnomes had the unique ability to transmit a particular high-pitched sound through a Faery whistle to call for their spritely services. "Gotta love taking the Faery." He gave the Gnome a fist bump.

Colin shook his head with quick, jerky movements, his enormous eyes growing rounder with fear.

"It's all good, my topside friend. You won't feel a thing." Spock placed the carved piccolo-style instrument between his lips and forcefully buzzed into the mouthpiece.

A barely perceptible trill pierced Alex's eardrums, making him wince. He glanced at the boy, whose terror was almost palpable. As Alex stared, Colin's knees gave way.

"Stand up!" Josiah jerked the boy upright. "You'll be fine. Keep your wits about you."

Through the window openings, the skylight above, and a couple of the bigger gaps in the wooden panels, phosphorescent puffs drifted into the barn like moonlit dust motes. They swirled around rafters and fluttered about the barn, casting a lemony glow in a shimmer of fireworks. Their jingling chatter reverberated like chimes in the wind. Old Ethan whinnied and stamped his hooves, which only egged on the mischievous Faeries.

Like a murmuration of starlings, the tiny orbs converged on the old stallion, spiraling about his neck, whisking his twitching ears, and zipping down his spine, sending his entire body into fearful spasms.

"It's okay, boy!" Alex called, lunging toward the horse, reaching out a comforting hand.

At the same time, Spock clapped his hands and yelled, "Hey, you hyperactive, oversized fireflies! That's enough. *Get over here.*"

"Keep it down." Alex ordered through gritted teeth.

The Faeries shifted mid-flight and zoomed to the clustered friends. The whole incident lasted less than a minute but left poor Old Ethan heaving like he'd sprinted a furlong.

Alex thought he might explode from exasperation. "Half the palace guard must've noticed the kamikaze comets headed into the stables. We need to get out of here."

A distant shout underscored the urgency.

Josiah and Finn caught Alex's eye in shared panic.

Spock blew another tune into the whistle, and the frenzied fluff began to circle the group as if riding the current of an invisible vortex. Their voices pinged nonsensically at first, but as the cloud of Faeries gained coordination, a distinct chant began to emerge. "To the woods! To the woods! Let's escape to the woods!"

Colin sagged against Josiah, and the warrior tugged him upright, only to have him collapse again. The boy had blacked out.

As the Faery-cyclone increased in speed, their chorus climbed in volume. Capes and feathers whipped about. Ears were covered to muffle the painful frequency, and heads were ducked in anticipation of the coming disappearance. Instantaneous transport felt a lot like a body-sized bandage being ripped off all at once.

Moments before impact, a voice shouted at the group from outside one of the windows. "Hey! What's going on in there?"

The answer looked like a lot like an old magic trick.

Now you see us, now you don't.

CHAPTER NINE

Alex

IN THE SAME JUMBLED INSTANT WHEN Alex heard a soldier shout from outside the barn, he felt the pull of the Faery transport on the very cells of his body. Before his brain could react to being discovered, he stood in a meager grove of evergreens and birch trees, blinking at the cloud of Faeries that now hovered above him like a swarm of radioactive bees.

He exhaled loudly, a mixture of relief and dread congealing inside. They'd escaped, but to where? And how long until the king's men found them since his dad would be immediately notified?

"Whew! Awesome timing, Sprighten Fey. Close call." Spock praised the Faeries—an important part of the delivery process—and the little creatures flew merrily about, their jingle-bell voices once again unintelligible.

One glowing orb hovered in front of Alex, its wings a blur of motion, tiny insect-meets-human face smiling as its arm-like appendages clapped. Alex gave it a nod and said, "Thanks," aware that these peculiar *little* creatures would make very creepy *big* creatures.

"Oh c'mon. On your feet!" Josiah's frustrated voice pulled Alex back to the group.

Colin drooped in the arms of the big warrior. The golden glow of the Faeries revealed platinum hair, damp with sweat, clinging to his slack-jawed, gag-wrapped face.

Josiah grimaced at the others. He released the boy, who slumped into a heap. "Kid was shaking like a rattlesnake's tail in the barn. Guess it freaked him out pretty bad. Might need some air." He leaned down and jerked the cloth gag loose.

"What're we going to do with him?" Finn gestured in frustration at the bundle of boy, who had begun to stir. "We can't have some frightened kid tagging along. He's a liability."

"I agree." Alex flicked a Faery off his dreads and nudged Spock with his knee. "Tell your little friends to buzz off, would ya? We don't need a spotlight announcing our presence to stray Trolls or whatever might be roaming the woods."

Spock yanked on Alex's cape. "Hey, you should probably dial it down and show some gratitude if you want to continue using their services."

"Right. Sorry." Alex looked at the Fey and waved. "Sorry!" he said louder. "You guys are the best. Thanks for the lift."

Their tinkling chimes rose in volume, which made their wattage glow brighter.

Spock clapped his hands together. "Thanks again. You guys rock! You're dismissed."

The Faeries spiraled into a tight knot above the group and suddenly vanished, leaving the runaways blinking in the gloomy light of the dusk-time forest. It took a moment for Alex's eyes to adjust. Soon, he made out three horses grazing on the undergrowth, about ten yards to his right.

His dappled-grey draft horse looked his way, munching a leafy plant. Gandalf had been given to Alex while he was reading, naturally, *The Lord of the Rings*. The gelding's wise gaze and silver-to-pewter coloring lent the horse an air of mystery and maturity befitting the wizardly character.

The other two shaggy-coated black drafts belonged to his parents—which meant Alex would be in deeper dung than ever, once he returned home. *No one* rode Ansyn, his father's horse, let alone removed him from the palace grounds without permission. Sage, a near-replica of her sire Ansyn, gave a soft whinny as if in greeting. Sage had inherited her dam's white muzzle and gentle personality, which set her apart from the temperamental Ansyn and made her perfectly suitable for her mistress, Sadie.

Dempsey swiped at his gnarly, muddy-blond hair, releasing a trapped Faery. The sprite corkscrewed skyward and disappeared.

"So, where are we?" Alex asked. "Glad to see our mounts made it."

"I'm not a frightened kid." The mound at Josiah's feet suddenly spoke and pushed awkwardly to a sitting position, wrists and ankles lashed together. "It—it's the Faeries. I—I've had a bad experience with them." Colin squared his shoulders and looked at the group, eyes ablaze with defiance once again. "But I'm fine as fish eggs now."

"Fish eggs?" Spock made a face.

Colin looked away. "It's a topside delicacy. Forget it."

"What you can forget is continuing on with us." Finn stooped and grasped the boy's elbow.

Alex placed a restraining hand on Finn's arm. "Leave him for now. We'll cut him loose once we're farther from Calamus. Don't need him helping my father's men to track us. Maybe Faeries weren't such a bright idea."

"They were quite *bright*, actually." Dempsey crossed his arms over his barrel chest. "May as well 'ave had the night watchman announce our departure with a blast on his horn."

"Hey!" Spock lifted his hands. "I'm the only one who had a plan, thank you very much. And we're here, aren't we? A good two leagues from Calamus." He made a slow turn, arms lifted. "Tah-dah! *Not* the palace."

"Maybe so." Alex would see how this played out before he felt indebted to the Gnome and his trained fireflies. "You'll have to forgive me if I'm not gushing with thanks for blabbing my problems to everyone and inviting yourselves along." He glowered at Colin, then the others. "There are now six of us, plus three horses, trying to elude my father's experienced trackers. Gotta say, I like my odds a lot better as a soloist."

Josiah spread his hands in a show of amenability. "I'm afraid you're stuck with us now."

"Plus, this is more fun, mate." Finn slung his arm around Alex's shoulders. "We always go on holiday together."

Alex grimaced. "This is no holiday. And if we're caught, *I'm* the one getting married, remember?"

"Indeed," Josiah said, ever the voice of reason. "Yet I think this puts you at a greater advantage than if you'd set off on your own, though I certainly wish we'd had time to plan ahead. Still, helping each other is what we do, so..." He shrugged.

"Whatever." Alex waited for Spock to situate himself on Dempsey's broad shoulder, then gave the Gnome an imploring look. "What now? Or *where* now, you two-footed compass?"

Spock crossed his compact arms, a parody of the Dwarf beneath him. "We're currently beyond the Kinleigh foothills, near Mila's Pass. There are some old tunnels in these parts. Tunnels through the mountainside to the Hinterlands. That's where we're headed." He nodded toward the grazing horses. "In fact, that's how they came to be here. They traversed one of the hidden tunnels near Calamus, which shortened their journey by half."

"And you think my father, King Xander, a man who loves to hunt and explore, knows nothing of these tunnels?" Alex asked.

"Has he ever mentioned them or shown them to you?" Spock challenged.

Alex thought a moment. His father had taken him on many expeditions and scouting trips all around the Kinleigh mountains, which protected the backside of Calamus like mounds of muscles on a giant's enveloping arm. Never had they trekked through tunnels, only enjoying the shelter of several deep caves on camping trips. "Not that I recall."

Spock winked. "Exactly."

Three horses and six passengers meandered from wide-open paths to narrow, overgrown trails in which the trees sketched a lacy silhouette against the muted sky. The horses slowed as the woods encroached, blocking out more of the paltry light.

The Gnome navigated astride Finn's shoulders, Ansyn surefooted beneath them. Spock's tiny fists held fast to the Nephilim's hair, prompting Finn to bark at Spock to "quit yanking!" every few minutes.

Alex doubled up with Dempsey on Gandalf. The Dwarf rode behind Alex, insisting on facing backward so he could easily cover the rear, if needed. His quiver of arrows bumped between their backs with all the comfort of a rolling pin.

It irritated Alex that his friends were so protective. They took his heir-to-the-throne status more seriously than he did. However, to avoid further delay, he allowed Finn and Spock to lead, Dempsey to play defense, and Josiah and the prisoner to bring up the rear.

Everyone rode bareback, and Alex questioned how long the horses could handle the chafing without padding and saddles. Still, he reminded himself, it beat walking. Alex sensed the kid studying him from behind with those unsettling, mismatched eyes. Perhaps Colin thought Alex's lack of wings equally unusual.

The friends had agreed to untie the boy's feet so he could straddle the horse, but his wrists remained tethered in front. When Josiah tried to remove the tattered, fingerless gloves, Colin had balled his fingers into fists and protested loudly. He calmed down when they threatened to gag him again, though he pleaded to leave the gloves in place. Josiah didn't see any harm in doing so and had deposited the kid on Sage's back.

Alex wondered what to do with the boy once they distanced themselves from the inevitable pursuit. Cast him off in the middle of the Hinterlands to fend for his scrawny self? What was Colin running from, and how had he found his way below ground? Who might be searching for him—putting the group in danger beyond that of Xander's army?

In past centuries, this world beneath the world was rarely stumbled upon by Topsiders—mostly spelunkers who had lost their way inside miles of topside caves. A bit of unfortunate exposure back when his parents first met had led to curiosity seekers traipsing about where few had previously dared to explore, ratcheting intrusions to an alarming number in Alex's lifetime.

Once discovered, the Topsiders would be relieved of any cameras or tracking technology before being sent back with good wishes and the gift of a canteen full of "special" tea. The Topsiders were instructed to drink the tea as soon as they were back inside their designated cave, in order to ward off any "dangerous foreign viruses" they may have been exposed to.

In reality, the tea caused short-term amnesia, wiping their memory of the Tethered World—though no one knew for sure how thoroughly it worked on each particular person. And, because the tea did indeed hold strong anti-viral properties, it was a half-truth of necessity. Fear of contracting some bizarre super-bug made people all too eager to return to safety and drink the life-saving brew.

"On ahead, past this ridge of rock," Spock hollered. The Gnome had migrated from Finn's shoulders to sit in front of the warrior, blocking Spock entirely from view. "There's a waterfall and a stream. That'll be Mila's Pass."

Finn clarified for the group by pointing ahead and to the left.

Water chattered in the distance, and Alex wondered whether the sound had accompanied them for some time or if it had only now reached his consciousness. He scanned the nearby foliage and sparse undergrowth, glad, for once, that the sky dome's ambient light didn't compel most species of plants to grow as large or prolific as authentic sunshine. The nighttime light filtered through the canopy and revealed a shadowy path.

Alex admired the contrast of the papery birch trees to the sheer granite cliff to his left. They stood like giant hashmarks against the dark rock. The smell of damp, decomposing earth grew stronger, as did the sound of bustling, busy water. In the near distance, he could make out where the wall of rock came to an abrupt end and the vegetation thickened along the banks of the stream.

As they approached, Spock said, "We lead our horses from here."

Alex halted Gandalf and waited for Dempsey to slide to the ground before dismounting. Instead, Dempsey vaulted over the horse's tail. Alex shook his head. "You're lucky the horse didn't kick you into next week, dismounting like that."

Dempsey waved him off with a "Nah" and reached for his pipe pouch.

"This isn't the place for smoke signals." Alex alighted and cocked his head at the Dwarf. "We don't need that sooty tobacco giving us away."

Dempsey frowned but didn't argue.

The group silently stretched their arms and legs as the horses nibbled the vegetation.

"I, um. Well..." Colin shifted from one foot to the other.

"Need the lavvy?" Finn replaced the lid on his canteen. Water droplets glinted from his wiry, red beard.

Colin's eyebrows puckered. "The what?"

"The lavatory. The toilet," Josiah said. He gestured at their surroundings. "Pick a tree. Any tree. In sight of us, obviously."

"I will not." Colin drew himself up. "That's barbaric."

Dempsey snorted. Finn hitched an eyebrow at Alex and Josiah.

"Well, your high-and-mightiness"—Finn gave the kid an elaborate bow— "allow us to unpack the royal, portable loo. Would you like to use it with the privacy screen in place, or shall I set it just beyond those trees?"

There were chuckles all around and the boy's face reddened.

"I'm not going to run off. I don't even know where I am." He held up his bound wrists. "Not to mention this ridiculous business. I'll be back." He did an about-face and strode toward a wide-trunked specimen.

"He can't get far," Josiah said.

"Bashful little guy," Spock observed.

Finn reached down and snatched the Gnome's beanie. "Who ya calling little?"

Spock set on the Nephilim, deftly climbing the giant's long leather boots and then his trousers and shirt. "Give it back. Give it to me!" The Gnome gave Finn's beard a yelp-inducing yank.

Alex threw up his hands. "Do you know the definition of 'keep it down'? Head start or not, let's avoid announcing our presence here."

Spock glared from Finn to Alex. "It's not as if you giant bird-men with your oversized equine are tiptoeing your way through the forest. Do you know how loud you guys even *breathe*?"

Colin rejoined them.

"If we can all act like adults," Spock went on, flicking a glance at Colin, "present company excluded, I'll tell you blokes what to expect. On the backside of this cliff we'll come to the waterfall that feeds this stream. The stream is slick and stony and difficult to cross, but its the way we gain access to a tunnel that burrows beneath the waterfall. We'll just have to choose the right place to negotiate it. For the horses sake as much as our own."

The group murmured their assent. Finn lifted Spock, setting him down without further provocation. The Gnome lumbered on, and Finn grabbed Sage's reins. Dempsey mumbled something about "blasted tall horses" and forged ahead, leaving Alex to collect Gandalf.

A sharp, slicing whistle drew everyone's attention to Josiah, who stood beside Ansyn. "Dempsey," he called, and jerked his head toward Colin.

Alex inwardly cringed at the shrill, exposing sound.

The Dwarf understood the signal and marched over to the boy. Dempsey looked Colin up and down. "I can break that bony body of yers like a twig." He snapped thick, calloused fingers. "Don't try anything funny."

Colin glowered and lifted his fettered, gloved hands. "I'll be testing your vigilance constantly." His large eyes rolled skyward. "I don't need a babysitter."

Josiah turned the kid toward the stream. "Let's go."

"Don't worry," Dempsey said, falling into stride beside Colin. "*Sittin'* on ya would be the last thing I'd think about doin' if ya get out of line."

Colin halted and flashed a sideways look at the Dwarf.

"You won't be talking like that once you see me fight."

The Dwarf gave a doubtful "Ha!" and spat on the ground. "Get yer wee legs a walkin' before I put yer big mouth to the test."

Alex had been watching the exchange. He clicked his tongue and led Gandalf to fall in behind Finn and Spock. There was something in Colin's unusual eyes that chilled Alex.

What might happen if they put that scrawny kid to the test?

CHAPTER TEN

Alex

THE POUNDING PLUMMET OF THE WATERFALL muted conversation as the group followed the wend of the stream, in search of a place to cross. The water hurtled over small, slick rocks and sprinted around jagged boulders. For the sake of the timorous horses and the squat Dwarf, they sought a calm, shallow crossing, that wouldn't require submersion.

Knee-high to a Nephilim was waist-high to a Dwarf, and fully soaked boots were best avoided by both. Though Josiah and Finn could, quite literally, wing it, Alex and the others preferred not to traipse about in soggy shoes. As always, Dempsey would risk drowning over the humiliation of being ferried or flown about by one of his taller companions.

An impressive mound of logs and limbs eventually revealed itself. A helpful beaver dam strangled the flow, exposing chunks of mossy rock jutting slightly above the water's tranquil surface. Possessing none of Dempsey's self-sufficiency, Spock wasted no time scaling Finn's boots, belt, and beard for safe passage. Giving their horses plenty of rein, the group picked their way across with only minor water splatters on boots and britches.

Safely on the opposite side, they made their way back to the distant curtain of water, raining down like liquid thunder. Alex wondered how he'd never heard mention of this unusually large waterfall, though "Mila's Pass" did ring familiar. Approaching the backside of the wedge-shaped wall of rock—and well out of sight from the first leg of their escape—the undercurrent of tension buzzing inside Alex began to dissipate.

Still, waterfall or not, the backside looked as impassable as the front. He hoped Spock hadn't been mistaken about the tunnel. What if it had collapsed since the Gnome last passed this way?

Tiny droplets of mist clung to the group as they drew near. Alex appreciated the chill it provided, waking his senses. Water cascaded from a height of about fifty feet, the ragged ledge from which it plunged causing the runnel to flare out, away from the cliff, before careening down the uneven surface of granite. He wrinkled his nose at the hint of sulfur that tinged the air.

Water wasn't the only thing blanketing the rock face. Gnarly tangles of vines tumbled from the top of the cliff like a mass of dreadlocks. Thick, ropey tentacles that seemed to twitch ever so slightly from the force of the nearby water.

As they closed in, however, Alex noticed a flutter of movement here and there, as if the tentacles were spasming, alive with nerves and sensing their approach. Was something clinging to the vines? Something...alive?

Bats.

Thousands of bats clutched the vines. Their upside-down bodies, a camouflaged match to the vegetation, created a blur of shifting, shivering movement.

The others obviously recognized the creatures as well. They collectively stopped and gaped at the squirming mass of bodies.

"It's all right!" Spock hollered above the din of the water, still seated on Finn's shoulder. "Bat-dragons are harmless. At least they will be, once I speak to them."

Did he say 'Bat-dragons'? Could they be the same creature as the Dragon-bats that Alex's nanny had used to scare him into obedience as a little boy?

"The Dragon-bats silently fly down the chimney and into your room, once you're asleep. If you get up, they will send scouts to alert me. If you try to leave your room, they will follow you and nip at your ears and nose and toes, to make you obey."

"Bats?" Colin gasped, mouth agape.

"Would these happen to be the same terrifying creatures as the Dragon-bats of my childhood?" Josiah asked. He and Finn and Alex had swapped stories about them over the years.

Spock sputtered a laugh. "Yes, indeed. But you can wipe that look off your face—all of you. They're cool. I promise they won't hurt a hair on your head."

Alex reached a protective hand to his neck. "I'm not exactly worried about my hair."

"Re-*lax*." Spock waved a dismissive hand. "They don't bite hard. Teeth are too small."

"They bite?" Colin squeaked.

"I'm kidding. No, no. They won't bite." Spock looked like he was enjoying himself. "They do puff smoke through their nostrils. It'll put you to sleep straightaway if you inhale it. They're not fire-breathing, though. Not that I've seen. They are simply small-scale Dragons the size of bats, not bats that look like Dragons, so Bat-dragon is the correct moniker for these little guys."

"Thanks fer the tutorial Professor Spock, but I don't do bats of any kind. Dragon or no." Dempsey's brows furrowed into a unibrow.

Spock punched his hands onto his hips. "If you guys could see yourselves." He shook his head. "Every one of you is bigger than me, and *I'm* bigger than these Bat-dragons. You must be forgetting my innate skill at talking to animals. Now, are we moving forward, or should we go back to Calamus and help Alex write his vows?"

Everyone turned to Alex, as if they couldn't quite decide.

"'Further up and further in,' as they say in Narnia," Alex said, pointing at the squirming wall of rock. "Let's soldier on and hope that a lifetime of horror stories are, indeed, false."

Finn extracted the Gnome from his shoulders and set him on the ground facing the group. "I'm going to let you and that consummate mouth of yours take the lead."

"Roots and fruits!" Spock shook his head and took a few backward steps. "Scared of a little rodent-sized Dragon..."

"Flyin' rodents. And too many to count, mind ya," Dempsey called after him, shuddering. "Trust me, I shall happily repeat yer little speech 'ere the next time ya encounter a wee spider and start blubberin' fer help."

Spock's smug smile dissolved. "Hey, everyone has their phobias." With a huff, he waddled over the rocky terrain to the Bat-dragons.

Dempsey chuckled. "Couldn't say whether he's more afraid of spiders or girls, to tell ya the truth."

The Gnome scrambled up a large hunk of stone and rubbed his hands together like he was cold. The agitated bodies of the Bat-dragons stilled in under a minute, though surely the coursing water drowned any potential sound made by his tiny digits.

The waterfall also drowned Spock's odd humming-thrumming talk that he did whenever he communicated with animals. It sounded the same to Alex, no matter what type of creature Spock spoke to. Apparently, there was a universal language between animals, and Gnomes spoke it fluently. Based on the behavior of these Bat-dragons, it seemed to be a language that transcended the volume of whatever might be churning nearby.

The prolific vines swayed beneath the twitchy mob. Then, as one, the Bat-dragons' tiny wings began to flutter. Like a vertical wave, the creatures swelled away from the cliff, carrying the vines in their taloned feet. With slow-motion precision, the veil was lifted and a black hole revealed.

The Bat-dragons continued to rise, a knotted cloud ascending past the top of the cliff. The cave beneath was huge. A few of the creatures broke away from the group and flew into the mouth of the tunnel, as if to say, "Follow us!"

Spock turned and gave a triumphant smirk. "You're welcome." He bowed, then hopped off the rock.

Alex squinted against the icy spray of water and held his breath at the dank smell of rotten eggs that radiated from the cave. A thrill of excitement shot through him as he led Gandalf into the stretch of darkness that lay before them. He might elude his father's soldiers after all.

Finn and Josiah wordlessly grasped their respective reins. Alex kept a wary eye on the unpredictable Bat-dragons even as he felt Gandalf's hesitation to enter the deep, dark cave.

The travelers crossed the threshold in silence. As the veil of vines descended behind them, Alex regretted his lack of a flashlight, having loaned it to Ellynn at some point and being unwilling to risk getting caught or questioned by trying to retrieve it. How long would it take to feel their way through the middle of a mountain?

Beams of light flared to life as Finn and Josiah worked their hand-crank flashlights that Alex had given them for Christmas, years earlier. The friends had been astonished by 'electric torches'—having played with those that Alex brought on camping trips over the years—and were thrilled to have such a novel device of their own. Now, Alex congratulated himself on his brilliant, childhood gift-giving skills.

His eyesight adjusted as they walked. Soon, sparse golden glimmers in the stone grew to puddles of glowing light. Granite in these parts contained phosphorous flecks that brought the walls and ceilings to life with glistening constellations. Here and there, jutting amber geodes offered more light, connected as they were to the crystalline dome of sky. Like the skydome above, which glowed from within, the geodes were powered by the energy of the Flaming Sword of Cherubythe in the far-off realm of Vituvia—where his Uncle Brock reigned as High King of the Gnomes and Spock's mother trained warriors.

Alex kicked at a large, prism-shaped chunk of ambient rock until it came loose and skittered ahead like an enormous, golden diamond. He snatched it up and held it aloft. Ellynn liked to call these temporary torches her "faery flashlights."

Once detached from the ground and the energy of The Sword, a geode would only glow for an hour or so. Alex hoped he and his friends would be well outside of the mountain by then.

The clomping footsteps and hoof falls, along with the sporadic drips of water, echoed around the travelers like an oddly syncopated jazz song. Alex liked the reverberating sounds. He liked jazz. His Uncle Brent had introduced Alex to his collection of jazz albums, which he reverently played on a retro turntable whenever the family visited.

Stray Bat-dragons flitted about whenever the travelers disturbed their sedentary stations. Though Alex knew something so small should be an unrealistic fear, years of horror stories were hard to suppress. He decided then and there that if he ever did marry and "produce an heir," he would not perpetuate the fearful tales of Bat-dragons.

The farther the group traveled, the more prolific the bright geodes and glittery granite grew. Flashlights became unnecessary and everyone marveled at the mineralized stars guiding their way. It was beautiful. And also quite frigid.

"This wretched cold is about to freeze my freckles off," Finn said to no one in particular.

"Maybe then we can stand to look at your face," Alex teased.

"Hmm. If it freezes freckles, maybe it'll freeze birthmarks too," Finn said, snorting a laugh.

No one laughed with him. Alex self-consciously felt his birthmark flame. Though he knew he'd walked right into that insult, neither Finn nor any of the others ever joked about the discolored patch that marked him. It was an unspoken taboo.

"Hey, sorry, man." Finn spoke quietly, though the tunnel amplified every sound. "That was out of line."

"It's fine." Alex's words were clipped, though his abrupt

spark of anger quieted.

"Why is it okay to insult Finn's freckles but not Alex's birthmark?" Colin asked, his voice shrill in the close space.

Alex stopped, jerking his horse to a standstill. Gandalf gave a protesting chuff.

Finn expelled a low whistle. "Look, kid, I insulted my own freckles. My freckles are my business. His birthmark is his. I shouldn't have said anything about it."

Before Colin could follow up with another question, Dempsey had his charge pinned against the wall of the tunnel. A glint at neck-height told the others that Dempsey's dagger rested against the naïve boy's throat.

"New rule, ya scrawny rodent," Dempsey spat. "No talkin' unless you've been asked a question or told to speak. Am I makin' meself clear? And you will refer to His Highness as Prince Alexander when speaking of 'im or to 'im. Got it?"

By the murky light, Alex saw the quick, shuddering nod that Colin gave.

"*That* would be a question, idjit!" Dempsey growled. "Am I makin' meself *clear*?"

"Y-yes, sir," Colin said. His eyes darted to Alex and he lifted his bound hands and pointed. "Except—"

"No! No exceptions. *We* make the exceptions. Not you," Dempsey said, evidently speaking through clenched teeth.

Alex wanted everyone to shut up, move on, and focus on something else. A slow-burning fire of frustration about *everything* had ignited inside his chest.

"*Except.*" Josiah repeated the word with deliberateness. "That birthmark of yours..." he trailed off as the others turned toward Alex. "I hate to say it, bro, but it's..."

"It's what?" Alex demanded, feeling it flush with heat, as if his head were a smokestack.

"*Dude*," Spock whispered. "Your birthmark is *glowing*."

CHAPTER ELEVEN

Alex

THE MORE THEY GAWKED AT ALEX, the more self-conscious he became, and the more his birthmark radiated. Even he could see it—a faint reddish gleam that partially fuzzed the vision in his right eye.

"What under God's green earth is happening to you?" Finn had closed the space between the two of them and now studied his friend from the side. Spock sat on the Nephilim's shoulder giving the impression of a two-headed giant.

Alex shoved them back. "Get out of my face." He sensed the mark glow brighter with the surge of adrenaline and anger. "Just—just quit staring at me. All of you! I don't know what's going on and I don't care. Let's get the hades out of this hole." He strode away, footfalls caustic against the stone. "None of this would be happening if you guys had minded your own business when I decided to leave—*on my own.*"

He heard their tentative steps following behind, alongside the clomp of horses' hooves. Realizing he'd failed to grab Gandalf's reins, he turned to see Josiah leading Sage and Gandalf, side by side. Alex snatched his horse's bridle and pulled him ahead, feeling Josiah's gaze following in fascination.

What was happening? Why was this happening? And why now? Alex kicked loose an overgrown geode from where it bloomed like a prismatic flower from a fissure in the wall. He snatched it up, illuminating the passage enough to reveal the curvature of ceiling and the snaking of the pathway ahead, its light catching the occasional flap of Bat-dragon wings as they skittered into the shadows.

He considered mounting Gandalf and riding off—there had been enough head room thus far—except he needed the physical exertion to stomp out his anger and humiliation. Not to mention the chill.

Alex tried to keep his focus on the progress through the mountain, rather than the dull gleam he could detect around his eye. The sparkling tunnels and glimmering geodes, he reminded himself, must be similar to the passageways his mother and her family had taken through Beacon Rock, the monolith that first brought them into the Tethered World twenty years earlier. He tried to distract himself by recalling details from the descriptions in her books. Weren't giant, glowing mushrooms involved?

Giant, glowing mushrooms. Giant, glowing birthmarks.

His jaw clenched, willing the thoughts away. Willing his skin to return to its bronze pallor. It had been a lengthy eight years since this bizarre phenomena had last manifested on his face. A singular incident he had kept so thoroughly to himself that he'd almost forgotten about it.

Why now?

Indeed, he'd always wondered–why then? Although the circumstances had been quite extraordinary, there was still no precedent, no logical explanation, for such a bizarre apparition.

Skin didn't glow in the dark. Phosphorous plants like giant mushrooms, firefly butts, geodes—even Dragon scales, according to his mother—those things could glow. But human skin? No. No way.

Except the faintly shimmering side of his face said otherwise.

Alex hoped he hadn't taken a wrong turn. Twice the passageway had forked, offering a smaller tunnel diverting from what appeared to be the main thoroughfare. He kept to the wider tunnels, and Spock—who had trekked this way before—didn't correct course.

Though he felt infernally cold inside this hollow shell of granite, he'd kept his mind off of the chill and off his birthmark—finally returned to its formerly dull state—by keeping an eye on a Bat-dragon that seemed to be keeping an eye on him. What he'd first assumed to be the frightened flight of various, lone Bat-dragons, disturbed by the group's intrusive presence, had eventually narrowed to the realization that it was but one individual critter.

Alex had glimpsed two greyish nubs—horns—on the heads of the various Bat-dragons they'd disturbed. This particular fellow looked different with the tip of one of its horns broken and blunted, making it distinct.

When Alex deliberated at yet another fork in the tunnel—Gandalf stamping the ground as if he, too, was cold—the miniature creature flew to the left and circled back, looping closer to Alex's head with each lap. Was it trying to show them the way? Could it be trusted?

"To the left," Spock spoke into the silence. "I think that little dude is trying to give you directions."

"You *think*?" Finn said. "Can't you speak to him in your gibberish and ask? My toes are numb and I'm ready to get out of this hole."

"Its body language is obvious, I don't need to ask," Spock replied.

Dempsey gave a skeptical grunt.

"We're going left." Alex wasn't ready for banter or conversation.

The Bat-dragon circled again, and Alex strode into the left-hand passage. Within a dozen yards, a faint golden light diffused the gloom. Gandalf saw it as well and increased his pace, head bobbing in anticipation.

"Glory be!" Dempsey called from behind. "I'm tired of lookin' at this horse's hinter-parts and I'm ready as a Yeti for a smoke of me pipe."

Striding out of the tunnel, Alex thought the dusktime skydome had never looked warmer and more welcoming. He released Gandalf, who wasted no time nosing into a clump of grass. The others tumbled out of the mountain in an exhale of bodies, hoofs, and wings.

Dempsey busied himself tamping tobacco into his pipe as he leaned against a tree trunk with a satisfied sigh. Spock sprawled onto a wide, bowl-shaped rock, whose mossy middle provided ample cushioning.

Josiah and Finn reached their lanky arms skyward, wings unfurling in a silvery-swath of feathers, while Colin looked on, seemingly unimpressed. Alex settled against a birch with one eye on the boy. He guessed that Colin had been around Nephilim before, since feathered appendages didn't make him look twice. Instead, the boy sat against the flat side of a chunk of granite, elbows on knees, his fettered wrists bridging the gap. One of his filthy, fingerless gloves was frayed;

a squiggle of yarn dangled temptingly. Alex imagined snagging the string to see how far it would unravel with one good yank.

He knew he needed to make Colin cough up his story, and he would demand answers soon enough. Safe as they seemed to be, Alex was determined to get moving after a brief rest. Cutting Colin loose this soon was premature. His father's men were excellent trackers. If they could sniff their way to the waterfall, the tunnel itself was a one-way road to where they sat. Colin could simply bide his time here, or tunnel back to Mila's pass to await their arrival and lead them to Alex's trail.

No, Alex would feel better with a bigger buffer zone. He only wished he had a defined destination—preferably one that would take him topside. Or, at least, lead him to something or someone who might relieve his father of his illness. Maybe there was a wise hermit living in isolation, brewing miraculous teas or growing medicinal mushrooms.

There had always been speculation surrounding who or what might live in the mysterious and relatively unexplored hinterlands. Early history claimed that these lands weren't always so wild and sparsely populated. Clusters of settlements once peppered most of the Tethered World, until the last dozen centuries or so. Dregs were rumored to live obscure lives in these parts. Creatures and people from all over the Tethered World who were disenchanted with the status quo, or maybe running from trouble, made their way to this unpopulated place.

Alex scanned the sparse woods for evidence of trails. Morning mist was beginning to coalesce and obscure the ground, weaving a wispy blanket that held secrets Alex couldn't penetrate. Though he'd lost grasp of time in the monotonous mountain, the developing haze meant dusktime light would be brightening to daylight soon.

"Should I take the first watch so you can rest?" Josiah now stood beside Alex's outstretched legs. "I can tether the boy to Finn and then switch after a couple of hours."

Alex looked away. He loathed the way his title made others feel the need to protect him. He wanted to take care of himself. Soon enough, he would do exactly that. "No. I'll stay on watch. We're not going to be here long enough to swap duty."

"But—"

"But nothing. I'm not tired. I'm..." He searched for something convincing to say. "I'm too wound up."

Finn sauntered over, gnawing on a hank of dried bison. "C'mon. We're nicely tucked away here. Unless your father is traveling with a Gnome who also knows these parts, you're not likely to be in any danger. I think we can all grab a cat nap."

"I wouldn't place any bets on that assumption. Even if my father is otherwise engaged today—no pun intended—his men are excellent trackers." Alex cracked his knuckles and clambered to his feet. "You guys grab a quick nap. I'll stay on lookout."

"Really, Alex," Josiah rubbed a thumb along the inky scruff of his jawline, "you should rest. I'm good for now."

Alex knew that Josiah loved sleep as much as he loved topside pizza. That is to say, more than life itself. Besides, he could see purple shadows beneath Josiah's eyes. "Nope. You sleep. Don't make me pull rank."

Josiah gave a doubtful smirk but didn't argue, dipping his head and backing away.

Finn stayed put, shifting his weight uneasily. "Listen, Alex. About what happened in the tunnel...I wanted to say how—"

"It's fine, Finn." Alex pressed his palms in the space between them. "I'm the one who overreacted. You were only following up my smackdown about your freckles with one of your own."

"No, no. I crossed a line." Finn shook his head, poked a thumb to his chest. "I'm sorry." He took a half step forward and stuck out his hand.

Alex clasped it, grinning. "Sheesh, we're turning into a couple of saps. Now go snooze while you can." He turned and climbed the jagged granite overhang that surrounded the mouth of the tunnel, knowing higher ground provided a better view.

He settled onto a slab of rock that formed a natural ledge about ten feet above his friends. From this vantage point, he could see into the foliage of birch and willows and evergreens, which—he noted—grew much thicker on this side of the foothills. The swirling mist danced around and between their trunks, giving the impression of trees sprouting from a gauzy ocean instead of the rocky ground.

What happened to the Bat-dragon who had led them through the tunnels to freedom? Was he out there somewhere, sitting on a limb watching Alex watch the others?

Dempsey's pungent pipe smoke mingled with the smell of

the decomposing earth and the herbal tang of growing greenery, drifting upward with the mist. It was a comforting combination. Alex leaned his head back, studying the skydome, deciding it looked a brighter already.

Man, what he wouldn't give to be looking up at a topside sunrise instead...

The next thing Alex knew, someone was shaking him awake.

CHAPTER TWELVE

Alex

ALEX AWOKE TO A TANGLE OF thoughts. He was instantly annoyed—at both himself for falling asleep and at whoever had the nerve to wake him by persistently plucking on his dreadlocks. He attempted to slap the interloper away, striking the air. The smell of sulfur prodded him fully awake.

He spied tiny, taloned feet, pewter scales, and leathery bat-like wings that kept the creature hovering like an annoying, oversized mosquito. Alex sat up and successfully batted it away. It landed on Alex's knee, pale green eyes scowling beneath its incongruent horns. Purplish smoke streamed from oblong nostrils like dueling chimneys, obscuring its reptilian snout. Head tilting, bird-like, it inspected Alex from one vertical pupil, then the other, revealing its crocodile-curved mouth. Fangs as fine as glass shards jutted over its lower lip in a permanent, insidious smile.

"It's *you*." Alex grumbled. He swept his gaze across the landscape of sleeping friends and grazing horses below. All was quiet, no thanks to his vigilance.

The Bat-dragon hopped onto the ledge beside Alex, peeking down, as if needing to confirm for itself that all was well.

"What are you looking at?" Alex whispered. "It's not *your* job to protect anyone." He waved a hand at the creature and it flapped out of reach. Then it launched itself and landed closer than before.

"Go back to your tunnel." Alex crossed his legs and rested his elbows on his knees, pointedly looking away.

The critter hopped onto Alex's right boot, facing him. Though the tips of the beast's wings had very bat-like claws that transformed the wings into a set of retractable arms, it also had another pair of scaly, lizard-like arms now clenched against its ribcage. The Bat-dragon managed to convey a look of irritation, magnified by faster, thicker smoke chugging from its nostrils.

"What?" Alex jostled his foot. Still, the creature clung to the leather boot. "Okay...*thanks*. Thanks for leading us out of the tunnels. Is that what you want?"

"Who're you talking to?" Josiah called from below.

Great. Alex had woken him. "Nobody. Go back to sleep."

"Nah. Couldn't sleep." Josiah unfolded himself from the base of a wide evergreen and turned to look up at Alex. "Sounded like you managed to catch a few winks, though. Not bad for someone who wasn't tired. I could hear you snoring from here." He chuckled and flicked his head so that his neck cracked and snapped.

Alex felt frustration clench inside his chest. Josiah had kept watch for him. Worse than that, his friend had expected him to fall asleep—with good reason, apparently.

Alex swiped at the smoke-churning irritant, knocking the critter sideways so that it cartwheeled off his boot. A yelp, followed by indignant chatter, erupted from the beast. It righted itself mid-air then levitated in front of Alex, spewing a flicker of fire from its mouth. Though it only breached the distance by half, Alex pulled back instinctively.

"Sheesh!" He leapt up. "You're crazy. Go away! Get out of here." Alex scrambled down the rocky face beside the tunnel. Hadn't Spock said that these freaky creatures *couldn't* breathe fire?

By now the others were awake and laughing at the commotion. The Bat-dragon continued to rant in its squeaky-hinge voice as it circled the group, finally landing on a nearby tree limb. Smoke encompassed its face in angry, lavender puffs.

Spock hurried to stand beneath it, speaking his animal-lingo, offering calming gestures and a soothing tone.

"I thought you said those things weren't fire-breathing," Alex spat, glaring at the Bat-dragon. "He's like a bleeping flame thrower."

"What got into him?" Colin asked, rubbing his eyes. His choppy platinum hair clung damply to the side of his face where he'd lain, his ankle tethered to Finn's.

"Hey!" Dempsey hollered, while fumbling to light his pipe. "The no yakkin' rule is still in place."

Finn reached for the leather strap that lashed his ankle

to Colin's. "Calm down, Dempsey."

Dempsey muttered to himself, jamming shreds of tobacco into his pipe.

"Listen." Finn squatted beside Colin and reached for the boy's wrists. "I'm going to untie your wrists for a few. I'm offering a tiny respite because, as you pointed out, you're outsized and outnumbered. If you dare try anything, however, I'll retie your arms *behind* your back and there won't be any relief for your scrawny wrists."

Colin gave Finn an appreciative nod.

As Finn worked the knot free, he suddenly clutched Colin's hands and brought them nearer, inspecting them. "What in the bottomless abyss is wrong with your fingers?" he asked.

Colin tried unsuccessfully to wrest his gloved hands away. "It's nothing. Forget about untying me."

Alex and the others gathered near. Colin's fingers were cobbled together in an attempt to hide them. Finn took both of Colin's hands in one of his own massive paws. With the other he untied the narrow leather binding.

Still holding Colin's wrists, Finn swiped the gloves off the boy, despite one last grasp that snagged the tattered gloves and turned them inside out.

The kid cursed then shoved his open, exposed palms at Finn's face, fingers spread wide. "There, ya happy? Take a good long look."

Alex could see scars threading between each of Colin's fingers, pink and lumpy, spilling onto his palms in varying degrees.

"Roots and fruits!" Dempsey sputtered around the pipe between his teeth.

Finn's voice was soft when he asked, "Colin, what happened to you? Who did this?"

A tear slipped from Colin's chocolate brown eye and he squeezed his eyelids shut, mumbling.

"What'd ya say, lad?" Finn spoke gently. "It's okay. You can tell us."

Colin only shook his head. Finn must have relaxed his grip because the young man retracted his arms from the Nephilim's grasp and folded them against his chest so that his hands burrowed into his armpits.

Finn gave the others a look of uncertainty, then placed a comforting hand on the boy's head before standing.

They readied their mounts, leaving Colin to collect himself.

Spock hopped from one chunk of rock to another until he stood on a decent-sized boulder a few feet from where the Bat-dragon crouched in the tree. The creature fluttered down from the limb to stand beside the Gnome, and the two chatted incoherently.

Alex checked Gandalf's hoofs for pebbles and debris. Colin's scars left Alex unsettled, but with the morning well underway, they needed to forge ahead. He imagined the commotion in the palace as everyone—who wasn't trying to locate him—readied themselves to greet the infamous wedding party from Éire House.

"Alex. Guys. We need to talk." Spock motioned them to come to where he and the Bat-dragon had been conversing atop the boulder.

Alex was glad for the distraction and headed over. He stopped mid-stride. "Where's our runaway?" Alex's gaze darted about, looking for Colin.

"Taking care of business," Dempsey called with a jerk of his chin. "Boy's got a bladder the size of an acorn. He's comin.'"

On cue, Colin stepped out of the trees, giving the Dwarf an irritated glare.

"Good." Spock crossed his arms and tipped his head toward their scaly companion. "Now then. Parsifal has some suggestions for the next leg of our journey."

"*Parsifal?*" Alex made a face. "What kind of a name is that?"

Spock shrugged. "*His* name. Parsifal Plinderpuff. Dragons always have names, extravagant ones, more often than not. That's his."

"Yeah. Awesome names like Smaug. Or Odyssey." Finn hid his laughter behind his fist. "Parsifal Blunderbuff? Really?"

"*Plin-der-puff.*" Spock enunciated each syllable as if speaking to a child.

Finn gave the Gnome a mocking thumbs-up.

"As I was saying," Spock went on, "Parsifal wishes to join us, Your Highness."

"Seriously?" Alex gave a frustrated toss of his hands and looked up at the skydome. "This isn't a traveling carnival. I don't need that bat tagging along too."

The Bat-dragon flitted to a branch that swooped above Alex's head. It snapped its smoking snout and chattered in scolding screeches. The beast was none too happy about something.

"Parsifal asks that you refrain from calling him a *bat*," Spock explained. "Says that the term 'Bat-dragon' is demeaning and we should toss it. Little dude has absolutely no relation to bats. He is a small species of Dragon. Therefore, 'Dragon' will suffice."

"Kripes. Would seem the pocket-sized beastie is also prone to drama and sulkiness," Dempsey said, giving said beastie a dark look.

"Fine, he's a Dragon," Alex agreed for the sake of expediency. "He can tag along if it means we can get out of here."

Spock offered a half bow in Alex's direction. "Terrific. Now it's your call, Alex. Do you want to navigate, or would you prefer to have Parsifal at the helm? He's familiar with these parts. My knowledge of the hinterlands ends right about here, unfortunately."

Alex felt a prick of frustration. He bulged his cheeks in a noisy exhale. "You're the one who knew about the tunnel and I assumed that meant you knew something about the hinterlands too." He offered a defeated shrug. "Obviously, I want distance between myself and Calamus. So if the Bat-dragon—excuse me, *Dragon*—can help direct us, then fine. If he knows of any friendly settlements farther out, people who might know about medicine...tell him to take us there."

Spock nodded. "Sure thing." He shoved his hands into his pockets. "Of course, most of the stories about the hinterlands have to do more with strange and unfriendly folks and wandering bands of Dregs. My grandpop had some rough encounters in these parts. Parsifal says their numbers have swelled. There are Trolls, Dwarves, Stygians, and even some disgruntled Nephilim living in some sort of feral community together. I'm guessing *they're* not hiding any medicinal miracles."

"Stygians!" Dempsey spat in the dirt at the mention of the common nickname for Dark Dwarves. These thickheaded miscreants were the dangerous nemeses of the Dwarves of Berganstroud in Dempsey's homeland.

Alex nodded. This was beginning to feel like an exhausting game of hide-and-seek. Hide from his bride. Hide from his father. Now, hide from the Dregs. "Fine." He gestured at the Dragon. "Probably best to avoid contact with anyone for now. If Parsifal can make that happen, then he can play navigator. Let's not waste time discussing it."

He made a beeline for Gandalf and nudged Dempsey as he passed. "You still riding with me?"

The others followed suit, grabbing rucksacks and canteens. Parsifal flew circles over the group. Once Alex sat astride Gandalf with Dempsey behind—feeling at ease enough to face forward this time—the little Dragon settled himself onto Alex's shoulder with a squawk.

"Hey! Get off me." Alex swatted at the creature. Parsifal flitted out of reach, then settled himself atop Alex's other shoulder.

"Mind yer passenger, laddie. 'Bout to shove me off Gandalf's backside," Dempsey groused, helping to shoo the Dragon away.

Finn and Spock nudged each other from atop Ansyn, clearly amused.

"Oh, one more thing," Spock said. "Little Dragon dude says it's also his duty to help protect King Xander's son. Like it or not."

"I don't *need* protecting." Did he emit some sort of signal that made others—or everyone—believe him to be weak? Alex didn't want special treatment. Was it asking too much to be treated like a normal, ordinary person?

A fuzzy blur gleamed from around his right eye, alerting Alex that his birthmark had gone neon again.

So much for ordinary.

CHAPTER THIRTEEN

Alex

"WHAT IN THE NAME OF WHITT Lake is that smell?" Alex asked, slowing Gandalf in the midst of a moss and fern quilted forest floor. They had been riding the better part of an hour through woods with undergrowth so green and lush, it almost hurt Alex's eyes to look at it.

It had been a blissfully uneventful ride thus far. Parsifal insisted the conglomeration of Tethered World outcasts—the Dregs—were tucked into a valley a league away from the tunnel. The Dragon led the group in the opposite direction where he knew of a spring-fed pond concealed within a grove of trees. Yet somehow Alex felt more tense than ever. The forest felt unnaturally quiet, and he couldn't shake the feeling of being watched.

The forest floor began to alternately slope and level out like a giant staircase, causing Gandalf to misstep as he picked his way down some of the steeper embankments. The sickening smell of rotten eggs assaulted the group as soon as the first descent presented itself. Faced with the noxious smell, Alex considered taking his chances with the Dregs. Everyone shared similarly sick expressions, using their tunic, shirt, or cape to cover their nose and mouth.

The diminutive Dragon, who sat on Finn's shoulder between occasional flights of fancy, jabbered loudly and coasted to the ground with a squawk. He hopped across the needle-strewn earth and began to play tug-o-war with a plump earthworm.

"Parsifal says that the smell comes from mist rising off of the pond just beyond this incline." Spock stuck out his tongue. "*Bleh.* Not sure that I can keep my lunch down if we get any closer."

Dempsey grunted from behind Alex. "Haven't eaten any

lunch meself, unless you've got a secret stash ya haven't been willin' to share." Alex could feel the Dwarf rub his paunchy stomach. "Could sure use a snack."

"If we're close to a decent-sized body of water," Alex said, "let's put it between us and our potential pursuers. The odor ought to keep anyone from sniffing us out. Then we can make camp and discuss our next move."

He glanced at Josiah, who looked slightly annoyed by Colin, now slumped against him, asleep. Josiah's free arm encircled the boy's shoulders to keep the kid from toppling forward as they descended.

Alex wouldn't want some stranger snuggled up against his chest. Then again, Josiah always had a soft spot for the underdog. He was kind and protective by nature, like his grandfather Gage. Josiah had shown Alex friendship at one of the lowest points of his life, at a time when Alex was busy pushing everyone away.

Finn lowered his cape from his face and said. "If you say so, boss. Really hoping the smell improves though or I'm gonna puke."

A victorious Parsifal launched himself off the ground, worm wriggling in his crocodile jaws, and perched on the leather rucksack that Finn had slung around his waist for lack of a saddle horn. The bulk of the pack bounced off the right side of the horse's flank, propelling the Dragon up and down with each hoof fall while he made quick work of the squirmy grub.

"We'll get used to it," Spock said from inside the collar of his shirt. "It's like going to the Sulphur Sea. Eventually you won't notice it."

Finn spoke from behind his cape, reminding Alex of a stereotypical vampire. "I've always wondered if the awful smell of the Sulphur Sea is responsible for how ghastly the average Ogre smells."

Alex pointed at his friend in a gesture of you're-onto-something. "Agree. They're surrounded by it on the island of Skellerwad, they drink it, and then they sweat it out as part of the water cycle. It's in their genes."

Many of the bodies of water in the Tethered World had that eggy-odor, because most water sources came from the bowels of the earth—and *bowels* weren't exactly known for their sweet smells. An abundance of fresh-smelling water was yet another thing that topside life had over life below ground.

Water that flowed through pipes, straight to the bathroom or kitchen, at the touch of a button or turn of a faucet...it was like a miracle that everyone in the modern world took for granted. Alex was impatient to have such luxury at his fingertips.

Colin roused, a bitter frown twisting his mouth as he jerked forward, looking ill. "Ugh! What *is* that?" He looked at the others, noticing their covered faces, and did the same with his grimy shirt.

Josiah chuckled. "It's your wake-up call."

Gandalf faltered as the slope tilted precariously. The horses huffed and pulled up short near the edge of a plunging, steep hill that disappeared into mist as thick as oatmeal.

"Good golly, Aunt Polly. What've we here?" Finn asked, peering into the all-engulfing white void at the front of the group.

Parsifal chirped and chattered, as the others squeezed beside Finn to look at the swirling, milky cloud. The mounts twitched their ears and stamped their hoofs, evidently as skittish as their riders.

"What's he yammering about?" Alex asked Spock.

The lower half of the Gnome's head emerged from inside his shirt and he gave the air a sniff, then cleared his throat. "Little lizard dude says the haze might burn off as the day goes on. He hasn't been this way often enough to know the water's habits."

"What's it like down there?" Alex asked. "Does this hill slope straight into the water? Or does it level out and provide a shoreline?"

Spock leaned toward Parsifal, who still roosted atop Finn's saddlebag, and the two conversed quietly. Then Spock straightened and explained, "Parsifal says it has an open, gravelly shore most of the way around, from what he recalls."

Finn placed his hands on his hips and slowly shook his head. "Not crazy about the idea of plunging blindly into that. Might walk into the waiting arms of a bunch of rabid Dregs."

Parsifal piped up again, wings aflutter.

"He doesn't think so," Spock interpreted.

"Not particularly reassurin'," Dempsey grumbled.

Spock shrugged. "We're in new territory. At least Parsifal has an idea of what we can expect. Plus, I'm starved."

The Dwarf nudged Alex. "Our boy's got a point. For the sake of some grub and a smoke, I say let's not sit 'ere like a slug on a log. Let's get down to that wretched pond."

Finn tossed Dempsey a dubious look. "You must be one of the seven dwarfs. Grumpy, I presume?"

"Wrong!" Dempsey shook his fist. "I'm the eighth Dwarf. M'name's Famished. Now let's get down this blasted hill and into that stinkin' mist before I stuff yer little bat-friend on the end of a spit and roast 'im over a fire."

CHAPTER FOURTEEN

Alex

WISPS OF FOG PIROUETTED OFF THE enormous glassy pond, twisting in a slow-motion dance. Alex watched the rogue swirls meander together like a ballet of departing spirits rising reluctantly heavenward. What physical phenomenon made one hazy patch stay on the water's surface while another swept up and away? Whatever it might be, at least the soupy steam was steadily evaporating, and the runaways could keep an eye out for any ragtag Dregs who might've trailed them.

He also wondered where to draw the line between a huge pond and a small lake. It had taken them over half an hour to skirt from one side to the other, though the mist certainly factored in.

"So what's your story, kid?" Alex shifted his gaze to Colin. He'd noticed the boy stealing furtive glances at him again, once they finally put Famished the Dwarf out of his misery. "Time to spill it. I'm confident we can leave you here without my father's men tracking you down anytime soon."

Colin shifted on the pebbly ground so that he angled in Alex's direction. Josiah sat between them, ankles crossed, leaning against a long, squat boulder that the three of them shared. "Leave me? Here? I really prefer to continue with you. I promise not to be a bother."

Dempsey gave a sardonic *hmph* around his mouthful of jerky. He paced the shore a few feet away, wary of what might creep out of the lingering haze. Spock had wandered into the shrubbery to look for mushrooms, while Parsifal busily chased the coiling tendrils of mist, swooping and looping over the pond. The horses wasted no time finding greenery to nibble.

At Colin's comment, Finn stopped skipping rocks at the water's edge and turned to face the three sitting against the hunk of granite.

Colin took in the sudden interest of the others, responding with his typical sullen glare.

"That's not your decision to make." Alex swiveled so he could rest one elbow on his knee, facing Colin. "You're a liability as far as I can see. You're too underwhelmingly small to be of any use. May as well have brought along my little sister."

Bright pink blotches bloomed on Colin's cheeks. With his choppy white-blond hair pointed in all directions, he reminded Alex of an anime character come to life.

"My money'd be on yer sister if it came to it." Dempsey chuckled, gesturing at Alex with his gnarled hunk of meat. "At least Ellynn's got some promisin' archery skills."

Colin crossed his arms and glared. "You don't know *what* kind of skills I have. So far all we've been doing is running. A skill shared in equal measure, from what I can see."

Alex arranged his features in a mockery of Colin's sneer. "Ooh. *Equal measure*," he mimicked. "Looks like we've got an educated runaway among us, guys."

Colin looked skyward and smacked one fist into the palm of the other hand. Knuckles popped one by one.

"Down, boy." Josiah patted Colin's head. "If you're gonna hang with us, you better learn to take your share of razzing."

Spock wandered up, cradling his beanie in the crook of his left arm like a basket, mushrooms overflowing. Popping one in his mouth, he caught the tense vibe and pulled up short.

"That's still a big and unlikely *if.*" Alex gave Josiah a cautioning look. "I still need to hear your tale of woe—there's an educated phrase for ya—before we decide whether to bring you or ditch you."

Colin pressed his lips together, his focus drifting to the water. Finn straddled a log that ran parallel to the shoreline, its tapered end void of all but nubby stumps where its limbs had decomposed. Spock scuttled over and settled himself atop Finn's boot, beanie of mushrooms clasped in his arms like a tub of popcorn at the movies.

Colin chewed the corner of his mouth before exhaling a loud puff of air. "Well, obviously I'm a Topsider."

Alex raised his brows, in a "yeah, so?" quirk.

Dempsey finished his jerky and grappled with his pipe paraphernalia. "And obviously you're no longer topside." He jabbed the tip of his pipe toward the crystalline skydome, tobacco pouch dangling from his other hand.

Parsifal alighted onto the log beside Finn.

Colin took in his rapt audience and flipped his palms upward, spreading his exposed, scarred fingers in a resigned gesture. "Not much to tell," he mumbled. "I—I was kidnapped as a child."

Josiah inhaled sharply. "Colin, that's...that's awful."

"So, *recently* then?" Alex said.

"*Alex*," Josiah said, incredulous. "That's not something to joke about."

Colin glowered at Alex. It was a long moment before he spoke again. "I was seven. My family and I were on...uh, holiday. We were swimming at the beach, and I—I sort of got separated from them. Had no idea where I was. Didn't know how to get back to them so I, y'know, wandered around." He lifted his unsettling eyes to Alex. "I was too afraid to speak to anyone. My mother had warned me about strangers, of course, so I was mistrustful of everyone I met."

Alex nodded, feeling worse and worse about how he'd treated this kid who had probably not been treated well in some time.

"I tried to blend in and act like I belonged while I figured out what to do. Finally, someone noticed me. They seemed to want to help me. By then I was starving. They offered me food." He pantomimed holding a dish out to the others. "Except they—they spoke a foreign language. So I didn't understand anything except that they wanted to feed me."

"Surely your parents and the police were scavenging the area for you, at that point," Josiah said.

Colin gnawed at a hangnail then gave a subtle shake of his head. "I don't really know." His gaze slid to his feet. "My parents didn't speak the language either, so..." He trailed off with a shrug. "That made things complicated. I finished eating, curled up in a chair, and fell asleep."

Spock stood and walked over to Colin, extending his mushroom-laden hat. "Language barrier or not, I'm sure your parents had the whole town looking for you. I mean, someone had to have spoken English, it's the university language. Or something."

Colin took a few mushrooms and gave a heavy, shrugging sigh. "I think you mean *universal* language." He popped the fungi in his mouth and looked to be steeling himself as he chewed and swallowed. "I only remember waking a few hours later to find myself tied up. An unwilling participant in some sort of ceremony. It was nighttime. I—well, my meal or beverage had been laced with something because I kept falling asleep, no matter how hard I fought it. I was trembling all over, partially from the cold. Partially, I believe, from some sort of reaction to what they gave me." Colin shivered, seeming to recall the chill. "I was strapped upright against something hard and cold. Between the drugs and the dark, I didn't know what was going on or where I was, other than outside, near the ocean. I could hear it."

"What makes you think it was a ceremony?" Alex asked. "Maybe you were their hostage and they planned to demand money for your safe return. I've read about that sort of thing."

Colin kept his eyes trained on the water. His silence said plenty, but finally he whispered. "They...they built a fire near me. There were cryptic symbols painted on their faces–and they painted mine as well." He looked at Josiah and Alex. "In their strange language they were chanting louder and louder until...well, until some Faeries appeared. They were vicious little mites. They stung me, or bit me, or both. Then they...took me away." He returned his attention to the water. "Which is why I didn't care for the Faeries in your barn last night."

Alex and Josiah exchanged mystified glances. What kind of Faeries had Colin encountered? Alex had never heard of such a thing. "Then what?" he asked, his tone softening.

Colin rested his elbows atop his knees, hands clasped, pale wrists sporting fading red stripes from the earlier restraints. "Then," he said, voice hard and bitter, "I found myself *here*, in this underground crypt, where I've lived not-so happily ever after."

Dempsey grunted. "Precisely *where* did this fairytale take place? You might be a young punk but ye're no seven-year-old kid. Where has a *Topsider* been hidin' fer years without none of us gettin' wind of it?"

The boy's nostrils flared with the flex of his jaw. "Don't really care to get into all that. Let's just say that I've been looking for a way to escape and return topside since I arrived. I finally managed it a few days ago, or so I thought." He gave Dempsey a scathing stare. "Looks like I've only managed to trade one set of captors for another."

"Not for long," Alex pressed himself off the ground, dusting sand off his breeches as he straightened. He looked down at the boy. "Because I'm not taking you with us. I can't."

"What? I—"

Alex pressed his hands toward the protesting boy. "I'm sorry. Really. I'm sorry about what happened to you. It was wrong. It was awful. You didn't deserve any of it. But I have enough problems of my own right now without adopting yours. I don't need another person coming after me in order to get to you. Maybe you can stay here. Join the Dregs or whatever. I bet they'd love the novelty of a Topsider in their offbeat tribe. Or find your way topside. You are finally *free*. We won't tell anyone about you, and you deny any knowledge of our whereabouts. Deal?" He extended his hand, trying to ignore the chorus of stricken faces. "Live long and prosper and all that."

Colin only lowered his tear-riddled face between the points of his knees. Josiah glanced at Alex over the wilting kid. A glance that said Alex was a heartless narcissist.

Too bad. This was supposed to be a private getaway. Not a therapeutic free-for-all.

No one spoke for a while, the silence amplifying the guilt that now throbbed through Alex like blood poisoning.

Colin eventually looked up, wiping his eyes. "Fine! Fine." He nodded, thoughtful. "I might be trapped in the middle of Middle Earth, but at least I'm free to go my own way. For that, I'm grateful."

"Alex," Spock said, shaking the last mushroom crumbs from his beanie before shoving it back onto his head. "Are ya sure we can't use an extra set of hands for—"

"Don't you mean an extra mouth to feed and another body to protect?" Alex squared off with his feet planted wide and arms crossed. "Sorry if it sounds heartless, but it's not practical. The kid said he *wanted* to escape. He did. We helped. Now he's free to go. I'd call this a happy ending."

Alex studied Colin's pensive profile, struck by how young and vulnerable the kid appeared. His chest gave a twang of uncertainty. Was turning the boy loose in this wilderness the right thing?

Colin's face changed in an instant, startling Alex. Eyes and mouth flung wide, the boy leapt to his feet. Alex instinctively took a step back, hand flying to the dagger at his waist. The others bounded up, weapons at the ready.

Ready to defend their prince.

Except Colin wasn't looking at Alex. His gaze intently focused across the water.

Alex followed the boy's stare, spying a metallic glint

between ghostly wisps of steam. His pulse rattled faster, though he wasn't sure what was out there beyond movement and metal.

Dempsey had an arrow nocked, ready to fly.

Colin splashed into the pond, ankle deep, as he scooped his arms in front of him like a conductor readying an orchestra. As the boy's flimsy limbs swept upward, so did the water at his feet. It gathered into a shimmering sheet of liquid, rising until it formed a curtain through which Alex could only glimpse light and shadow.

"What in the name of Beacon Rock?" Dempsey shouted.

The boy slung his arms forward. The water responded by rushing ahead with such speed and force that the small lake became a muddy waterhole. Most of the liquid swelled into a vertical wall, leaving rocks and muck and many a floundering fish in its wake.

Colin clapped his hands together. The water gave a corresponding *crack* as it instantaneously froze and shattered, before flinging itself forward when Colin gestured with his arms. Icy shards careened toward the opposite bank, where Alex now spied a threatening rabble—a wild, spear-waving group of Dregs.

Shouts and roars of anger arose from across the chasm, even as the displaced water pooled back into its mucky footprint, somehow melting as fast as it had frozen. The Dregs's crazed gesticulating gave evidence of wounds inflicted by the ninja ice.

"Run!" Colin ordered, turning his back on the chaos he had inexplicably created. He jumped over the fallen log and stopped long enough to look back at the stunned group of runaways. "C'mon! Let's go. Now!"

They shook themselves from their stupors and clambered for supplies and horses, blinking in awestruck silence at one another.

Alex grabbed Gandalf's bridle and tugged the horse toward the cover of trees, where Colin stood waving them on. Confusion and wonder churned inside Alex. Though he couldn't process what just happened, he understood two things with clarity—Colin was no ordinary Topsider, and the boy would *definitely* be joining them.

CHAPTER FIFTEEN

Ellynn

ELLYNN STABBED AT HER BOWL OF oatmeal, spearing a brandyberry with the tip of her spoon. A tiny explosion of deep orange nectar leaked between the cobble of oats and milk. She watched the abstract design take shape while stealing glances at her mother across the table.

Bruised half-moons eclipsed Sadie's eyes, tattling on the exhaustion of yesterday's funeral, followed by a night of unrest. In the wee hours of morning, guards had alerted the household to the presence of Faery activity and missing horses. It took another hour to learn that Alex was no longer in bed, let alone on the palace grounds.

Ellynn had missed the mayhem entirely, having been found safely in her bed and, therefore, left to sleep the night away. A bitter disappointment. Her personal attendant, a Dwarf named Trinny, filled Ellynn in on all the details. Now, questions were bursting faster than Ellynn could pop each and every brandyberry, though her mother's bedraggled appearance made her hesitate.

"Any idea where Alex went?" she asked, shoveling a spoonful of oatmeal into her mouth, attempting indifference. The funeral schedule and emotions of the past several days had kept Ellynn from her usual covert attention to her brother's movements. Spying on him and his friends kept palace life from becoming dull, since she lacked friends her own age within the palace walls.

Her mother rested her elbow on the table beside her untouched oatmeal, bandaged palm pressed against her forehead, eyes closed. "I've no idea, love."

Ellynn swallowed another spoonful and another question. Her mom looked awful. Pushing for details would only stress her out more.

Worth it.

"Why is Grandmama Lucia so angry? Is she upset about Alex leaving?" This had been perplexing Ellynn since her grandmother had stormed past in the corridor, clutching her taffeta skirt with one hand while grasping her satin robe with the other. Ellynn had rubbernecked after the receding figure, noticing her grandmother's ruffled and rumpled wings—recently dyed a pewter-to-charcoal ombre, which befitted her status as grieving widow more than her previous turquoise feathers. Since the fashion-conscious diva never stepped from her quarters without being wrapped and tied with a bow, Ellynn thought she might be hallucinating this half-dressed version of the woman.

Her mother only blinked, seemingly glazed and dazed.

"Mom?" Ellynn snapped her fingers hoping to penetrate her mother's foggy focus. "Hel-*looo*."

"Huh?" Sadie flinched. "Sorry?"

"I asked if you know why Grandmama Lucia is so mad," Ellynn repeated.

"Oh. Hard to say." She absentmindedly scooped a spoonful of oatmeal and let it slip back into the bowl with a wet *plop*. "Your grandmother has had a lot going on with the funeral and all the dignitaries. Who knows?"

"*You* know." Ellynn twined her fingers together, tenting them atop her oatmeal. "I saw the look you gave her. Or, actually, the non-look. You were trying so hard to act impassive, you reminded me of, like, a waxed figure of yourself."

Her mother's mouth twisted into what Ellynn called a frowny-smile. "So many questions. You remind me of your Aunt Sophie when she was young. Always trying to figure out what the grown-ups are up to."

She was avoiding Ellynn's question, but Ellynn would play along if it could help with intel. "I'm almost grown myself." As if to prove her point, she unfolded the cloth napkin that had been placed beside her bowl and arranged it on her lap. "Only four more years until my seventeenth birthday and my own Feast of Ascension."

Her mom grunted a laugh and pinched the bridge of her nose. "Don't be in such a hurry, pet. Enjoy your childhood. You can never get it back." She expelled a forlorn sigh. "You know, I'd go back—"

"I know, I know," Ellynn cut in, stopping herself mid eye-roll since *that* particular reaction always got her into trouble. "You'd go back and have a do-over if you could. You were a timid scaredy cat, etcetera, etcetera."

Her mom's soft chuckle surprised Ellynn, who had expected her to be irritated.

"And here I thought moving to a land filled with Nephilim and Gnomes would finally make me interesting." She shrugged. "Turns out, I'm plain predictable."

"Seriously, Mom." Ellynn leaned against the chair and felt the slight ache in her wingbuds, reminding her that transformation was right around the corner. "I'm not a kid anymore. I can handle the truth about what's going on. Alex goes off with his friends all the time. Why is everyone suddenly panicked about it? And why did Lucia charge past us like an angry bull?"

"*Grandmama* Lucia," corrected her mother, grasping the cup of tea like it might be someone's neck. It sloshed over the rim as she lifted it to her lips.

This time Ellynn couldn't suppress the eye-roll. "Why? She's my step-grandmother. We're not blood related and we aren't exactly fond of each other. Why pretend?" That wasn't entirely true. The two used to have the occasional tea party together when Ellynn was younger. Lucia had even let Ellynn play with her make-up once in a while. But since Magnum spent the last few years becoming a public embarrassment, Lucia's focus had turned fully toward damage control with her son.

Ellynn also struggled to think of Magnum as her uncle. His place in her life felt more like a houseguest who wouldn't leave and go back to where he belonged. She might as well be a piece of palace furniture for all the notice he paid her. For some reason, Magnum concentrated his attention—and torment—on Alex. He was an expert bully who knew how to avoid detection, his particular flavor of abuse being more mental than physical, though not exclusively.

For each time the bully had been caught, Ellynn knew of a half-dozen other incidents he'd gotten away with. Her constant surveillance of Alex and his friends meant she knew the good, the bad, and the ugly. Most of the time, Magnum's meanness surfaced as verbal jabs and putdowns or annoying practical jokes. A slow wearing down of Alex's nerves and patience. When things became seriously heated between them, Ellynn had found subtle ways to interrupt, or she'd seek out a servant or guard and give them reasons to fetch one or the other, and thus lessen the chance of a brawl. These interventions helped Ellynn justify spying as an important palace safety measure.

She never directly intervened, knowing there would be consequences for spying on her brother. The last thing she wanted was to be assigned a chaperone or some other version of a babysitter. Then she'd be forced to behave like a proper princess. Not happening.

Of course, Lucia always took the side of her beloved son. No one in the Land of the Ancients nor the Tethered World— nay, the realm, nor the planet—was as clever, witty, strong, or handsome as Lucia's precious progeny. Ellynn believed her grandmother's real love was herself, however. Magnum's behavior made *Lucia* look bad, so she was protecting her reputation more than anything else.

Had Magnum turned up last night? Maybe that's why Alex took off. And maybe that's why Lucia looked like she could turn rock into magma with her blazing eyes.

Ellynn's mom set her tea down and leveled her gaze across the table. "You will call her *Grandmama* Lucia because it is what you've been told to call her. It's a show of respect for her role in our family, regardless of whether or not you approve of her as such."

Ellynn glanced away from her mother's frustrated, weary stare, making an effort to tame the angry thoughts that would surely etch havoc onto her face. "*Grandmama* Lucia..." she said in a strained, polite voice. "Do you know why she was so upset? Did Uncle Magnum come home?"

Sadie pushed her chair away from the table. The screech of wooden legs across the stone floor snapped Ellynn's attention back to her mom. Her mother's lips were pressed into a tight line, but she didn't stand, only looked back at Ellynn as if weighing whether to answer or shut down all the nosy questions, straightaway.

Ellynn wondered why she always managed to push people to their limits. She only wanted to be included, but everyone continued to treat her as if she were an immature child.

"All right," her mother said, and turned her palms up as if surrendering to Ellynn's curiosity. "It's like this. Before King Aviel died, he...he arranged a marriage for your brother."

Ellynn dropped her spoon into her bowl and pushed her

own chair back, springing to her feet. "He what?" How had she missed *this* tidbit of news? "You're kidding me. Tell me you're kidding."

"Oh, I wish I were." Her mom slumped back in her chair. "It gets worse, I'm afraid."

"What could be worse than that?" Ellynn leaned onto the table, arms locked, bracing.

Eyes squeezed shut, her mother spoke in a pained voice. "Due to some, um, circumstances beyond his control, the courier from Éire House—you know, the Irish Nephilim settlement—was greatly delayed. He arrived yesterday. Just in time to warn us that the princess and her family should be here *today*."

Ellynn's eyes went wide. "Today?" She pointed at the table. "Like *today*, today?"

Her mother looked at her through hooded lids. "Is there another kind?"

"Well." Ellynn flicked her hands up and then settled them on her hips. "I guess we know why Alex took off. Can't say I blame him." At least that explained a few pieces of the puzzle. There was still the one question that loomed. "And Grandmama Lucia..." Ellynn cocked an eyebrow at her mother in that way which others said looked so much like her father. "Why does this development leave her in such a tizzy? Is she mad that her precious Magnum isn't the one getting to wed this mystery bride?"

"Likely because his leaving makes her look bad to her long-lost family. I really don't believe jealousy is an issue. These are her people, after all. And Magnum wouldn't be expected to marry his second cousin."

Ellynn cringed. "*Ew.*"

Her mom clasped her hands and leaned in, lowering her voice. "Lucia had a hand in arranging this marriage. She undoubtedly influenced your grandfather to pursue it as his health declined. When we discovered Alex was missing in the middle of the night, she went ballistic. Went so far as to claim I was behind it." She shook her head and did her own version of an eye-roll. "Accused me of hiding him or helping him slip away. I didn't want to get into it with her again when we saw her this morning. That's why I looked so strange, I suppose."

Ellynn felt a swell of pride. Her mother was *confiding* in her. Not merely sharing plans for a surprise party or venting her frustration with bothersome protocol. This was something important. As if she finally recognized that Ellynn was growing up and could be trusted. It felt good.

"I see," Ellynn said, afraid to say too much lest her mother retreat.

Her mom looked over both shoulders, as if making sure they were alone. Odd because the royal family was never alone, unless they were in their bed chamber. Otherwise, there was always a servant or assistant or *somebody* nearby, ready to meet any possible needs. Here in the dining room the wiry, shy kitchen maid Raechel stood unobtrusively beside the door, as always.

Ellynn gravitated forward. What was her mother about to divulge?

"Here's the thing." Her mom's voice dropped lower still. "I learned, only this morning, that the queen *despises* her side of the family. Apparently, her uncle arranged her marriage to King Aviel, behind her back, to get her off his hands. She's never confided in me, but the way she brags about the land of Brihndle, where she lived, and the beauty of the palace and gardens, gave me the impression that she'd left a fairytale life to come endure Calamus. Apparently not."

Ellynn pulled back enough to give her mother a quizzical look. "So, what does that have to do with Alex? Why would she care about his disappearance if she actually hates them?"

Her mom gave a slow shake of her head. "Like I said, probably because it makes her look bad. This marriage, strange and sudden as it is, is still *her* idea. The invitation to this family whom she despises came from her and Aviel. It's all quite peculiar. Everything is shifting so quickly it's like a puzzle whose picture is changing every time I try to piece it together."

CHAPTER SIXTEEN

Sadie

SADIE WATCHED ELLYNN SASHAY FROM THE family dining room, as nimble and fluid as a ballerina. Her daughter seemed buoyant with the events from the night and the revelations of the morning. No longer a child. Not quite a woman. Ellynn was a beautiful, bold young lady who had inherited her Aunt Sophie's adventuresome, inquisitive nature. The change seemed so sudden that it made Sadie sad. How had she missed her daughter's metamorphosis?

The girl had always been a stunner. Olive skin. Glossy curls. Those frosty blue eyes that she inherited from her father and grandfather. And, oh! Xander was such a protective fatherly mess around her. It made Sadie melt a little every time she watched them together.

What was he going to do when Ellynn's wings developed and she could fly off on a whim? Clip them, most likely. Well, maybe not. That was considered a shameful, unthinkable punishment in these parts, especially since the royals were the ones sporting the wings.

"Shall I clear the table, your ladyship?" Raechel asked, pulling Sadie out of her familial musings.

"Oh! Yes, thank you." Sadie nodded and stood. She'd barely touched her breakfast and felt wasteful. "Sorry. I—I didn't have an appetite."

Raechel offered a timid smile and shook her head, reaching for Ellynn's half-eaten bowl of oatmeal. "No need to apologize. 'Twas a long night, I hear." She busied herself collecting the breakfast things.

Sadie noticed how Raechel's thinning, oily feathers drooped along the floor so that the bottom few inches were now a dingy brown and spiderwebbed with lint and, probably, spiderwebs. Raechel was a commoner whose wings had provided her a position in the palace.

"Raechel, are you well?" Sadie asked. Her conscience pointed a guilty finger at herself for being so wrapped up in her own world that she'd failed to notice the welfare of those that took such excellent care of it.

When she and Xander had married, *entitlement* was something Sadie was determined not to cultivate. Xander had always been gracious and appreciative. A charming characteristic that allowed him to see past the insecure Topsider Sadie had once been—though he claimed to have never noticed that side of her, since their early interactions involved myriad near-death experiences.

At the time, his graciousness was likely an overreaction to his condescending and uncharitable mother, Estancia.

Xander was not proud of the woman Estancia had become before her death, although he always maintained that her intentions had once been noble, despite her brusque personality. Sadie didn't think it necessary to add to his disappointment in his late mother by sharing her own unflattering insights.

Raechel's gaunt face now reddened at Sadie's question. "Who? M-me?" she sputtered. "Why, yes. Of course. Why wouldn't I be well?"

That might be the most Sadie had heard the girl say. She gave Raechel her best, motherly smile, hoping to put the nervous-nellie at ease. "I'm only asking because you're so thin. And your wings," she fluttered her fingers at the girl, "seem a bit, well, unkempt."

"Oh, dear." Pink splotches crept into her cheeks. She placed her hands behind her back and swept her wings forward so they framed her lower body. Tilting her head, she looked from one to the other, then released them with a shrug. "I—I never pay attention to my feathers, I'm afraid." She huffed tendrils of dirty blond hair from her forehead. "I barely bother with my hair and I can *see* most of it. I suppose my feathers are looking forlorn from disuse. Couldn't guess the last time I took flight. No time for such fancies."

Sadie frowned. "I'm sorry to hear that. Those of us

without wings would love to know the freedom of flight that you are blessed with. You need regular exercise. I'll speak to Miss Hyacinth about it."

"No, no. That won't be necessary." Raechel looked ashen and flustered at the mention of the housekeeping supervisor. The maid blustered about, stacking dishes onto a tray. "I thank you for your concern, m'lady. Truly, I wouldn't know what to do with myself if I could be so leisurely."

Sadie *tsked* but didn't have time to argue. Princess Larkin and her entourage from Éire House would be arriving at some point, and Sadie needed to disguise her up-all-night appearance.

As she made her way back to her quarters, she couldn't help wondering how her life may have turned out had she remained topside. Would she be rushing kids off to school about now? Or would she have homeschooled, like her parents? Maybe she would've had a career—something involving writing or books, of course—and, right at this very moment, she would be grabbing her cup of chai and heading out the door in a rush, late to an appointment with a rare book collector.

Sadie liked to play this mental game on occasion. The "what would I be doing at this instant if I lived topside?" game. It wasn't that she *wanted* to live topside. She had no regrets about moving to Calamus and marrying her very own Prince Charming. Still, the boring, bookish, safe Sadie continued to rummage about on the inside.

Thankfully, peaceful palace life offered plenty of mundane moments of its own. Sadie managed to keep insulated from most of the politics. Her sister and brother, Sophie and Brock, were more entrenched in such matters. Sophie had become High King Brock's Royal Adviser in neighboring Vituvia. The two of them were always doing something diplomatic or ministerial together.

Sadie approached the door to her and Xander's quarters and stopped short. Where was Blaylock, their daytime chamber-guard? The heavy oak, arched door looked strangely naked without someone stationed beside it. *Well, even a guard has bodily functions. He's probably taking care of business.*

Sadie hauled the door open and strode into the sitting

room, looking ahead at the double doors that led to her bedroom.

Whumph!

She was suddenly face down with a mouthful of fleece.

"Ugh." *That hurt.* At least she'd face-planted onto the sherpa rug instead of the stone floor. She pawed at the wooly hair that stuck to her tongue. What had she tripped on? Maybe in her rush she'd tripped on the rug. Her neck shot through with pain and she winced as an instant headache sprang to life. Her bandaged hand stung from the weight of the fall.

"Ouch." She closed her eyes and took her time pressing up to her elbows. After a moment, she glanced to her left.

An instant, icy shock washed over her. Blaylock's face lay inches from her own, eyes wide, terrified, and unseeing.

CHAPTER SEVETEEN

Sadie

SADIE SCREAMED AND LURCHED AWAY, LANDING on her back with a fresh stab of pain. Ignoring her throbbing skull, she struggled upright on unsteady legs. Was Blaylock's attacker still here? Was Xander similarly prone somewhere inside their bedroom?

She stepped over the guard's jutting, booted foot which, she realized, had been the cause of her tumble. Looking into the hallway and seeing no one, she gave a distressed screech.

"Help! Someone help!" The sound a drill between her ears. She swiveled back to the sitting room, heart thudding as she took in the prone figure of the ruddy-faced guard who had greeted her with a respectful "Good morning, m'lady" less than two hours earlier.

Though she felt certain he was dead, she knelt, avoiding his stare, intending to check for a pulse. That's when she noticed the blood.

A deep, crimson swath of Blaylock's blood made a streaky half-rainbow that revealed the guard's trajectory to the floor where he now lay, back against the wall. It had seeped into the ivory fur of the sheepskin rug, tinging it a rusty-pink. With a gulp, she placed two fingers on his neck—a courtesy born of respect rather than optimism.

Sadie didn't see an incriminating weapon, though it might be concealed beneath the bulk of Blaylock's body. Commander Gage would soon come, she told herself, and do a thorough investigation.

Though she knew Xander had a busy morning scheduled, she wanted assurance that he wasn't slumped inside their room in a similar state. The dark, sticky texture of Blaylock's blood meant the deed hadn't *just* occurred. The murderer had likely fled long before Sadie returned—at least, that's what she wanted to believe.

Whoever killed the guard obviously needed him out of the way so they could get inside the quarters of the new king. There were plenty of places to hide in the enormous space. Sadie stood, her body pulsating with suppressed panic as she took careful steps toward her room.

She stopped in the threshold of the oak doors that opened into the bedchamber. Leaning against the door jamb, she took in the state of things, thankful to see no sign of her husband. She strained to hear the slightest noise, a rustle of clothing or an inhale of breath. All was silent. The place felt deserted, if that were possible, though someone had obviously ricocheted around the room searching for something. Drawers were dumped on the floor, both of their wardrobes stood ajar, items of clothing in disarray. Their feather mattress was shoved halfway off the bed. Even the tapestries on the wall hung crooked, as if someone had given them a good shake. What did this person—or *persons*—want?

An old, protective instinct kicked in. Sadie covered her right ring-finger with her left hand, feeling the twined gold ring press into her palm. Could they be after this petite but powerful piece of jewelry and what it protected?

Surely not. Her seemingly ordinary ring was one of the Tethered World's best kept secrets. Whoever murdered Blaylock and tore through this room must've had something else in mind, though Sadie couldn't guess what was worth the taking of someone's life. In the corridor outside, she heard footsteps approaching.

"Hey! In here!" she yelled. "Help! I need help!"

Footsteps swelled in tempo, and soon Raechel and an older maid, Avalen, appeared. Avalen rounded the corner, her arms full of clean linens. The bundle fell to the floor as she, too, tripped over Blaylock's protruding foot. Behind her, Raechel pulled up short, a mop in one hand and a bucket in the other. Its sudsy water sloshed onto Avalen's prone legs.

"Oh, dear!" Raechel and Sadie both exclaimed.

Sadie dashed to Avalen's side, mentally berating herself for not nudging the offending boot out of the way. At least the mound of linens had broken the woman's fall and obscured the shock of being face to face with the guard's empty, staring eyes. "Are you okay?"

Avalen nodded and pressed her ample body up onto her hands and knees. "Yes, m'lady."

"Oh, dear hosts of heaven!" Raechel dropped both mop

and bucket, the latter of which landed on Blaylock's boot and tipped its remaining contents onto Avalen's feet, legs, linens, and the floor. Raechel gaped as her gaze traveled the bloody path across the wall and down to where Blaylock lay.

Avalen yelped at the sudden flood of water. "Roots and fruits!" She lumbered to her sopping feet as Sadie attempted to help. "We've made heaps more work for—*wahhh!*"

Sadie winced at Avalen's shriek of surprise, which was immediately amplified by Raechel's delayed scream of horror. Her headache ramped into migraine territory, and Sadie covered her ears. "Ladies! Please! Calm down." When the volume didn't change, she released her ears and pressed her hands in the air between the maids. "Get hold of yourselves. *Right now.*"

Raechel's hand clamped over her mouth as her scream sputtered out alongside Avalen's own shrill siren. Their collective focus now magnetized to the trickle of water wending its way across the floor and diluting Blaylock's blood.

"Thank you." Sadie inhaled deeply, aware she must assert her authority before things further devolved. She took a couple of squelching steps so that she stood in the middle of the puddle, between both women. "Obviously something horrible has happened. Still, we must keep our wits, ladies."

They looked at each other, a trio of stricken faces.

"Here, now." Avalen broke the silence, her voice hoarse and choked with tears. "I'll use these sheets and blankets to soak up this mess."

Sadie nodded. "Yes. Good idea." She looked at Raechel. "Please, find Commander Gage. He's probably practicing formations on the lawn with his regiment, preparing for our guests. Hopefully King Xander is with him. If not, find him as well."

Raechel nodded and looked relieved to have something to do elsewhere. "Yes, Princess—beggin' your pardon, *Queen*—Sadie. Right away."

As the maid turned to leave, Sadie noticed the poor girl's wings once again. The dingy, dragging feathers were now tinted an awful, brownish pink—an unintentional ombré the color of watered-down blood.

CHAPTER EIGHTEEN

Alex

"*HOW* DID YOU DO THAT?" ALEX gripped Colin by his narrow shoulders and shook the scrawny boy with each word. "How did you acquire such power? Tell me!"

Colin winced at the giant who held him, his face a mixture of fear and defiance. "It's—it's my own power, n-nothing special," he sputtered.

Alex and friends had encircled the runaway, demanding answers.

Dempsey balled his meaty fist and shook it. "How gullible do we look, Topsider?"

Colin attempted to twist out of Alex's grasp, to no avail. "C'mon. Let go! You should be thanking me for helping you."

This was true.

The Dregs had not pursued the runaways. Parsifal had stayed behind, perched in a tree out of sight, while the rest had mounted up and hoofed it through the woods. When the Dragon finally caught up, he reported, through Spock's interpretive skills, that most of the Dregs had sustained multiple cuts and abrasions from the shattering ice, whilst all had expressed fear of this "water warlock" who had conjured the attack as they turned tail in retreat.

The group had continued to put distance between themselves and the pond. The forested mountainside grew steadily steeper, slowing their efforts. The horses had begun to chuff and snort from the climb when they came upon a gaping hole in the rocky cliffside. More of a sideways crater than a cave, it provided a shallow, concealed shelter for horses and people alike.

As soon as they'd corralled themselves inside, Alex vaulted from Gandalf and yanked the boy off Sage's back. The others had wasted no time in joining the prince's interrogation.

"You some sort of wizard?" Josiah asked, scrutinizing the boy's face as if he might discover a lightning bolt-shaped scar on his forehead.

Colin shook his head and tried yet again to free himself from Alex's grasp. "No. No, I'm not. Nothing like that. Would you just—seriously! Just let *go* of me," he said, his shrill voice pitching soprano.

"Take it easy on the kid," Finn said. "It's not like he's going to run off. And," he chuckled, "I do believe the boy gave us fair warning, didn't he? Told us we'd be impressed if we saw him fight. I'd say he impressed us all right. Even if he does squawk like a girl."

Alex glared at the kid and his unusual eyes. They were disconcerting for sure, yet not nearly as disconcerting as his stunt at the lake. With a little shove, Alex released the boy. "Fine." He made a sweeping gesture at Colin. "Now, explain yourself."

Colin's lips compressed and he inhaled deeply. "I...I'll try. I don't entirely understand it myself. But ever since that day at the beach, I've had this strange relationship with water. It...it does my bidding. Somehow."

"Somehow?" Josiah arched an eyebrow. "Could you be more specific?"

Colin dropped his gaze to the ground and poked at the aggregate with his boot. "I thought it was a coincidence at first. A rain shower started spitting at me when I had wandered to a deserted stretch of beach. I was already miserable, desperate, cold, scared. Separated from my family. I sorta wished—well, I did wish—that the weather wouldn't make things worse by raining on me. It was a light rain, and I had my head down as I walked, so it took me a minute to realize that, somehow, the rain was avoiding me. I thought it might be my imagination. So, I stopped walking and stood still, waiting to feel the tiny flecks of water on my skin. I remained dry, even after standing there for several minutes as the shower intensified. Not a drop of water landed on me. There was even a dry spot on the ground where I stood."

His gaze traveled the group as if he hoped to see their faces awash with mutual understanding. They only blinked back, unconvinced.

"And. Um." He shoved his hands into his pockets and shrugged. "This one time, after I'd been taken below, I was working hard, sweating from exertion. There were a dozen or so kids like myself forced to do manual labor on this farm where they kept us. I spoke out of turn at some point and was *detained,* you could say. They forced me to stand in one place while I waited for the headmaster to come by and administer my punishment. There was a cow trough a few feet from where I stood, all hot and sweaty. When I wished that the water would douse me and cool me off...suddenly, it did. I stood there blinking, dripping wet. Soaked yet delighted. The men, my captors, thought one of the cows had somehow sloshed it, but I knew differently. I made a tentative connection with those two events. After that, I tested my theory, privately. And, over time, I learned to control water more precisely. Even the temperature. I can make it ice cold or boiling hot. I'm like a— a water sculptor or something."

"Or a water warlock, like the Dregs claimed," Dempsey said. "Sounds 'bout right."

Colin dragged a filthy hand across his choppy nest of hair. "Fine. If there's such a thing, then I suppose I'd fit the description."

"And you've no idea how you came to possess this special ability? One day you're a normal kid, and then you have a bad case of separation anxiety and—*abracadabra*—you're a magician." Alex stood, hands on his hips, and looked Colin up and down. "Colin the water-whisperer."

Colin tossed his hands in the air. "That's me."

Finn fingered his rusty beard and shifted toward the boy. "Do you think it had anything to do with that strange ritual that happened to you? With the Faeries?"

"No. The incident with the rain happened *before* I was captured."

"Well..." Finn tapped his chin thoughtfully. "Maybe you always had this ability, but you didn't know it."

An odd expression flitted across the boy's features. "Maybe so." Colin looked down and resumed kicking the pebbles.

"Well, I for one am glad to have you on the team," Spock said, poking a finger in the air. He had remained on Ansyn's back. "I think we all owe you a heap of thanks, right boys?"

Silence.

The Gnome cleared his throat. "*Right?*"

Alex offered a half-hearted nod.

Colin glanced up, a cynical grin threatening his usual scowl.

Parsifal chirped from where he dangled, upside down, on the rocky ceiling above. He looked more bat-like than ever in this setting.

"I must agree," Spock responded. The Gnome gave a little snicker and turned his attention to Alex. "Parsifal wishes to point out that that wasn't a proper thank you."

Alex felt tempted to snatch the Gnome from his literal high-horse and lob him at the cheeky Dragon. Instead, he snapped a curt "thanks" in Colin's direction.

"At your service, Your Majesty." Colin twirled his hand and offered an exaggerated bow. "Let's strike a deal, shall we? Permit me to tag along as you leave your bride standing at the altar, and I'll continue to employ my water-sculpting skills as necessary, on your *royal* behalf." He extended his right hand.

Great...another person who thinks I need their protection. Alex glowered at the kid, anger prickling through him, aware that his birthmark had just begun to glow.

CHAPTER NINETEEN

Ellynn

ELLYNN HELD HER BREATH AS SHE pressed her left eye against the gap between wood panels. The wall space in her grandparents' parlor had never been a favorite eavesdropping spot. She found the view of the room too restrictive—revealing a mere sliver of carved chair with the edge of the table beside it—and boring to boot. On the rare occasions she'd meandered the inner-palace walls to this position, it was rarer still to find anyone occupying the space, though twice she'd manage to observe her grandmother taking afternoon tea with her lady-in-waiting, Katheryn. Their dull conversations about clothing or silent games of cards nearly put Ellynn to sleep.

Today, however, curiosity held Ellyn in its orbit. She had gravitated to the person who had a mysterious connection to all the strange developments of the last twenty-four hours. Sure enough, she could slightly make out the sheen of Grandmama Lucia's navy taffeta skirt, her fingers curved and white-knuckled around the carved wooden armrest of the chair. Ellynn noticed that her grandmother wasn't wearing her emerald-encrusted wedding band. Had she forgotten to put it on in the craziness of the day, or was she ready to forget King Aviel? Either way, it kindled a spark of indignation that her grandmother could be so thoughtless.

"...this is a good thing?" Katheryn's voice lifted in question, though Ellynn hadn't gotten situated in time to hear what the lady-in-waiting was asking about. The formidable woman sat somewhere outside of Ellynn's limited view.

Each member of the royal family had their personal attendants. Ellynn and her mother enjoyed the company of two Dwarves from Calamus, Trinny and Joanie, and her brother and father sort of shared Tassitus, the shortest Nephilim Ellynn had ever met. Guys were more low-maintenance, Ellynn guessed. But Katheryn—or *Kat* to Lucia—was part of her grandmother's entourage from the land of Brihndle years before. The woman was as prickly as Grandmama Lucia. The two were like a couple of walking, talking cacti.

"Actually, yes. Now that I've had time to consider it, I *may* have overreacted," her grandmother replied. "If I'd shared our arrangements with Magnum all along, he never would have run off and missed the show. Still, a plan as important as this...well, we all know how a couple goblets of mead can loosen Magnum's lips. And 'the man dost loveth his mead,' as they say. Still, he would be all over our arrangement, spurned as he is from either throne. The latest lead on his whereabouts sounds promising, however. If I could only get word to him."

Katheryn made a sound of agreement. "Indeed. Getting him here before your Uncle Odhran leaves will be the trick."

"Yes. I know. Alas, I remain an optimist at heart."

Ellynn had to stifle a laugh. *An optimist disguised as a fault-finding control freak, maybe.*

"And now Brady—er, Alex." Grandmama Lucia's pale hand gave a dismissive flick. "Whatever his name is. He's run off as well. Such chaos makes for tediously constructed lies. I don't like to reinforce my uncle's perception that getting rid of me as he did—banishing me to this—this United Nations of folklore, crawling with Gnomes and Dwarves and even Ogres— was a good idea. Odhran will insinuate blame for unruly children and Aviel's death. He *wants* me to believe I'm weak and impotent—exactly how he described my father once Odhran's coup was a success."

"I'm not sure if *coup* is quite the right word, Your Grace."

"Oh, shut it, Kat." Grandmama Lucia's fist pounded the chair. "What else would you call what my uncle did—leaving my father unprotected while the palace was under siege? It was nothing short of a passive-aggressive *coup*. Odhran had sworn to protect my father to the death. *Odhran's* death, not the other way around."

"He left to help defend the castle—"

"And now you're defending *him*? Enough!" Grandmama Lucia ordered. "Odhran abandoned my father. He may not have been the one to do the deed, but his absence cost my father his life. Father was weakened from pneumonia and barely had strength to wield a sword. My uncle knew that."

Ellynn heard Katheryn sigh and shift, her pointy black boot sliding into Ellynn's limited viewpoint.

"And *I* know that." Katheryn said, her voice slipping into its usual wheedling tone. "I'm on your side. Always. I hope *you* know that."

"And since my mother was a commoner," Grandmama Lucia went on, as if Katheryn hadn't spoken, "Odhran knew his lineage would outweigh my own in the eyes of the Supreme Council. No doubt he promised favors if they saw things his way. Well, I've been patient. And I'm finally going to get back what's mine."

"Absolutely," Katheryn said. "Your reckoning is at hand. I'm confident that's so. And I honestly don't find Alex's disappearance to be a problem. It saves us the trouble of preventing the marriage ourselves. He did you a favor."

Prevent the marriage? Had Ellynn heard that correctly? Hadn't her mother explained that this whole matrimonial fiasco was Grandmama Lucia's idea?

"I agree. There's always an upside to these surprising little twists. It complicates some things while it simplifies others." Grandmama Lucia pointed at the floor and jabbed for emphasis. "Maker knows that I've bided my time. I did what I had to do to get Odhran and Clodagh to Calamus, and I will see this thing through. Alexander Brady is only one of many moving parts."

Katheryn hummed her agreement. "And if Xander's men are able to retrieve the flightless imbecile quickly, what then? We need a plan for various scenarios. I hate that we didn't learn of your uncle's impending arrival any sooner than the day-of. We are ill-prepared, I fear."

How dare these two speak of her brother like this! A protective fury swelled in Ellynn's chest, and she concentrated on controlling her breathing, not wanting to risk being overheard behind the wall. She grasped the tiny book charm at her neck, pressing the pad of her thumb into its open pages, calming herself.

"The timing *is* unfortunate," her grandmother replied. "You must prevail upon our network for any information once my uncle arrives. Remind them how we deal with disloyalty. Gouldor has his orders and he won't dare defy me. He understands how close he came to losing his position after Aviel's death. You should've seen him beg for his job. Despicable. However, after thinking it through, I believe his unique set of skills will continue to be an asset to our cause. My mercy has only ingratiated him to me all the more. Which means if Alex returns"—and here, Grandmama Lucia leaned forward so that Ellynn could see the sneering frown on her jutting chin—"we go back to our original course of action. Either way, tragedy befalls my uncle and I am that much closer to getting my kingdom back."

"I will convey your wisdom to each of our operatives, personally, Your Highness," Katheryn cooed.

Grandmama Lucia made a noise normally heard when someone savors a tasty bite of food. "Odhran won't be extending his influence to this side of the globe, as he no doubt plans to do. When my stratagem succeeds, it'll be the other way around."

Katheryn's fingers came into view as she gave Lucia's hand a supportive pat. "Patience and planning will finally pay off. His coming here under the guise of a wedding is a brilliant distraction, Alex or no Alex."

"He probably assumes time has healed our differences," her grandmother said, scoffing. "I'm certain he's salivating at the prospects of marrying off his precious daughter to expand his seat of power, all the while keeping it away from me. Another slap in my face. Another way in which he can keep an eye on me, too, no doubt. Well, he's going to regret he ever agreed to this marriage, by the time I get my revenge."

"Indeed. He's a loathesome—"

Bam-bam-bam!

Ellynn jumped at the loud wallop on the parlor door.

"Your Majesty!" boomed a voice from the other side.

"I said *no one* is to disturb me, Florentino," Grandmama Lucia yelled back.

"It's an emergency, my queen," came the gruff reply.

Ellynn readjusted her position, switching to the other eye to relieve the kink in her neck. Her grandmother's erect body, now on her feet and facing the door, filled her vision. A fragment of protruding elbows, and eyelids at an indignant half-mast from the haughty tilt of her head.

The creak of the door could be heard, and Ellynn imagined the big, burly form of Florentino filling the space as completely as the carved wooden door itself.

"Blaylock is dead. They found his body in King Xander's chambers moments ago." The hardened soldier stated this as offhandedly as he would announce dinner. "I'm afraid I must place you on protective lockdown while my men search your quarters."

Blaylock? Dead! What did this mean for her parents? Ellynn's heart stampeded recklessly and she shifted backward a fraction, as if the pounding might give her away.

"If you feel I'm in danger, then do your job and keep close. I'm not going to wait around, today of all days." Grandmama Lucia smoothed a hand over her glossy hair, the ends brushing her collarbone. "You do realize my uncle may descend on us at any moment."

"I'm afraid I must insist," Florentino said, nonplussed. "This won't take long. It's for your safety."

Ellyn heard heavy footfalls and watched several soldiers sweep past in quick succession.

"They've got five minutes." Her grandmother's icy empirical tone left no room for debate.

"Shouldn't take long, Your Grace."

Silence descended, and Ellynn itched to retreat from the enclosed space and assure herself of her parent's safety. Why would someone kill Blaylock while he was on duty, unless it was to get to her mother and father?

To her horror, something else was, quite literally, itching. An impending sneeze prickled her sinuses. Ellynn leaned against the wall behind her, hand flying to her twitchy nose as she inched sideways, uselessly pleading with her body's impulses.

Then, it happened. A muffled yet audible: *cheh!*

Cover blown, Ellynn took off, fingers brushing the narrow walls to guide her, feet flying as fast as she dared without a candle.

But not before she heard Florentino bellow, "Hey! Who's there?"

CHAPTER TWENTY

Alex

SOMETHING PRESSED AGAINST ALEX'S FACE, CATAPULTING him from sleep to hysteria. He couldn't breathe. He couldn't move. He couldn't see a thing or remember where he was.

As he writhed beneath the calloused hand that enveloped the bottom half of his face, it came to him that he lay deep within a cave where he and his friends had bedded down for the night, after journeying roundabout foothills for several hours. Alex dug his fingers into the furry arm that pinned him down, confirming his suspicion that his attacker was a Troll. Was he a Dreg or merely a troublemaking Troll who'd wandered far from his home in Craventhrall?

The scratchy *zing* of flint being struck was followed by a faint flame somewhere in the vicinity of Alex's feet. The indistinct features of a pitch-black Troll loomed into view, a mountain of fur whose face was turned toward the blossoming glow of what Alex assumed to be a torch catching fire.

How many Trolls were here? Had a rogue gang stumbled on their cave? Josiah and the others must be in a similar state, otherwise they'd be wrestling this miscreant to the ground.

"I'll help each of you bind and gag the bird-men," said a low-pitched voice. "Those of you with scrawnier prey should be able to manage on your own. Just make sure you incapacitate the water-warlock first."

Dregs!

In his struggle to breathe, Alex had succeeded in slipping his nose above the grasp of the big ape's fingers. Memories of another time and another pressing hand asserted themselves in his mind. A nauseous flutter disturbed his stomach, and he pushed the image aside, telling himself to focus on his present predicament.

With effort, Alex forced himself to save energy for whatever came next. He obviously couldn't remove this living, breathing boulder. The Troll—known to Alex's mother's side of the family as a Sasquatch, Bigfoot, or Yeti—had pinned Alex's legs beneath one of his own like a felled tree.

The change in tension must've alerted the ugly ape, because he shifted his focus back to Alex's face. Beady black eyes studied him from beneath a heavy brow. Torchlight reflected in twin golden specks, but otherwise his eyes were two obsidian marbles.

Alex heard grunts and snarls from the others as bodies struggled against their captors. From deeper within the cave, a horse snuffled and stomped.

"Ah, so that's what they did with their mounts," said the same deep voice. "That'll make our trek back much easier. Won't have to carry all the dead weight ourselves."

Dead weight?

"Don't worry," the Yeti whispered, his putrid breath making Alex's stomach pick up where it had left off. "Not gonna hurt you. Not yet. The Overlord will decide what to do with you." He wobbled his head one way, then the other, as if considering possible outcomes. "*Thennn,* maybe I will hurt you. And I will enjoy it." A yellowed fang glinted from between leathery, grinning lips.

Alex did his best to will laser-beams from his eyes, longing for some sort of superpower found in his mother's old movies. As if mustering a feeble response to this thought, a faint glow began to emanate from Alex's birthmark.

The big thug caught sight of the spectacle and withdrew his clammy paw like he'd been burned. Before the Troll could recover, Alex instinctively gave the big ape a head-butt to beat all head-butts.

And it was lights out for Alex.

His head throbbed. Then again, so did his wrists. And his mouth. Taking inventory, Alex realized he was bound and gagged and slung over his captor's shoulder like a sandbag. So much for getting caught by his *father's* men. Things had definitely taken a turn for the dreadful. And what was that garlicky smell? He wondered if the awful odor was what had brought him back to consciousness. Some sort of cruel and powerful smelling-salts.

Before he knew which way was up, Alex was hoisted upright and straddling the back of one of the horses. At least this was familiar territory—and way better than being carried about on the shoulders of Bigfoot. Maybe he could manage an escape.

That notion died a quick death as Alex realized that, though his feet weren't tied together, each foot was connected by a short rope to his tethered hands, effectively hobbling him in a fetal position. Holding the horse's mane with swollen, numbing fingers was the only thing that would keep him from falling off sideways or forward onto the horse's neck. He recognized the sleek ebony of his father's horse, Ansyn, beneath him.

"Don't get any ideas, freak," said the Troll. "I'll have the reins."

Alex glared at the vile creature, noticing with satisfaction the enormous goose egg that now protruded from the center of the Troll's forehead. Apparently, Alex had hit his mark and then some.

The Troll stepped beside Ansyn's bridle and Alex cringed to see his friends similarly hamstrung and incapacitated. Josiah wriggled in the arms of a light brown Troll, who staggered beneath the Nephilim's uncooperative brawn. The Yeti tried to leverage Josiah up onto Gandalf's back, but the horse sensed the danger and shifted away from the Troll with a loud snort.

"Be still, ya big beast!" A silvery Troll stepped over and grabbed Gandalf's reins, giving them a violent yank. The steed whinnied and tried to pull his head up and away.

Alex recognized the Troll's deep voice as the one giving orders inside the cave. "Shtaab!" Alex hollered, attempting a gagged command at the brute to stop hurting his horse.

Josiah managed to plant his feet against Gandalf's flank, preventing his captor from seating him. Alex wasn't sure whether to cheer or tell him to save his strength for a legitimate possibility of escape. The gag prevented either.

The light-brown Troll wrestled Josiah into a chokehold.

"Easy, Skeeva," the silver Troll-boss ordered. "There's a fine line between unconscious and dead."

Josiah's body went limp. The light-brown Troll—Skeeva—gave a grunt of satisfaction before hoisting Josiah astride Gandalf's back while the Troll-boss gripped the horses bridle.

The Nephilim tumbled forward like some discarded, oversized puppet, face-planting onto Gandalf's mane. Josiah's disheveled wing feathers stuck up at odd angles, his cape twisting down the center of his back.

Alex watched his friend's ribcage expand with breath, and Alex let out his own, relieved. Skeeva busied himself securing Josiah's limp, top-heavy form to the horse's back.

In the commotion, mild-mannered Sage had been laden with her Nephilim cargo. Finn huddled over Sage in the same awkward manner as Alex, another nondescript brown Troll gripping Sage's reins while absentmindedly gnawing a fingernail. Finn's gaze latched onto Alex's. The two exchanged an angry, indignant conversation without words. Alex noticed the addition of a rope around his friend's middle, securing his wings to his torso.

Boisterous, blustering complaints suddenly boiled over from Dempsey—an incomprehensible diatribe that seemed to amuse the tawny Troll who was tying Dempsey and Colin together with a rope. A gnarly Ogre held the two captives in place, by the scruff of their necks. His beefy body glistened with sweat. Alex decided that this big, ugly giant must be the source of the stench.

Across one of the Ogre's bulging shoulders drooped Alex's backpack. It wriggled like a sack of snakes. Evidently, Spock was traveling in steerage. Alex could only hope that the pack provided a bit of an air filter for the poor Gnome. Being up close and personal to Ogre stench was as pleasant as hugging a skunk.

Alex gave his fettered hands and feet a frustrated jerk, garbling a gagged curse on the Dregs. He felt responsible for his friends' predicament, even though he had planned for a solo adventure. Still, the gang had interjected themselves with honorable intentions, and look where it had landed them.

An ache of gratitude and guilt settled inside. Gratitude for their friendship. Guilt over a sense of relief for not facing these Dregs on his own.

Despite the precarious situation, Alex couldn't *quite* concede that things might've been better if he'd stayed home to wed a stranger.

CHAPTER TWENTY-ONE

Alex

"ALEX! ALEX! WAKE UP, MAN."

Alex heard someone calling him. A rushing sound—water, maybe?—drowned the voice, giving it a distant quality.

"*Alex.* C'mon. They're coming for you."

Finn's voice amplified, suddenly much clearer and much closer. Alex groaned, struggling to open his eyes, which, he could feel, were swollen shut. The rushing noise grew faint, but continued as a subdued throbbing inside his skull, keeping rhythm with his heartbeat.

"Who's...coming?" Alex croaked, his throat dry as dirt. The night came back in a blur of painful images. The ambush. The kidnapping. Traveling with cramped muscles, aching wrists, numb fingers, and the possibility of toppling to the ground with every hitch and stumble of the horse. A feat that groggy Josiah had managed twice.

The second tumble earned him a severe choking and a promise from the Ogre that if it happened again he'd "gets a holds of yous and pummels yous until I turns yous into a droopy chicken-bird."

Ogres were not known for their elocution.

Though Alex had managed to keep himself atop Ansyn—and awake—for the several-hour journey on narrow switchbacks and into a steeply hidden valley, he was nevertheless rewarded with a pummeling of his own, for reasons unknown, once they arrived at their destination. Fishbreath Skeeva had taken to smacking him, open-palmed, on the temples and square in the eyes. Repeatedly.

Alex knew it could've been worse. As in—*much* harder. The Troll was merely playing to injure, like a cat swipes at a mouse enough to keep it running and squealing. Hobbled as he was, Alex couldn't run. And his squeals were more like groans and moans from behind the saliva-soaked gag.

Waking now, he guessed he'd passed out at some point. Game over. Despite the bruises and swelling, he was relieved to find the gag and the ropes were no longer in place. He pushed himself upright, even as Finn clasped his shoulders to help.

"Dude, your eyes look like a couple of those pot-stickers your mom makes. Can you see me?"

Alex gave Finn a feeble push. "Do you mind? I feel rotten enough without your disgusting culinary comparisons." He tried to open his eyes but couldn't manage more than a sliver of sight, making it hard to see beyond a few feet.

Finn lunged into Alex's field of vision, squinting. "So, can you see me?"

Alex nodded. "Barely."

"Well, you need to try to shake off the mental fog." Finn gripped Alex's shoulders again and made Alex look at him. "I heard the guards talking about taking 'the freak without the wings' to see the Overlord ." One side of his mouth pulled down, apologetically. "Sorry, mate. Their words, not mine."

Alex gave a little nod, careful not to goad his headache. He studied Finn enough to make out a patch of hair missing from his beard, along with a black eye of his own. "You're not going to win over any Dreg maidens in your state, either. Guess I wasn't the only one that had the snot beat out of me."

Finn smirked and gingerly tapped the raw, exposed skin on his chin. "You weren't. We all enjoyed a welcome-to-the-hinterlands thrashing, but you definitely got the worst of it."

"Where are the others?" Alex looked around the rock-hewn cell. Dim light filtered in from a lengthy gash in the granite ceiling—too high for them to reach and too narrow to breach if they could. Since even this distant glow hurt his battered eyes, he avoided looking up.

The puddle of light that spilled down illuminated the center of the cave-like cell and diffused into the shadows. The space was small, maybe ten by ten, Alex and Finn the only two prisoners. Some straw littered one side of the roughly circular room, a small boulder offered an apparent place to sit. A heavy wooden door with a tiny square window, the only way in or out. A squat bucket was tipped over beside the door, exposing its empty insides.

"I don't know." Finn shook his head. "I assume they're in nearby cells, although I haven't called out to confirm it. Only woke a few minutes ago myself. I heard voices outside, heard them talking about you, and woke you."

Alex turned his head and spit, tasting coppery blood. A brownish glob of spittle made a slug-like trek down the nearby wall. "Any guesses at who this so-called *overlord* might be? I knew the hinterlands were filled with roaming gangs of outcasts, but I've never heard anything about their being organized beneath some sort of leader."

"News to me too." Finn shrugged. "Still, whoever he—or she—might be, they've got, what? Trolls and Ogres in their ranks. Who else did you notice yesterday by the lake?"

"Pretty sure I saw a Stygian or two—" Alex's thoughts were swallowed up in a fit of coughing. He really needed some water.

Finn whacked Alex on the back as if that might lubricate his throat. The distant screech of a door being opened, compelling a burst of wild howls and barking, discouraging further conversation. The friends looked at each other and then at the door to their cell.

"Time to meet this mysterious Overlord," Alex whispered.

Alex shuffled along between the two Yetis who'd come to retrieve him. They'd shackled his feet together, which made him walk with mincing, stumbling steps as he tried to keep up with their massive strides. Worse, they'd bound his hands behind him, each taking an elbow in their enormous grip so that they half-dragged him along between them.

Despite the brutes leading him past other cells, no familiar voices called out as he passed. Alex longed to look for his friends but couldn't glimpse much beyond the pillars of fur beside him, even if his eyes had been functioning and healthy.

The prisoner's passageway connected to another, a slightly wider one via the screeching door. With the ear-splitting squeal of hinges came a fresh flurry of barks and growls and slobbery snarls. The corridor was lit by the flicker of torches and smelled of dirt and dung and the distinct tang of blood. All manner of ferocious snouts and fangs chomped hungrily at the passersby through narrow bars. In his shortsighted state, Alex couldn't identify the beasts, which gave them a nightmarish quality.

The Trolls ignored the salivating savages and Alex felt oddly thankful to be wedged between their ample bodies as they made their way through Satan's personal zoo. By the time they turned a corner into a quieter passage, Alex had worked up a sweat. Salty streams trickled into his puffy, tender eyes making them close involuntarily. The urge to rub his face against the matted, absorbent fur of one of his captors was nearly overwhelming.

He squinted at what appeared to be steep stairs at the end of the corridor, awash in faint light from an opening above. The steps were crudely chiseled from the rock wall until they met with the opening which, Alex assumed, must be a giant hole in the ground above them.

"Where are we?" he mumbled, not really expecting an answer.

"Shut up," said the Troll on his left.

He was a mottled grey creature, while the one on Alex's right was tawny brown—fur color seemed the only difference he could discern in these beasts. Both sported filthy, ragged looking loincloths, strung across their hips.

At the stairway, the grey Troll released his grip to climb the narrow, near-vertical steps. The tawny Troll gave Alex a shove to go next, then followed behind. Encumbered as he was with chains and shackles, the steps were a challenge. If each stair tread hadn't been so deep—no doubt to accommodate Dregs of the Bigfoot variety—Alex would have feared tumbling off sideways.

Despite his careful ascent, he lost his footing and tripped onto the gravelly ground as he tried to clear the opening. Before he could react to the exfoliating effects of the grit, the grey Troll heaved Alex upright with an impatient expletive. Alex squinted against the brightness of the skydome, trying to ignore the fresh throb of pain in his face and concentrate on deciphering his location.

The tawny Troll emerged from the hole like an ugly, oversized rabbit materializing from a magician's hat. Beside the opening, a narrow monolithic rock stood sentry, reminding Alex of the standing stones near Aunt Jules's farmhouse in Ireland. A pang of longing and homesickness surfaced at the thought. What he wouldn't give to go back to that time, that place, and his aunt who was so full of patience and kindness. What would Aunt Jules have to say about his recent choices and predicament? Something like 'choices have consequences,' no doubt.

The big apes tipped the enormous rock flat, sealing the opening in the ground. The three resumed their silent, speedy pace. Alex attempted to get his bearings. Maybe he could escape and return with help, if he could find some sort of landmark that stood out. They were in a narrow valley, though the rising cliffs on either side were more foothill than mountain. Thanks to his swollen lids and splitting headache, he couldn't distinguish one tree or boulder from another.

After several stumbles over small rocks and broken limbs, Alex found it best to watch his step, in order to avoid getting his arms wrenched from their sockets by the guards. Every time he tripped, they yanked him hard, and not always in the same direction. His long, narrow feet looked alarmingly scrawny beside the wide, rectangular bipeds flanking him. They made his size fifteens look petite.

"So, who's this so-called Overlord?" Alex asked, hoping to glean any information he could. "I thought the hinterlands were full of creatures disillusioned with the trappings of normal life. Wouldn't that include having some tyrant lording over you?"

The grey Troll gave a grunt. "The Overlord is not like other rulers. He—"

"Shut it, Churkull," the tawny Troll barked. "We're not supposed to talk to the prisoners."

"But he's not a prisoner he's—"

"I said, shut it!" The tawny Troll stopped and pivoted so that he faced the other Troll, Churkull, nose to nose.

"*You* shut it, Sarcoptes," Churkull said. "You're not in charge."

"Hang on! I'm *not* a prisoner?" Alex found that almost funny. "Then I'll thank you to take your big paws off—"

"You can shut it too," Churkull snarled, poking Alex in the chest with one thick finger. "Don't bother us with useless questions."

Alex withheld several smart remarks, deciding silence might be best in the presence of Dense and Denser. The two resumed their trek at such a swift pace, Alex spent half the time dangling between them, parallel to the ground, scrambling for purchase. Thankfully, he didn't have long to stumble through this particular dance. They steered Alex toward the cliff on the right. As they approached, one of the shadowy clefts crystallized in Alex's vision to become an opening in the rock.

Another Troll stepped from the opening. Alex guessed he was higher up the food-chain based on his clothing. Unlike

Dense and Denser in their furry birthday suits and loincloths, this nut-brown Troll sported an open, black vest and a matching pair of drawstring trousers. A tan leather baldric peeked from beneath the vest, angled across his broad chest, ensconcing a curved scimitar in a scabbard at his side.

The bumbling escorts saluted without releasing their hold on Alex's arms, which meant they used opposite hands for the gesture.

Definitely dense.

The uniformed guard gave an answering grunt and stepped back into the shadows. "The prisoner has arrived," he barked.

Alex smirked at Churkull. "He must be talking about someone else since I'm *not* a prisoner."

The Troll only tightened his grip on Alex's arm. They stepped into the mouth of the cave and Alex felt disconcerted by the sudden darkness. He heard the screech of hinges and then a torchlit tunnel revealed itself as a door pressed open. The silhouettes of two more guards stood right inside.

"I'll take him from here, chumps," the uniformed guard said. "You two need to feed the animals and make sure the other prisoners get some water."

In unison, Dense and Denser shoved Alex through the door. Once again, he lost his footing. Since he no longer had the benefit of the Trolls to keep him upright, he flew forward, chains clattering, and broke his fall with his shoulder. *That's gonna leave a mark.*

Alex struggled to get his knees beneath him without the use of his hands, half-expecting the guard to hoist him upright. Instead, one of the soldiers flanking the door gave Alex's backside a shove with his foot, sending Alex sprawling onto his face amid menacing laugher. He gritted his teeth, as much to keep his anger in check as to deal with the pain. In particular, the stab of pain from biting his tongue when he face-planted. He swallowed the tinny taste of blood and attempted another grapple to get upright.

This time the uniformed guard made an impatient-sounding snarl and grabbed Alex by the bicep, hauling him to his feet. After what had just taken place, Alex didn't mind.

No sooner had he found his footing and turned toward the burly brute beside him than the big ape let out a gasp and jumped back.

Alex twisted around, thinking something worse than a

Troll must have come up behind him. The two guards were still there, standing beside the door. Suddenly they, too, lurched back, looking at him wide-eyed.

That's when Alex noticed the glow emanating from around his right eye. Blast it. What was up with his stupid birthmark? Why had it decided to self-activate again? He decided to use it to his advantage.

Alex turned back to the uniformed guard. "What are you staring at, Chewbacca? My light-saber skin freaking you out?"

The Yeti blinked—surely as confused by the Star Wars reference as he was Alex's birthmark.

"Yeah. That's right. Fear the face!" Alex stomped his foot and the guard flinched, much to Alex's satisfaction.

Recovering, the Troll had his scimitar point-to-nose on Alex in a flash. "Fear this, you freakish, flightless excuse for a Nephilim." He pressed the tip of it into the fleshy part of Alex's sniffer. "Douse your flaming face, freak."

Alex flushed, vexed by his lack of autonomy, which caused his traitorous birthmark to glow all the brighter. *I am a freak.* He swallowed back the rest of his bitter thoughts, concentrating on the needle-like prick at the end of his nose. Shame and embarrassment slowly dialed down the wattage on his face.

"Walk," the Troll demanded, stepping aside and gesturing at the corridor.

Alex shuffled forward. A distinct pressure between his shoulder blades alerted him to the scimitar's new point of reference. Torches offered their flailing flicker of light to the tall, narrow tunnel. Soon, Alex's birthmark no longer contributed to the ambiance. A few openings shot off to one side or another but were much too small for Troll or Nephilim. They were Dwarf size.

Alex guessed that Dwarves had created this labyrinth. Tunneling was their particular talent. This sort of mountain dwelling took years, if not decades, to hone. These unsavory Dregs probably found a long-abandoned fortress to call their own.

"Keep straight," the Troll barked.

Ahead, an intersection of passageways converged into a wide, circular opening. A knot of Trolls sprang apart, saluting. Then Alex realized that one of the three wasn't a Troll at all.

He was Nephilim.

CHAPTER TWENTY-TWO

Alex

Alex's gaze was magnetized to the rogue Nephilim soldier. Did he recognize this traitor?

The Troll prodding Alex along expelled a frustrated grunt. "The time for superficial soldiering has passed, you lazy oafs," the Troll shouted from behind. "The Overlord expects professional behavior. You'll each be brought before the disciplinary council when my business with this interloper is finished."

Each guard hurried to station himself between the openings of the other passageways that spoked off of the intersection. Alex continued to stare at the Nephilim as he passed, ignoring the throb of his swollen eyes. The soldier kept his focus trained ahead. Alex couldn't place the grizzled old man's face. A ferocious-looking scar spliced his forehead, through his right eyebrow. The man's salt-and-pepper hair and stubble matched his salt-and-pepper wings, which looked to be in a permanent state of molt.

How long had it been since this ossified guy had lived in Calamus? When did he abandon King Aviel and become a defector?

A beat-up wooden door loomed on the opposite end of a narrow passageway layered with a filthy rug that might have once been red.

Beside the door, like a watchman hewed from the heart of the mountain, stood an enormous Ogre. Torchlight glinted off his perspiring dome, a beacon of flesh that drew the eye. Though Alex had been to the isle of Skellerwad once, and knew a few friendly Ogres back home, he'd seen none as massive as this spectacle. His bicep eclipsed Alex's head, dreads included. The thick-necked mound of muscle was every bit of nine feet tall.

The Ogre's garlicky body odor assaulted Alex from the opposite end of the corridor and made last night's stinking Ogre encounter seem pleasant. Alex held his breath as they waited for the giant to open the door, but the mighty stench asserted its foulness nonetheless.

"Great granite gravestones, Babel! Do us all a favor and *bathe*," the Troll said, sputtering into a cough.

Babel? As in "Tower of," obviously.

Alex exhaled as they stepped into a cool stone chamber. Its length gave the room the illusion of being narrow, yet it was wide enough to be flanked by a half dozen guards stationed in the shadows. They stood sentry along the walls to Alex's left and right. He could make out two Dwarves—Dark Dwarves, if he had to guess—two Trolls, and two Ogres standing in size progression and facing their creature counterpart. A vaulted ceiling gave the room a cathedral-like quality, enhanced by a blaze of torches along the far back wall, opposite Alex, providing the only source of light.

Also opposite was a platform. And on that platform sat the silhouette of someone seated on a large, throne-like chair. The one who called himself Overlord, Alex surmised, though he couldn't make out features or details due to the backlighting. He could, however, easily identify the two sentinels on either side of the throne. Their robe-like garments and feathered appendages gave them the angelic-warrior appearance that this narcissistic tyrant was no doubt hoping to achieve. Instead of bodyguards, this guy employed guardian angels.

Except Alex knew they were no angels. They could only be more traitorous Nephilim.

"Approach!" ordered someone from the platform.

A shove in the back—thankfully by hand rather than sword tip—made Alex stagger forward on his pilgrimage. Having grown up in palace life, he was familiar with the way leaders sought to create an intimidating presence for both enemies and dignitaries alike. He hoped he might wield his princely persuasion to convince this mystery man that he was the latter, rather than the former.

As he approached, Alex noted that this Overlord wielded power over a ragtag kingdom. Not only was this quasi throne room as unimpressive as a storage room in the palace of Calamus, but none of the soldiers wore a uniform that matched the other. A weapon was the only thing they had in common, and each of those seemed to be of personal preference in size and placement.

"Head down as you walk, plebeian," said the Troll at Alex's back. "You will kneel, head bowed, when you stand before the Overlord, and you will not speak or look elsewhere unless you are told. Got it?"

Alex didn't think Sasquatch required an answer, so he lowered his gaze to the iron-colored stone at his feet, but not before he pegged one of the Nephilim flanking the throne as female. *Interesting.*

When he caught sight of the dais, he dropped painfully onto both knees, wishing he had enough slack between his feet to take a knee with dignity.

A low, cynical chuckle rippled from the throne in an increasing swell. As the volume picked up, the hair on the back of Alex's neck bristled in response.

He knew that laugh.

Alex jerked his head up.

The Troll shoved his head down. "I *said*—"

"Leave him be, Vetch. My little troublemaker of a nephew wasn't expecting a family reunion."

Alex lifted his chin and straightened his back, staring at his uncle Magnum with the full-on fury of seventeen years of loathing.

CHAPTER TWENTY-THREE

Sadie

XANDER KISSED THE TOP OF SADIE'S head. They stood on the balcony outside their bedchamber while Gage and his men continued to thoroughly comb the palace—though for whom or what, no one knew for certain. It was procedure. One made all the more urgent with the impending arrival of King Odhran's family and retinue.

Sadie felt herself relax into the familiar, protective strength of her husband. It had been one of the longest nights and most stressful mornings that she'd experienced since her earliest exploits into the Tethered World. The past month had given her many opportunities to comfort her husband as he watched his father's life ebb away. She only now realized how much she'd missed being on the receiving end.

When Xander enveloped her like this, Sadie felt like a small and precious pearl being safely shielded within its oyster shell. They fit together so perfectly.

Mmm. How she needed this chance to catch her breath and revivify. While their room was being pieced together from its upheaval, and the awful reminders of Blaylock's murder were being purged from their parlor, Sadie allowed some of her husband's strength to fortify her.

"I'm sorry you had to be the one to discover Blaylock, Princess," Xander whispered against her hair. He had always called her Princess, long before she was anything except a topside teenager. "I am so, *so* thankful it wasn't you. Had you been here when the intruder came…"

She felt him shake his head against the top of her own. Sadie gave his back a reassuring squeeze. Her hands were snuggled beneath his wings, feeling their silky softness blanketing her fingers. "Me too. But it's awful to lose Blaylock."

Now she felt the pressure of a nod. "It is," Xander agreed.

"He was a great man. And a good man. Those aren't always the same thing. Still, selfishly, I am relieved that you, dear, are safe."

He pressed her shoulders back and looked her in the eye. "I've been so emotionally wrapped up in my father's failing health and fearing for my own..." He grimaced. His icy-blue eyes were red-rimmed and tearful. "I've not been much of anything to you besides a royal pain in the apothecary. You've had to nurse my father and listen to me carry on about the unfairness of it all like an overgrown child."

Sadie giggled. "The apothecary, eh? That's a new one." She slid her left palm across his rough, stubbly cheek and swept the pad of her thumb across his lower lip. "I haven't minded, whatsoever."

Xander arched a disbelieving eyebrow. "*Right.*"

"Okay. Maybe a little." She gave a one-shoulder shrug. "Mostly when I hadn't slept much and you were a grouch."

Xander blinked in false innocence. "Me? A grouch?" He chuckled and reached for her wrist, pulling her hand from his cheek, inspecting her palm. "No more bandage, I see. Skin looks much better." He kissed her palm.

"Still a little tender," Sadie said, warming to his touch. "The bandage was becoming more irritating than the burn." Her fingers moved from his grasp to the back of his neck and she pulled his face down to hers. "Come here grouch."

Xander laughed, his lips vibrating against hers, pulling away to kiss the tip of her nose. "I've let circumstances dictate my moods for too long."

Sadie leaned against his chest and nodded. "I'm guilty too. We've both self-isolated."

She heard him swallow. "I don't know about you, but I feel like Lucia wants to use this wedding as a way to force us back to the past...or, at least, the dynamic between all of us after the tragedy with Alex and her son. The look in her eyes when she was explaining this crazy plan that Father agreed to—a plan I wouldn't have believed if I hadn't seen the papers written in his hand and signed with his signet."

"*Ahem.*"

Sadie and Xander turned to find Commander Gage standing in the doorway between the balcony and their bedchamber, arrayed in his military uniform and cape. The bronzed prosthesis of his left arm, and his freckled balding head, reflected the luminous amber light of the skydome, giving him a regal, statue-like appearance.

He offered a little bow. "King Odhran and his company are nearing the crossing point of the River Gambrell, your Highness. Unfortunately, the murderer remains at large. Most of the palace and grounds have been searched. A few of my men are still in the aqueducts. Tassitus is conducting a thorough search of the cellar and crypts in the lower regions."

"Whoever did the deed is not some criminal who crept in and out. They're one of our own, they fit in." Xander released Sadie and stepped to the balcony as if he might spot the guilty party. "That makes them all the more dangerous and much more difficult to discover."

CHAPTER TWENTY-FOUR

Sadie

BECAUSE ALEX AND COMPANY HAD ABSCONDED with Sage and Ansyn, much to Xander's overt displeasure, Sadie and he were forced to ride other horses. Sadie sat astride Cricket, a laidback chestnut, hoping the equine's calm might seep up through the saddle.

She took a steadying breath, annoyed to feel so jumpy about the arrival of their guests. Such visits were rare and, despite the reasons behind it, should inspire mild anticipation. Perhaps if this one wasn't instigated by Lucia and involving Alexander, things would be different.

Shrugging away anxious thoughts, Sadie adjusted the simple, wavy circlet crown that offered a more comfortable fit than the jewel-encrusted monstrosities demanded by more formal pageantry. Joanie had worked her magic on Sadie with a quick herbal mask for her puffy eyes and a simple French braid to disguise her bedhead. Ironic, since Sadie was only in bed a few hours the previous night.

A stable hand proffered the reins, and Sadie nudged Cricket away from the portico to join the other members of court. She spotted Xander and Lucia on their mounts, aside from the others, the tension between them visible despite the distance.

Lucia did not acknowledge Sadie's approach, though Sadie was in her line of sight. *As per usual.*

Xander noticed Sadie, however, and his face softened, morphing from frustrated to subtly flirtatious. He briefly wiggled his eyebrows, then returned his focus to his stepmother.

"…so insulting," Lucia was saying. Beneath her billowing, indigo-blue dress, Old Ethan snorted and fidgeted. She had never been comfortable on horseback, probably because she wasn't in absolute control, and thus preferred the oldest and slowest horse in the herd. "How can I possibly excuse Brady Alexander's absence to my uncle?"

"You've had plenty of practice making excuses for Magnum." Xander shrugged. "I'm sure you'll think of something."

Lucia's features iced over, and she turned Old Ethan and trotted away.

"Looks like I missed the fireworks," Sadie said.

"Oh, it wasn't too bad. I'm fireproof with that conniving woman."

The blast of a distant horn announced the approach of King Odhran and company. Xander sighed and Sadie watched his protocol-mask settle on his features. "You ready for this?"

Sadie gave him a lopsided grin. "I'd feel a lot better about it if Alex hadn't disappeared. With all of the chaos of the morning, you and I haven't had a chance to discuss our *official* explanation."

He scratched his jaw. "Yeah. I've been giving that some thought. 'Diplomatic honesty' is the term my father employed for this sort of delicate conversation. Ultimately this is Lucia's predicament, which means it's up to her to explain Alex's disappearance. I told her as much, though I'm wondering if that was particularly wise."

"Hmm, same here." Sadie nudged Cricket to keep pace with Xander's steed. "Sure wish we at least had an inkling of his whereabouts. Makes me nervous that your men haven't come back with any word. Unlike Magnum, Alex took off with four friends and three horses. I figured scouts would've found something by now."

Xander fingered his crown, seating it onto his long braids more securely. "Me too." He twisted in the saddle and scanned the dozen or so riders who were headed to greet their guests in the courtyard. "Speaking of whereabouts...have you seen Ellynn?"

CHAPTER TWENTY-FIVE

Alex

"WHAT'S THE MATTER, BRATTY BRADY?" MAGNUM leaned onto his elbows to stare down at Alex, who was forced to remain kneeling beneath the heavy hand of the Troll called Vetch. "You don't look pleased to see your ol' Uncle Mag-*nificent.*" He swayed back against his throne with a maniacal laugh.

And here I thought things couldn't get worse...

In a blink, Magnum's laughter ceased and he glowered down at Alex. "So, Brady, why were you and your little friends trespassing on my land? Hmm? Did the king send you to find his absentee son, or were you and your posse merely looking for trouble?"

Alex only glared, his breathing labored as he struggled to keep his temper in check. He hoped his birthmark would remain in the 'off' position as he scrambled to make sense of the bizarre scenario. Magnum had only been MIA for three or four months. How had he managed to pull together this shabby little kingdom of loyal Dregs? Surely, he'd been arranging things for some time, covertly, on his many excursions from Calamus. Though his earlier jaunts typically lasted a week or two, Alex had always welcomed the peaceful atmosphere left in Magnum's wake. *So this is what he's been up to...*

Despite his puffy-eyed tunnel vision, Alex had no trouble recognizing the familiar smirk of satisfaction on his uncle's face. That amber-eyed condescending stare—so similar to Lucia's—focused its repugnance on Alex. His cynical grin was framed by coffee-colored curls that caught the torchlight in coppery glints. Sporting a deep burgundy tunic trimmed in braided gold, and black breeches that tucked snuggly into a fine looking pair of matching leather boots, Magnum played the part of dashing despot quite well.

"Ah, no worries. We can discuss the nitty-gritty details after my men here pay each of your friends a private visit." Magnum crossed his legs, clearly carefree. "Thought you might ease my conscience by allowing me to skip the unsavory step of physical torture, but..." He shrugged and looked to the hulking figures on either side of him. "Who am I to look out for their wellbeing if you're willing to let them suffer to spite me with your silence?"

Before Alex could respond, Magnum shot to his feet and clapped his hands. Alex flinched at the sudden, piercing report. The Ogre stationed against the left wall lumbered toward the platform, his large bare feet slapping the stone so that a sharp echo pinged throughout the rock-hewn room.

Magnum gestured at a door near to where the Ogre had stood. "Deke, fetch the girl and bring her here."

CHAPTER TWENTY-SIX

Sadie

INDEED, WHERE WAS ELLYNN? SADIE KEPT scanning their company, checking to see whether her daughter had slipped in late. Palace life was often a solitary, rather boring affair, especially for children. A visit from another Nephilim kingdom happened once in a lifetime, if that. Ellynn would not want to miss it. Surely Trinny wouldn't let her. Something wasn't right, though answers would have to wait.

A ram's horn trumpeted *long-short-long-short* to herald the arrival of Éire House at the palace gates. The Calamus company arranged themselves into a U-shape in the courtyard to receive their guests. Lucia, Xander, and Sadie maneuvered to the center while the aristocratic counsel fanned out on either side. Gage held the purple and black standard of Calamus from his mount stationed in front of Xander, its shield boasting intersecting swords atop a large, vertical feather with a cross-shaped tip.

Sadie glimpsed the telltale sign of the approaching travelers in the ghostly dust that drifted above the courtyard walls and her pulse elevated in response. King Odhran and his entourage had managed a daunting journey and were poised to discover that Alex had run from his royal responsibilities.

These strangers seemed as fearsome and exotic to Sadie as the tales of their Nephilim ancestors. Pagan Nephilim explorers sailed to the Northern Atlantic islands as early as the eighteenth century B.C. These winged Titans inspired awe among the natives, birthing Celtic legends that evolved to fantastical proportions through ages of oral storytelling.

Referred to as "the shining ones," generations of Nephilim enjoyed god-like status. This allowed them—the Tuatha Dé Danann—to flourish for hundreds of years before being driven into hiding. During the Middle Ages, most recanted their pagan beliefs. Of course, the Biblical account of Nephilim went *much* further back to a much darker time—but those beings seemed to embody little relation to the modern-day Nephilim thousands of years hence.

Though Lucia herself had come from Brihndle in Mooredbelow—the Tethered World equivalent within the depths of Ireland,—she volunteered little information about her homeland. Mostly, she boasted of its superiority to Calamus in all facets from food to fanfare. She had never elaborated on her journey to Calamus, though it was surely arduous. Sadie was curious to learn how the coming retinue managed, horses and all, to travel here from across the ocean. Dragons? Faeries? Flight? Likely a combination.

The staccato clomp of hoofs drew Sadie's attention to the cobbled path that led from the palace gates into the courtyard. Their guests had arrived!

Steeds sporting wild, gnarled manes carried an array of riders decked in furs and weaponry, a fitting manifestation of Sadie's preconceived ideas. The lead rider trotted ahead carrying the standard of Éire House–an offset, charcoal-colored cross, known as Brigid's Cross, dominated the center of a jade green flag. Between each of the cross's four spokes sat a black, five-pointed star.

Sadie heard Lucia suck in her breath and gave the woman a sideways glance. Was that rapture or contempt on her face? Her steely veneer made it hard to read. After nearly two decades of separation, surely the woman was thrilled about the reunion. Perhaps homesickness had created the monster-in-law that Lucia had slowly become. Sadie had glimmers of memory from a time when things were less contentious between Lucia, Xander, and herself.

"Greetings, Pacific House of Tuatha Dé," said the chiseled Nephilim soldier holding the verdant flag ahead of the entourage. Dirty blond hair billowed over his shoulders in a tangle of waves. A black five-pointed star tattooed the temple of his left eye, as if one of the stars on the standard had dislodged and landed there. Despite his fierce and rather bedraggled appearance, he gave an affable bow. "Éire House offers their greetings and come bearing gifts to celebrate the union of two great Tuatha Dé families. Hail to the Tethered World from the Land of Moored-below."

The company trotted to a stop behind the soldier. Horses and riders alike were festooned with leathered armor and chainmail, embellished with cording of deep gold and ribbons of emerald and ebony. Of the dozen or more riders, some wore capes of fur, others layers of animal skin.

It was almost too much for Sadie to take in. She found herself relieved that this encounter was of a friendly nature, a touch intimidated by their display of tempestuous pageantry. She scanned their weathered, tired faces. Which one was Larkin? Sadie had to admit that the girl's name was charming. Maybe because it sounded like a bird. Maybe because it was similar to her own maiden name—Larcen.

As royal parents, they may not be able to give their son the freedom to choose his own bride—*thank you for that, King Aviel*—yet Sadie remained hopeful that the bride-to-be was a roundabout answer to a lifetime of motherly prayers. Maybe not the answer she had expected, but an answer all the same.

Would this family still want Alex to wed their daughter once they learned he'd run away? His actions certainly didn't lend themselves to a good first impression of the family, nor of himself.

A cloud-grey horse strode forward, nosing past the soldier with the flag. On its back sat a herculean man with a silver walrus-style mustache, a matching mass of beard sprawled half way down his chest, and one thick salt-and-pepper braid tumbled over his left shoulder. Though broad and muscular, he was made broader still by a layer of blubber that softened his bowling ball-sized biceps and settled around his middle. Snowy wing-feathers peaked from beneath a cape made of plush, chocolaty fur. In his meaty right hand, he clutched a spear, easily five feet long, that spiraled to a forked spike on the end.

Lose your trident, Poseidon?

Sadie fought the urge to shrink back when his penetrating, cerulean eyes swept her way. His fleshy mouth curved into a frown amplified by the droopy mustache that framed it. When his gaze lit on Xander, his frown downgraded to a grimace. He swiveled his head, taking in the others, his gaze quickly snapping back to Lucia.

"Is that you, Lucia?" the man asked, his voice deep, his Irish inflection surprisingly faint. Wiry brows knotted, then one corner of his mouth tweaked upward. "It is! It is. You've...changed." His gaze traversed the length of her. "You've aged."

Lucia's lips clenched, nostrils flaring in silent dissent. A sprout of compassion unfurled in Sadie's heart. So much for happy family reunions. The hostility between niece and uncle felt as dense as the morning mist. If the words "you've aged" were the best this man could offer after a couple of decades, Sadie wasn't eager to unite Alex with this family.

"Same could be said of you, dear uncle." Lucia's head tilted into her customary I'm-superior-to-you posture. She looked down her nose at the bulwark of a man. "Time can be a tyrant."

"Lucia!" A booming voice cleaved through the tension. Another pale horse came alongside the king's. A colossal woman sat astride, full figured in leather breeches, laced boots, and a blousy linen shirt. The disapproval on her middle-aged features made Odhran look almost approachable. "As peevish as ever, I see. Has the favorable marriage *we* arranged for ya—a marriage to the most respected Nephilim king in all of the tethered realms—done nothin' to make that tongue of yers more diplomatic?" She spoke with a brogue so heavy, so full of rolling Rs and clipped words, Sadie found the woman difficult to understand.

Lucia leveled her gaze on the strawberry-blond giantess with wings to match. "No more than your marriage has sweetened your bitter tongue, obviously, Aunt Clodagh."

"King Odhran. Queen Clodagh. Welcome to Calamus." Xander's jovial greeting sounded forced. He prodded his horse forward.

Sadie joined him, mindful to leave a space for Lucia to be seen and to join them if she wished. They were off to a rough start, and that before any news of Alex's disappearance had surfaced. Goodness!

And where was her future daughter-in-law? Sadie's gaze swept across Éire House, hoping to glimpse Princess Larkin, wondering if she might recognize her by the family scowl.

"It is an honor to have the esteemed Éire House in our midst, Cousin." Xander proffered a nod.

Though 'cousin' was a designation used between monarchs as a show of camaraderie, implying a shared type of kinship, Sadie noted how King Odhran recoiled, ever so slightly.

"Surely ye're not King Aviel?" Queen Clodagh snapped, looking him up and down with eyes the color of jadeite. "Ye're much too young and..." she trailed off, brows peaked as if to say, *you know.*

Xander blinked but kept his tone cordial. "You are correct, Queen Clodagh. I am Xander. *King* Alexander, to be precise. This is my wife, Queen Sadie. My father, King Aviel, unfortunately passed four days ago."

Sadie saw a disapproving cringe flick across Odhran's features, settling into a mild shock, similar to Clodagh's. Having shipped Lucia to Calamus with a handful of attendants—like some deluxe model mail-order bride—Sadie guessed these two hadn't considered that the king of Calamus might come with more melanin in his skin than themselves. Without the benefit of photography or television, every in-person introduction came with the need to reconcile one's expectations with reality.

King Odhran and his wife shared an incredulous frown. "King Aviel is *dead*?" Odhran lifted one wiry brow and looked past Xander, at his niece.

Lucia clasped a hand to her throat and looked back through hooded eyes. "Indeed. I am newly widowed. I regret that you did not get to meet the man you used to wash your hands of your responsibility toward my father." She leveled her gaze on her uncle. "Though I suppose I should, indeed, be thankful for how things worked out. Aviel was a good man and a noble king."

Sadie's heart warmed toward Lucia another degree. Though she hoped Lucia's praise was sincere, Sadie also understood that she meant to imply that Odhran was neither good nor noble.

To his credit, Odhran didn't bristle, but rather appeared to have recovered his royal manners. "Then it is our loss, indeed. Éire House extends our condolences to Pacific House. We regret that our presence here comes so soon after your misfortune. We hope we're not a burden to your household."

"Of course not," Sadie said, employing her most welcoming smile. "Your presence will surely lift our spirits. It's such a rarity to have guests from afar."

"Come." Xander extended his hand. "This is not the manner in which we should share the affairs of our houses. Let us refresh your horses and allow you to refresh yourselves. I know you've had a grueling excursion. There will be time enough to exchange stories this evening." With that, he turned his horse toward the palace.

Though Sadie felt certain that the young, auburn-haired woman she'd spied was indeed the bride-to-be—there were few females among the party—she withheld her curiosity. Since Alex could not be produced at the moment, further introductions might best be saved for a smaller audience.

Sadie nudged Cricket to turn and found herself looking directly at Lucia. The woman stared into the middle distance, lost in thought. Was that a swell of emotion glossing her amber eyes? Sadie wondered about the wounds Lucia had become so adept at hiding. Maybe Lucia's rough edges were more scar tissue than sandpaper.

She rode past Lucia who suddenly glanced at Sadie, façade momentarily neglected. Was that a plea for help that Sadie glimpsed in Lucia's fleeting glance? Perhaps it wasn't scar tissue either. More like scabs...fragile, painful, and easily disturbed.

CHAPTER TWENTY-SEVEN

Ellynn

"PLEASE, DON'T TELL MY MOM AND dad, Trinny. *Please.*" Ellynn winced at the sharp sting of alcohol splashing her leg. "*Ohhh. Ouch.*" She bit her lip and cracked one eye at the foamy pink sludge dripping down her right shin onto a towel spread beneath her on the bathroom floor.

"Serves ya right, ya little tunnel rat," Trinny scolded, jabbing a clean rag at Ellynn's wound, ignoring the girl's yelp and twitch with each rough pass. "What've I told ya about spyin' on people, eavesdroppin' where ye've no business listenin'. It's dangerous. It's rude. It's *wrong.*" The Dwarf grabbed Ellynn's ankle and lifted it close to her face, scrutinizing the fillet of skin that striped the length of her shinbone. "And a princess, to boot! Shame on you, Ellynn Jules. Shame. On. You." She pointed the disgusting, blood-stained rag at her patient.

Ellynn blinked back tears, determined not to cry. "I know. It's just. Well..."—and here, the tears leaked out against her will—"no one tells me anything. No one bothered to wake me last night when Alex left. Grandmama Lucia is acting like—like an apocalyptic wasp. If I'm *ever* going to know what's really going on around here, it's up to me to find out."

Trinny kept her gaze trained on Ellynn's shin, applying a thick, gooey green salve, then wrapping her leg with a clean linen bandage. "Mmhm. Ya keep a tellin' yerself that, youngin'. *Poor* Ellynn! How is it that the kingdom of Calamus isn't reportin' to her Royal Teenage Majesty? Leaves me baffled, it does."

Ellynn crossed her arms, aware of her raw, scraped palms, which would be harder to keep hidden than her shin, despite being less mangled. She glared at her lady-in-waiting whom—Ellynn resentfully understood—functioned more like a nanny or chaperone. Still, Trinny was usually on *her* side.

Trinny tucked the tail end of the bandage into itself. "Now then, if ya don't want me tellin' yer ma or da, ya best be explainin' how ya came by such a spectacular laceration. I'll be the judge of whether or not yer parents need to know." The Dwarf shifted her mauve tunic and sat back, facing her charge, leather moccasin boots outstretched, crossed at the ankle.

Ellynn eyed her disapproving caregiver, weighing how much to reveal. The woman might be strict, but Ellynn knew that Trinny loved her fiercely. Most of the time the two got on more like sisters. Still, if Ellynn stepped out of line, the little lady didn't hesitate to pop off like an arrow from a crossbow.

"Well? Out with it!" Trinny flicked her hand between them.

Ellynn gave a weary sigh. "Fine." She reached for the book charm at her neck, rubbing the tiny V of the open pages. "Mother told me about Alex. Why he ran away. Y'know. Because of having to get married."

Trinny pressed a palm at Ellynn. "Wait, wait. *Whoa.* So...ye were *told* about Alex's predicament before this happened?" She swirled her finger indicating Ellynn's wounded leg. "I could've sworn ya told me, just a wee bit ago, that the only way ya learned anything was by eavesdroppin' on all of us tightlipped adults. So which is it?"

Ellynn looked away, a flush warming her neck. She hitched her shoulder. "I guess I'm told a few things. Here and there." She turned a self-pitying blue-eyed gaze back to Trinny. "But usually it's after the fact, or it's the overly simplified 'kid' version. I still have to read between the lines and piece together what's *really* going on or—"

"No, ya don't!" Trinny interrupted. "If yer parents don't give ya the full-blown version with all the gory details, there's a reason. Ya need to respect that. One day ye will be a mother yerself and ye will understand. I can promise ya that."

Ellynn had heard this speech before. Though she thought it sounded like a bunch of grownup doublespeak for "none of your business," she left space for the possibility of thinking, *my parents were right.* Only because she, herself, hated to be wrong.

"Fine," Ellynn said, then sighed. "I'm sure that's true. Or, at least, it was true, when I was little. I'm thirteen, now, and still getting the five-year-old version of things."

Trinny pursed her mouth, looking thoughtful. "All right.

I'll give ya that. Maybe yer skinny little self 'as been a growin' while the rest of us weren't lookin'. Maybe we need to start givin' ya the thirteen-year-old version, eh?"

A grateful smile sprang to Ellynn's lips. "Yes. I can handle it. I can handle more than anyone gives me credit for. I watched my grandfather die before my eyes. And watched my grandmother freak out and shoot daggers from her eyeballs at everyone in the room. Me included. I mean, if that doesn't shatter my childhood innocence, I'm living in a granite bubble."

Trinny threw her head back and guffawed. "Sheesh! Ye're a hoot sometimes." She composed herself and cleared her throat. "Now then, out with it."

"Okay. Well...I wanted to figure out why Grandmama Lucia was so angry. She'd given Mom such a dark look this morning." Ellynn studied her raspy, red palms as she gave a shortened version of what she'd overheard. Anger flared afresh as she relayed insulting comments about Alex, Lucia's desire for revenge, and puzzling phrases like "press our network for information."

Trinny sat wide-eyed and slack-jawed, as Ellynn went on to describe Florentino's interruption. "When he told grandmother that Blaylock was dead, I—I was *so* afraid..." At this, she trailed off, a catch in her throat with the return of the fear she felt for her parents. "I ran. I didn't grab my candle. I just ran." Her voice was barely a whisper. "I don't use those passageways very often and forgot about a small set of steps that connects to an older part of the palace. I tripped and..." she gestured to her leg.

"Oh, Ellynn!" Trinny set upon her neck, drawing Ellynn to her shoulder. "Ya poor dear. Ya must've been crazy with worry." She pulled back and looked Ellynn in the eye. "Fer now, I'll keep yer secret, the best I can. Seein' that this happened on account of yer distress. But much of what ya overheard is treacherous and must be looked into. I'll be thinkin' hard about what to do, and how I might conceal yer bein' the one to bring it to my attention. Probably safer that way anyhow. I am concerned that ye may've left a candle burnin' in the passageway, however."

Ellynn swiped her tears away and gave a thick sniff. "It blew out as I ran past."

"Very well." Trinny lifted a finger between them, then used it to point at Ellynn's shin and hands. "Now then, I can't help it if yer parents notice yer hands or yer leg. Promise to tell the truth to yer ma or da, if they question ya. Understood?"

Ellynn nodded. "Fair enough."

"And no more of yer foolish pussyfootin' about. Next time—*if* ye're a big enough idjit to sneak about again—next time, I'll take ya to yer parents meself. Straightaway. Is that as clear as the crystal-domed sky?"

Another nod.

In the distance, a ram horn sounded a series of blasts, announcing the approach of visitors. A rare and beloved sound to Ellynn's ears.

"Oh, no!" Ellynn clambered to her feet, flinching at the pain in her tender leg. "I'm missing the arrival of Éire House."

Trinny stood and took Ellynn gently by the wrist and turned her hand over to inspect the wound. "Hang on, missy. Before ya go, I need ya to wash yer hands and rub that salve into yer palms. Ye're goin' to miss their arrival either way. There's no time to get through this enormous palace and to the courtyard. Don't ya worry, they'll be a buzzin' about inside in no time."

Ellynn pulled free. "My hands are fine, Trinny. Thanks for fixing me up."

She didn't look back as she left her bedchamber and scurried down the hall toward the library.

Ellynn knew a shortcut.

CHAPTER TWENTY-EIGHT

Alex

Girl? What girl?

Alex watched Deke, the Ogre, emerge from the side door, the squirming backside of someone wedged beneath his hulking arm. Once Deke deposited the fitful form at the feet of Magnum, Alex recognized the pitiful soul.

Colin!

Colin's unusual eyes found Alex, a zigzag of tears streaking the boy's dirty cheeks. His nose glistened with snot and his lower lip was fat and busted wide, a dark blotch of blood crusting beneath it in a half-moon.

Alex held no affection for the runaway, but Colin had saved their collective backsides yesterday and didn't deserve to be caught up in Alex's family drama. Magnum was a bully who enjoyed a good game of cat and rat, just for laughs.

"I can't get *aaany* information from this Topsider." Magnum prodded Colin with the toe of his boot. "She's tougher than she looks."

Colin closed his eyes as Magnum spoke, turning his head so that his forehead rested against the stone floor.

Why was Magnum referring to Colin as a girl? Was his uncle trying to degrade the slender boy, much like he degraded Alex by calling him Bratty Brady?

Magnum swooped off his throne, wrenched Colin up by his neck, and stood, allowing the teen to dangle and writhe like a fish out of water. Colin clawed at the fingers that squeezed his neck like a clamp.

"Where did you find her, Brady?" His uncle took a step forward so that Colin's twisting body managed to land a stray kick across Alex's jaw.

Alex reeled backward, grabbing at his face with one hand, shielding himself from Colin's flailing body parts with the other.

Laughter bubbled up from the on-looking oafs, and Magnum shoved Colin forward, his feet pummeling Alex's head and shoulders. When the boy realized what was happening, he drew his legs up beneath him.

Magnum snickered then returned to sit on his roughhewn throne. He plopped Colin onto his lap like some oversized child's toy. "I'll ask you one more time, dear nephew. What's up with the Topsider? Where did you find this ugly little girl and why is she traipsing about my realm with the likes of you and your lowlife friends?"

Alex looked from Magnum to Colin and back. Though a deluge of curses threatened to break the barrier of Alex's tongue, he swallowed them, managing one seething word. "*Girl?*"

Magnum quirked his brows in mock shock. "Yes. *Girl.* Don't tell me you were fooled by her hack of a haircut and the boy's breeches." His uncle guffawed. "If so, you really are as stupid as you look."

Alex stared at Colin, hoping to convey the question—is this true? Maybe it was Alex's swollen eye, or maybe it was the boy's—girl's?—stubbornness, but Alex couldn't fetch a response from the Topsider.

Magnum stroked Colin's hair. The kid recoiled, eyes crimped closed, a bright bead of blood bursting from the scowling, scabbed lip. Alex watched a tear slip down the mysterious runaway's cheek and discovered he had the capacity to despise his uncle even more.

"When my men told me of this Topsider's so-called talents at the lake, I felt it imperative to subdue any threat." Magnum gave an exaggerated sigh. "You know the trouble we've had with Topsiders sneaking into the Tethered World over the years. Bringing weapons or cameras or other forbidden objects. My men had to search the wretch to ensure our safety. Didn't take them long to report back that the prisoner was without weapons and...and wasn't quite what *he* made out to be. He was a *she.*"

All at once, Alex recognized the truth. The soft planes of Colin's face...the baggy, ill-fitted clothing...the privacy demanded when nature called. The pieces synthesized into a picture that suddenly made sense. He inhaled sharply, stung by shock.

Said prisoner curled her shoulders around her ears, head turned away from Magnum, as if she hoped to fold into herself and disappear. Magnum touched her cheek and, with elaborate tenderness, traced a tear to the corner of her mouth.

"Nope. Not at all. Not a boy. Not a man. Not a male." Magnum grabbed the back of Colin's neck again and her eyes snapped open. "A scrawny little girl is who we have on our hands. One who seems to have an important skillset that I simply *must* persuade her to employ."

Alex was struggling to complete the paradigm shift—*he* was actually a *she*—but couldn't quite get there. He caught her gaze again and perceived the tiniest of nods, confirming the truth. His sister's face materialized before him, sparking an ember of protectiveness toward the poor girl. If this were Ellynn, what would he do about it?

Considering his chains and the surrounding thugs, probably not much, he decided. At least...not yet.

CHAPTER TWENTY-NINE

Alex

"WHY IN THE NAME OF WHITT Lake would you try to pass yourself off as a *boy*?" Alex hissed, tempted to shake the truth out of Colin—or whatever her name might be—like coins trapped inside a Topsider's piggybank. Not that he could reach her from across the table.

They sat facing each other, wrists clamped to a filthy, splintered tabletop by matching sets of crudely welded cuffs. The girl's wrists so thin they required the addition of ropes to bind them together on the far-side of the restraints, scarred fingers turning purple. She sat curled on her knees atop a stool brought to hoist her petite body high enough to reach the bonds.

Her sour-faced glare told Alex she wouldn't be offering up her secrets. Jaw flexed, he looked toward Vetch, guarding the pockmarked wooden door. Somewhere outside of this medieval interrogation room, Magnum was probably preening himself in preparation for his grand entrance, allowing his captives to sweat it out for a bit. The swine did everything for maximum effect.

The door hinges squealed to life. Babel, the enormous, odorous Ogre, hunkered through the doorway and shuffled in like a walking bag of boulders. His garlicky aura soon enveloped the room, and Alex reflexively ducked his head, longing to clamp a hand over his face.

Vetch coughed before cussing at the giant while thrashing his arms as if that might dilute the smell. Finally, the Troll covered his face with the crook of his hairy arm and glared at Babel, who now towered over the table, looking between the two prisoners.

The Ogre placed fists on hips, exposing his sweat-matted hairy pits, providing maximum impact. Babel's ample stomach protruded from between the open flaps of a too-small vest. The fraying, greyish fabric clearly doubled as a bib, based on the assorted food smudges staining it. He wore long, mud-colored drawstring shorts—probably meant to be trousers on anyone else. A thick chain encircled his waist, disappearing beneath the dip of his belly. It dangled with a variety of tools and implements like an overgrown version of Alex's Aunt Nicole's charm bracelet. Alex knew there was nothing charming about any of *these* gadgets, however; they were used strictly to inflict painful persuasion.

Enduring torture hadn't been on the list of what Alex expected during his little diversion from Calamus. Marriage to a total stranger suddenly held more appeal than he'd thought possible. How drastically circumstances could change in a day.

Choices have consequences. Great-Aunt Jules's old idiom asserted itself again. Though he'd grown tired of hearing it as a kid, Alex now appreciated its accuracy.

Magnum finally strode into the room, arms spread wide, with an obnoxiously cheery, "Miss me?" He pulled up short with a curse, one hand pinching his nose, raven wings twitching as if he might fly from the reeking room.

"Hey, mister barf body." He coughed and gestured at the giant. "Leave your tools here and go drown yourself in a vat of molten lava so the world can breathe again."

Babel's features crumpled, lower lip and belly simultaneously poking forward, an apparent wounded soul. Eyes downcast—likely on his belly—his thick fingers fumbled with the clasp on the chain as he mumbled under his breath. "Nobuhn lubba muh. Nobuhn."

"Let's go, Babel," Magnum barked from behind his hand. "No one cares. Get out!"

Perhaps the Ogre's name had more to do with the oaf's thick-tongued talk than his comparative size to the tower of Babel. Though Alex was happy to see the foul creature depart, he felt a twinge of sympathy for him too. Somewhere deep inside, the mountainous monster had feelings, and his uncle had thoroughly trashed them.

Magnum swatted the air, exhaling loudly. "Great founts of flatulence! My apologies to you both." He gave a theatrical bow toward the table. "I wouldn't subject my worst enemy to that repugnant refuse. Oh wait"—he took a step back and pulled a mockingly shocked face—"you *are* my worst enemy!"

He brayed in his abrasive donkey-doofus laugh, and Alex found he had a limitless capacity for loathing the man.

Magnum tilted his head toward Vetch, and Alex watched his uncle's false animation morph into a cold, seething animosity. "Shut the door and grab the tools. These two aren't going anywhere so there's no need to guard the door. Let's begin with the splitchet."

Vetch removed the requested tool and left the rest of the chained implements on the floor where Babel had abandoned them.

Alex swallowed. What did his insane uncle plan to do? Splitchets were similar to a vise, but with a sharp, curved hook where the upper clamp would be. As the vise tightens, the hook corkscrews into a piece of wood—or, in this case, a human extremity, Alex guessed.

Magnum made a big show of dragging another stool from the corner of the near-barren room and plunking it at the end of the table, perpendicular to Alex and the girl. Alex felt her intense gaze and turned to see her startling eyes pleading with his own. What did she want from him? She'd kept her secrets close, including her gender, which meant he had nothing to divulge. Except, perhaps, the story of how she came to be in the Tethered World, which might be as false as her male persona.

"Isn't this cozy?" Magnum straddled the stool, leaning onto his elbows within reach of his two prisoners. "Now, this is how our little *soirée* is going to work. I'm going to ask mystery-girl some questions and, if she refuses to answer, Vetch here is going to hurt you." He winked at Alex as if the two had conjured up this dandy plan together.

Alex recalled a time when Magnum and he got into a scuffle over the last piece of cake from one of King Aviel's birthday celebrations, back in their early teens. *I'm the king's son*, Magnum had said, grabbing Alex's hand, which had been reaching for the plate laden with a delicious slice of strawberry cake. *But I'm the firstborn son of his firstborn son*, Alex had replied. *I am heir to the throne, not you!* He had punched Magnum square in his smug face, hard enough to break his nose. Magnum had reeled backward as Alex swiped the cake, shoved it in his mouth, and ran. He had licked his fingers gleefully, even as his conscience condemned him—about the lie of being firstborn, not the punch in the nose.

Granted, Alex had probably deserved the beating

Magnum gave him once his uncle caught up with him. Still, Alex had no problem imagining the sweet smack of his fist connecting to Magnum's conceited face once again. Could feel the satisfying impact of knuckles crumpling against his nose and scraping across his teeth. The memory kept Alex focused on the slight crook in his uncle's snout, a consolation prize from that childhood victory.

Vetch uncurled Alex's fingers and sandwiched his palm in the vise-like tool of torture. Alex felt the curved spike of the splitchet bear down with a firm, measured prick, stopping short of breaking the skin. Shackled wrists gave Alex zero leverage to fight or squirm away, so he gnashed his teeth together and sent up a flimsy prayer to the God from whom he was currently estranged.

Magnum abruptly straightened and raked his fingers through his wavy hair. He peeled it off his damp neck. "Whew! It's blistering in here. Vetch, remind me to get one of my Dwarves to dig a sky-vent or two in the ceiling. I can't think straight when it's this hot. No telling what I might be capable of." He barked a laugh.

Vetch gave an impatient grunt, as if he, too, was ready for Magnum to finish with the theatrics.

"Anyway." Magnum released his hair and covered the girl's nearest hand with his own. "Let's get this game underway, shall we?" He squeezed her unresponsive fingers. "You *do* understand how this works, yeah? You answer my questions, and Brady escapes torture."

The girl refused to meet his gaze but nodded.

"Good, good. Now, to be clear, there is no love lost between my nephew and myself. If you don't want to answer, no problem. It'll be my pleasure to watch him writhe in pain each time that corkscrew drives deeper into his skin." He stretched his forearm so it paralleled Alex's arm. "Same skin tone, we two. We're both a mix of coffee and cream. More like brothers with only two years between us." He slid his arm away, leaning in to the girl, dropping his voice. "Ironically, Brady here *killed* both his own brother and mine. A killer twice over. Did he tell you that? Which means we've grown up with some bad, *bad* blood between us—regardless of the family blood that, unfortunately, links us together. You think we look alike?"

The girl didn't move or answer. If she was shocked by Magnum's revelation, Alex couldn't tell.

"Except Brady here has a *topside* mother—small, scrawny, not much to look at. Though he did inherit her amazingly dull flightlessness. Tries to impress the girls on the basketball court since he can't fly any higher than he can jump. Mother always said that only a *real* Nephilim should inherit the throne and the realm of Calamus. Yet somehow this basketball playing buffoon gets all the goodies." Magnum slid a sideways gaze at Alex. "Assuming you outlive your dear old daddy."

Alex felt a jolt of wariness. Did Magnum know about the fever dreams? If so, that would make the unexplainable affliction a lot less mysterious. Either way, Alex felt his own temperature on an uptick, and it wasn't because of the stifling, airless room.

Magnum had perfected the art of needling Alex, and Alex had perfected the art of tamping down his anger like gunpowder—until it exploded.

This time it came as no surprise when Alex's birthmark began to burn bright.

CHAPTER THIRTY

Alex

"YOU'VE MOVED TO A WHOLE NEW level of Nephilim freakishness!" Magnum released the girl and clamped his hand on Alex's chin to scrutinize the anomaly. "Roots and fruits, Brady. How in the—? I mean, when did this—?" He shoved Alex away with a curse and sat back, shaking his head. "I'm gonna have to keep you alive if only to enjoy your new trick. It's *literally* brilliant. Does it do anything impressive, or does it just light up and draw attention to your glaring deformity—as if someone might accidentally overlook it?"

"His name is Alex."

Alex started at the sound of her voice. Her soft, raspy tone at odds with his uncle's cynical droning.

Magnum gave an exaggerated blink before turning his attention to the girl. "She speaks."

"You keep calling him Brady," she said, her voice stronger this time. "His name is Alex."

Magnum closed his eyes and grinned. When they slowly peeled open, he looked at Alex. "Well, well. Bratty Brady is no more, huh? Trying to get a fresh start. Leave behind that failed attempt from your grief-stricken mother to push you into your legendary, but *dead*, uncle Brady's shoes." He nodded. "I can see it. Probably not a bad idea."

"The only uncle who should be dead is *you*." Alex glared, his vision blurred by the growing glow around his eye. If there wasn't a corkscrew twisting into his hand, he felt certain he could bust out of the rusty cuffs with the sheer force of his anger. "Don't you ever get tired of hearing yourself yammer on? I'm about to screw this splitchet into my own hand to be relieved from the pain of listening to you."

"I'm more than happy to help," Vetch said, tweaking the metal knob enough to draw a bead of blood. "Do not insult the Overlord."

"The *Overlord.*" The girl spat back the moniker. "The *bully* would be more accurate. Getting everyone else to do your dirty work. You're disgusting."

Magnum's hand flinched. Alex braced himself to witness a backhanded slap, but suddenly his uncle laughed.

"Ah, well. You're entitled to your opinion." He spread his fingers, palms up. "I'm comfortable with 'disgusting.' Whatever it takes to get the job done."

He drummed his fingers and grinned, clearly amused by the new development. "So," he gestured at Alex, "you prefer *Alex*, now. Got it. I will, of course, have to come up with a catchy nickname like Bratty Brady. Something will come to me soon enough, no doubt."

Magnum gave Alex a catty smile and then turned it on the girl. "And how about you? What's your name, water witch? Surely it's not Colin."

Silence stretched for several seconds. The girl's gaze remained riveted to the table, her lips a slash of severity. Magnum gave a tiny flick of his pinky finger and—

"*Ahh!*" Alex howled as the spike spiraled further into his hand. Blood radiated crimson spokes across his skin. It dripped between his knuckles like hot, gushing tears.

"Tymbrelle!" the girl called, fingers flying open as if she could reach across the table and stop the torture. "My name is Tymbrelle."

"That's better." Magnum retrieved her hand once again, rubbing his thumb along her index finger. "Okay, Tymbrelle, why don't you explain how a Topsider like you ended up in our little pocket of the earth?"

Tymbrelle. Alex mentally tried her name on for size in an effort to blunt the persistent stab of pain. As she reiterated her story of getting lost on the beach, being drugged, and the encounter with the stinging Faeries, Alex tried to picture it playing out with a *girl*, this time. A girl named Tymbrelle. A girl who probably had flowing corn-silk hair before she butchered it to disguise herself. And whose mismatched eyes might play off as enigmatic and cool, rather than unsettling and odd, given the right context.

"And these Faeries," Magnum said, "they brought you where?"

Alex waited, knowing that this was where Colin—er— Tymbrelle's story had turned vague, only hinting at being someone's slave and discovering her gift with water.

Another flick of Magnum's finger.

Alex yelped as the splitchet dialed down producing a fresh surge of blood.

"Okay, wait." Tymbrelle grimaced and turned a pleading look to Magnum. "How about I promise to tell you *everything* if you stop hurting Alex? I swear to tell you anything you want to know. Answer any question."

"Darling, *I'm* not hurting him. You are." Magnum looked at the girl, his gaze as tender as two shards of glass. "As long as you answer my questions, Vetch here will have no reason to screw that splitchet into Alex's hand. It's a very efficient system. Plus, you're in no position to make any type of deal. So, get on with it."

"Fine." Tymbrelle nodded coolly and tossed Alex an apologetic look, as if his predicament was somehow her fault. "The Faeries took me to Moored-below. In, y'know, Ireland. Or, below it, anyway. It's not nearly so big as the Tethered World. I was taken to a farm. It was filled with maybe a hundred kids. Kids that had been taken from the streets of Dublin, Galway, Belfast. All the big cities. Mostly runaways. Some were immigrants who didn't speak much English."

She looked questioningly at Alex. He felt her demeanor shift, preferring to tell him her story, ignoring Magnum. Alex gave her an encouraging nod.

"We were forced to work on this farm, which was more like an encampment. They barely fed us. Potatoes, usually. We were beaten at anyone's whim. Kids would disappear suddenly, never seen again. Rumors were rampant—none of them good. Kids sent away to be used as slaves in different parts of the world."

"Yeah, yeah," Magnum said, gesturing her on. "I get the idea. So how did you escape from there and end up here?"

"Sometimes..." She trailed off and took a steadying breath. "Sometimes people came and inspected us kids, like cattle, and chose who they wanted. That's what happened to me."

Alex felt horrible for how he'd treated her since they'd met.

Tymbrelle swallowed and cleared her throat. "I need water. I've had nothing to eat or drink since yesterday."

Magnum cocked an eyebrow. "You really expect me to offer water to a water witch?"

"Ugh, please." Tymbrelle rolled her eyes. "I'm dehydrated.

How much damage could I possibly inflict with a small cup of water?" She offered Magnum a flinty stare. "Plus, I'm no witch."

Magnum laced his fingers together, evidently unmoved. "Your story. Now. Or Alex here gets a new body piercing."

Tymbrelle resettled her attention on Alex, nostrils flaring like an incensed animal. "A couple came to the camp and chose me and another girl. We were taken to their cottage on the outskirts of Brihndle. A third girl was already living there. She'd been selected from the camp when the couple had last visited. The three of us were close in age—between seven and ten years old. I was the youngest."

As Alex listened, he tried to imagine Tymbrelle with all the trappings of a girl, but he struggled to see past the nest of hair and layers of dirt.

"The couple trained us in etiquette, social graces, the history of Éire House, and whatnot." She shifted her gaze back to the table and made meager gestures with her tethered hands. "After about six months, someone from King Odhran's court came to visit. They interviewed us privately. Inspected us. Quizzed us. Had us do everything from curtsy to pour tea. In the end, they chose me."

Alex's stomach clenched at the mention of Éire House.

Magnum squinted, giving Tymbrelle a once over. "Chose you for what?"

"To be taken to the castle for further training." She closed her eyes as if to shut everything out. "To be lady-in-waiting to the princess of Brihndle. Princess Larkin."

Alex felt the room tilt. Somehow, he had run off with Princess Larkin's closest confidant and most faithful attendant. He had no idea how this might further complicate matters between Pacific House and Éire House, but if the two of them made it back alive, it wouldn't look good for either.

Tymbrelle emitted a meaningful look from across the table, revealing that she understood the implications as well.

"Lucky *you*. You've moved from peasant life to palace life" Magnum made a big show of cracking his knuckles and then his neck, letting his wings rustle about as if he was miserably stiff from sitting for so long. "And these scars?" He grabbed her thumb and roughly pried it back, exposing its marred ridge of skin. "Surely they came along after you landed in this prestigious position, or they wouldn't have hired you. Royal households generally prefer an illusion of perfection.

Although," he cut his gaze to Alex, "there's not much a royal family can do about deformities from birth."

Tymbrelle retracted her fingers, fisting them.

Alex bristled, anger fueling his birthmark with the glow of hot embers. Magnum's lips curled at the sight, clearly relishing Alex's discomfort. Tymbrelle's own gaze softened and looked back at him with pity. Alex resented this as much as Magnum's incredulous stare but reminded himself she meant well.

As if aware of Alex's thoughts, the girl flushed and looked away. "I was burned, okay? I don't care to talk about it." Her eyes widened, clearly remembering the cost of her earlier refusal. "No, wait—I will! I *will* talk about it." She gave Alex a panicked look. "There's really not much to tell. It was an accident. There was a fire in Princess Larkin's room. A kerosene lamp tipped. I tried to put it out..."

She trailed off, tracing her left thumb along the ridge of scars on the outside of her index finger.

"Wow. Touching and tragic." Magnum's tone was flat. "I was hoping for something more cataclysmic. Let's skip to the part where you ended up with my idiotic nephew and came to be trespassing on my property."

Alex resisted the urge to scoff at such an outlandish claim. *His* property?

Magnum somehow sensed the doubtful vibes. He frowned at Alex. "I can hear those cogs moving in your noggin there, nephew." He reached out and knocked firmly on Alex's head. "You're thinking I might be putting a shiny spin on my situation here."

Alex kept his gaze on the wall behind Tymbrelle, seething at Magnum's smug tone.

"Just you wait, *Alex*." Magnum said Alex's name with thick and bitter disdain. "You'll soon understand that this kingdom of Astra—*my* kingdom—is the new realm to be reckoned with. It's shocking, really, what I've accomplished here in a short time. Stick around and you'll see. Not that I'm really giving you a choice." He nodded at Tymbrelle. "On with the rest of your little fairytale."

Astra? Alex bit back a scoff. He knew enough Latin to know that the word had something to do with the stars. Apparently, Magnum had been busy building his own ill-assorted galaxy.

"Fine," Tymbrelle continued. "Nothing much to tell until

King Odhran received a message from King Aviel and Queen Lucia, desiring—"

Smack! Magnum whacked the tabletop, making each of them jump.

"*Ah!*" Alex yelped. Vetch had accidentally nudged the nob in reaction.

"Mummy and Daddy-dear are part of this fairytale?" Magnum leaned closer. "This *is* fascinating. Go on."

"So..." Tymbrelle looked askance at the bully but continued. "Your *parents*, then, were wanting to arrange a marriage." Her eyes darted to Alex, apologetically. "To their grandson. They wanted to unite their houses by marrying their grandson to Princess Larkin."

Magnum tossed his head back and brayed with laughter, letting it ebb into a slow and menacing applause that he directed at Alex. "Wow. Alex, a married man. I...I can't picture it, if I'm honest. But, hey, I'm guessing you can't either, which is why you're here. The bachelor ran off and left his girl at the altar."

"Your parents are apparently more invested in *my* future than yours," Alex said with a smirk.

Magnum gave an incredulous grunt. "My future is here. In *my* kingdom. You think I'd exchange Astra for anything you have?" He made a sound of disgust. "Forget it. My ambitions are bigger than a bunch of diplomatic niceties to maintain affairs of state. I'm free to forge my own way. Marry whom I choose. One day I'll return to Calamus as an equal to my father. I don't need my parents' help to get there. You, on the other hand, need all the help you can get. I hear arranged marriages are ideal for people with something to hide. Like flightlessness. Or blazing birthmarks."

Alex didn't take the bait. He studied the bloody map of his hand, noticing the contrast of blood against skin. Should he tell Magnum about the death of his father, King Aviel? No, not like this. It felt disrespectful to his grandfather's memory, and it would likely miss its mark anyway. Magnum cared for none except himself.

I killed the wrong one. The thought plowed through Alex's mind, unbidden. He shoved it aside, shame and justification warring within his heart.

Magnum focused on Tymbrelle. "Pardon my little rant. You were saying?"

"Umm." Tymbrelle looked at Magnum like a wounded

mouse might warily eye a cat bearing a first aid kit. "I—I traveled to Calamus with King Odhran's royal retinue. A dozen in all. Larkin and I wouldn't be going back, obviously. I was being forced to relocate to another strange place, against my will. When we finally arrived in the more civilized part of the Tethered World, I...I ran away."

"But why?" Magnum looked from her to Alex and back. "Why leave a perfectly good fairytale? No doubt your real parents considered you dead, years ago. Good luck finding them anyway. Instead...it almost looks as if the two of you ran off together." He gave a nefarious chuckle and reached to give her hand a playful squeeze. "*Almost.* Here's the thing. I don't believe you're being honest with us."

Tymbrelle stared at him with undisguised repugnance.

Magnum narrowed his eyes as sweat trickled down his temples and beaded on his upper lip. "Do I need to inflict some pain on my nephew to keep you from lying?"

"No! But, I *did*. I did run away." The girl leaned away from her overbearing captor. "That *is* the truth."

Magnum bared his teeth in a snarl of disdain and shot to his feet, stool toppling with a loud *clunk*. Both Alex and Tymbrelle flinched as Magnum swooped into the girl's personal space, sweat splatting the tabletop and flecking her arms.

"You sure about that?" Magnum's voice held a tone of warning. "Is that the story you *really* want to stake Alex's life and limb on?"

Tymbrelle winced, trapped in Magnum's maniacal grasp. She shook her head in rapid denial. Alex looked between them, confused.

"I know why you were brought to Calamus," Magnum continued in a low, menacing tone. "I know of King Odhran's plan for Calamus. He's the reason I'm here, after all. And so, little orphan Topsider, tell the truth! Your little trick with the water gave it all away."

Tymbrelle's attention shifted back to Alex, and he studied her face for clues. What could Magnum know about this strange girl and her trick with the water? What was supposed to happen in Calamus? And what was that flicker of defiance he saw in her eyes? The atmosphere shifted. Alex couldn't determine if it was a result of Magnum's strange rantings or the contemptuous spark that now burned in Tymbrelle's gaze.

"It wasn't a trick." Tymbrelle's tone was biting. "*See?*"

She curled her fingers around Magnum's hand. He began

to writhe and choke, free-hand groping for the edge of the table to steady his quickly stiffening body. Alex watched, incredulous, as every rivulet of perspiration froze, trapping his uncle in an opaque, organic web. Even Magnum's eyeballs glazed over like two frosted amber marbles.

Vetch backed away, hands lifted, eyes pleading. "Hey, I'm only following orders. I don't want any trouble."

"Oh, right." Tymbrelle nodded at the predicament that was Alex's tortured hand. "Sure, you don't. Get over here and remove that horrible thing. Then take these shackles off us both. Or—or I'll shoot poisonous tears from my eyes, straight into yours. And blind you."

Alex could tell she was making this up on the fly, though Vetch obviously believed her. The Troll gave a pitiful whimper and fumbled with the splitchet until it retracted enough to slide safely away from Alex's hand. Then he fished a key from his trouser pocket. Shaking fingers led to several near-misses with the lock, but he eventually succeeded.

His hands free, Alex eyed Magnum, ready to defend himself. Could his uncle resist what was happening in any way? It didn't appear so. He only hovered over the table, a specter's statue, face fearful and aghast, skin pale as a corpse.

Vetch rounded the table, approaching Tymbrelle with the key while simultaneously shrinking from her. If Trolls had a tail, his would've been between his legs.

"Hurry up!" Tymbrelle hissed. "And don't dream of trying anything stupid."

Alex probed his injured hand. The puncture wound was starting to coagulate and, thankfully, wasn't deep. It throbbed dully as he reached across the table and worked loose the ropes around the girl's wrists, a bit of an undertaking since she still grasped his uncle's fingers and Vetch was unlocking the cuffs.

Cool air radiated from Magnum's close proximity. Alex grappled with the chemistry—or was it physics?—of this seeming impossibility. Though science had never been his best subject, he didn't believe there was a chemical reaction that could explain this.

When Tymbrelle was free from cuffs and rope, she stayed put, fingers gripping the giant, winged ice sculpture. "Now listen, Vetch. You and Alex are going to shift Magnum over so I can clamp him into a restraint. Then you're going to march us out of here as if that's exactly what you've been ordered to do." She gave a wry chuckle. "I mean, that *is* exactly what you've been ordered to do. Right now. By me. While this power-hungry maniac thaws out in here, you're going to help us collect our friends, our horses, and some food and water, then send us safely on our way. If you attempt to alert anyone to what happened, I will summon every drop of water in my body and yours and fry us both like bacon. Am I making myself clear?"

"Oh, yes! Yes. Absolutely." Vetch offered her a bow. And then another.

"Enough, Sasquatch," Alex said. "Help me move this iceberg uncle of mine and lead us out of here without raising suspicions. Got it?" He crossed to where the tool belt lay, snatching free a sheathed knife and sliding it into his trouser pocket. "I'll be keeping this close at hand too," he added, knowing how lame it sounded in comparison to what Tymbrelle could whip up with a few drops of water. Or sweat.

"Got it." Vetch nodded and offered what was probably meant to be an eager smile, though it looked more like a sneer with his leathery lips and yellowed fangs. "I'll help get your party on its way. I don't want any problems."

"Excellent," Tymbrelle said with false cheer. She stood and kicked her stool out of the way. Arm at an uncomfortable angle as she stretched to keep her grip.

Vetch and Alex scooted Magnum's frozen form to where her stool had been. They could only clamp his right wrist into a cuff, as his other was grasping air—formerly the table edge—hovering near his side.

"Perfect." Tymbrelle gave a satisfied nod. "When I let go of his fingers, he will, unfortunately, begin to thaw. Vetch, you are to lock the door behind us when we leave. I can't say how long the effects will last, so I'm going to *watch* you lock it. Then, we get our friends. We leave. You leave us alone. We leave you alone. We all live happily ever after, yes?"

Vetch nodded again. "Yes. I mean, yes ma'am." He gave a hurried bow, as if for good measure.

"Good. Very good." She offered Alex an optimistic grin, but he could read an anxious question in her eyes. One that pulsed inside of him as well...

Could they really pull this off?

CHAPTER THIRTY-ONE

Ellynn

ELLYNN TRIED NOT TO STARE. REALLY.

But it was hard to overlook the gulps and slurps and burps, the laughter and jesting, which percolated through the Great Hall from the retinue of foreign guests. Even King Odhran and Queen Clodagh frequently chewed with their mouths open, though they couldn't compete with their royal guards and attendants sitting at the long row of tables perpendicular to the high table. Éire House was so different from Pacific House! They were boisterous, colorful, and rough around the edges, as if ancient, time-traveling Vikings had arrived in the future.

By the time Ellynn had left Trinny and made her way outside earlier in the day—even with her shortcut—the visitors were dismounting and following Xander and Sadie inside. Realizing how unpresentable she looked in her rumpled yellow dress with its oblong stain of blood on her skirt from where she'd clamped a hand over her injured shin, Ellynn had remained in the shadows, mesmerized. Then she'd rushed back to her room to change, and none too soon since her mother had come looking for her. Ellynn claimed to have lost track of time...which was true enough, and she did her best to keep her injured palms from her mother's observant eye.

It had been a truly torturous afternoon spent wiling away the hours until the banquet. Finally, Trinny arrived to ready her for dinner, chattering on excitedly about the exotic guests until Ellynn's parents come to collect her.

Inside the Great Hall, Ellynn felt tingly with anticipation as the visitors were announced and seated. Sizzling platters of roasted pheasant with a kaleidoscope of vegetables made for an impressive and tantalizing display, the savory aroma reminding Ellynn of family Christmas feasts. Once her father had blessed the meal and taken his first bite, Éire House had set upon their food like crows on corn.

The only person who seemed mindful of not chewing like an animal was Princess Larkin. The plain yet pleasant girl sat directly across from Ellynn and had barely lifted her gaze from her plate, providing Ellynn with an excellent view of Larkin's wiry, russet tresses. Someone had expertly plaited her hair into a complex circular pattern around her head.

Ellynn tried to catch the girl's eye whenever she glanced up to answer questions posed by Ellynn's parents. Several times Larkin didn't respond until prompted by a jab from Queen Clodagh's neighboring elbow. Her wide-set, grey-green eyes would look first at her mother, as if seeking permission, and then to Sadie and Xander, as round and terrified as a startled foal as she eked out her answer. She seemed wholly overwhelmed and much too cautious for the likes of Alex.

Larkin did have something in common with him though. She was also s royal without wings. Ellynn hadn't seen the girl from behind to determine the presence of wingbuds, but surely she was past the age of metamorphosis if she was expected to wed. Though Larkin didn't look much older than herself, Ellynn guessed the girl's painful shyness made her seem younger. Studying Larkin—as brandyberry shortcake and cream made the rounds—Ellynn concluded that she was either a wingless Nephilim in need of a growth spurt, or a plain, vanilla Topsider. If the former, then perhaps a late bloomer? If the latter, then how had she come to be a part of Éire House?

Ellynn, as always, was brimming with questions. Hopefully the princess would warm up eventually, and the two could chat.

"It's a shame yer son did a legger," Queen Clodagh said in her loud and lilting Irish brogue. "We were lookin' forward to seein' our darlin' daughter beside her future husband. Imaginin' how our grand-babes might look."

Princess Larkin choked on a bite of cake and reached for her water goblet.

"I dare say those future grands will look a little different than we imagined," King Odhran groused.

"Perhaps if you'd made any effort to get to know the widower king of Calamus, whom you covertly contacted with an offer of my hand, you would not be surprised by his ethnicity," Grandmama Lucia said. "Although your little corner of the underworld includes many shades of *pale*, you shouldn't expect the wider world to be so."

For once, Ellynn was proud of her grandmother's sharp opinion. She was also shocked to learn that the woman had come to Calamus in much the same way as Larkin—as a complete stranger with no choice in the matter.

"You know firsthand what an ordeal it is to get from Moored-below to the Tethered World." King Odhran scarfed a forkful of shortcake that left a halo of whipped cream along the edge of his enormous mustache. "Tis a trip one undertakes only once in a lifetime."

Ellynn found it hard to take him seriously with his paint-dipped-paintbrush facial hair. She caught Larkin smirking as well. Their gazes met—at long last—and both shared a tentative smile. The girl's lovely eyes reminded Ellynn of a stormy Irish sea.

"An undertaking you wanted to reserve for the remote possibility of Aunt Clodagh finally giving you an heir that could marry into another royal household," Grandmama Lucia replied, smiling coolly. "Guess your wildest dreams have come true, Uncle. Lucky you."

King Odhran's ruddy cheeks flushed deep pink, making his silvery hair look bright and luminous in contrast. "Listen here, Lucia." He speared a brandyberry with his fork and pointed it at his niece. "I did right by you."

"That's right, y'ungrateful little shrew. Yer father didn't do us any favors when he was king." Queen Clodagh hooked a thumb at herself, her eyes like two hard green peas narrowing in on Lucia. "We owed ya nothin' when yer da passed. Exactly what *he* gave *us*. Still, when the news of King Aviel's loss reached our kingdom, we knew such a marriage would be beneficial fer ya. We had yer welfare in mind."

"And beneficial for you too, no doubt—removing me far from my home and from *my* kingdom," Lucia said. "I must say how strange it is that word of your pregnancy never reached us. I realize communication is slow between realms, but nine months and over sixteen years without mention in any correspondence? It's as if Larkin materialized from nowhere. Faeries drop her at your castle door perhaps?"

Xander cleared his throat. "No matter. The lovely Larkin is here, and I'm sorry our son Alexander is not. As I explained, the messenger reached us only yesterday, the same day Alex took an excursion with his friends. Hopefully my men will soon catch up to share the happy news, so he and Larkin may get acquainted.”

“Seems strange that he should plan a holiday the same day as his grandfather’s funeral.” Odhran quirked one bushy brow and, thankfully, wiped his mustache clean with his cloth napkin.

“Simply a spontaneous decision.” Xander shifted and placed his arm around Sadie’s shoulders. “Stress and sadness and all.”

“Yes,” Sadie chimed. “Terrible timing. Thankfully Xander’s men are *on* it.”

Ellynn cringed at her mother’s hollow sounding cheerfulness. Her brother had left her parents in the sticky position of walking the fine line between polite truth and blunt insult.

One of Odhran’s guards approached the table. The one whom Ellynn had seen carrying the bright yellow standard of Éire House earlier today. The star tattoo that sprawled across his brow bone reminded Ellynn of a pirate’s eyepatch gone askew. He looked menacing. Despite his dirty blond hair, his wing feathers were as dark as black coffee. The whole effect was disconcerting, and Ellynn instinctively disliked him.

He crouched between King Odhran and Queen Clodagh, who had turned to watch his approach at a nod in his direction from Xander. Heads together, voices low, the three held a brief conversation. Whatever was being said must not have been happy news. The king stiffened and the queen inhaled sharply.

Once finished, the soldier stood but did not leave. He crossed his massive arms across his leather jerkin, his face a wary mask whose sights settled somewhere above the hosts’ side of the table.

Odhran leveled his gaze on Lucia, then shifted it to Xander. Beefy fists gave a constrained *thump* on either side of his dessert plate, causing a small yet seismic shifting of utensils. “General Izaiah brings disturbing news to me. I wonder why I should be hearing it from him, rather than you?”

Ellynn’s heartbeat rippled. Alex’s secret escape was about to be exposed.

“I guess that depends on what news your general shared. Perhaps it is mere palace gossip.” Xander kept his arm around Sadie, clearly unruffled by their bristling guests.

From the corner of her eye, Ellynn noticed her father’s thumb stroking her mother’s shoulder. Everything must be fine. Or, maybe, it was to the benefit of a king or queen to always act and react as if it were.

Queen Clodagh scoffed at Xander's offhanded comment. "I doubt yer staff would manufacture a *murder*."

Oh, that. Ellynn felt ashamed for forgetting about poor Blaylock's demise.

"One of your personal bodyguards was taken out today. Or is that a palace ghost story meant to scare my men?" King Odhran's mustache quavered, his lips compressed within its bushy depths.

Xander nodded once. "Indeed, it's true. Yet again, I must apologize that your arrival coincided with other unexpected events. I assure you that this tragedy has nothing to do with you."

General Izaiah gave a skeptical grunt but kept his intense blue eyes trained ahead.

"A king's trusted and professionally trained guard is not easily taken out." Odhran slid his fists forward so that he hunched across the table. "Especially in the king's own quarters. Do you expect us to rest easy with this news? Have you apprehended the murderer, or must we sleep with one eye open?"

"How you sleep is your business," Xander quipped. "The death of one of my men is *none* of your business. It would seem the murderer was making a point to *me*, seeing that he attacked my man in my room. I'm happy to assign extra men to guard your quarters if that would allow you to close both of your eyes in slumber, however."

"As if that would give us peace." Odhran waggled his head, disapproving brows obscuring his eyes. "You could be assigning a murderer to our quarters for all you know."

Xander removed his arm from Sadie's shoulder and stood, which prompted Odhran and Clodagh to stand as well. The chatter in the hall sputtered out, and the eyes of all latched upon the two kings.

Commander Gage and General Merrik approached, followed by two of Odhran's men and one of his female warriors. Were the two kingdoms going to battle it out rather than join their families? Ellynn glanced at Larkin, who looked back, eyes wide with dread. Ellynn slid her hand across the table, palm up, a gesture of solidarity.

Larkin tentatively grasped it in her own.

Sadie stood and placed a calming hand on her husband's arm.

Ellynn sensed her father taking the tiniest step back from the edge. Then another, as he released a resigned-sounding exhale. Ellynn gave Larkin's fingers a reassuring squeeze.

"Forgive me, Cousin Odhran, my new friend." Xander shook his head, eyes closed in a lengthy blink.

Gage and Merrik drew near with care, looking less likely to jump in with swords blazing to defend their master.

"It has been a rather intense week, which does not come close to describing the past twenty-four hours. A funeral. Grieving the loss of my father. Family and diplomats leaving us at the same time a messenger brings word of your arrival. And this morning...a murder." He sighed. "I'm drained and exhausted, but that's no excuse for being a poor host. I can appreciate your concern, and hope to put you at ease."

Ellynn watched as King Odhran and Queen Clodagh visibly decompressed, sympathy softening their hard edges. She spared a glance at Larkin, who was staring at Xander with shining, compassionate eyes.

The girl blinked and a tear escaped. Larkin pulled her hand free and used the cloth napkin to dab at her face, turning pink with embarrassment. This girl was way too emotional for her brother, Ellynn decided, though that was a better quality than a stoic, rigid woman like Grandmama Lucia. Couldn't Alex marry someone in between metallic and mushy? Someone more like their mother?

King Odhran gave a slow, understanding nod. His wife seemed to take her cue from him and twined her fingers together in front of her, the challenge in her eyes retreating.

"*New friend.*" Odhran's walrus mustache fanned out, implying a grin. "I like the sound of that. I desire that, actually. I would like our houses to be joined in happiness. In peace. It is unfortunate that our arrival timed so poorly with your father's passing and other matters. You are tired, and, for different reasons, so are we. Not the best time to discuss weighty issues, is it, Cousin? Please." He extended his arm across the table. "Accept our condolences and know that we hope for a long and happy relationship together."

Xander dipped his head and clasped Odhran's forearm. "As do we. I believe a good night's sleep is our wisest course of action, considering. How can we ensure you and your family feel safe in your quarters? Please. Name it."

CHAPTER THIRTY-TWO

Alex

ALEX AND TYMBRELLE FOLLOWED ON VETCH'S hairy heels as the Yeti marched them through passageways with an authoritative stride, playing his part convincingly. It probably didn't hurt that Tymbrelle was holding a half-filled wooden cup of water someone carelessly left on a side table near the interrogation room.

Vetch had a momentary meltdown when Tymbrelle snatched it up while he locked the door.

"Don't make me use it," Tymbrelle had warned. "Pull yourself together and act natural or else."

Vetch readily complied, and the three made it outside with no more than a few sidelong glances from Magnum's minions. Vetch barked, "Don't question your superiors!" at a bald Nephilim warrior who asked too many questions. Alex turned to look at the weathered old traitor, feeling an odd mixture of anger and curiosity. Was he so unhappy in Calamus that he willingly deserted it for this godforsaken place?

Beneath the bright skydome, the two followed Vetch to the stable, which looked ready to reenact the Nativity scene. Formerly a shallow cave, its size had been expanded by an extension of mud and straw walls, with a thatched roof protruding from the front like a covered porch circa the Dark Ages.

Inside the gloomy interior, Vetch approached the sprawled form of a Dark Dwarf bedded down in filthy straw, snoring softly. The Troll gave the slumbering curmudgeon a wallop in the rear with his full-sized foot.

"*Yowch!*" The Dark Dwarf, half asleep, scrambled to his feet with a few choice words and a collection of sticks and straw protruding from hair and clothing. He swiped at the drool trailing across the sallow skin of his face. "What's the problem? Can't a fella catch a nap?"

In the recesses of the cave, horses nickered and stamped at the disturbance. Alex wondered who placed this hunched halfling in charge of animals the size of horses.

Vetch grabbed the derelict by the front clasp of his tattered cloak and yanked him nose-to-nose. "No, imbecile. A fella can't catch a nap when he's supposed to be working. I will report this to the Overlord ." Vetch released the Stygian with a small shove that propelled him back onto the bed of straw. "Now fetch the horses belonging to our guests and ready them for travel."

The Dark Dwarf glanced at Alex and Tymbrelle as if only now registering their presence. His beady eyes grew large. "These are the trespassers!" He squinted at Vetch. "Why'd ya call them guests?"

The Troll stepped closer. "The Overlord said to release them. That's all you need to know. Now *go*." He pointed at the back of the cave.

The Stygian mumbled something unintelligible, spat into the straw, and waddled into the shadows.

Vetch turned to find Tymbrelle trailing her finger in the water cup clasped to her chest. She sucked the moisture from her fingertip and met Vetch's apprehensive stare with a syrupy smile.

"Well done. Now, let's go get the others," she said.

Alex continued to be impressed by her confidence and quick thinking. Yet again, this twiggy Topsider was the one with the plan and the power to make things happen. Loathsome old fears resurfaced that he had spent a lifetime tamping down. Failure. Uselessness. Ineptitude. The latter, a former vocabulary word that had lodged itself in his cranium as soon as he memorized it, thanks to its close resemblance to his life.

Though Alex knew better than to expect miracles or magic when he changed his name from Brady, his heart had secretly yearned for something to shift on the inside. Something profound. Instead, this waif-like Topsider—or whatever she was, with her weird relationship to water—showed up and saved the day. Saved *his* day, and that more than once, like some sort of preternatural superhero from one of his mother's dystopian novels. How dare she be so cliché? Shouldn't he be the one saving the damsel in distress? Well...maybe that was cliché, as well.

Still, he resented her, even as he admitted that he needed her.

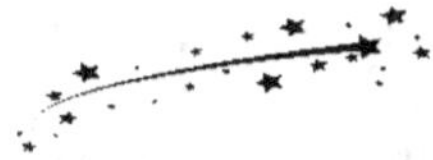

"Dude! My mind is *blown*." Spock paced a tight circle between his tall compatriots. The reunited friends huddled just inside the woods at the open end of the U-shaped valley, waiting for Tymbrelle and Vetch to return with the horses.

Tymbrelle had suggested their hodgepodge crew take cover and get up to speed with Alex while she accompanied Vetch back to the stable, cup of water in hand. Alex gave his friends the short version of events, main points being that Magnum was the mysterious Overlord, and Colin was really Tymbrelle—as in *he* was really a *she*.

Spock snatched his beanie from his head, revealing a purplish knot near his right temple. He smacked the hat against his leg, clearly astonished. "I mean, she totally had me fooled."

"Keep yer voice down," Dempsey said in such a fierce whisper he matched Spock in volume. A sprawling pea-green bruise claimed the bridge of his nose like a bullseye, and two front teeth were chipped. "We're not free of this flea-bitten place yet." He set to scratching his ample middle with both hands. "I ain't goin' back in there. They'll have to kill me if they can catch me. Worst night's sleep I've had in me life. And they took me pipe! I'm about to crawl out of me skin with the wantin' of it."

"I suspected she was a—a *she*," Josiah said in his calm, thoughtful way, his words slurry thanks to a split upper lip. A blotchy necklace of bruises encircled his neck. "Sort of suspected it back at the barn, to be honest." He fingered his whiskers, which were flirting with becoming a beard from lack of a razor.

All of them were a scruffy, dirty, beat-up bunch, but Alex knew they'd gotten off easy. Why had Magnum restrained his henchmen? His uncle didn't do anything without a reason that would ultimately serve himself.

"What gave it away?" Finn asked, his swollen eye now a painful purple.

Josiah shrugged. "Her voice, first off. When she tumbled out of the blankets and started protesting, I thought she was a raspy-voiced girl. Still...she disguised herself well enough, and I bought into her scrappy-teenage-boy persona. The more

I studied her, though. Listened to her speak. Her need for privacy..." He trailed off with a shrug.

"Sheesh. That should've tipped us all off," Alex said, squinting through the trees at some sort of commotion happening across the glen.

It was Tymbrelle on horseback, galloping like a locomotive atop Sage. She was yelling, one hand gesticulating madly, too far away to be understood. Alex stared, aware of Josiah and Finn shifting and straining to see beside him.

"What in the name of Beacon Rock...?" Dempsey muttered.

All at once it became clear. Dregs were in pursuit!

Vetch trailed behind Tymbrelle, the gap growing wider by the second as he struggled to keep up on foot, holding the bridles of the other two horses as they trotted fitfully on either side. A pack of angry Dregs pursued them, pouring from the mountainous clefts and swiftly closing the gap.

"Uh-oh. Your ice-sculptured uncle must've liquidized back to life," Spock said.

"Blast it!" Dempsey stomped. "They kept our weapons, and we're sorely outnumbered. We're gonna have to leg it."

Tymbrelle closed in, her face stricken. Behind her, Vetch let out a yelp of pain and went down, an arrow lodged between his shoulder blades.

"Maker help us!" Spock hollered, scaling up Finn's leg. "They're killing their own."

The two horses galloped off in different directions as the mob of infuriated Dregs swelled.

Tymbrelle dismounted from Sage before the horse pulled up short. "Flee into the woods! One horse isn't going to do us any good. Run!"

Sage whinnied and snorted and cantered off along the tree line. The others turned to run. Alex waited for Tymbrelle, feeling a tug of protectiveness despite his earlier resentment. He snatched her hand and yanked her along behind, finally stopping to scoop her up so he could use his seven-foot stride to their advantage.

"Put me down! I can manage."

She kicked and squirmed, but he ignored her. He needed to pay attention to where he was going, not look back to make sure she was keeping up. Alex jumped over fallen logs, weaved around trees, ducked low limbs, and scanned ahead to keep sight of the others and look for possible paths of escape. The

Dregs' distant shouts were no longer so distant, and panic shot him through with adrenaline.

Dempsey struggled to keep pace. His stride was compact and unnaturally quick—and only good in short bursts. Now he huffed and grumbled, his legs stutter-stepping beneath him.

Alex whistled at Finn and Josiah, who were several yards ahead. Finn had Spock tucked beneath his arm as firmly as a football headed for the end-zone. The Nephilim friends turned and took in Dempsey's state, circling back to hook opposite arms beneath the Dwarf's armpits to carry him along.

Dempsey's legs churned in protest. "Put me down! Put me down, you hybrid, half-breed bullies!"

From behind, the first sounds of twigs snapping and rocks crunching reached them, fueling a new surge of energy. The Dregs had penetrated the woods.

A crow darted from a nearby tree, swooping so close to Alex that he drew back involuntarily. It flew ahead of Dempsey and company, landing on a branch several yards in front of the approaching group.

That's when Alex realized the ungainly bird was no crow. Parsifal the Dragon had waited for them.

Finn and Josiah stopped to allow the chattering creature a moment to converse with Spock. Alex had almost caught up and could hear Spock explaining something that Alex couldn't make out over his own huffing breath and noisy footfalls. He had barely rejoined them when Finn and Josiah took off again. Alex mutely followed, assuming the clever creature was leading them to safety—or, at least, somewhere that would give them a fighting chance.

The sounds coming from the Dregs steadily increased. Alex risked a look backward and gasped to see scattered dark shapes weaving between and around the tree trunks like newly hatched spiders of nightmarish proportions. Guttural, slobbery snarls became distinct, sending a wave of dread through Alex.

The Dregs had brought their mongrel mutts.

Parsifal kept slightly ahead, landing on tree limbs with a squawk so the group would be sure to notice. After ten minutes of this game, he stayed put, his nostrils churning out violet smoke in feverish puffs.

Beneath him, a shallow yet steady stream of water meandered between the trees.

"Yes!" Tymbrelle sprang from Alex's arms before he could

process what Parsifal was carrying on about. "Get on the other side of this creek. Hurry!"

Logic snapped into place, and Alex and the others hopped over the runnel of water. He prayed it would be enough H2O to defend them from the vicious attack barreling their way. Even now, the enormous, mangy dogs were straining at their leashes, close enough that Alex could see their gnashing, salivating jowls.

Bitterness bristled against gratefulness as Alex realized that Tymbrelle was about to save the day, yet again. Save *his* day, more precisely. If Josiah and Finn really wanted, they could fly away, Tymbrelle, Dempsey, and Spock in tow—except they were too loyal to abandon *him*. Which meant Alex's physical limitations were what kept them all in danger.

And that danger had teeth and fangs and claws, not to mention *numbers*, on their side. Alex needed a miracle big enough to save himself and his friends. Like it or not, Tymbrelle seemed to be the diminutive guardian angel sent to perform precisely that on behalf of three angel-men—those with *and* without wings.

Impotent anger rippled through Alex, setting his birthmark aglow once again. Dimly, at first, and brighter with each hateful acknowledgment of his bizarre irregularities. A distant part of his mind snickered at how his new "fiancé" would react if she could see the frightened and freakish man she was expected to marry.

Tymbrelle squatted beside the narrow stream and plunged her hands into the water. As if in slow motion, Alex watched how her actions registered on the faces of their attackers. Trolls, Dark Dwarves, and a smattering of Ogres went wide-eyed and began to slow their pace. Clearly Tymbrelle had a reputation.

The hounds, which looked more like wolves than domesticated dogs, strained against their leather lead ropes, three canines in all. The Trolls handling the dogs leaned back, digging their heels in, not ten yards away. A few of their cronies actually turned to hightail it out of there.

Tymbrelle swept her arms into a high arc as she stood, flecking Alex and the others with chilled droplets in the process. The length of the stream responded to her touch and movements with a great, vertical leap.

A liquid wall of water grew before their eyes, but not before one of the ferocious hounds broke free of its restraint and leapt headlong over the rising tide. Some base, raw instinct shot through Alex with lightning speed. A spark of strength that began as a spike of pain in his birthmark, traveled through his arm, and ended with a powerful punch to the dog's snarling, frothing jaw.

The impact flung the beast up and onto its back. It landed with a yowl on a burgeoning spike of ice, impaled by the rising sheet of frozen water as it severed the sightline between friend and foe. Shouts of terror and surprise rang out from both parties, and Alex hoped this stunt would be enough to keep them safe.

The dog had gone limp on impact, then the heat of its body quickly melted the ice that incased him. He slithered down the frozen wall and landed with a heavy thump near Alex's feet, trailing a deep scarlet smear down the sheet of ice.

Through the jagged hole left by the dog's body, Alex saw that most of the Dregs were retreating. Cries of "powerful magic" and "water witchery" rang clear. One Stygian and three Trolls continued to stand their ground, bold enough to point their sword or dagger at the glacial wall and take tentative steps forward. The remaining canines clamored to pounce.

"Can you shatter this wall and send the pieces flying, like you did at the lake?" Alex asked Tymbrelle. "That should take care of who's left."

Tymbrelle grinned, arms held high, unable to see what was happening from her shorter vantage point. "Your wish is my command, Your Highness." She winked her coppery-green eye at him. With one hand she made a slicing motion while clawing at the air with the other. The top portion of the glazed water splintered into icy blades that shot forward and pierced the hides of the four Dregs. The lower half of the wall remained protectively in place, precisely where she'd sliced the air.

Alex saw the Dark Dwarf topple, writhing and bleeding, his face hatch-marked by small incisions where jagged shards delivered their damage before melting. The three Trolls cried out and stumbled backward in various states of pain and injury. One of them, a fair-furred Yeti, looked particularly gruesome as deep scarlet stains blossomed across his hide like hideous polka dots.

The three Trolls staggered off, shouting commands at the dogs, who followed bleeding and whimpering at the ends of their leashes. The Stygian was left to fend for himself—and, most likely, die alone.

"Great glacial geysers, Batman!" Spock quipped, ever a fan of Topsider superheroes. "That was an impressive show."

Tymbrelle's arms remained lifted in command of her water wonders. She tossed a glance over her shoulder. "Batman? What's that?" Her arms quivered, body trembled. "Am I finished here? My arms are about to turn into slug blubber."

"Yeah, it's over." Alex swiped a hand across his face, wondering why he was sweating when Tymbrelle was the one doing the work.

The girl crumpled to the ground as she released her arms, a painful groan escaping her lips. "That sapped the sap out of me." Her head lolled sideways, and she noticed the dead dog lying a few feet away. "Ugh!" She retreated, rolling a few times in the opposite direction. "That's so creepy."

The remaining wall of water began to thaw, chunks of ice sliding free with a plunk.

Josiah stepped to where the dog lay and took a knee beside it. "Maker have mercy, Alex. What did you hit him with? A brick?" He grabbed a busted branch from the ground and poked at the dog's muzzle.

Alex flexed his fist, remembering the explosion of knuckles to jaw. It had happened so instinctively the impact had barely registered with the rest of his body. He knelt beside the mutt.

The dog's head was snapped back at an unnatural angle. Several of its teeth were smashed into its palate, blood and bone giving way to fur like a small bomb had detonated.

Dempsey whistled, long and low.

"Wow," Alex said, looking from the hound back to his fist. "That's a skill set I didn't know about."

Finn gave a rumbling laugh. "Guess I won't be picking fights with your skinny self anymore."

"Dude. *You* must be Batman," Spock said. "We'll call Tymbrelle Wonder Woman instead."

"Who is this Batman?" Tymbrelle called from her prone position. "Instead of a Dragon-bat, is he a man-bat?"

Spock chuckled, "No, no. It's...it's a topside thing. Never mind."

The meager creek was chattering back to life as the last remnants of ice succumbed to liquid. A soft moan from the other side of the shallow bank shifted everyone's focus. The Dark Dwarf lay flat on his back, limbs splayed. Brownish saliva burbled around his lips in foamy bubbles. His thumb twitched.

"You think he's going to live?" Josiah whispered.

"If so, we might need to send Alex to finish him off," Spock said, shaking his fist.

As they watched, the Stygian's head sagged and a deep gash across his neck gaped open, spilling a scarlet tide. His body stilled.

"Good riddance," Finn said. Then he turned to Tymbrelle, who had pushed herself into a sitting position. "And well done, once again, to our new friend and defender Colin-Tymbrelle. The incredible worker of water wonders."

Josiah, Spock, and Dempsey gave a spontaneous smatter of applause, belatedly joined by Alex.

The girl lumbered to her feet, scowling. "Death isn't something to celebrate."

"It is when the choice is us or them, lass." Dempsey hopped onto a rock protruding from the water, then leapt to the other side, grabbing up a lengthy twig as he approached the dead Styg. He used it to poke the pasty-faced creature in the jowl several times. The Stygian didn't move.

Alex and the others watched as, ever so slowly, Dempsey crouched beside the Dark Dwarf, pinched the blade of the dagger between his fingers, and slid the hilt out of the Stygian's grasp. They released a collective sigh as their friend stood, victorious, and shoved the dagger into his belt.

"One weapon is better than none," he said.

A crashing and smashing of branches broke the relative calm. All eyes darted to the canopy of trees, bodies shifting into their instinctive defense-mode.

Two rogue Nephilim Dregs landed with a battle cry, wings unfurled, swords flashing.

CHAPTER THIRTY-THREE

Ellynn

"WELL, ISN'T THIS COZY?" QUEEN CLODAGH remarked, picking up her teacup and giving the contents a sniff. Her pinky finger suddenly popped skyward, as if it had overslept on National Etiquette Day. Her strawberry tresses were swept into a spiraling bun atop her head, which emphasized her full-moon face, waxing above a constellation of ruffles across the bodice of her dress.

Ellynn watched as Princess Larkin lifted her own cup and saucer, her pinky finger unfurling like a slow-motion instant replay of her mother beside her. With not-so furtive glances, the princess constantly monitored Queen Clodagh for social cues, leaving Ellynn to believe the poor girl didn't get out much. At least she had offered Ellynn a shy smile this morning, already an improvement from last night's banquet. Her pale green dress set off her eyes, its square neckline a frame to her delicate gold necklace dangling with a tiny bumblebee pendant.

Ellynn's mother hoped a brunch invitation in the family parlor— strictly for the ladies—would be a conduit for more relaxed and casual conversation. Assuming Alex would be retrieved soon, her mom hoped they could move past the tension of the previous night and learn to be more comfortable with one another before the nuptials. Ellynn couldn't help but hope that Alex would continue to elude his trackers.

Catching her mother's eye and sharing a subtle smile, Ellynn wondered how long it might take for Clodagh and Larkin to act comfortable around each other, let alone the rest of them. The two seemed as wooden as the chairs on which they sat.

In the center of the table, a bowl of brandyberries and cream nestled beside freshly whipped butter, overflowing its butter dish, waiting to be paired with a steaming platter of cloth-wrapped pastries. Between Ellynn's mom and Larkin, an empty space awaited Grandmama Lucia. As always, Ellynn's grandmother was determined to do things her way or not at all.

Ellynn's mother gestured at the steaming cup in Queen Clodagh's hand. "It's Irish breakfast tea. We always bring back several tins whenever we visit *Inis Chléire*. Thought it might make you feel at home."

The pug-nosed woman gave her cup a sniff, then took a slurpy sip. "'Tis delightful."

Her sour expression said otherwise. Sadie only smiled and slid the platter of pastries closer to mother and daughter. "Please, have a sausage and mushroom scone. No one makes savory breakfast scones like our Raechel."

Ellynn noticed Raechel's flush of pride as she stood beside the tea service waiting to refill a cup or offer more cream and sugar. The tea and pastries filled the room with comforting smells that reminded Ellynn of breakfasts at the old farmhouse on *Inis Chléire*—herbal, salty, buttery, and delicious.

Clodagh used petite silver tongs to select one scone, then another, placing them on a china plate sporting the sword-and-feather Pacific House crest in its center. Larkin followed suit. Clodagh slathered butter on top then picked one up and bit into it, eyes rolling in obvious delight. Then, spying her fork, she replaced the scone and retrieved the provided utensil—but not before Larkin had bitten into her own scone, further mimicking her mother all the way through fork retrieval.

Ellynn sipped her tea to avoid giggling. The two seemed more like a mother-daughter comedy team than royal houseguests. Maybe they did things differently in Moored-below. Being a smaller, more isolated kingdom probably didn't give them many chances to entertain. Or maybe manners were different there. Regardless, Ellynn's heart wilted at the thought of Alex being stuck with this painfully self-conscious girl. Awkwardness wasn't any way to launch into happily-ever-after.

"You know what?" Ellynn's mom placed her fork on the table. "I see no reason to use a fork on a perfectly good handheld pastry. You two have the right idea." She picked up her scone and took a mouthful. "Even *tastes* better this way. Like pizza."

Judging from their blank stares, Éire House had been deprived of the euphoria associated with Italian food. *That explains a lot*, thought Ellynn. Of course, exotic food perks were one advantage of having a Topsider for a mother.

"Morning all." Grandmama Lucia breezed in, accompanied by Katheryn toting paper and quill beneath her arm.

Her grandmother placed an affectionate hand on Ellynn's shoulder, and Ellynn had to suppress a flinch of surprise at the uncharacteristic gesture. She glanced up in time to see the woman incline her head to Queen Clodagh.

"I trust you slept well, Auntie?" Grandmama Lucia asked.

Auntie? Wow, she was laying it on thick.

Queen Clodagh stopped mid-chew, nodded, and offered a strained grin to Lucia with crumb-encrusted lips. Ellynn felt a twinge of secondhand embarrassment for the woman. At least she'd had enough sense not to speak with her mouth full— though that hadn't stopped her the night before.

Raechel scurried over to pull out Lucia's chair. With exaggerated motions, Lucia swept her pewter-meets-black wings away from her iron-grey skirt before sitting down. Being in mourning suited her grandmother, Ellynn decided. All those dark, stony colors.

Katheryn made herself comfortable at a side table.

Grandmama Lucia flashed Sadie a smile. "Lovely idea, gathering for brunch."

Ellynn nearly spit out her tea. *Who are you and what have you done with my grandmother?*

Grandmama Lucia picked up the tongs and helped herself to a scone as Raechel poured tea into a cup and placed it on a saucer. Without discussion, everyone knew the rules had suddenly changed. Scones would henceforth be eaten with a fork.

"Why is everyone so quiet?" Her grandmother arched a well-defined brow. "It's just us girls. Let's get to know each other."

Us *girls*? Ellynn would bet the royal treasury that her grandmother had never referred to herself as a *girl*, even when she slept with stuffed animals.

"Auntie Clodagh...we *do* have years and years to catch up on." Grandmama Lucia lifted her teacup and smiled sweetly across the table. "Let's start from the exciting moment when you learned you were with child. We can compare notes. I remember being beyond tired when I was pregnant, and hungry enough to eat a bear. How was pregnancy for you?" She brought her cup to her lips, *sans* pinky, and took a silent sip.

Queen Clodagh's complexion tinged a deep rose. Her emerald eyes leveled, laser-like, on Grandmama Lucia's face. "I'm no fool, Lucia. Quit playin' coy and say what ya mean."

Princess Larkin became instantly and deeply fascinated with her teacup, holding it in front of her like it might sprout branches to conceal her entirely.

Why was Grandmama Lucia so determined to make things uncomfortable for her own aunt and cousin? Wasn't this whole prearranged marriage thing partly *her* idea? It made no sense.

"You presume to know me well enough to know what I intend to say." Grandmama Lucia set her cup down, fake smile affixed. "So, please, answer for me, since you're such a mind reader."

Uh oh. Ellynn wriggled in her seat and tried to suppress her eager, darting gaze that didn't want to miss anyone's reaction.

"I shan't deign to answer a question ye're too timid to ask." Clodagh gave Grandmama Lucia a smug smile and took an enormous bite of scone, ignoring the fork that sat poised for duty.

Grandmama Lucia stiffened. Queen Clodagh might be less refined than her niece, but the two definitely shared the same stubborn streak.

Her grandmother took a slow, nostril-flaring inhale. "Fine. I'll be blunt." She flicked a disdainful glance at Princess Larkin, who still cowered behind her cup, elbows planted on the tabletop for the long haul. "This girl isn't of royal Nephilim blood. I doubt she's even a flightless Nephilim commoner. If I were to guess, Larkin is naught but an ordinary Topsider. She has no claim to Éire House because she's neither Nephilim nor your daughter. Have you so little pride in our bloodline that you would allow such an unremarkable shrew to hold title and influence in our kingdom? Or is it merely that you despise me so?"

Larkin sputtered her sip of tea and clattered the cup onto the saucer, sloshing its contents with an, "Oh, golly." She mopped at the mess with her cloth napkin before seeking shelter behind its white fabric, coughing.

"Ellynn, why don't you take Princess Larkin here to your quarters and show her your, uh, rock collection," her mother said, without looking at Ellynn.

"But I don't have a—"

"Go outside and get one, then." Her mom's sharp gaze shifted to Ellynn, giving her a tight, because-I-said-so smile. "No time like the present."

Ellynn sat, unmoving, bitterly disappointed to once again be dismissed like a child who must be shielded from the smallest of conflicts. So unfair.

Finally, Ellynn gave a curt nod. "Come on." She stood and marched toward the door. Fingers curled into fists, Ellynn stopped and turned to her mother. She couldn't tame her dark, sullen glare, feeling like the girl who had just learned that Christmas had been cancelled.

CHAPTER THIRTY-FOUR

Sadie

SADIE WATCHED THE GIRLS LEAVE, BOTH of their faces flushed for very different reasons.

"Step-mama," Sadie said, using the ridiculous name that Lucia insisted Sadie call her when *Queen Lucia* wouldn't do. "You might have chosen a better time—"

"*Don't*, Sadie." Lucia pressed a palm in Sadie's direction. "I'm not interested in playing nice. Larkin's a big girl. About to be married. I believe she could've handled a forthright conversation. But since *you* have belittled her in your own protective way, she will have to wait to hear it from Clodagh"

Sadie felt her stomach clench, knowing what Lucia said rang true. Although, to her mind, *protectiveness* seemed kinder than Lucia's brand of brutal honesty.

Clodagh offered Sadie a tight smile. "Thanks for yer discretion, Sadie." Then she loosed a bitter glare on Lucia. "Not that I owe ya any explanation...Larkin *is* our daughter. Odhran and I could not conceive. Thus we chose to continue our family in another way—adoption. Eventually, however, we were blessed with a wee *bairn* of our own. Colin came along shortly after Larkin's adoption. Unlike yer unpredictable offspring, Colin is a good boy who shall be worthy of the throne."

Sadie sensed the chill emanating from Lucia. Clodagh glowered back, equally arctic with her cold and cutting jade-stone eyes. Sadie leaned away, wary of getting caught in the maelstrom.

"Leave Magnum out of it," Lucia hissed, pointing at Clodagh for emphasis. "Regardless of your legal papers, Larkin has zero royal blood. If I'd known, I would've proposed my *own* son in marriage, since they are not true cousins. Brihndle is my *father's* kingdom, after all, though you've been busy erasing any memory of him since he died. Furthermore, why haven't I heard about this Colin, until now? Our kingdoms share news and correspondence."

Before Clodagh could reply, Lucia reloaded. "And really, I find it most peculiar that you should adopt a daughter first. Why not a son to carry on your royal lineage? It's not as if you knew that you would eventually conceive a child of your own, let alone that he would be a boy."

"That's none of yer concern," proclaimed Queen Clodagh with finality. She crossed her arms over her ample bosom. "Yer nothin' more than the daughter of a slain king and a commoner, with no place to talk about less than *royal* blood."

Lucia reeled back, as if slapped. Sadie, too, felt the sting of Clodagh's accusations, suddenly protective of Lucia. What had happened to cause them to shun her so? And what was this about Lucia's mother...she was a *commoner*? Had King Aviel known this before he agreed to marry her? Sadie supposed Lucia's wings dispelled any hints of her mother's heritage.

"I see." Lucia's voice was low and measured. She pursed her lips and glanced at Katheryn, who sat with quill at the ready, face impassive. "In that case, I don't know why you would agree to have this precious daughter of yours unite with my dead husband's grandson. Brady Alexander's mother is not even a *Nephilim* commoner—Sadie is a Topsider."

Sadie lost the thread of sympathy she'd picked up on Lucia's behalf. Though her opinions about Sadie's topside roots were not news, the woman's lack of diplomacy and discretion continued to scale new summits.

Queen Clodagh laced her fingers together on the table and leaned in. "Actually, I take comfort in the fact that Sadie's son has absolutely no connection to ya beyond the proximity of 'is bedchamber. And, as ya well know, there are precious few occasions fer marriage between royal houses in our rather disconnected realms, so these nuptials offer a unique opportunity." The stern-faced woman jutted her chin to Sadie. "I have it on good authority that Sadie's family lineage is noble by way of their God-given appointment as topside overseers. 'Er brother inherited the Vituvian throne, did he not? Besides, I've no real issue with bloodlines or I would not have chosen to adopt."

Sadie was surprised that this far-flung stranger had knowledge of the Larcen family's formerly secret connection to the Tethered World. Word may travel slowly in these parts but, clearly, it traveled.

Lucia gave a disdainful grunt, as if everything now made sense. With teeth clenched in a snarling semblance of a smile, she calmly pushed her chair back and stood. "I see. It is only *my* bloodline with which you take issue. Very well. I shall excuse myself and allow you and the mother of the groom here to make your plans."

Queen Clodagh held Lucia's gaze with cool indifference. Sadie believed the two women were having two completely different conversations beneath their frigid, self-possessed exteriors.

With a curt nod, Lucia turned and strode from the room, Katheryn hurrying to keep up.

CHAPTER THIRTY-FIVE

Alex

PANIC SHOT THROUGH ALEX AS HE sized up their predicament. It might be two Nephilim Dregs against the six of them, but the dead Stygian's dagger was the singular weapon between them. Hand-to-sword combat wasn't anything Alex had trained for yet, let alone cared to try.

He recognized the weatherworn old Nephilim from the belly of the fortress, though he hadn't previously seen the hulking Asian fellow, his youthful face a chisel of angles and planes that made him look like a Hollywood martial arts movie star. Had he traveled here from a Far East Nephilim settlement? Alex would have remembered such a distinct, fierce face in Calamus, had they crossed paths. The Asiatic House had kept well to itself over the centuries.

From the corner of Alex's eye, he noticed Tymbrelle inching toward the creek.

"Don't move," the Asian angel-man ordered, his English heavily touched by a Far East accent. He pointed his sword at the girl. "Keep away from the water, little witch. The Overlord wants all of you returned alive. Be smart. Turn around and head back to the citadel."

Josiah and Finn unfurled their wings and stepped closer. Alex felt his friends angling in to protect him. *Not this time.* He took a step forward too.

"What plans does my uncle have for you Nephilim traitors?" Alex asked. "He must've bribed you losers with something extraordinary."

"Shut up!" The older warrior shifted toward Alex, sword tip targeting Alex's chest. "Start walking or we'll carve up one of your expendable friends. *That* is something the Overlord will allow, if it will provide you with the necessary motivation."

No one moved.

Alex held the old warrior's gaze and shook his head. "Not happening. Swords or not, you're outnumbered. So take your chances." A gleam of light fuzzed the edge of his vision, skin prickling around his eye.

Here we go again.

The old Nephilim blinked and gaped at Alex, eyes wide. "What in the...?"

The Asian inhaled sharply.

"That's right." Alex decided to play his oddity off as some sort of superpower. "We have weapons you know nothing about."

"Indeed we do!" Finn chimed, moving his hand to his back, likely hoping to give the impression he was armed.

Josiah followed his lead, and Dempsey withdrew his newly acquired dagger.

The traitors exchanged a dubious glance. Josiah and Finn used the distraction to attack. Josiah leapt into the air, ink-black feathers carrying him high enough to press the sole of one boot against the Asian warrior's fist, the other hooked behind his forearm, trapping the man's wrist in between. The Dreg dropped onto one knee, forearm bent backward, barely keeping a grip on his sword.

Holding himself aloft, Josiah rerouted to deliver a kick to the traitor's temple. The stricken Nephilim spun sideways to the ground with a cry of pain.

Alex gave a layup-worthy leap, closing the distance and landing on the Asian's wrist, pinning it to the ground. With an angry, primitive growl, Alex ground his heel so that the man was forced to release the weapon. Alex snatched it up, pointing the sword at its former owner, while keeping his weight on the turncoat's wrist. "Take a good look at my fiery face. It'll be the last thing you see, traitor!"

Meanwhile, Finn and Dempsey had charged the older warrior. Dempsey used his dagger to block the Nephilim's slashing sword that plunged toward the Dwarf's head. In an instant, Finn rushed headlong into the renegade's solar plexus, knocking him off of his feet. The two grappled on the ground as Dempsey stood over them, obstructing the man's attempts to dice and slice Finn at close quarters.

In the process, Spock had tumbled from Finn's shoulders and landed, across the traitor's eyes like a fat, blinding barnacle. The Gnome grasped the man's salt-and-pepper hair in one fist and pummeled him with the other.

The chaos left the old Nephilim swinging his sword blindly until Dempsey managed to knock it from his hand. Like lightning, the Dwarf snatched it up.

Josiah assessed the situation, apparently confident of the outcome. "Going airborne to make sure they don't have any friends headed our way," he said to no one in particular, fluttering off through a gap in the treed canopy.

Finn pinned the old warrior's shoulders beneath his knees and pushed Spock off the man's head. "Thanks, mate. I'll take it from here." Then he set upon the traitor's face with his knuckles as the Dreg writhed and bucked beneath him.

Dempsey whistled at Finn, then lobbed the Stygian's purloined dagger for Finn to use. He caught it by the hilt and flicked it to rest beneath the old warrior's jaw.

"Don't even twitch," Finn said, sneering at the rough-hewn Nephilim.

Dempsey reinforced the effect by flashing the man's own sword blade in his face.

Alex felt like laughing. In under two minutes they'd disarmed their opponents. Not necessarily the outcome he had expected, even with their decent odds. He lowered the sword until it poked the Asian warrior's Adam's apple. "Bummer to be you."

The defeated Dreg flexed his jaw, lips pressed tight.

Tymbrelle stood beside the creek, fingers curled into her choppy platinum hair, making it stick out more than it already did. Her chest heaved with unsteady breaths. She caught Alex's eye, and her face settled into a look of relief, hands dropping to her sides. "Oh, thank goodness! You guys were amazing. I felt so helpless. I couldn't attack them without hurting all of you."

Alex felt like he had leveled the score between them, or at least narrowed the gap. He and his friends had managed this victory without her fancy-shmancy waterworks.

Josiah returned, touching down where he had taken off, wings retracting as he walked to where Alex stood with sword in hand. Its point had extracted a small bead of blood from the defeated warrior's neck.

"Looks like these guys were the clean-up crew. Didn't see anyone else approaching," Josiah said.

Alex nodded, drawn to the chiseled face of his enemy, surprised to see tears trekking the planes of the man's face. The ninja was *crying?*

"Shall we kill these traitorous no-goodniks?" Dempsey asked. "Or merely incapacitate them?"

Alex felt everyone's expectant gaze on him. The Asian soldier's eyes were closed while the perplexing tears continued to flow. Was this warrior so weak? Maybe he lacked the flint-hard training that General Gage gave his men.

Training that Alex was expected to begin in earnest, now that he had reached manhood. Although he was practically born with a sword in his hand, combat training took second place to schoolwork, with the exception of annual tournaments between school years. Now, as he stared down at this subversive renegade, Alex felt a wave of retroactive dismay. He'd just experienced his first battle with a legitimate enemy. Never in his lifetime would he have guessed that his first fight to the finish would be with another Nephilim.

Though relieved to have subdued the reprobates, did Alex have the guts to see this situation through? In Calamus, these men would be imprisoned and put on trial. Under the circumstances, dragging two prisoners along, as Alex and crew continued to sort out their current situation, wasn't viable. Which left only one, very disturbing, option.

Alex studied the pained face of the man beneath him. His almond eyes opened, and he looked back with a mixture of pleading and resignation. Did he have a family who loved him and would miss him? He was exceptionally far removed from his homeland.

Probably doesn't have a family, Alex decided. Which might make the punishment to be meted out a little easier for Alex's soul to bear.

He swallowed back a bitter, regretful lump and pronounced, "In Calamus, traitors are executed. Your tears don't move me, you coward." And Alex readied the sword to strike the Asian Judas with a kiss of steel.

The warrior suddenly rolled, wrenching his arm from beneath Alex's boot with a loud screech of pain. Alex lost his footing, tumbling backwards like a rug had been pulled from beneath him. Josiah immediately leapt onto the traitor's back, wresting him into a headlock amidst a swirl of feathers.

Alex regained his balance, sword at the ready, when he heard the debilitating *crack* of the traitor's neck. Josiah glanced back at Alex, clearly surprised and disturbed by what he'd done. Alex guessed that his friend hadn't meant to take it so far, at least not yet.

The hulking warrior went limp, and Josiah released him, rolling off the Asian man's winged back and onto his own. His hand flew to his mouth as if he might be ill.

No, Alex thought, Josiah definitely wasn't ready for that.

A screech of pain brought Alex round to where the older warrior lay, now every bit as lifeless as his compatriot. Finn stood over the man's prone form, eyes glancing from the blood-slicked dagger to the growing, scarlet stain on the Nephilim's chest, as if he couldn't reconcile the two. Dempsey and Spock stood on either side of Finn in silent contemplation.

Behind him, Alex heard Tymbrelle sobbing softly.

Alex held Tymbrelle against his chest, feeling awkward yet obligated to comfort her. He wrestled with his own emotional stew, knowing the choice had been to kill or be killed. A part of him would always wonder if there may have been a way out that wouldn't have included bloodshed.

Finn and Josiah had already dragged the old warrior's body beneath some thick vegetation to keep any scouts from learning his fate too quickly. Dempsey and Spock stood over the other Nephilim's prone form, pointing at something. The Dwarf looked up and trilled a sharp whistle through his teeth, waving the others over.

"Dempsey wants to show us something, Tymbrelle," Alex whispered, pulling away, glad to see her tears no longer trickled out.

She blinked wet lashes at him, her mismatched eyes luminous and lovely behind the pooling tears. Alex shoved the thought away, appalled to notice such a thing under the circumstances.

Tymbrelle nodded and sniffed. "Sorry. This...this excursion hasn't turned out quite like I'd hoped."

Alex smirked. "Tell me about it." He made to turn away, but she grabbed his forearm.

"Wait. Please."

"Yeah?"

The girl sighed and bit her lower lip as if determined to speak. Her bloodshot yet beautiful eyes searched Alex's face expectantly.

Alex shifted beneath her scrutiny, annoyed that he now

had a running narration in his brain that included words like *luminous, lovely,* and *beautiful.* "Well, what is it?"

Tymbrelle puffed her cheeks, exhaling. She reached a hand toward his face, standing on tiptoes to touch her fingertips to his cheekbone.

To his birthmark.

He flinched and pulled back—a galvanized current rippling around his eye. "What the—"

"No! Don't," she said. "Let me..." Her fingertips whispering across his skin.

Alex hoped the guys weren't watching. *Fat chance.* He took a half-step back, gently removing her hand. This was getting weird.

A wry grin twitched one side of her mouth, but she let her hand drop and tilted her head. "You...you don't remember me, do you?"

CHAPTER THIRTY-SIX

Alex

"Remember you?" Alex looked down at Tymbrelle's imploring face. Her touch had brought a flash of memory. Memory of another unusual girl encountered one very unusual night. But, no. That was categorically impossible.

Tymbrelle quirked an eyebrow at him. "Yes. From *Inis Chléire*. The comet? The shed? You—you must remember me."

I remember trying to forget.

Alex studied her, studying him. Could she really be the girl he'd written off as the childhood equivalent of an invisible friend—if only to keep from driving himself crazy with worry over her fate? He tumbled the words in his mind, feeling the weight of each like a punch to his gut. *Inis Chléire.* Comet. Shed. Trigger-words from a strange and mysterious night he had denied himself access to, burying the memory like something better left dead. Had it been resurrected? Did it— did *she*—now stand before him with blond hair and mismatched eyes?

That night was one of several that Alex never wanted to revisit. One of those life-jarring events he was determined to leave in the past along with his childhood name, Brady Alexander.

Funny thing about working so hard to forget...those things have a way of searing themselves into the subconscious. A brand on your brain that eventually finds its way back to the one who sent it out to pasture.

CHAPTER THIRTY-SEVEN

Alex
Then

A SCINTILLATING STAR—A METEOR—CAREENS across the night sky. A silver dragon with a brilliant tail of fire takes aim at the small spit of land in the southernmost part of Ireland. Nine-year-old Brady Alexander is too awestruck to fear the incoming comet as it sets the sky ablaze. But he feels the impact deep within his lanky Nephilim bones the moment it strikes.

Amazing, almost magical things seem to happen whenever he spends time on *Inis Chléire* with his Great great Aunt Jules, but tonight's stargazing event is beyond anything he could have imagined.

"Listen, cherub. Y'know this 'ere island like a satellite map." Aunt Jules grips Brady's hand in gnarled, liver-spotted fingers. "I need ya to see what happened yonder. I'd go meself but these arthritic knees won't make it. Seems to've hit near-about the standin' stones, although I can't say fer certain in the dark."

"Wait. You're sending *me* to investigate? Right now?" Brady Alexander is certain he's misunderstood.

"I wouldn't send ya if I didn't feel t'was important. We just witnessed somethin' special, lovey. Once in a lifetime special." Aunt Jules steers him toward the gravel driveway. "No doubt there will be others out and about investigatin' what the blazes hit us. Nose about the best ya can, but don't interfere with the authorities. Keep out of sight and learn what ya can. I'll be waitin' to hear all about it."

"But what should I be looking *for*? A glowing piece of rock?"

Her wrinkles pleat into a smile. "That may indeed be what ya find, chipmunk. Though it may be somethin' else entirely." She pulls a small flashlight from her cardigan pocket and hands it to him. "Somethin' that spectacular is like a special delivery from the heavens. Seems worth investigatin' if ya ask me.

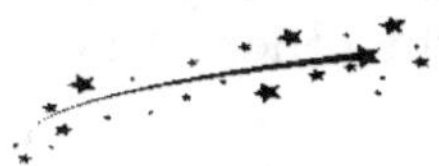

Brady Alexander leans against the wall inside the old cowshed weighing what he should do next. Light from emergency vehicles filters through the window opening beside him, illuminating the O'Driscoll's field beyond. He turns off the flashlight—or, 'torch', as his Aunt Jules would call it. How is it that she just *happened* to have the flashlight in her pocket anyway? It's almost as if she was expecting the unexpected tonight...

A creak and a squeak makes Brady catch his breath. He listens, forcing his brain to think *mouse* instead of *zombie*. The only sounds continue to come from the search efforts outside. Soldiering on, he shifts to peek out the window, ignoring the upside-down crate others have likely used for a step up.

A half-dozen men sweep the area, flashlights in hand, murmuring softly in their mix of Irish and English. An emergency SUV lumbers farther into the field, pointing its headlights at the bruised landscape, its glare now head-on to the window of the shed, obstructed only by the jack-o-lantern teeth of the two upright standing stones.

The stones are huge and, according to Aunt Jules, have been there since the time of the pyramids. They were once part of a circle, she explained, like Stonehenge, but now there are only four rocks left—two upright stones and two that fell many years ago. They're covered with earth and growth, tucked beneath a blanket of grass like enormous coffins in shallow graves.

Churned-up rocks and dirt create a deep gash that begins on one side of the standing stones and splices the length of the field in the direction of the sea. A gust of wind barrels into Brady's face, peppering him with dust.

He recoils. Eyes stinging, mouth gritty, he turns from the window and spits, rubbing his eyes against his sleeve and fumbling his flashlight in the process. He sinks down, eyes closing involuntarily. He blinks and rubs some more.

A muted *bump*—footsteps?—forces his eyelids open. Is someone coming to the cowshed? Scrunching against the wall, he hopes the bales of hay between him and the doorway provide cover from any probing lights. The glare from the headlights still lingers in his retina. His irritated right eye waters fiercely, and he swipes at it with one hand while groping for the flashlight with the other.

Thump.

The sound definitely came from *inside* the shed. He stiffens, hearing it again, louder. Closer. Someone, or something, is creeping to where he sits.

"Who's there?" Brady whispers. He doesn't know if he should hope the sound came from a varmint or a person. Either seems terrifying in this shadowy barn. "Hello?"

A soft whimper. A sniffle.

Crying?

The soft *puh-puh-puh* of feet—or maybe hands and feet—padding across the hay-strewn floor. Coming closer.

Heart walloping, Brady presses himself against the wall, feeling his wingbuds complain in pain. His fingers frisk across the ground in search of the dropped flashlight. Where is the blasted thing? Doesn't help that his eyes won't stop watering.

"Huh-loo," whispers a voice. A young voice, like his, though heavily accented.

"Who are you?" Brady whispers back. He feels a little better knowing the stranger is a kid. A girl, if he had to guess.

His eyes are clearing and he can make out a hand—fingers curling into the straw—and part of a forearm, twig-skinny and looking pink in the reddish glow of light pooling between them.

Brady blinks, aware that this source of light is not angling in through the window. It is, somehow, billowing between himself and this stranger, low to the ground. He swivels his head, wondering if the flashlight turned on when it fell, landing behind some fabric or something that might obscure it. He'd feel a lot calmer if he could retrieve it.

The reddish glow follows his movements. Weird.

"Huh-loo," the voice tries again.

Brady whips back round, confused by the stranger and the strange light. Is this—whatever *it* is—what Aunt Jules expects him to find?

"Who are you?" he hisses at the arm, and now a knee, that is crawling closer. He lifts his gaze, which somehow shifts the pale red light onto the owner of the hand and knee. A young girl. Scrawny. Long, tangled hair that is probably blond but appears pink in the mystifying glow.

She cocks her head and crawls closer, her shoulders gleaming and bare. In fact, her whole torso is bare. Not necessarily strange for a kid as young as she is—younger than him, he decides, but older than his six-year-old sister. Still, how strange to be half dressed on a chilly night. He glimpses a striped towel wrapped around her waist.

"Whoo ah yoo?" She asks in her strange accent.

"I asked you first."

"I ahhsked yoo fuhrst," she replies breathily, sitting back on her heels and crossing her arms like Brady.

He shakes his head. The red light wobbles too. "No you didn't!"

"Nuho yoo didhunt." She shakes her head.

Ugh! The little brat is copying him. He hates it when his sister plays this dumb game.

Brady angrily looks away. The red light moves too, glowing brighter, more vivid in front of his right eye than his left. In fact, the glow appears to be coming *from* his right eye. Brady takes to closing one eyelid, then the other, trying to understand. He holds his hand a few inches in front of his left eye, then his right. The obvious difference makes him feel a little panicky. What's going on?

The panic somehow surges the wattage, and the light blazes like the neon sign at the petrol station. He can feel a prickly warmth on the skin around his eye.

His birthmark!

A tap on his shoulder interrupts his growing alarm.

"*What.*" It isn't a question. Brady turns to see the girl only inches away. The curious light throws shadows across her face. The shadows shrink and stretch with each anxious jerk of his head as he attempts to distance himself from this weird girl and turn off the perplexing light by sheer force of will.

What does this mean? Is this God's punishment for what Brady did to his uncle?

Yes. That must be it! Somehow, this knowledge calms him a little. Brady deserves to be punished, and Aunt Jules always says that God works in mysterious ways.

Surely this is the most mysterious ever. Aunt Jules must've known this would happen. Probably worked it out with the Maker ahead of time. The two were pretty tight.

Of course...that falling star must have been a signal. It had been his auntie's idea for him to come stay with her on

Inis Chléire for the summer. Since he is too young to go to jail, this flaming face of his must be a supernatural punishment.

The girl corners him. Brady doesn't remember moving, but finds that he's stuck against a crate of glass milk jugs. Something smells like fish. He's pretty sure it's the girl.

The girl brushes her fingers across his cheekbone, soft as one of his father's feathers.

Brady doesn't move—beyond wrinkling his nose at her fishy breath. He doesn't want her touching him. If he shoves her away he's probably going to get into bigger trouble with God. Maybe Brady's whole body will glow if he isn't careful.

He offers the girl a hesitant smile, deciding to play along.

She withdraws her fingers while keeping her face uncomfortably close—fishiness and all—her gaze seeming to memorize him.

"Do you speak English?" he asks.

"Doo yoo spayk Englush."

He tries again. "Do you speak Irish? *An bhfuil Gaeilge agat?*" Brady knows a few Irish phrases from his many visits to the island.

"Gaway-ahl-geh a-goot," she attempts to repeat. Suddenly, she sits back on her haunches and tips her head toward the shed door.

Brady looks in that direction about the time he registers footsteps approaching. Someone must have heard them talking. Or, more likely, they noticed the glow from his blasted birthmark and came to investigate.

He shoves the girl out of the way, rougher than he intends, and dives beneath a sawhorse draped with old blankets and a canvas tarp.

The girl cries out and rights herself, then, none too quietly, scampers after him.

"In here! Someone's in O'Driscoll's shed."

Brady recognizes Mr. MacAndre's voice. The strange girl is on her belly, trying to shimmy beneath the sawhorse beside Brady.

"There! I see someone's legs. It's a wee child."

A torch beam slices through the shadows and Brady turns his face, afraid his blazing beacon will give him away. He can sense it shining brighter in the anxiety of the moment. Although he feels badly about the girl, he can't help her now. She's been caught. Besides...she really seems lost. Maybe Mr. MacAndre can help her find her house. Her family must be vacationing on the island.

The desperate zing of nails scraping the stone beneath the straw makes Brady cringe. Mr. MacAndre must be pulling her away by the ankles. Brady resists the urge to peek.

"What have we here?" Mr. MacAndre out-volumes the girl's frightened cries. "Hey, hey, lass. It's okay now. Calm down."

The girl is sobbing and screeching. Brady can't stand it. He covers his upturned ear and presses the other to the ground. Hadn't his father always taught him to stand up for the weak? To protect his little sister? Is this any different? Guilt and fear paralyze him as the girl's cries grow fainter. She will be better off, he tells himself. What can *he* do? He's only a kid himself.

The cowshed grows quiet, and the murmur of the adults seems to shift in a way that says the others are curious about the girl. With the return of calmer breaths and a normal pulse, Brady's glow-in-the-dark face finally switches off. Relief washes over him.

Thank You, God, thank You! Please don't ever let this happen again. I'll do anything. Anything! I'm so sorry about what happened to my uncle. And I'm sorry if I was supposed to help that girl, but I didn't know how. Please, don't let this happen to my face again. I learned my lesson. I promise!

Stinging tears replace the dull burn of his birthmark until Brady cries himself to sleep.

CHAPTER THIRTY-EIGHT

Alex

OH, YES, ALEX REMEMBERED. IN THE fleeting time-warp way that one can recollect hours and days in seconds...

He remembered waking in the wee hours of the morning on the shed floor. Remembered wanting to forget the girl, despite the desperate claw marks that mocked him as he crawled from his hiding place. Remembered the horror of what happened with his birthmark.

Remembered making his way back to the old farmhouse to find his aunt asleep in her rocking chair in front of the cold, peat-burning fireplace. Remembered how she pleaded with him in the morning, to tell her what happened. Remembered refusing to tell her anything. Remembered the defeat and disappointment he saw in her eyes and the guilt that heaped on top of his other guilt for being the source of that pain.

Yes, Alex remembered...and ever since, he'd been trying to forget. Forget that night—forget this girl—because he couldn't wrap his mind around any of it.

He thought he had succeeded, more or less. Until now.

Tymbrelle looked at him with those imploring—and, okay, *beautiful* eyes—and it all came back like a splash of water waking him from a dream. *'You don't remember me, do you?'*

"Nope." Alex shook his head. "Don't know what you're talking about. Sorry." He absolutely couldn't go there right now. Maybe never.

Tymbrelle narrowed her gaze. "I don't believe you," she hissed.

"Hey, Alex!" Finn called. "You've *got* to see this."

Relieved by the distraction, Alex trotted to where his friends stood hovering over the body of the Asian soldier.

He heard Tymbrelle give an angry huff.

"Lover's quarrel?" Dempsey's mustache stretched into a lopsided grin as Alex approached.

"Shut it." Alex scowled.

Josiah was squatting beside the dead Nephilim's torso. He lifted the warrior's limp arm, hand drooping like a willow branch.

"Dude! What did you do to this guy's wrist?" Spock pointed at the damaged limb.

That's when Alex noticed that the soldier's hand wasn't the only thing drooping. The guy's wrist was flattened so that it was nearly as wide as his hand, and it dangled at a near ninety-degree angle from halfway up the forearm. The traitor's limb resembled a grotesque pancake more than a body part.

Alex blinked and shook his head. "Whoa! How did that happen?"

"You tell us," Finn said, elbowing Alex in the ribs. "That's your footwork. We found him like this."

Alex stared, not comprehending.

"Now we know why he was crying." Josiah sighed and let the arm flop back to the ground with a sickening *thunk*.

As one, the friends cringed at the unnatural angle of the soldier's arm where it lay. Alex's stomach churned.

"I don't see how I could've crushed his arm to that extent." He shook his head. "Something else must've happened between then and now."

Finn gave a mirthless chuckle. "Yeah, like he ran it through a homemade pasta maker." He clapped Alex on the back. "I think you've been holding back, buddy. First the hound. Now this. I'm gonna take it easy on you from now on."

"Let's get him moved so we can get out of here." Josiah stood. "Finn, take the other arm. Alex, mind grabbing his ankles?"

Alex wordlessly did his part. He couldn't tear his gaze from the disfigured mess at the end of the dead man's arm. Had he really inflicted that damage? Remembering the dog's mangled muzzle made him acknowledge the possibility. Where had such superhuman strength come from?

He glanced at Tymbrelle, remembering their uncomfortable conversation. Was she the common thread? His birthmark only switched on in *her* vicinity. That's probably why it hadn't happened since that night in the cowshed. Now this phenomenal strength had asserted itself. He recalled how the skin around his eye felt pricked with electricity right before his fist met the snout of the hound, and again when he was fighting the Nephilim Dregs. The glow and his surreal strength...the two things had to be connected.

Make that *three* things, he thought, studying the strange girl—the girl who could turn water into a deadly weapon. Tymbrelle definitely had more secrets.

A loud jabber from a nearby branch made the group turn their attention to Parsifal, hanging upside down before making a fluttery dismount onto a chunk of rock. He gave an animated oration.

Spock answered the Dragon and then explained, "Parsifal isn't familiar with this area. He explored as much as possible since our capture last night, but he continued to loop back to the valley to look for us, unable to travel far. He found tunnels in the hills up ahead and they're pretty extensive, though he didn't have time to fully explore them."

"More of a plan than we've got at the moment." Josiah lifted a questioning brow at the others. "Certainly don't need to camp out this close to Alex's deranged uncle."

Alex nodded. "Agree. Let's move."

It took the better part of a wonderfully boring hour for Parsifal to lead the group to a particular outcropping of foothills. The forest had grown in density as they trekked, providing both concealment and a slow, steady release for Alex's anxiety.

Fragments of the perplexing night in the cowshed surfaced while he mentally combed through details of the last few days—all while avoiding Tymbrelle's questioning, insistent stare. The farther they journeyed into the woods, the more the barrage of thoughts slowed to a manageable, contemplative pace. He knew the priority was getting as far from Magnum as possible. There would be time for answers later.

Parsifal probed a ragged granite ridge that swelled as high as the treetops. He traveled the length of it, flitting from branch to branch, apparently looking for the opening he had discovered. At last he squawked and fluttered to the ground in front of a gash that Alex might have missed if he wasn't looking for it. The rock puckered in on itself, giving way to a large but easy-to-overlook tunnel, further disguised by a wide oak growing in front of it.

"Sweet!" Finn said, sizing it up. "Nicely hidden. This rock looks like one of those cookies you brought back from Portland, Alex. The ones with the silly paper message inside."

"A fortune cookie," Alex said, finding that the folds in the rock did, indeed, look like a super-sized fortune cookie.

"Exactly." Finn stepped behind the tree and peeked into the opening. "Let's hope this part of our journey is a little more *fortunate* than the first half." He grinned and leaned against the wide trunk. "See what I did there?"

"Yeah," Dempsey grumbled. "You assumed we're only halfway done with this 'ere expedition. I don't know about you lads, but I've had me fill of adventure and am ready to head home. We've got no food. No water. No horses. And, maybe worst of all, I haven't got me pipe. This is about as fun as sticking thorns beneath me fingernails and calling it a manicure."

"Could be worse." Spock slid off of Finn's shoulder and down his arm, before dropping to the ground next to Parsifal. "At least we've got some weaponry now."

Dempsey made a noise that conveyed how unimpressed he was with this uptick.

"What would you know about a manicure?" Tymbrelle eased closer to the group. It was the first time she had spoken since the incident at the creek.

Alex risked a sideways glance at the girl. No one volunteered an answer.

"That reminds me." Alex plunged his hand into his pocket and retrieved the sheathed blade he had deposited there—and forgotten—when Vetch helped them escape. "Grabbed this on my way out of the citadel and forgot about it in the ensuing craziness—unfortunately. Guess I'm not used to carrying a pocket-size weapon, though it would've been better than nothing. Here." He offered it to the Gnome. "It's more your size."

"Thanks!" Spock took the proffered knife and sheath, inspected them briefly, then slid the combo into the waistband of his jeans.

"Even if we wanted to call it off and head home, we don't know which way home is yet, Demps," Josiah said.

Dempsey waved him off. "Yeah, yeah. I'm merely givin' y'blokes notice. Soon as I see a way back, I plan to take it."

"Noted." Josiah dipped his head. "Glad to know the extent to which you have our backs."

Dempsey muttered something unintelligible and waddled past Finn to inspect the tunnel.

Alex jerked a chin at the Dwarf. "I think our grouchy friend here is wrestling with nicotine withdrawals."

"Maybe those Dregs did you a favor," Finn said. "Haven't you heard that smoking is a danger to your health?"

"So is friendship, of late, Finnegan," Dempsey groused. "Can we skip the lecture and get on with it?"

Parsifal chattered at Spock, who nodded and translated. "Little Dragon dude says we'll have to walk awhile before we find some glowing geodes to light our way. Said he'll use his fire-breathing skills to help us maneuver until we can get our hands on some."

"Good to know," Alex said. "I was wondering about that since we've lost our supplies."

Parsifal flitted past Dempsey, who turned with a grunt to follow. Everyone filed inside. Alex waited for Tymbrelle to enter, then brought up the rear.

She flashed a brief, intense gaze at him, and his mind careened back to the cowshed. He remembered the young girl with an equally intense stare. How she'd studied him, copied him, and cried out to him before being dragged away. Her terrorized scream had haunted Alex for months after their encounter.

Now, inexplicably, she had come back into his life. Had saved his life. Had triggered his birthmark and seemed to have awakened some primal strength from deep within. It was too much to contemplate.

The damp, earthy smell of the tunnel worked to calm Alex's mind as he trekked after his friends. He welcomed the cool air against his skin. With effort, he pulled his thoughts to the present problem of escape.

The echo of footsteps was soon accented by the uneven tempo of water droplets pinging against the granite ground. At the front of the procession, Parsifal produced a flickering tongue of fire with each combustible exhale. It provided a flash of bluish-orange light revealing bite-sized glimpses of the narrow, rocky passageway.

Alex could make out little more than the direction he needed to keep moving. He found Tymbrelle's pale hair a helpful beacon in the dim glow cast by the Dragon. The flaxen strands glinted enough to help Alex pace his long-legged stride so he wasn't walking on her heels.

The passage echoed, as all tunnels do, filling his ears with the dissonant harmony of footfalls, spattering water, huffing breath, and the occasional unintelligible mumble from Dempsey. Alex noted that tunnels and cathedrals seemed to have similar effects on people. Chatter felt unnatural and exceptionally loud.

At last he began to glimpse the occasional blister of light glowing in the granite walls. Like bright breadcrumbs that provided direction, tiny, glowing geodes made an appearance in the vein of rock. As they traveled, the geodes increased in size and frequency, allowing Parsifal to ease up on his fire-breathing, though the rocks were still too embedded to break off and use for a torch.

As long as the path was lit, Alex didn't much care where the light came from. What struck him as odd was the lack of intersecting passageways. Such tunnels were, as far as he knew, manmade. Or Dwarf-made, anyway. He had never been inside such a lengthy stone corridor that offered zero alternative routes. This made escape options limited to *forward*, if Magnum's Dregs tracked them here. Whoever built this passage seemed to have one goal in mind—getting to the other side.

What if it spit them right back into Magnum's lair?

CHAPTER THIRTY-NINE

Ellynn

"WELL, THAT WAS AWKWARD. AND RUDE." ELLYNN STOLE a sidelong glimpse at Larkin as they hurried down the long corridor, leaving brunch behind. No sense pretending everything was dandy.

Princess Larkin gave a nervous chuckle but said nothing. Freed from the complicated braids of the night before, her glossy auburn hair fell in patterned waves around her face. She used it to shield her eyes from Ellynn's persistent glances.

Ellynn heard the echo of staccato footsteps far behind them and turned to see her grandmother and Katheryn storming out of the family parlor before stopping to whisper in sharp, unintelligible tones, heads together.

Blast it! As much as she wanted to crack open the timid shell of this strange girl beside her, Ellynn's secret-spy self wanted to know what her grandmother was up to even more. Though she understood Trinny's stern warning—that Ellynn should not be listening in on private conversations—the things she had accidentally-on-purpose overheard the day before felt weighty and important. They had bothered her all night.

She recalled Grandmama Lucia's prediction that *"...tragedy will strike Éire House before the two strangers can say I do."* Didn't Ellynn have a responsibility toward Larkin and her family to know, and prevent, whatever vengeful plans her grandmother was brewing?

Grabbing Larkin by her sleeve, she led the girl into a reading alcove, hoping to overhear something insightful. The deeply recessed stone niche was flanked by large ferns and held a violet settee with a set of narrow end-tables that offered a rotating selection of books. Ellynn had spent many an afternoon stretched out with a favorite read, tucked away yet still connected to the comings and goings around her. She'd overheard a good bit of palace gossip right here, concealed in plain sight.

"Let's chat," Ellynn offered, sweeping a hand toward the well-worn sofa.

Larkin, of course, didn't protest, only tucked her flouncy skirt beneath her and perched on the edge, hands clasped over her knees as if she might be a good-natured gargoyle.

Ellynn plopped down beside her, making the springs squeak and Larkin bounce. "Oops. Sorry." She hoped her grandmother was too far away to notice.

Larkin rubbed her palms across her knees and took a deep breath.

"You okay?" Ellynn asked, feeling a pang of guilt that she hadn't removed this flustered girl further from the verbal assaults of Grandmama Lucia.

Larkin bit her lip and nodded. "Thank you for—"

"Wait!" Ellynn interrupted, holding up a finger. She could hear footsteps approaching, along with her grandmother's voice gaining clarity. With quick, silent movements, Ellynn snatched a book from the table and opened it, shoving it between herself and Larkin, pressing the girl close with an arm slung around her shoulder. Playing along, Larkin tentatively pinched the other side of the book like it might burn to the touch.

Maybe Grandmama Lucia would be so preoccupied with her conversation, she wouldn't notice the two girls *obviously* engrossed in this book...five minutes after leaving breakfast.

"...need to fetch Gouldor," her grandmother was saying. "Order him to my parlor. If you see Florentino, send him my way too. Though I'll also send one of my quarter guards to track him down when I get back, regardless."

The two women strode past, arms linked and heads bent, oblivious to the girls a few yards away. Grandmama Lucia was nearest the alcove with Katheryn on her other side. The pair stopped walking just past the niche, which conveniently hid the girls behind a pedestaled fern. At this, Larkin began to tremble so violently she nearly pulled the book from Ellynn's grasp.

"Lucia, I've got your back." Katheryn's body angled slightly toward the girls, a hand on Lucia's elbow. "I always have. We came here with a long-term vision of getting your kingdom back. We've been patient. We've got our people in place. Don't let Clodagh's words shift the target. *Nothing* has changed."

"Except the added slap by their adopting that limp little Larkin. I'm certain she's nothing but a tall Topsider. A Topsider, presuming to represent my father's kingdom and attempting to marry into Aviel's family. A double insult!" Grandmama Lucia pulled free from Katheryn's grasp and placed her hands on her hips. "It's as if they chose the weakest, wormiest person in the world strictly to insult me. Well, it worked! Not that she's any threat. She'll be easy enough to flick out of the way." Lucia gave a grunt of disgust. "They could've at least found a worthy contender. I bet they've put up with that insipid child all in hopes of parading her under my nose one day. If they believe their little shepherd girl has the power to take down Goliath..." she trailed off into cynical laughter. "Wow, have they underestimated *me*."

Ellynn wanted to both crawl under a rock and throw one at her grandmother. Could this have turned out any worse?

Larkin did, finally, yank the book from Ellynn's fingers. She lowered it, flipped it, and lifted it back up. That's when Ellynn realized they had been holding the thing upside down because now...it wasn't. Larkin's levelheadedness surprised her.

"You're right, you're right," Katheryn said, leaning in and speaking slowly, like a parent to a child. "All the more reason to maintain your focus. Proactive, not reactive, remember? Let's not forget that there's no need for a wedding. You wanted to entice your aunt and uncle away from Moored-below to the Tethered World. You've accomplished that. You still have the upper hand, Your Grace. Now, why not head to your quarters and rest while you can before we set these wheels of vengeance in motion?" She lowered her voice and practically purred as she added, "You know it'll be *delicious*. Keep your—*uh-oh*."

Katheryn spotted the girls.

Ellynn felt her stomach drop. She and Katheryn locked gazes through the fern fronds, and Katheryn's eyes went round. Ellynn made an instant and silent promise to God that she would never go out of her way to eavesdrop again, if only...

Grandmama Lucia turned with a sharp gasp, eyes aflame when she saw Ellynn and Larkin. "*What* in the name of Lake Alethia are you doing here, little girl?" She marched around the fern and grabbed Ellynn by the wrist, yanking her to her feet. "Your mother sent you to your room."

Ellynn bit back a yelp of pain as Larkin let out a squeal loud enough for both of them. "I—I'm sorry! We sat here instead." Ellynn gestured feebly at the couch. "Seemed private. How was I to know—"

"Oh, don't give me *that*." Her grandmother spoke through clenched teeth, a menacing sway to her head as she leaned in. "Wouldn't surprise me if you were the little *rat* I heard in the walls yesterday."

Ellynn willed her face to have no reaction.

Her grandmother's looming sneer didn't waiver as she probed Ellynn with her cat-like eyes. "Mmhm. I'm right. I can read it on your face, Ellynn Jules."

Ellynn gave a feeble shake of the head, though she was half-tempted to confess then and there. Except, Grandmama Lucia looked so vicious, Ellynn feared her reaction. Plus, the hateful things the woman had spouted, both yesterday and today…they were very dangerous things. Ellynn felt devoured by panic and dread and uncertainty.

Larkin had curled into the settee like a snail into its shell. Katheryn lunged at the girl, her long, bony fingers wrapping around Larkin's upper arm, the book tumbling onto the floor. "On your feet—and quit blubbering!"

Ellynn hadn't even noticed the girl crying. Her own heart beat so loudly it seemed trapped between her ears, blocking other sounds. Except the sizzle of her grandmother's fiery words.

"Here's what's going to happen." Lucia flicked her index finger straight, like a switchblade, directing her polished nail at Ellynn's face. "You two will not breathe a word of anything you may have heard. *Not a word*. In return—"

The slamming of a door, somewhere down the hall, morphed her grandmother from werewolf to woman, like a cloud obscuring a full moon. She straightened and released Ellynn, taking a half step back. Katheryn did the same.

Clasping her hands in front of her waist, face contorted into a pained smile, Grandmama Lucia spoke in a low, strained voice. "And in return, I let both sets of your parents *live*. Got it?"

Ellynn and Larkin said nothing. Lucia looked at Katheryn, who gave an encouraging nod.

"I have people, sworn to my agenda, all over this castle," she went on. "They will watch you and report to me. If either of you breathe a word of this to anyone, even your stupid horses, I shall know about it."

Footsteps approached and stopped, making the four of them acknowledge the intruder.

Tassitus!

Ellynn felt a wave of relief cooling her hot fear. Had he overheard Lucia's threats? Doubtful since she had been talking in such careful, muted tones. Still, as Xander's personal attendant, Tassitus was charged with having his eyes and ears on the pulse of the palace. Could he sense Ellynn's quaking, terrorized heart?

"Everything okay?" He drew out the first word as if he knew it wasn't. His concerned, sharp gaze bounced between Ellynn and her grandmother.

"We are fine, Tassitus." Grandmama Lucia's smile looked more like a snarl. "Don't let our *tête-à-tête* interrupt your work." She made a shooing motion. "Off you go, little one."

"Ellynn? You good?" Tassitus gave her a probing look, ignoring Grandmama Lucia's insult about his compact physique. Most people assumed he was a Topsider.

Ellynn hoped her expression conveyed that she wasn't at all good. Still, she gave a hesitant nod. "Fine."

Tassitus looked from Ellynn to Larkin to Katheryn to Grandmama Lucia.

"Your job is to follow orders, Tassitus. *I* am telling you to leave." Grandmama Lucia clamped a hand on Ellynn's shoulder. "My granddaughter and I are experiencing one of those life lessons. That's all. I'm sure Ellynn will agree that our chat has been productive. Right, dear?"

Ellynn held Tassitus's reassuring stare and nodded.

"Very well." He took a step back and inclined his head. "I'll leave you ladies to it." He turned and continued on his way.

Ellynn watched him leave, praying he understood her silent plea for help.

"You better hope that nosy gnat keeps his mouth shut," Grandmama Lucia said. "Because it doesn't matter *who* does the blabbing around here." She aimed her blistering glare at Larkin. "I'm prepared to do whatever I must to get my...my...my *goodness*. Where did you get that?"

Ellynn reeled at her grandmother's sudden change of topic. The woman's sharp features shifted from angry to suspicious as she took a step toward the pitiable form of Larkin. The girl would surely have fainted if Katheryn hadn't grasped her elbow.

With surprising gentleness, Grandmama Lucia grasped the bumblebee pendant at Larkin's neck, causing the girl to flinch and list against Katheryn.

"Be still. I'm not going to hurt you," she ordered, flipping the pendant over and inspecting the back. "Where did this come from?"

"Uh, well." Larkin gulped. Her frightened gaze darted to Ellynn and back.

"Well, *what?*"

"It belonged to my mother. M-my birthmother." Larkin's voice was a tremulous whisper. "It's the only thing I have of hers."

The necklace slipped from Grandmama Lucia's fingers and she took a step back, her eyes sweeping over the girl as if seeing her for the first time. "It can't be." She shook her head. "Impossible."

With that, Grandmama Lucia turned and hurried away.

Katheryn stood opened mouth, clearly as bewildered as the girls. She made to dash off after her mistress, then stopped and pointed a warning finger at Ellynn. "Remember, the safety of your families depends on complete silence." She targeted Larkin with her accusing finger. "From both of you."

CHAPTER FORTY

Ellynn

"YA POOR DEAR! WHATEVER IS THE matter?" Trinny grasped Larkin's hand as Ellynn led the distraught girl into her bedchamber. "Let me get ya some tea."

"No thanks, Trinny." Ellynn didn't wait to see whether Larkin needed tea—that mysterious, universal tonic—because the two needed to talk. Now. "If you wouldn't mind leaving us alone. We, uh, have something to discuss."

Trinny released her grasp and stopped walking, clearly perturbed by the dismissal. "Leave Larkin in this state? I should think not. She doesn't appear fit to discuss the weather."

"It's okay," Larkin said between shuddering breaths. "Ellynn is right. We must talk."

Ellynn felt sorely tempted to tell Trinny everything, certain the loyal Dwarf was not one of her grandmother's minions. For now, however, she and Larkin needed to get on the same page about what happened and what they were going to do about it.

Trinny pursed her lips and eyed them both. "Hope this has nothin' to do with yesterday's nonsense, Ellynn Jules."

Ellynn felt a twinge of self-reproach, knowing the current circumstance to be a roundabout continuation of the one Trinny had so recently doctored. "Not exactly. We...have a situation, that's all."

"Not exactly? Well what *exactly* is the situation?" Trinny grasped her wide hips, elbows akimbo. "I'm not leavin' without a more satisfactory response."

Ellynn felt angry impatience building. She glanced at Larkin, who had collapsed into a cushiony chair beside the fireplace. "It's a private matter, and I'm taking care of it. Plus, you're supposed to assist *me*. That's what a lady-in-waiting does." The snobbery of her words—and their similarity to her grandmother's belittling remarks to Tassitus—filled Ellynn with shame and self-loathing. She clamped a hand over her mouth. "I—I'm sorry, Trinny. That was uncalled—"

"Well, now! If that's how ya feel, Yer High-and-Mightiness, then by all means, excuse me." Trinny gave an exaggerated curtsy. "Someone of yer station certainly shouldn't trifle with the wisdom and concern of a friend who used to change yer nappies."

"Wait, Trinny. I didn't mean it," Ellynn pleaded, reaching for the Dwarf as she turned to leave. "*Please.* I just...I *need* to talk to Larkin, okay?" Tears tumbled down her cheeks, choking off her words.

Trinny crossed her arms and turned in a slow about-face. "Very well. I shall return shortly to check on ya both." She aimed a scolding finger at Ellynn. "But if ya ever speak to me in such a manner again, I'll be packin' me bags and movin' back to Berganstroud before ya can blow yer snotty nose. Understood?"

Ellynn nodded, relieved. When the bedroom door closed, Ellynn dashed to Larkin, squatting beside the chair. The girl's round face looked rounder still, splotchy and puffy as it was from crying.

"Hey...I, um, I know we don't know each other. Like, whatsoever." Ellynn placed a hand on the girl's knee. "Still, I want you to know I'm sorry I asked you to stop in that spot, instead of coming straight to my room. We could've avoided that whole mess. And, I'm sorry about—"

"I'd rather know where I stand with your grandmother." Larkin's voice was stronger than Ellynn expected. "I'm quite aware of where I stand in Éire House. Believe me."

That was the most Ellyn had heard Princess Larkin say. Ellynn liked the girl's soft, lilting accent. Sinking onto the floor, Ellynn leaned her shoulder against the padded chair leg. "You should know that my grandmother—step-grandmother, really—doesn't even like *me*, most days, so don't take what she says personally. Lately, she's stuck-up and rude to everyone except her lady-in-waiting and her precious son Magnum. She was only *kind* of nice to Grandfather Aviel, and he was her husband, not to mention the king."

Larkin met Ellynn's gaze, the girl's grey-green eyes losing their angry edge. She sniffed and wiped her nose with the back of her hand. "She does seem overtly critical."

Ellynn nodded. "Precisely. What she said about you and your parents..." Ellynn trailed off, uncertain she should mention it. "I don't know your parents, but they seem much nicer than her."

Larkin uncurled her legs and leaned her forearms onto her knees, close to Ellynn. "It's...it's very complicated between us at the moment. That's all I can say."

Ellynn nodded as though she understood, despite her own relationship with her parents being completely opposite. Still, if they sent her off to marry a stranger, she could foresee plenty of issues. "I'm sure adoption comes with its own set of complications, without the added pressures of a royal family."

"That's putting it in polite terms." Larkin's mouth twisted as if tasting something bitter. "I've never learned what happened to my birthparents. They refuse to discuss the details. Like I told your grandmother, this necklace is my only connection to my birth-mum." She gingerly grasped the tiny bumblebee.

The action made Ellynn grasp at her own book charm. "My necklace used to belong to my mother as well. I would feel naked without it. I can imagine how precious your necklace is to you."

Larkin nodded and gave Ellynn a lopsided smile. "I wondered about that little book. I like that we're both wearing something that belonged to our mums. Makes me feel more, um, normal? I guess. Still, I don't understand your grandmother's reaction to it."

Ellynn gave an agreeable nod. "*So* weird."

With a sigh, Larkin sank into the chair.

After a moment, Ellynn ventured back to the most pressing particulars. "So, what should we do? Personally, I can't sit back and pretend I didn't hear what we heard." She absentmindedly twisted her skirt around her finger, recalling her grandmother's foreboding threat to their families. "And yet, I don't want to endanger our families by saying something."

"Do you really think she has spies everywhere?" Larkin glanced around as if she might catch someone in the act.

Ellynn gave a slow, thoughtful nod. "She definitely has people loyal to her. My guess is that she's exaggerating to scare us."

"What exactly *do* we know? I'm not sure that we have anything specific to report." Larkin leaned her forehead against her palm, causing her long, wavy hair to veil her face.

"Your grandmother feels cheated. Apparently, *I'm* in her way. Yet what does that mean for me? Even if your brother comes home, it doesn't sound like there will be a wedding—not if your grandmother has her way—which is fine with me, and probably your brother too."

Ellynn offered a thumbs-up. "Safe assumption. I'd feel exactly the same, though one day I might not have a say in the matter, either. Princess hazards, right?" Ellynn was hoping to lighten the mood, though Larkin looked lost in thought. Judging by the girl's quavering lips, they were sad thoughts. "You okay?"

Larkin gave a shrug that conveyed numbness and resignation. "I'm not certain I know what okay feels like anymore. I've never had any say or control over my life. Why should this be any different?"

Ellynn didn't know how to respond but hoped a change of subject might help. "Mind if I ask you a question?"

"Sure. Although I might not answer."

"Fair enough." She shifted so her back was against the chair. "You *are* a Topsider, aren't you?"

"Can't fool you," Larkin said with a note of disgust. "Isn't your mum a Topsider? It appears things turned out well enough for her."

"Sure, except she wasn't obligated to marry my dad. They married for love. Long story." Ellynn popped off her shoes and wiggled her toes. "Do you remember anything about life before Brihndle?"

"Nothing. And I'm not the only Topsider in Brihndle—or the rest of Moored-below. I've seen things that muddle the line between adopting and kidnapping, in my opinion. Still, I have no power to do anything about it."

Ellynn nodded. "Right. Especially when the royal family is involved. Can I tell you something?"

Larkin gave a soft chuckle. "I get the impression you're the type to say whatever you want. In a nice way, of course."

Ellynn flushed, aware that she was, as always, overly inquisitive. "Sorry. I...I was only thinking that you're a lot different when you're not with your mother. You're so shy and unsure of yourself around her, but you're easy to talk to now. By the way, that was quick thinking with the upside-down book. Not that we fooled anyone."

"No need to apologize." Larkin twined her fingers together and dropped them in her lap. "Especially since you're right.

It's...it's not easy when my mum has such exacting expectations. Let's just say I don't feel particularly well-suited for them. Being a Topsider among giants—no offense—makes me feel inadequate, regardless of any title."

Ellynn felt a rush of excitement. Larkin and Alex seemed more well-suited by the minute. She swiveled onto her knees, facing the princess, scraped palms reminding her that she needed to move more carefully. "You've no idea how much you've got in common with my brother. He's always getting into trouble for, y'know, not meeting expectations. Plus—well, he might be mad for my telling you this, but...Alex doesn't have any wings. He's a flightless Nephilim."

Larkin's features flitted from surprise to concern to amused.

"Hmm." Larkin quirked a half grin. "I wonder if my royal parents have withheld this from me or if your grandmother withheld that detail from them. Regardless, you heard what she said—she has no intention of there being a wedding. So how should we handle her threats? We can't guess who your grandmother has working for her, but I've no doubt she meant what she told us—she'll remove anything, or anyone, standing in her way."

Ellynn gave a slow nod. "Seems like our choices are to say nothing and let my grandmother push you around and right out of the picture. Or say something to try to prevent her from pushing you around and, potentially, unleash her evil twin on both our families."

"She has an evil twin?" Larkin looked horrified.

Ellynn shook her head and chuckled. "No. That's a topside expression my mom uses. Means there're two sides to my grandmother. Mean and meaner."

"Ah, well, good to know she doesn't have an evil sister locked in a dungeon waiting to feel useful. I've seen enough strange things in Moored-below that it wouldn't surprise me."

"She hasn't always been such an unpleasant grump. She was nice when I was little." Ellynn waved away the memory. "Anyway, those are the options, right? She either comes after you or she comes after you and everyone else. Sheesh."

Larkin expelled a noisy breath. "Sounds like the first option is the safest."

"Safest for me and my family, maybe. What about you?" Ellynn reached a hand to Larkin's knee and gave it squeeze. "Sorry, but we're in this together."

"You're sweet, Ellynn," Larkin said. "But if we don't tell anyone, *I'm* the only one in danger. Of some sort. At least we've been made aware of it—thanks to your idea of sitting in the alcove. That gives me an advantage. If we tell someone, and she finds out and hurts a lot of people, I'll never forgive myself."

Ellynn sat back on her heels and crossed her arms. "If I don't say something, *I'll* never forgive *myself.* Especially if something happens to you and I could've prevented it. We need to tell someone."

"No..." Larkin trailed off, shaking her head thoughtfully. "No, listen. As long as I don't marry your brother, I'm safe. Thinking back, *that* was the crux of the threat towards me. And since he's not here, I'm safe. Even if he returns, I'll refuse, so I'm no threat."

"I don't know. She's obviously been planning her revenge for some time, and the way she acted when she saw your necklace—not a good sign."

"Look, the immediate threat is my marrying your brother." Larkin flushed and kept her gaze averted. "And...my parents didn't exactly come here without an agenda, Ellynn. They have their secrets—secrets they don't realize I'm privy to. As you know, servants talk."

"Like what?"

"I can't risk talking to you any more than we can risk talking to someone about your grandmother. We're all pieces in a political chess game. No one has altruistic motives here."

Ellynn felt overwhelmed by the unfairness of the situation. She stood, hands fisted in protest. "If we keep quiet it only makes it easier for everyone to do their dirty work." She jabbed her finger in the air. "Like a kidnapper who tells you not to scream or they'll hurt you. They're going to hurt you no matter what, but if they can keep you quiet, no one knows what they're doing, which means no one will stop them. So if we speak up, we can spoil everyone's selfish plans. The kidnapper loses."

"Ellynn! Are ya ready fer some tea, dear?" Trinny called through the door.

The girls looked at one another, wide eyed. Ellynn could read Larkin's imploring stare. Should she tell? Should they ride it out? Did Trinny overhear anything? Her palms went clammy as her mind bounced between questions.

Larkin leaned in and whispered, "Let's keep what we

know to ourselves for now. It's safest for all of us. Meanwhile, I'll think on it."

Before Ellynn could respond, the bedroom door swung open and Trinny stood there, holding a tray laden with teacups and a teapot. Behind her stood Tassitus.

Behind him, filling the doorway with his protective presence, stood Ellynn's father.

CHAPTER FORTY-ONE

Alex

"DID YOU SAY SOMETHING?" TYMBRELLE PULLED up short, causing Alex to sidestep to avoid her.

"Quit doing that," he said, smacking his shoulder into the stone passageway.

"Doing what? This is the first time I've stopped since we walked into this giant worm hole."

Between the phosphorescent glow of the granite and the prolific amber geodes sprouting like mushrooms, it wasn't hard to see the annoyed dip of the girl's brow and the impatient set of her jaw.

"Yeah, well, you've no idea how often you slow down, making me trip over myself to avoid stepping on you." Alex glanced at the receding figures of the others. "Let's go."

Tymbrelle huffed and continued walking. "It's not my fault you're twice my size."

"Not my fault you're vertically challenged."

"You two havin' a lover's quarrel back there?" Dempsey called from around a bend.

"That wasn't funny the first time you said it, Demps. Lay off," Alex barked. "Excuse the Dwarf," he added to Tymbrelle. "He's probably jealous. He's used to looking at the kneecaps of most of the ladies in Calamus, so you're closer to his size than most."

Tymbrelle chuckled. "I bet. But, really, what did you say a moment ago?"

"Nothing."

"You must be mumbling to yourself then, because I heard *something*." They walked a few yards when she stopped abruptly once again. "Okay, quit messing with me."

Again, he swerved around the girl. "Roots and fruits! What are you talking about? You're the one tripping me up again."

"I'm not deaf," Tymbrelle said, placing her hands on her hips. "You were perfectly clear this time."

Alex looked her up and down. "Oh, yeah? You mind telling me what I said so I'll recognize it the next time I say it?"

"Murderer!"

This time, they both heard it. Alex gaped at the girl, who reflected his stricken expression.

A beat, and then they both searched the space around them for an intruder. Alex stepped away from Tymbrelle, unsheathing the sword that had once belonged to the Asian Dreg.

"Show yourself!" he yelled, hoping to alert his friends, who had continued on in apparent oblivion.

"Murderer!" The voice seemed to come from everywhere in the acoustics of the tunnel. *"You are a murderer."*

"I was only protecting us from being attacked by you Dregs!" Tymbrelle said, her gaze flitting about and finding no one.

Alex signaled for her to get behind him. "Same here. Those traitorous Nephilim attacked us first. Now show yourself and fight like a man." Alex made a slow circle, sword at the ready, keeping Tymbrelle tucked behind him with his other arm. Where were his guys?

"I'm not talking about *today*, Prince Brady," hissed the nasally, disembodied voice. "I'm talking about your very nature. You are not the first-born son of the first-born son, are you?"

A Leprechaun!

"All right, *Leprechaun.* Show yourself, since you're feeling brave enough to sling such insults at the heir to the Calamus throne." Alex hoped he had more conviction in his words than he felt in his heart concerning his princely rights.

A snicker. *"Ooh.* You got me. But not as well as I've got you, murderer. You can't really be blamed for what happened at birth, I suppose. Now what you did to your Uncle Barron—*that* took guts for a nine-year-old kid. Needed to rid yourself of any competition it would seem."

Behind him, Alex felt Tymbrelle stiffen.

"Shut up!" Alex yelled. "I'm not going to defend my actions to a Leprechaun."

"No?" This time the evil chuckle was joined by a menacing chorus of snickering voices. "How about a *host* of Leprechauns?"

Suddenly the passageway filled with the diminutive bodies of the treasonous, trickster creatures. Ceilings, walls, and floor flashed with the glint of their blades as they clung to crevices and stood atop large geodes. Their bearded faces etched a dark, menacing contrast to the whites of their eyes and sheen of their pointy teeth—some snarling, some smiling hungrily.

Alex swallowed hard, his mind reeling through a short list of possible escape scenarios. He might be ten times their size, but he couldn't take on fifty of the little demons. Farther down the tunnel, he heard the sound of ringing metal and shouts associated with combat. It would seem the others had found themselves in a similar situation, though he liked their combined chances better than his own.

"Here's how this is going to go down," the original voice explained.

It took Alex a moment to distinguish which of the creatures was doing the talking. He finally spotted an older, fox-faced fellow sitting on a ledge of rock, casually cleaning his thumbnail with a small dagger. His pointy features framed a cynical smirk. He waited for Alex to notice him and gave a little nod.

"The Overlord wants the girl," the Leprechaun explained. "He said to tell you that your time will come. It seems he wants to reserve *that* pleasure for himself. For now, you send the girl with us and we'll leave you and your friends to scurry away, life and limbs intact."

The clang of swords grew fainter. Alex assumed that driving his friends farther into the tunnel must be part of the vermin's strategy.

"Ouch!" Tymbrelle jerked against Alex and he spun, keeping her pressed to his back. Several Leprechauns, daggers drawn, clung to the wall.

"Got her!" one of them said, lifting his blade to reveal a dark smudge of liquid on its tip.

A quick well-practiced flick of Alex's sword knocked the dagger from the offending Leprechaun's grasp. The twerp's eyes grew wide, especially after the tip of Alex's weapon circled back to his face.

From above and below, the Leprechauns nearest to Alex shifted his way, their needle-like blades precariously close to head, neck, legs, and feet.

"Don't be as stupid as you are flightless," the fox-faced

fellow said. "Drop your blade, step away from the girl, and—"

"*Ahhh!*"

A pained cry carried from deep within the tunnel. Was that Dempsey? Alex's heart hammered angrily, fueled by a fresh and infinite repugnance for Magnum. This wouldn't end well.

Amid the gleam of the geodes and the phosphorous granite, Alex hadn't noticed when his birthmark began to glow, but there it was. Blooming brighter as fury coursed through him.

"Ah, the famous glowing face-target!" Fox-face giggled. "So glad I get to see that with my own eyes. You *are* a freak of nature, exactly like the Overlord said."

Rage clawed through Alex. Magnum had belittled him and, usually, bested him their entire lives. Now he'd spread his poisonous hatred to these Dregs to make insulting Alex an all-inclusive pastime.

Alex reacted with the only option he could summon.

Grasping Tymbrelle's arm, he yanked her in front of his body and held his sword to her throat. "I'll kill the girl myself if you don't call off your gang right this minute."

CHAPTER FORTY-TWO

Alex

"Alex! What are you—"

"Shut up, Tymbrelle!" Alex ordered. "If Magnum thinks you're so valuable, then he'll spare us all to save you."

"C'mon now, freak-face. You expect me to believe you're willing to hurt your little girlfriend to test your uncle?" the Leprechaun asked.

"She's not my girlfriend. In fact, she's only been a liability since she showed up uninvited. Besides, I am, indeed, a murderer. No sense denying it." Alex pressed Tymbrelle's wriggling body against himself. He leaned in and snarled, "Be still!"

She made a sound of disgust but calmed herself. "This is how you thank me for saving you and your sorry friends?"

"I think you're bluffing." Fox-face hopped onto a nearby chunk of rock, waggling his weapon at Alex and the girl. Blades glinted all around, reflecting the ambient light in a constellation of aggression.

"You willing to bet on that?" Alex shifted his free hand from Tymbrelle's shoulder to her chin, jerking her head up to expose the pale column of her neck to the edge of the blade. He took a step toward the mouthy Leprechaun. "What's it going to be, huh? How much does my uncle value this water magician? I get the last word, this time."

Fox-face only narrowed his greedy-eyed glare. "If you're willing to kill the girl to get away, then why not give her to me, fool? You'll be on your way without her blood on your hands, and your uncle gets what he wants."

Tymbrelle huffed against Alex's chest, breathing hard and sobbing quietly. "Don't do this, Alex. Listen to him. Let me go with him, and we'll both walk away from here."

"Shut up!" Alex dragged his clammy hand up from her

chin, pressing it across her mouth. Strength surged through him, and he trembled to keep it in check. "You're assuming it would bother me to walk away with her blood on my hands. What's one more death to me, huh?"

The Leprechaun's smug look faltered, and Alex pressed the advantage. "I am finished with giving Magnum what he wants. This water-witch is my insurance that I get what *I* want for once. So take your minions and get the hades out of here. After you tell my psycho uncle the bad news, make sure to let him know that his father, King Aviel, died last week. Sent to an early grave by his selfish, ungrateful son."

Tymbrelle whimpered. Alex could still make out the distant sound of the others engaged with more of the pint-sized henchmen. His heart thudded. Thoughts scrambled for clarity. The only thing he knew for sure was that he couldn't— wouldn't—let his uncle push him around for one more moment.

Tymbrelle's legs buckled and she slipped, causing the sword to slash into her neck—superficially, Alex felt certain.

"Stand up!" he snapped. If he hadn't been pressing her so tightly against himself, and had she slipped any harder or farther, it would have been disastrous.

She yelped against his hand, then found her footing. His glance flitted to a bloody rivulet that meandered the length of the inclined sword blade toward his white-knuckled grip on the hilt.

Fox-face looked unsure, eyes darting from Alex's face to the bloodied sword to his fellow hooligans.

"You really want to mess with me?" Alex asked, his voice a vicious shout in the stony acoustics. "I'm happy to prove that my uncle isn't the only ruthless, crazed tyrant in the family!"

Alex felt what he guessed to be wet, warm tears dripping onto his hand. Tymbrelle attempted to shake her head *no,* but he pressed her head against his chest. She gave a feral growl.

Fox-face held Alex's gaze. His birthmark surged, blurring his periphery. Sounds from down the passageway made both of them glance to where several Leprechauns sprinted into their midst. Their patchwork jackets were torn, one had a sleeve ripped off revealing a gash on his forearm. Several more Leprechauns rushed in from behind, bloodied and bruised, as the sound of heavy footfalls echoed from deeper in the tunnel.

Pandemonium rippled through the ranks of Leprechauns as their anxious and pulverized counterparts poured into the corridor, shouting in alarm.

Alex couldn't make sense of what was happening or why. The atmosphere shifted from menacing to panic-stricken. He kept his grip on Tymbrelle and backed into the granite wall as the Leprechauns around him leapt to the ground. They were a blur of uncoordinated limbs for a moment, as they shouted and ran back and forth.

Grateful for the diversion, he dipped his head near Tymbrelle's ear. "I won't hurt you, but they need to believe that I will."

If the girl replied, her answer was lost in the tempestuous chatter that ricocheted through the stone cylinder.

Alex couldn't decipher the reason for their fear. Should he be afraid as well? The loud smack of footsteps—large ones—reverberated in his chest. Had they stumbled into a dragon's lair and awakened the beast?

In a moment, he had his answer.

As Leprechauns scattered, leaving Tymbrelle listing against him, a lumbering Ogre emerged. He swiped and kicked at the skittering Leprechauns, who were doing their best to outrun each other, not hesitating to push a fellow Leprechaun into harm's way to further their own escape.

Fox-face stepped into the fray and shouted orders and expletives at his comrades, none of whom seemed to be listening. Alex lost sight of him in the flood of frenetic activity.

As if collectively remembering their unique superpower, the clambering Leprechauns flickered out of sight in random succession. The sound of their footfalls continued to scuttle and dash away as they yowled and cursed at each other at full volume.

Alex lowered the sword from the girl's throat, ready to thrust it at the approaching Neanderthal. By the murky light of the tunnel, the enormous Ogre revealed himself to be none other than Babel, the odiferous oaf from Magnum's citadel. He appeared to be enjoying his game of Leprechaun pinball, swiping at the air, kicking at the ground, and occasionally connecting with one of the fleeing, unseen creatures by sheer luck.

Alex had the strange impression that if he remained still and silent, the galumphing giant would lumber right past. As the Leprechauns' footsteps and voices petered out, Alex hoped the Ogre would keep following them right out of the tunnel.

But he did not.

As the last of the shrieking Leprechauns faded away, Babel stopped his rampage, having just tramped past Alex and Tymbrelle. He turned and zeroed in on them, making it clear that he had been aware of their presence all along. Alex swallowed and pointed his sword at the brute, a small part of his mind registering that something about the Ogre had changed—he no longer smelled like a bumper crop of rancid garlic.

A noisy shuffle came from the depth of the tunnel, where Babel had appeared from minutes before. Josiah, Finn, Dempsey, and Spock shambled out, looking weary yet wonderfully alive.

Alex, emboldened by their presence, pointed his sword at the giant. "Out of our way, Ogre! You're outnumbered."

The Ogre blinked at Alex, looking at the sword as if he'd never laid eyes on such an object.

"Alex!" Finn said. "It's okay. *He's* okay. He's on our side."

Alex didn't move. Finn wasn't making sense.

"Fwend," Babel said, in a bullfrog croak.

Alex kept his sword at the ready, glancing at Finn, who had trotted ahead of the others.

"He saved us back there," Finn said breathlessly. "We were overwhelmed by the bearded rodents. Babel came along and started clearing house. He only targeted the Leprechauns, helping us drive them back."

Alex looked from Finn to Babel to the others coming up behind Finn, bruised and raw. Dempsey gripped his left bicep. Blood oozed between his fingers.

Alex blinked, his adrenaline plummeting into a bone-tired relief. He let his sword clank to the stone floor and glanced down at Tymbrelle. He still grasped her mouth and chin in his left hand, stiff and sweaty. Her eyes met his, accusing and wounded, her face an unusual hue of pale violet by light of the geodes. He looked, wide-eyed from her glare to his fingers, a ripple of nausea contorting his stomach.

Stepping away, Alex released her, grasping his wrist with his right hand, looking at his left palm as if it had acted without his knowledge. Tymbrelle stumbled into Finn, gulping in lungfuls of air.

Alex's face slackened and he took another step backward, bumping into the wall. Tymbrelle stared at him, brimming with disdain. She held his gaze as her fingertips probed the sticky, red gash at her neck.

"I—I'm sorry." Alex rasped. He stretched his hand toward the stricken girl. "I didn't—didn't mean to... I'm *so* sorry."

Babel stepped toward them, wringing his fat, sweaty digits like a nervous child. "Fwend," he repeated, though everyone remained riveted on Alex's meltdown.

Alex curled his hand into a fist and pressed it against his mouth, sinking to his knees. He had nearly suffocated Tymbrelle. Had bullied her to comply as he bluffed his way through the situation with no consideration for her and no thought of his past, appalling actions.

Was he some sort of sociopath? Was unintentional killing an intrinsic part of him—as uncontrollable and twisted as his glowing birthmark? A lifetime of overheard accusations and self-condemnation clouded his mind, as dark and dangerous as a topside tornado. Alex wasn't worthy of these friends, let alone his royal lineage.

A torrent of shame pummeled him. Gut-wrenching sobs surfaced from eight years of pressed down, dammed up, and denied emotions. Their horrific, haunted cry echoed through the granite chamber.

CHAPTER FORTY-THREE

Ellynn

"Dad!" Ellynn took an unconscious step back, unsure if she could keep Larkin's secret under the weight of her father's imploring stare.

Trinny ushered Tassitus and Ellynn's father inside and set about pouring cups of tea. The two men made a beeline for the girls.

Larkin's timid disposition descended like a veil, somehow diminishing her even as she stood to receive their guests. "King Xander." Larkin offered a small curtsy.

Ellynn's father nodded. "Please, take a seat."

Tassitus dragged another chair and ottoman near to the fireplace.

Her dad took a seat and gestured at the wingback that flanked the hearth opposite Larkin. "Join us, Ellynn."

Ellynn swallowed and sat, unsure of what might come out of her mouth. She watched Tassitus perch on the ottoman, happy to distract herself by looking anywhere other than her father's piercing blue eyes. Though she possessed a matching set of irises, her dad's frosty gaze never failed to unnerve her. The incongruence of those eyes set against his deep caramel skin, his mass of black braids, and his broad shoulders assured Ellynn that her own pearly blues would never have quite the intimidating effect on others.

Trinny brought a cup and saucer to Larkin, who accepted them without comment. She held them in front of her face as she had during brunch.

Ellynn followed suit when Trinny offered her a cup.

"Would ya like me to wait outside, Yer Majesty?" Trinny asked.

"Perhaps in the hallway?" Ellynn's father replied. "Don't go far. We may need a woman's touch."

Trinny curtsied and scooted out of the room.

"Tassitus tells me that you looked quite distressed when he saw you and Princess Larkin earlier. Grandmama Lucia appeared to have you cornered. Is everything okay?" Her father looked from Ellynn to Larkin and back.

Ellynn took a lengthy sip of tea, aware that her hand was trembling. Before she could muster a satisfying response, Larkin surprised her by speaking up.

"Ellynn was standing up for me." Larkin's voice sounded tinny and tremulous.

"*Right.*" Ellynn gushed. Wait, was she?

"Why was that?" Her dad leaned into the space between them. "What was said that left you looking terrorized"—he tipped his head toward Tassitus—"according to Tassitus here?"

Tassitus leveled his gaze on Ellynn, his lips pressed so that his square jaw flexed and looked boxier than ever. "C'mon, kiddo. Your body language screamed for help. What was really going on?"

"Um..." Ellynn glanced at Larkin, conflicted about how to answer. Should she keep their secret?

Larkin lowered her cup and saucer, clearing her throat. "Ellynn's grandmother made her feelings about me quite clear. They weren't particularly flattering."

"I didn't get the impression that Queen Lucia was standing there merely to insult you, Princess Larkin, though I don't doubt that she's willing to freely share her opinions," Tassitus said, his eyes kind. He looked back to Ellynn. "I had the distinct impression that your grandmother was threatening you in some way."

Since it wasn't a question, did he require a response? Ellynn's heart revved as she rehearsed the very real threats her grandmother had made. How could Ellynn agree to help that awful woman keep such secrets?

"Look," Xander said, spreading his fingers palms up. "Tassitus had just explained what he happened upon—to the best of his knowledge—when Trinny crossed my path. She told us about Larkin crying. And about what *you* so disrespectfully said to her, Ellynn Jules." He pointed at his daughter and gave a disappointed shake of his head. "If I ever hear of anything similar coming out of your mouth, you'll wish you'd been born mute. Got it?"

Ellynn gave a hurried, guilty nod. A fresh wave of self-disgust washed over her, and a tear plunged down her cheek.

"So." Her father sat back and crossed his arms, studying the girls. "I don't have all day. There's a kingdom to run and royal guests to entertain, as you well know. However, I'm happy to give Tassitus the day off to sit here and wait on the truth if that's what it takes. Sooner or later it will be exposed. So let's make it sooner, shall we?"

Larkin exchanged a nervous glance with Ellynn, who thought she saw determination in Larkin's stormy green eyes.

"This is a personal matter," Princess Larkin said, her voice steadier and stronger. "Although I appreciate your concern, King Xander, I've asked Ellynn to keep the matter to herself. I'd appreciate it if you'd respect that."

Xander and Tassitus looked at each other and exchanged a subtle eyebrow quirk, which Ellynn had seen them share on many occasions.

"Very well." Xander gave the princess a hesitant nod. "I suppose it would be rude to insist my daughter divulge something you've expressly asked her to keep in confidence." He leaned forward again, elbows on his knees. "However. If you two have knowledge of something that may put you or others in danger..."

He let the sentence dangle there, looking at Larkin until she squirmed, twisting her hands in her lap.

"If you feel threatened in any way, you must speak up," Tassitus added, finishing Xander's sentence. "Don't wait for someone to stumble across a situation like I did today. Next time there may not be anyone around to intervene."

Xander nodded in agreement. "You're certain there's nothing you wish to tell us?"

Ellynn swallowed and didn't meet his gaze. This was, ultimately, Larkin's call. She would stick by the girl's decision for as long as it seemed to make sense.

"Nothing," Larkin said. "Thank you for your concern."

Xander stood. "Very well. I'll see you ladies at dinner." He turned and headed for the door.

Tassitus offered a curt bow and followed.

When the door closed, Ellynn let out a noisy breath. She glanced at Larkin.

Larkin gave a nervous, tight-lipped smile, seemingly pleased with herself. "Well!" She lifted her teacup toward Ellynn in a gesture of salute. "Our secret remains safe. Thank you for keeping it."

Ellynn halfheartedly lifted her teacup in response. If this was truly the right thing to do, why did she suddenly feel so sick?

CHAPTER FORTY-FOUR

Alex

THE ACHE IN ALEX'S HEART FELT as fresh and raw as though some beast had clawed through his chest to expose the throbbing, meaty muscle.

Maybe it had. Maybe Alex himself was the beast.

Still on his knees, he unfurled his fingers and stared at his rigid, splayed hands. Hands that had killed once. Hands that seemed to have their own muscle-memory, ready to unwittingly do it again. Dual images asserted themselves.

His hand on Tymbrelle's mouth. Covering, smothering.

His hand on Uncle Barron's mouth. Covering, smothering...suffocating, killing. Barron deflating against Alex's body so suddenly. One moment, curious and trilling with laughter. The next, limp and listless.

Alex looked at Tymbrelle's questioning face, scouring it for assurance that she was, indeed, okay. That she was alive and breathing. That he hadn't snuffed out the girl's fierce spirit the way he'd snuffed out Barron's buoyant soul.

Confusion and concern now softened Tymbrelle's edge of anger. She took a tentative step, as if approaching a wounded animal. Alex's tear-blurred vision broadened to take in the others and found anxious consternation reflected in each.

A harrowing specter suddenly materialized beside Tymbrelle. Alex's eyes went wide as Uncle Barron's swaying body stood in silent accusation, eyes rolled back to reveal their eggy whiteness, mouth open in a silent, final gasp.

No! It wasn't possible. Alex swiped at his eyes with the back of his hands. He blinked and willed the haunting apparition to disappear. It did not.

"What do you want?" Alex shouted, scrabbling onto unsteady legs. "Why are you here?"

"Alex."

Someone spoke his name. Was that Barron? Could the dead speak to the living?

"*Alex.*" Finn waved his arms in the space between them.

Alex blinked at his friends, who were converging on him. Everyone except Tymbrelle moved to surround him with reassuring arms and words. Tymbrelle remained rooted, mismatched eyes scrutinizing, puzzling out his behavior.

Where was Barron? Alex scanned those clustered around him, but Barron was not among the living. Never had been.

Alex couldn't breathe. He needed air. He needed to be alone. His friends didn't know what he was capable of. The subject had always been off limits.

Alex knew. He knew his secrets. He knew they were better off without him. Safer, for certain.

With a clumsy effort, he struggled to his feet. Finn and Josiah attempted to steady him from either side. He shrugged them off. "I—I need to go." He shook his head and stepped away from his friends. "You guys never should've come with me. Just...just go back to Calamus."

"You're not running away *again*, are you?" Tymbrelle stepped between Alex and the passageway.

He glared at the intrepid girl, his glance darting from her face to her blood-smeared neck. "So the runaway is going to lecture me about running away? That's rich."

Tymbrelle crossed her arms and cocked her head. "Actually, I'm running toward something. I want to go home— a place I've been kept from against my will. You are running *from* home. Except you're really running from your past. Certainly from yourself. That's a race you're going to lose every time."

Alex staggered backward. Her words—their truth— winded him. He felt the weight of that truth and, suddenly, it exhausted him. He reached for the tunnel wall and leaned against it without breaking eye contact with Tymbrelle. How had she understood his problem with such pinpoint precision? Alex felt as if a bandage had been ripped away, exposing an ugly and festering wound. A wound that really needed to be aired out in order to heal.

Could he do that? Did he dare go there?

What about the other truth he and Tymbrelle shared? Their first encounter the night of the meteor was another subject Alex had been running from.

Alex released a lengthy, disconsolate sigh and grabbed a

fistful of dreads. It felt like all the fight—or maybe it was the *flight*—had gone out of him. He looked at his friends. Friends who had stuck by him without ever truly knowing what happened to Barron eight years earlier. Probably left to believe some twisted version of the truth, thanks to palace gossip.

Beaten, bruised, and filthy faces looked back with a mixture of expectancy and uncertainty. Including one new face whom Alex wouldn't exactly call a friend but who seemed to need a "fwend."

Spock had already made himself comfortable on the big Ogre's shoulder.

"Guess it's time I told you guys what really happened to my uncle Barron." Alex sat on a rocky ledge, lowering himself on legs as unsteady as his voice.

He noticed the others cycle through a quick series of glances, revealing a flash of bridled disbelief. No doubt they had expected a lifetime ban on this subject. Beyond this subtle exchange no one so much as flinched, as if they feared he might change his mind lest they move.

Alex looked away, disliking what he read on their faces. He suddenly felt very worn and very old. Was he really only seventeen? The weight of a lifetime of failure must have aged him exponentially on the inside. He was heavy and depleted, deep into his marrow. It would crush him if he didn't free himself from the weight of it.

"My father took us camping." Alex decided to launch the boat before he changed his mind. "Barron and Magnum and me. They were my dad's half-brothers, but he had always been more like an uncle to them because, you know, he's old. King Aviel started a second family about the same time my dad began his own."

Tymbrelle was the first to settle onto the stone floor, elbows encircling her knees. She caught Alex's eye and gave him an encouraging nod. As if her movement broke some sort of spell, Finn moved to kneel beside Dempsey and set about tearing a piece of fabric from his own cape to use as a bandage on the Dwarf's bleeding bicep.

Alex sailed on. "The three of us were so close in age, we were the ones like siblings. We certainly played and fought with each other like brothers. Barron was the oldest. Although he had nearly three years on me, I always had a couple of inches on him. Something to do with his being premature and always kind of sickly left him small for his age. Which of course roused the bully in Magnum—he's always one to sniff out the weak and vulnerable, as you know. Which meant Barron and I hung out, avoiding Magnum as much as possible."

Alex waited as the others sat on the ground or leaned onto hunks of protruding rock, shadows playing unflattering games on their curious faces by light of the luminescent cave. It brought to mind the molten embers of the campfire from that awful night eight years earlier.

Allowing his memories to drift back there, untethered, felt terrifying. He had constructed such a careful barrier around that event—a minefield of memories that he no longer allowed himself to tread across. After it happened, he spent the following year in self-inflicted torture, reliving that moment to change the outcome. He finally had to nail up a No Trespassing sign and avoid it altogether.

Could he venture back across that boundary and survive?

"Barron and I would have preferred ditching Magnum," Alex went on, his gaze returning to the ground between his feet. "I think my dad believed he could teach Magnum some manners and respect, since those things were no longer enforced in King Aviel's old age, and certainly not by Lucia. They were both overly protective of Barron's frailty while being way too dismissive of Magnum's bullying behavior."

"Guess it's safe t'say none of those manners ever sunk into Magnum's thick skull," Dempsey said, lifting his arm to inspect Finn's handiwork.

"Obviously not," Alex replied. "Though when he was around my father, Magnum was on his best behavior. That's the only thing that made these outings bearable. Of course, that didn't mean Barron and I welcomed him into our confidence. We still kept an us-versus-him mentality whenever Magnum was near."

"Pretty much the way it is whenever we're all hanging out." Josiah scooped up a handful of pebbles and began to toss them at a glowing geode protruding from the cave wall opposite where he sat.

"Yep," Alex agreed. "So, anyway, my dad built this nice campfire. We roasted fish that we'd caught in the stream and fell asleep listening to one of my dad's tales."

Dempsey moaned at the mention of fish, but Alex ignored him. "Something woke me up. I've no idea what. Sleeping outside always comes with strange noises. I lay there, close to dozing off again, when I heard something very peculiar."

Alex could read the curiosity on his friends' faces. He wasn't sure if he was doing the right thing by building the suspense. This was not a story with a happy ending.

"I heard someone *singing*. Somewhere deep in the woods, a good distance from our campsite, someone was flat-out singing, heart and soul." Alex could remember the strange, almost haunting sensation as the faint song reached his ears. "I sat up on my elbow, wondering if I was imagining it. That's when I noticed that Magnum wasn't on his sleeping pallet. I assumed he had heard the voice too and went to investigate, but I wanted to know what was going on for myself. I woke Barron with a finger to his lips and signaled for us to sneak away in search of the crooner. The closer we came to the sound, the clearer it became that Magnum was the one singing his lungs out."

Alex recalled the moment when he and Barron realized that Magnum and the midnight singer were one and the same. "Barron and I looked at each other in shock. We started laughing so hard I thought we both might have an accident. We were still a good ways off at this point and were careful not to bust our guts too loudly. We didn't want to alert Magnum and spoil the concert."

"Magnum, singing." Finn shook his head. "I really can't picture it, kid or not."

Alex gestured at Finn and nodded. "Exactly. Which is why we had to see it for ourselves. We got ourselves under control and crept closer. From between the branches of a downed tree we could see him standing on this big slab of granite we'd passed earlier in the day. It made a perfect stage. Magnum held a broken limb like a microphone—having watched enough of my mother's old movies with me over the years, I suppose."

Spock grabbed the beanie off his head and smacked it against his other hand. "What I wouldn't give to have been a faery on a flower and seen this for myself."

"We crept pretty close, staying behind the protruding limbs, keeping out of sight. It was dusktime, of course, so there was barely enough light to make out details, while being dark enough for us to keep concealed in the shadows of tree branches." Alex felt his heart thump hard and heavy against his ribs as he recalled what happened next. "Except Barron wouldn't quit laughing. He could be like that. Once he got started, it tended to keep bubbling up until he was crying for laughing so hard. Usually I laughed right along with him, but I knew he was about to give us away and our fun would be over. So, I...well, I..."

There was no easy, off-handed way for Alex to explain what happened next. He swallowed, squeezing his eyes shut against the all-too clear picture he carried in his mind. "I grabbed Barron. I covered his mouth with my hand and pressed him against my side to keep him from shrugging me off and collapsing in a heap of giggles as he was prone to do. When Magnum finally finished his song, I released Barron so we could clap. So we could, you know, embarrass the pants off him. But Barron slumped over in front of me. He didn't move. He..."

Alex looked up at his friends, his eyes darting from one to the other, his hands cupped in front of his chest as if showing them how empty he felt. "He was slumped. And he didn't move. And he wasn't breathing. I had, somehow"—tears blurred Alex's vision as he stared at his empty hands and turned them over, inspecting them front and back—"I had smothered him. Suffocated him. He'd been trying to grab my hand away from his mouth, and I had just pressed him harder and harder against me, determined to let Magnum finish his song before we made a peep and..."

Alex pressed his empty palms to his face and dropped his head with a loud sob. "I killed him."

CHAPTER FORTY-FIVE

Sadie

SADIE NUDGED XANDER WITH HER FOOT for the umpteenth time. He snored terribly when he was exhausted, which kept his equally exhausted wife from sleeping at all. A beastly snort had startled her from sleep sometime earlier. Now Sadie sat propped against several pillows, rechargeable book light aglow, and a well-worn copy of *The Princess Bride* resting on her lap.

Xander responded to her nudge by shifting his body, which only cranked his snore volume by several jolting notches.

Sadie shook her head and whispered a theatrical "Inconceivable!" before slipping out of bed, pillow clutched beneath her arm, reading material abandoned on the bedside table. She padded to the sitting room and arranged herself on the velvet divan, grabbing the quilt she'd left draped across it for these frequent occasions.

Pulling the quilt to her chin, she thought about the disastrous day, glad to bid it good riddance. After the brunchy brouhaha between Queen Clodagh and Lucia...and after hearing how both Tassitus and Trinny had encountered a very shaken pair of teenage girls...Queen Clodagh and King Odhran claimed travel-lag and took dinner in their quarters, avoiding Pacific House entirely.

The atmosphere in the palace felt thick with tension and mistrust—not the ideal ingredients for festive occasions. The possible nuptials were fragile at best, and that was probably *for* the best. Sadie cringed to imagine Alex stuck in forced courting conversations with the painfully shy and incredibly bland Larkin.

Perhaps it would prove providential that he had run off. Meanwhile, what was that conniving Lucia up to? What had she realistically expected from her estranged family once they were under the same roof? Why had she been in favor of this betrothal in the first place?

So many unanswered questions. Sadie wished her sister Sophie were here to discuss them together. Her younger sister was clever and fearless—which, of course, made her an excellent right-hand woman for their quiet, contemplative brother Brock, High King of Vituvia. His intuitive autism and Sophie's gregarious personality provided a perfect partnership of wisdom and grace for the realm. But sometimes Sadie really needed her sister. Either sister, really. Except Nicole lived topside, even farther out of reach.

Sadie yawned and snuggled into her pillow, when a soft rumble from outside the main door pricked her ears. The night guard, Hartwell, was speaking to someone. Merrik, by the sound of it.

"...all three of them, reins dragging in the dirt," Merrik was saying. "But no Brady Alexander and friends. They're still missing."

Sadie was on her feet and pulling the door open before Merrik could continue. Both he and Hartwell startled in surprise.

"Your Majesty," Merrik said. He and the other guard shot to attention before offering a curt bow.

"Gentlemen." Sadie nodded, suddenly aware that she must be quite the vision of bedhead and rumpled pajamas. She folded her arms across her chest and rubbed at her biceps self-consciously.

"Are you in need of something, Your Grace? Are you unwell?" Hartwell asked in his soft, resonant voice.

"Uh, no." Sadie shook her head. "I was, y'know, sleeping in the parlor because Xander is snoring. I heard you mention Brady—er—Alex?"

Merrik dipped his head. "Yes, my queen. Sorry to have awakened you."

"It's fine. I wasn't asleep. Please, tell me your news."

"Well..." Merrik trailed off and hitched his shoulder. "It's not much. Only the horses returned. No riders. One of them— in fact, it was your horse, Sage—had an arrow tangled in her mane. No harm to the animal, thank the Maker."

Sadie covered her mouth with her hand. Had Alex been shot off the back of one of the horses? Had he and his friends been attacked and now lay wounded—or worse—somewhere?

Merrik grimaced, seeming to read her troubled thoughts.

"There's no way to predict what this means, Your Highness. Please don't jump to any conclusions."

Sadie nodded, unconvinced. She lowered her hand and put on a brave face. "Is there anything else?"

Merrik and Hartwell exchanged a fleeting glance.

"Actually, there is." Merrik's mouth pressed into a flat, unhappy line.

Sadie steeled herself. Middle of the night news was never good—with the exception of healthy newborns.

"King Odhran and Queen Clodagh are ill. I summoned Gouldor for them earlier. They were, um...regurgitating their supper," Merrik said. "I'm afraid they're accusing us—or, at least, *someone* here—of poisoning them."

Sadie exhaled loudly and shook her head. "Oh, lovely. Those poor people." Sadie glanced back at her bedroom upon hearing a telltale groan. "Let me wake Xander. He needs to know. You two wait here."

Before the heavy door closed, a prickly sweat crept across her scalp. From the bedroom came wave upon wave of moans, each billowing louder and longer than the last.

"*Neverrr...*"

Sadie dashed inside, hoping she could wake Xander from yet another fever-dream without needing to call the men standing guard. Xander did not want anyone to know that he now suffered from the same fate that killed his father.

"Xander!" Sadie gave his shoulders a firm shake. "Wake up, babe. It's only a dream."

"I said I won't do it!" Xander swiped his arm up from beneath the quilt and whacked it across her shoulder, flinging Sadie onto the floor. She landed hard, the air expelled from her lungs.

Rasping wheezes gripped her chest as Sadie fought for breath and to remain calm. Her back ached from how she'd landed, even as she writhed across the floor wrangling for air. A loud, whooshing "*Aww-huh,*" blasted from her throat as her lungs finally expanded.

Merrik and Hartwell rushed into the room right as Sadie rolled onto her side, coughing and gasping. Both had their swords at the ready as they converged, gazes scouring the space for an intruder.

"Help Xander," Merrik barked, coming to kneel beside Sadie, lifting her upright. "What happened m'lady? Were you attacked?"

Sadie's oxygen-starved groan morphed into a cynical giggle. "You could say that." She leaned on Merrik and got to her feet, pointing at the culprit in bed.

Hartwell had Xander pinned beneath his own massive frame. The two were near-equal in stature. "Wake up, Your Majesty! That's it. Open your eyes. It's only a dream."

"Get off of me!" Xander ordered.

The guard released his grip and stood, looking at Xander warily.

Outside, the skydome had sifted dawn into the room by degrees, revealing Xander's deep caramel skin, slick with sweat. He sat up, the blanket pooling around his waist, bare chest heaving. Since the onset of the dreams, he slept without a nightshirt as the apt-named illness brought on intermittent fevers. Now he blinked at the audience of three who blinked back at him.

His brows twitched together when he met Sadie's gaze. "Was I having another—"

"Bad dream," she finished for him, nodding. "Yes. A nightmare." She sat beside him on the bed. "I couldn't wake you. Thankfully these two came to my aid."

She glanced at Merrik with a pointed *leave-it-at-that* sort of look. Xander would never forgive himself for tossing Sadie to the ground.

The gruff soldier nodded. "Must've been a nasty one. You okay, Your Highness?"

"Yes," Xander said, a little too forcefully. He looked from Merrik to the guard. "Why are both of you standing guard tonight?"

Merrik took two steps forward. "I was not on duty, Sire. I had merely come to deliver some news when we heard you cry out."

"News?"

Sadie touched the small of her husband's back. "The horses returned. Without Alex or the others, unfortunately."

Xander looked at her. "And how do you know that, if you were in bed?"

Sweet mother of Sasquatch. Sadie did *not* feel like explaining that just now. "Because I was in the parlor. You were snoring." She waved a hand at the air. "Doesn't matter. I overheard Merrik talking to Hartwell, and then you cried out. They came in to help wake you."

Xander's silver-blue eyes probed Sadie's chocolate ones.

"Did I hurt you?" His voice was low.

She winked. "I'm fine."

He held her stare a moment then nodded. "So...no Alexander. And no sign of his friends?" He looked at Merrik again.

Merrik shook his head. "No. Only the horses making their way home from wherever they had been. Sage had an arrow tangled in her mane, but it only grazed her withers. They were in otherwise good shape."

"An arrow?" Xander slid from beneath the covers and stood, his drawstring pajamas twisted around his hips. "I want to have a look."

Merrik glanced at Hartwell. "Fetch the arrow from Commander Gage. He was in the stables last I saw him."

"I'll go to the stables myself," Xander said, heading to his wardrobe. "I'd like to see the condition of the horses."

"I've more news to deliver, Your Grace," Merrik said. "Allow Hartwell to retrieve the arrow, if you don't mind. I assure you, Ansyn and the others look no worse for the wear."

Xander stopped walking and slowly turned to Merrik. "Very well."

Hartwell saluted and trotted from the room.

Merrik watched him leave and then turned to Xander.

"Well?" Xander asked.

Sadie closed her eyes and sank back onto Xander's pillow, feeling the leftover warmth of his body seeping through her pajamas. If only she could doze off and wake up when all these problems had resolved themselves.

"Before I get into that, I need to ask you something, Your Majesty. Please be honest with me."

Sadie cracked open her eyelids and studied Merrik who now looked at Xander, grim-faced.

"What is it?" Xander growled.

Merrik's chest expanded beneath his leather jerkin. He glanced up, then refocused on Xander. "Are you—are you having fever dreams like your father?"

CHAPTER FORTY-SIX

Ellynn

PANIC AND CONFUSION DREW ELLYNN FROM a deep sleep. Someone's hand smothered her mouth and their unyielding arm pressed around her torso, pinning her own arms to her side. Ellynn kicked and arched her back the instant her mind registered her predicament.

"*Shhh!*" It was a command to cooperate, not a plea to calm down.

The paltry light that filtered through Ellynn's window illuminated the severe angles of Katheryn's face. Ellynn stared into the lady-in-waiting's aloof eyes, able to read their cold, forbidding warning despite the low light. The woman was strong. Her hand a clamp over Ellynn's mouth, her arm an iron strap around Ellynn's middle. At least Ellynn's nose was exposed, allowing her to breathe.

She stilled, looking back at Katheryn with contempt.

"That's right. You are at *my* mercy," Katheryn whispered, her tone scolding, as if Ellynn had transgressed in some way by her mere existence. "I'm only here to make a point. I've already paid a visit to your little friend Larkin."

Ellynn bit back a gasp, fearing she'd failed to protect Larkin by agreeing to keep their secret.

"I'm going to tell you the same thing I told her." Katheryn leaned in closer. "In case you were wondering whether your grandmama was exaggerating, hear this—we know you spoke to your father and Tassitus. We also know that you and the girl wisely held your tongues. I'm here to assure you that there's nothing you can do, in secret or otherwise, that won't get back to me. As you see, I've gotten past your guard, as well as the guards in the visitors' quarters where Larkin sleeps. Do not trifle with me. Understand?"

Ellynn nodded, wrinkling her nose at the woman's stale breath.

"You passed the test today, Ellynn. This visit is to prove that anything less than your compliance will be made known and punishment henceforth meted out. Understood?"

Ellynn nodded again.

"Good," Katheryn said. "Now, go back to sleep and pretend you never saw me."

Ellynn gave another nod, which set loose tears that had welled in her eyes. Katheryn abruptly stood and left, quiet as a shadow.

Heart hurtling out of control, Ellynn pressed a hand against her chest as if that organ might turn loose. She took several gasping breaths to collect herself.

"There's nothing you can do, in secret or otherwise, that won't get back to me." Ellynn heard the echo of Katheryn's warning and believed it.

She knew with certainty that her grandmother must be stopped, whatever it might cost.

CHAPTER FORTY-SEVEN

Alex

ALEX KNELT BESIDE THE MIRROR-LIKE cerulean water of a small and perfectly round pond. Smooth white stones surrounded the hidden pool and were unlike anything Alex had ever seen. It looked entirely out of place.

Though Alex hadn't planned on stopping once he finally fumbled his way out of the endless tunnel—leaving his friends behind with a warning not to follow—it felt good to catch his breath and still his mind in this peaceful place. The luminous water practically glowed, vivid and otherworldly. Alex thought it might be a trick of the eyes, the water being in such contrast to the bright rocks, which encircled the tiny body of water like jewels on a necklace. The undisturbed surface provided a pristine mirror, reflecting Alex's image as perfectly as any looking glass.

He grabbed a few of the pearly rocks and studied them closely. Indeed, they appeared to be pearls, if he were to guess, though that was impossible. There was neither ocean nor oysters in the Tethered World. And even if there was, oysters didn't create perfectly uniform pearls the size and shape of a slightly used bar of soap.

Had the pond been larger, the stones would've been perfect for skipping. He settled for slipping a few into his pocket for further contemplation and, perhaps, to make a gift of them to Ellynn once he returned.

If he returned.

His hotfooted trek out of the tunnel had left him mentally and physically drained. Once outside, he'd slowed his pace and kept right on walking. The twisting thoughts and instant replays that flitted through his grey matter had finally settled on the only thing that rang true: his friends and family were better off without him.

Now, kneeling before this private oasis, he remembered one of Great-Aunt Jules's quirky idioms. He'd never quite understood it, but it now made perfect sense.

"Wherever ya go, there ya are. So ya best make friends with yerself, pet."

A change of name might have been a start, yet it could never change what he had done. Alex was still stuck with Alex. He still had to find a way to live with what he did to Barron, what he did to Tymbrelle when he turned his back on her in Ireland, and what he nearly did to her today.

How strange that she'd come back into his life. How pathetic that he had managed to hurt her twice, unwittingly or not.

Was it mere coincidence that they had crossed paths these two times? Did coincidence exist? Alex couldn't say. He knew his parents believed the Maker had a hand in such things, but Alex wasn't sure about Him either. If meeting Tymbrelle as a child had been some sort of test—one that came with a do-over, giving Alex a second chance—he had failed big time.

He had failed both times.

Alex let his gaze wander to his reflection in the bright blue pool. He rubbed a thumb along his jawline, feeling the scruff of his sparse beard.

"Ouch!" he said aloud, his jaw bruised and painful. Leaning into his reflection, Alex couldn't see what had hurt so badly. In fact, he couldn't see anything wrong with his face at all, though his left cheekbone and eye socket were still swollen in his peripheral vision.

"What...?" Tilting his head side to side, his reflection following, he saw neither scrape nor bruise nor flaw—well, except for his birthmark. How could this be? The pummeling of the past couple of days could be dully felt without touching any of the abrasions. Still, his reflection was as pristine as the water.

As he studied his reflected image, he noticed a set of protracted wings at his back. Silvery feathers that arced above the horizon of his shoulders. This was some sort of trick or mirage, of course. A hallucination? He didn't want to shatter the illusion by thinking about it too hard, only enjoy the magic of the moment.

Surely that's what it was, right?

Magic?

CHAPTER FORTY-EIGHT

Ellynn

ELLYNN SLIPPED ON A PAIR OF jeans and a tie-dyed T-shirt that once belonged to her mother. Ellynn knew how much Grandmama Lucia loathed topside clothing, so it seemed fitting to make a silent statement of protest after Katheryn's terrifying visit on her grandmother's behalf.

Ellynn couldn't go back to sleep, and she guessed Larkin couldn't either. They needed to chat.

But where? Where would it be safe? How was it possible that here, in Ellynn's own room, someone had overheard what was said between her and her father, Tassitus, Trinny, and Larkin? Was someone besides her utilizing the labyrinth of hidden passageways in the castle? Or was there a mole hiding in plain sight? If so, who could it be? It wasn't her father or Larkin, but Tassitus or Trinny seemed equally preposterous. No matter how she plugged in one or the other as a spy for Lucia, she had no imagination for it.

The guard, perhaps? Who had been standing guard yesterday? Larkin and she had been so distraught after their confrontation with Lucia that she hadn't paid attention when she brought Larkin to her room. That was the only possibility that fit, so Ellynn determined to have any private conversations elsewhere.

But *where* elsewhere?

The best idea seemed to be the basketball court. No one could trail them without notice. And it would give the girls a legit reason to head off by themselves without looking suspicious.

Ellynn tried to squeeze her feet into last year's tennis shoes. Nope. It was time for a new pair. She settled for her favorite ankle-high moccasins, appreciating the supple leather that silenced her footsteps.

Slipping from her bedroom, she took note of who was standing duty. A broad, no-necked female soldier stood beside the door. Ellynn's overnight guard was most often a woman. Judging by her heavy lids, Ellynn's exit had awakened her.

"Good morning, Gladney. Rise and shine." Ellynn smiled at the guard in a way that said *I see you.* If this woman was doing any tattling on Ellynn, then Ellynn wanted to be able to return the favor. Not that Ellynn could blame the woman for sleeping on the job. What could be more snooze-worthy than watching over a closed door all night long?

The hallway curved enough for Ellynn to be out of Gladney's line of sight before she entered her brother's bedroom. He had a basketball lurking somewhere in that jungle. She stepped over miscellaneous items, most belonging to the inside-out clothing variety. What a slob! Ellynn guessed that Alex's last-minute escape contributed to the current chaos.

Despite the mess, two basketballs adorned the wicker creel their mother had placed in the corner to keep them contained. Wonder of wonders...that was easy, considering the clutter.

Inside the creel Ellynn also found Alex's phone. She snatched it up, thinking to mess around with it for a few minutes of rare screen time. Larkin would think the phone terribly interesting, no doubt. Except...it was as dead as a rock, which didn't surprise her. If it had been charged, Alex wouldn't have left it. Returning the phone, Ellynn shoved a basketball beneath her arm and turned to leave.

She caught sight of herself in the full-length mirror beside the wardrobe and had to smile at her reflection. Between the jeans, T-shirt, and basketball, she had the teenage-Topsider look *down*. Though she wasn't as enamored with topside life as her brother, she still loved to visit and feel like she fit in. Today's reflection revealed a teenager who could stride into most any topside school and look like one of the other kids.

Except...

Except for the wingbuds at her back. She noticed that they throbbed with a dull ache. Were they swelling? Twisting toward the mirror, she tried to see her back. Between heaps of coiled hair and the weak morning light, Ellynn decided she could have a dorsal fin back there and not know it.

With great sadness, she realized her topside days were numbered. Once her wings emerged, she could no longer visit her mother's family topside, except to hide out in their aunt's old farmhouse in Ireland. She recalled family "vacations" with her father in tow. He had to stay in or near the secluded stone house or disguise his wings with a giant pouch-like cape that enveloped his feathers top to bottom. Still...a seven-foot-tall black man wearing a cape tended to stand out worse than a unicorn in a herd of donkeys, so that particular disguise was saved for twilight walks or emergencies.

Ellynn had known, in a distant sort of way, that she would eventually succumb to the same fate. Still, since it hadn't happened for Alex, it made her own changes feel...remote.

Now, she was struck by the looming reality of her plumage and its implication on her topside freedom. Seized by a desperate desire to visit somewhere—anywhere—while she still could, she left the room to find Larkin.

A crazy idea was brewing that Ellynn couldn't quite acknowledge. Careless thoughts flitted like moths to a bright light.

If she and Larkin were topside, they'd be out of Grandmama Lucia's reach.

CHAPTER FORTY-NINE

Alex

ALEX BLINKED BACK TO CONSCIOUSNESS, AWARE of gentle pressure on his arm. He'd been having a delicious dream of flight. True Nephilim flight with a surge of wings undulating from his back and carrying him to the heights of the skydome.

The bitter truth asserted itself now as he looked up at Tymbrelle, who was studying him.

Wait, hadn't he left this girl back in the tunnel?

Alex pressed upright and looked roundabout, trying to recall the current state of calamity he'd escaped from before falling asleep. Despite ditching his friends in the mountain tunnel, they now lay scattered in mossy spots or curled into the curve of tree roots. A set of enormous, calloused feet stuck out from beneath a huge fern frond. Apparently, Babel had been invited to tag along with these bloodhounds. *Wonderful.*

"We need to talk, Alex." Tymbrelle had shifted onto her heels while Alex took inventory. Her voice was low, urgent. "It's my shift on lookout. I waited for everyone to fall asleep before I woke you. I'm sorry. I know you're tired, and I know you didn't want us to follow you, but too bad. You're stuck with us." She motioned at the space between herself and Alex. "I think it's time for some honesty between you and me. Ready or not."

Alex rubbed the shoulder he'd been lying on, to buy some time. Glancing past his feet, he saw the gleaming pool of water nearby, continuing to look out of place. Had he passed out? The last thing he remembered was looking at his reflection and seeing wings...uh, no, that had obviously been a part of his dream of flying. So strange how he'd gone to sleep right here.

"*Hello.* I wasn't planning on this being a one-sided conversation." Tymbrelle scooted closer and dropped her voice further. "Look, you and I have a history together. Quit denying it."

Despite feeling disoriented, Alex made an effort to look at her and engage. "Sorry. I...I'm trying to piece together what led me here. I *do*, however, recall asking you guys to leave me alone."

The girl gave him a crooked grin. "Like I said, too bad. You didn't think we would let you run off and have all the fun without us, did you?"

Alex couldn't quell a half-hearted smile. "Yeah, I like hogging all the excitement, like imprisonment and possible dismemberment by Leprechaun." He stifled a yawn. "Guess I underestimated how much you guys enjoy hanging out with me."

Josiah stirred and mumbled something from where he lay. Alex pointed to a pair of birch trees farther from the group. "Let's move over there so we can speak freely."

Tymbrelle nodded and followed. The two sat facing each other, backs against papery white trunks.

Alex wasn't sure what good it would do to discuss their fleeting childhood encounter, but after spilling his guts about Barron, it sounded manageable.

"I know you remember me, Alex." Tymbrelle hugged her knees and rested her chin on top of them. Her large, lustrous eyes holding his gaze.

Alex gave a single nod.

"That's it? That's all you can give me when you met me the very night I lost my family and was taken away? You've no thoughts on how *now*, in the Maker's mysterious plan, I've been thrust back into your life?"

Alex looked away, swallowing down a sudden swell of emotions. Did the same God who allowed Alex to kill Barron, who did not give Alex the ability to fly, who let this girl be kidnapped and taken underground...Did that God also cause Alex and Tymbrelle to meet again after all these years? If so—and it *did* seem like something, or Someone, greater than coincidence must be at work here—there must be a reason. What might that be? Did Alex really want to know?

He glanced back at Tymbrelle, who waited expectantly, head cocked, brows raised. There was something about the way her shock of blond hair framed her heart-shaped face at the moment that made Alex see the girl, truly, as a girl. A young woman, actually, who had a delicate beauty rather than an impish, boyish air. He wondered how he hadn't seen that *Colin* was actually female right off. It seemed obvious now.

"I remember," he whispered. "I've never forgotten. I...I always wondered what happened to you. Now I know how badly I failed you." He gave a wry laugh. "If God brought us together again, perhaps He wants to make sure I realize what my cowardice cost you."

Tymbrelle pressed her lips together as if she was trying to prevent herself from saying something she'd regret.

"What?" Alex asked. "Don't tell me you haven't wondered what would've happened if I'd helped you. If I'd hidden you beside me or gone after you when those men grabbed you. Your life may have turned out differently. Better than what you ended up with, anyway."

Tymbrelle unclasped her hands and ran one of them through her hair. "Look, there's more to that night than I've shared with you. What happened between us—or didn't happen—was really insignificant compared to the rest."

Alex's mouth went dry. "What? You mean those men did other things to you, worse things, than what you described? Is that supposed to make me feel better?"

Tymbrelle rolled her eyes. "Really, Alex, would you quit making everything about *your* shortcomings and failures? You are not the source of everyone's problems, contrary to your martyr complex."

"Hey, where do you get—"

"Let me finish!" She held up a hand, her voice growing louder. She grimaced and scrambled over on all fours so that she sat beside him. "I'm going to tell you my side of it. How *I* saw what happened. How *I* remember that night. Don't put words in my mouth."

Alex leaned his head against the tree and looked at her. "Fair enough."

Tymbrelle squeezed the bridge of her nose and let out a wearisome sigh. "The story I told you about the day I disappeared—the one I've been telling everyone for so long I could almost believe it myself—isn't exactly the truth."

CHAPTER FIFTY

Tymbrelle
Then

"*TYMBRELLE*." CADENCE HISSES. "GET BACK DOWN here. Don't be stupid."

Tymbrelle feels a tug on her tail fluke. She shakes out of her sister's grasp and propels herself closer to the water's surface, hovering inches beneath the liquid plane. Arms outstretched, she rotates her wrists in a slow, oscillating rhythm, allowing the webbing between her fingers to steady her. Would she finally see a shooting star? Zosimus, their pod chief and navigator, told of many such wonders to be seen in the night's sky this evening. He allowed the pod to crest the water briefly, right before dark, but they weren't allowed to linger.

"Such tempting wonders are dangers to our kind," he had said. "Keep your curious little ones close and deep. Adults...well, watch with caution. I understand how heavenly signs have a certain fascination or attraction. Still, such things are best approached with care."

Afterwards, Mother was preoccupied with plans for time spent in the company of the dashing and daring Triian. No doubt the two of them looked forward to a romantic evening in a remote cove where they could watch the heavens and frolic in the Atlantic. Ever since their mother's three-moon cycle of mourning had passed, Triian has spent a lot of time in her company.

The sisters were seeing a completely different side of their mother. Where once she'd been reserved and careful in the presence of their overbearing and caustic father, she soon shed that identity like a hermit crab changing shells. With Triian's besotted interest in her, their mother had become increasingly flattered by his attention and saved little time for

Tymbrelle and Cadence. Claimed she was rediscovering the joy and freedom of being a Mermaid—though Tymbrelle felt as if she'd lost her Mer-mother in the wake of such self-discovery.

Earlier in the evening she had placed the girls on a bed of kelp for their nightly interlude—the closest thing Mer-folk come to sleeping. She'd caressed their cheeks with a light touch, her golden hair dancing about her lovely face like rays of sunshine.

"Remember what Zosimus said, girls." She blew a kiss to each of them. "See you at newdawn." She swam up and away, her undulating turquoise-green tail waving a languid goodbye.

When all was dark and the tide had shifted directions, Tymbrelle tried to coax her sister into ascending to watch the heavenly wonders with her. Cadence, though older by three years and bigger by a tail fin, was forever timid and tame. Tymbrelle thinks the two of them are like the two sides of their mother, before and after their father's death. Where Cadence is meek and careful, Tymbrelle is bold and cavalier. So it is no surprise that her sister wanted to cower in the kelp while Tymbrelle enjoyed the heavenly wonders on display.

The stars hover temptingly out of reach. Magnified and winking metallically from above the water's surface, Tymbrelle watches with a tingle of anticipation. It is too much to hope that a heavenly host might actually fling itself to earth—let alone near enough for the young Merrow to put the legends of old to the test—yet perhaps she would at least catch sight of a star that has turned loose from its place in its sea of stardom. Zosimus said that it would be a night in which many stars would traverse the heavens, but Tymbrelle thinks it will take a miracle to see even one from her watery vantage point.

If she can be certain that no Land-folk are near, she might be brave enough to peek her head out of the water to get a better view. As bold as she is, she's petrified of Land-folk after what happened to her father. She knows that they also watch the heavens and will likely be outside transfixed by the phenomenon. She can't risk being spotted, even if they might assume her bobbing head to be that of a sea lion or seal.

The heavens suddenly vanish as her body is yanked into the depths again. Tymbrelle struggles against it, knowing it's her sister's futile attempt at reining her in. The two are in a constant battle of wills. Tymbrelle's usually dominates. She isn't sure why Cadence bothers anymore.

The older girl's hands grasp Tymbrelle's tail and steadily

pulls her down, hand over hand, until her sister grips Tymbrelle's tiny waist. Tymbrelle stops resisting and crosses her arms over her skin-meets-scales chest, glaring at her big sister. Like everything else in the nighttime water, Cadence appears in shades of grey.

That is until she activates her luminescence. To emphasize her fierce displeasure at Tymbrelle's headstrong behavior, Cadence allows her scales, her webbing, her gills, and her green eyes to illuminate at a low wattage. A swath of seaweed belted about her waist divides the length of her glinting torso in a way that reminds Tymbrelle of the Land-folk clothing that she's caught glimpses of. Since when did her sister experiment with Mer-fashion?

"I told you to get back down here. You're being foolish," Cadence says in the clicks and chirps of Mer-language.

"Quit your glow-show, Cadence! You're going to draw predators here and leave us swimming for our lives." Tymbrelle is jealous of her sister's newfound ability to light up like a star beneath the water. Cadence began her metamorphosis into adulthood on the last moon cycle and takes every opportunity to flaunt her developing attributes.

"Oh! Maybe so." Cadence returns to her muted grey self. "You still can't go up there. You heard what Zosimus said. Quit putting yourself in danger. I'm not coming after your scaly backside if you get spotted by Land-folk or, *worse*, turned into one."

Tymbrelle swipes at her swirling hair, which is still visibly pale despite the water's depths. She's amazed by how easy it is to make her sister do what *she* wants. They have very few predators, and Zosimus knows how to plan around the migration habits of any species that might dare attack the fearsome Mer-folk. Still Cadence, as always, wants to play it safe. Exactly what Tymbrelle counts on by preying on her sister's fears.

"If you don't want to watch the heavens, fine, but I won't be cowering under the water with you." Tymbrelle cocks her eyebrow. "Didn't you listen to what *else* Zosimus said? Tonight's activity only happens once in a lifetime. This might be my only chance to see such a thing, and I'm not about to miss it. Besides, what do you think mother and her new Merman are up to? I'll bet you three pearls and a conch shell they're off in some remote spot watching the display."

Cadence's face is obscured by a curious, striped

mackerel, which she swats away. "Of course I know what's going on with them. I can only hope Triian will protect her since I can't. But I can protect *you*." In one swift movement she grasps one dangling end of the seaweed belt and begins to wrap it around Tymbrelle's wrist to tether Tymbrelle to herself.

"Hey!" Tymbrelle squeaks. She tries to twist out of Cadence's grip. "What are you doing? Let me go!"

"We've lost our father and have all but lost our mother to Triian's charms. I'm not losing you too." Cadence struggles to hold Tymbrelle's wrist with one hand while securing the crude binding with the other.

A bright light abruptly illuminates the murky depths and draws the girls' attention to the surface. Something golden and galvanized streaks above, announcing its presence like a molten sphere hurled from the sun itself.

Tymbrelle feels her sister hesitate. She shoots upward, out of Cadence's reach, and toward the fizzing, flying object.

"Hey!" Cadence shouts from below.

She's too slow.

The celestial traveler explodes into a thousand gilded sparks and rains atop the water like liquid sunshine. Tymbrelle glides silently into its shimmering wake, breaking the surface with a great gasp as lungs take over and gills seal shut. It is an impulsive move with instantaneous consequences.

Below the surface, Tymbrelle thrusts her tail just as her fluke separates into a pair of kicking legs.

CHAPTER FIFTY-ONE

"I SWAM TO THE SHORE IN a panic." Tymbrelle squeezed her eyes shut and shook her head as if in disbelief of her own tale. "I'd heard the legends, the interlude stories, the histories of our ancestors that everyone believed to be a mix of myth and fact. Although I secretly hoped that the rumors were true...I didn't, deep down, think it could happen."

Tymbrelle looked at Alex. In her eyes he saw the years of regret that haunted her because of that one, split-second decision. Boy, could he identify with that. "Looks like it happened," he whispered.

"It sure did."

"So, you—you're a *Mermaid*." Alex scoured her face as if she might be wearing a disguise. "I didn't think Mermaids existed."

She suppressed a giggle. "Why, because Nephilim are taken so seriously topside? Your kind are as much a myth as mine. More so, in fact. There are legends of Mer-folk the world over, but if people don't believe the sacred scriptures they've never even heard of you, or your stories."

"Actually, they have." Alex picked up a twig and rolled it between his palms. "They gave us different names and assigned godhood to us instead—there were some pretty nefarious Nephilim back in the day. Like the Irish legends of the Tuatha Dé Danann and the Greek gods."

Tymbrelle nodded. "Yes, true. Hadn't thought of it that way."

"So..." He gestured at her with the short stick. "You made up the rest of the story then? I mean, I saw Mr. MacAndre take you away, obviously. You weren't literally kidnapped, though."

Tymbrelle swallowed and her mouth turned down. "Unfortunately, that part is true. The men. The ceremony and the Faeries. All that. I needed a plausible reason for how I got separated from my family. In a way, I *was* lost on the beach. Lost and trapped in a human body around people whose language I didn't understand. I ran to the nearest building that looked deserted. The building where I met you. Inside I found something to wrap around my cold, bare body and then pressed myself into the far corner, frightened and completely overwhelmed."

"Wow," Alex said, eyebrows raised. "So, when we met...you had only gotten there a few minutes before me. That's crazy."

Tymbrelle bumped his shoulder with her own. "You were the first human I had any real contact with. Beyond a few previous curiosity sightings from the safety of the water."

He nudged her back, liking the warmth of her arm against his.

"I was relieved because you were about my size. Though I'd always been frightened of Land-folk, other kids fascinated me and I knew, instinctively, that a child would be a safe way to have contact with the world outside of the ocean. Children or elderly people, really. Except whenever I saw children, parents were inevitably nearby. Anyway, it was a relief to meet you first. A gift from the Maker, I'm certain. Also, the man who found me there—Mr. MacAndre—he was kind. Other men were the ones who took me away, pretending to help me."

Learning that didn't make Alex feel any better about it.

She placed a hand on his arm. "Why did you come to that barn in the first place, Alex? What were you doing alone in that building in the middle of the night?"

"My Aunt Jules asked me to investigate the place where the meteor struck," Alex said. "She thought it was an important sign from God and wanted me to check it out. Almost like she'd been expecting it."

"What did you tell her?" She removed her hand and clasped them on her lap.

Alex heaved a long sigh. "I, well, I refused to talk about it afterward, actually."

"Why?"

"Because, how could I admit that I found you and couldn't help you? This was only a few months after my Uncle Barron...you know. After he died. *That* was my fault. All I could think about, as I heard them drag you away, was my little sister Ellynn. It was as if I had personally failed to protect her when I failed to protect you.”

“Oh, Alex. It was not—”

“What if *you* were the thing—or person—she expected me to discover?” he went on. “How could I admit that I messed that up? Plus, there was that thing with my birthmark.” He shook his head, disgusted. “You know, until this recent failure of an adventure, that night in the cowshed was the only time my birthmark had ever lit up. I still have no idea why or how. I’m guessing it has something to do with *you*.”

“It’s not me.” Tymbrelle said with a quiet assurance. “Not exactly, anyway.”

“What’s that supposed to mean?” He studied her. “Do you know what’s causing it?”

“I watched you from my spot in the shadows of the, uh, *cowshed*, as you call it. I watched you looking out the window at the men investigating where the star skidded before crashing into the water.” Tymbrelle reached for his hand. She squeezed his fingers. “I saw the wind blow dust into your eyes. I remember it clearly. You turned and sank to the ground to blink it free. Your *eyes*, Alex. It blew into your eyes and then your birthmark glowed. At the time I thought all Land-folk must have the ability to make their faces glow. Like the luminance that adult Mer-folk possess.” She chuckled softy.

Alex grimaced, trying to see the connection. He decided he liked the feel of her hand on his. It felt like kindness and a bit of a distraction. “Not seeing how dirt in my eye has any connection to my birthmark glowing.”

“No. Not dirt.” She sat up straight and looked at him intently. “Or not *only* dirt, anyway.”

“What do you mean?”

“Stardust, Alex! Stardust.”

CHAPTER FIFTY-TWO

Ellynn

ELLYNN PULLED UP SHORT AT THE sound of voices. She rounded the corner to the guest quarters to visit Larkin, when she caught sight of her mother speaking to the massive, tattooed guard Izaiah. She retreated to spy from the corner.

Why was her mother up and about already? It was barely dawn. There must be a new set of problems on her mom's plate.

Ellynn bit her lip, thinking through her options. Would it really be wise to escape topside and worry her mother with another disappearance? She seemed the embodiment of stress lately. Ellynn leaned against the wall and knew her impulsive plan must be kept as a last resort.

For now, she needed to speak to Larkin. The basketball court idea was still the best way to do that. Would her mother tell her it was too early to visit and send her away until later? Only one way to find out...

Ellynn strode confidently around the corner, basketball propped against her hip, as if she always began her mornings with a brisk game of one-on-one.

Her mother caught sight of Ellynn and did a double take. Izaiah turned as well, brows rumpled together as if it had already been a long day. His piercing blue eyes, accented by that black star tattoo, left Ellynn unsettled.

"Morning," Ellynn whispered, offering a little wave.

Her mom stifled a yawn and gave Ellynn a once-over. "Kind of early, isn't it? And since when do you play basketball?"

So much for casually fooling the natives. Ellynn gave a little shrug. "Couldn't sleep. Thought I might introduce Larkin to her future husband's favorite sport."

Her mother raised a skeptical brow. "At daybreak? Uh huh, sure."

"*Mom.*" Ellynn frowned, lips forming an indignant pout.

"Thanks a lot. I'm just happy to have another girl to hang out with."

"Whatever." Her mother gave a dismissive wave. "I don't have time to parse out your *obvious* ulterior motives at the moment. It doesn't matter, since Larkin is in no shape to do anything. Apparently, our guests are ill. General Izaiah was explaining the situation."

Izaiah gave a grunt of acknowledgement. "Actually, Larkin has been spared any stomach issues. She didn't touch her supper last night, which is why we believe there was a problem with the food. It appears we should employ a royal food taster or cupbearer." His tattooed scowl revealed his obvious suspicion.

"That's awful." Ellynn tensed, squeezing the basketball against her hip. Had someone done this on purpose? Or was the food spoiled? She assumed they'd all eaten the same meal. The king and queen were travel weary, and their food had been served in their quarters. "If Larkin isn't sick, may I at least go and visit her in her room? I won't drag her outside to play basketball unless she wants to go." Insisting wasn't the same as dragging, right?

The huge soldier's scowl softened a bit, as if considering. Ellynn decided the man must look fierce even when he was asleep. Between his weatherworn face and the dark star staining his brow, it couldn't be helped.

"Maybe in a bit, Ellynn," her mother said. "It's really too early."

"Actually, she's up and about," Izaiah replied. "I'm sure she'd welcome the company. I think she's upset about her parents' taking ill—she asked how they were feeling before I ran into your mother."

Ellynn gave the big man a grateful smile. He seemed nice enough beneath that gruff exterior.

"All right," her mom replied. "You win. Just be quiet. Don't disturb her parents. They've been up most of the night. Gouldor finally gave them something that soothed their stomachs so they could sleep."

Oh, I bet he did. Remembering Grandmama Lucia's secretive whispers about Gouldor being in her pocket, Ellynn felt a twinge of guilt. Maybe she should tell her mother everything. Maybe her grandmother was wasting no time getting her revenge on Éire House. At least Larkin had been spared from whatever made her parents sick.

"I'll be quiet. Pinky-promise." Ellynn raised her fist and waggled her little finger, setting aside her guilt until she and Larkin could talk.

"She's in the last room on the left." Izaiah opened the arched door for Ellynn, and she slipped into the guest corridor. Her nose wrinkled at the sour smell. Perhaps the staff had been sick along with the king and queen.

Guards stood beside each of the three doors on her left, decked in the emerald and black uniforms of Éire House. She recalled Katheryn's boasting about everyone in the palace reporting to Lucia. Were *these* guards working for her grandmother as well, or were they loyal to their king?

She approached the last door on the left, aware of the jowly faced soldier eyeing her topside clothing and the basketball with a questioning brow.

"I'm here to visit Princess Larkin," she whispered.

"Let me see if she's receivin' visitors, Yer Grace." His thick brogue made him more fascinating than fear-inducing, in Ellynn's opinion.

He went inside and returned in less than a minute, holding the door open for her.

As soon as he shut the door, Ellynn rushed across the room. Larkin watched her from puffy, pink eyes. The girl was curled into an overstuffed chair beside the hearth, enveloped in a knobby, beige quilt. Someone had recently stoked the fire and it felt invitingly warm.

Plopping the ball on the bed, Ellynn went to Larkin's side. "So…" she touched Larkin's arm. "Guessing we both had a real-life nightmare come for a visit."

Larkin's eyes widened. "You too?" Her voice was a hoarse whisper.

Ellynn nodded. "I'm so, *so* sorry this is happening. What should we do?"

Larkin looked away, her face hardening. "Nothing. You heard that crazy woman. They're watching and listening. Thankfully we did the right thing yesterday."

"I guess." Ellynn couldn't say what she really thought in case "that crazy woman" was listening again. "Sorry to hear about your parents getting sick. Glad you're okay though."

"Seems suspicious, right? Why would that happen if we're cooperating?" Larkin made a sound of disgust.

Ellynn stood, knowing it would be too hard to talk in code or be careful enough to communicate meaningfully inside the palace. They needed to head to the basketball court. At least the skydome had fully brightened. It wouldn't look too questionable. "Alrighty. Get dressed in something you can run around in. You're going to learn to play basketball."

Larkin frowned. "Basketball? I was thinking about breakfast. Not exercise."

"C'mon. Wouldn't you rather work up an appetite?" Ellynn widened her eyes and made a gesture of impatience. Couldn't the girl guess that Ellynn was using this as cover? "Trust me. It'll be fun."

"I don't play basketball." Larkin didn't move.

Barking bumblebees! Ellynn pressed a hand to her forehead and offered Larkin a fake smile. "You should, though. It's Alex's favorite sport. Why don't I show you the basketball court and give you a few pointers, o-*kay*?"

Finally, understanding sparked and she nodded. "Right. Sure, let's do that. It'll be grand."

Ellynn responded with a genuine smile, plucking the basketball off the messy bed. "Yes. Yes, it will."

"Anything for my dear fiancé," Larkin said, walking to the wardrobe and flinging the doors open. "Let's see what's inside that will pass as sporty."

Ellynn crossed the room to stand beside Larkin, looking at an array of dresses and more dresses, stuffed inside. "Uh, do you even own a pair of jeans or trousers?"

Larkin snickered. "I believe I packed one pair in case we went riding." She stood on tiptoe and eyed the shelf suspended above the dresses. "Here they are." She snatched a pair of olive-colored breeches from the shelf, followed by a knitted sweater that was much too nice for shooting hoops.

"Kinda fancy," Ellynn observed.

Larkin shrugged and stepped behind the changing screen in the corner. "It's all I've got."

"Do you need help getting dressed?" Ellynn asked. "I noticed you don't have a lady-in-waiting—I'm sure you do back in Brihndle, though. I mean, I get dressed by myself all the time because my mother insists we do as much as we can for ourselves. She'll only let Trinny help with my hair or complicated dresses. Other princesses have help, of course. At least, they do in books. Not like I've really hung out with other girls like me before. I'm assuming..."

Ellynn trailed off. She was babbling.

Larkin stepped out dressed in the pants and sweater, both

on the snug side. She had a strange, determined set to her features that made Ellynn bite back the rest of her thoughts.

"I can manage fine without a lady-in-waiting," Larkin said, her words clipped.

"Well, yes, of course." Ellynn smiled, hoping to ease whatever tension her friend was feeling. Apparently, this topic was a sore spot.

A sound from behind made Ellynn turn in time to see the door to Larkin's room being flung wide and Grandmama Lucia striding inside. The jowly Éire House guard hurried in with an uncertain bow in Larkin's direction and announced, "*Err...*Her Majesty, the Dowager Queen."

"You may leave," Ellynn's grandmother said, amber eyes latching onto Larkin.

The soldier appeared all too glad to make a hasty exit. Grandmama Lucia glanced at Larkin, then Ellynn.

Ellynn expected to be dismissed, but her grandmother offered an almost pleasant grin.

"I see you two have hit it off well enough," Lucia said. "Did you girls have a sleepover?"

Neither girl replied.

Grandmama Lucia took a step toward Larkin, who cowered into herself while, courageously, remaining rooted in place. Ellynn made a beeline to her friend's side. Whatever her grandmother had planned, Larkin wouldn't be on the receiving end by herself.

Her grandmother neither scowled nor threatened the girls. Ellynn clasped Larkin's hand as the towering woman bent down and inspected, once again, the golden bumblebee necklace. Grandmama Lucia's pale, lithe fingers grasped the pendant, evoking a shudder from Larkin.

Ellynn watched her grandmother scrutinize the tiny insect as if it might come to life. She flipped the pendant over and seemed to be memorizing its delicate details. When Lucia's gaze slid back to Larkin, Ellynn was close enough to see the glint of tears pooling in her grandmother's eyes.

Ellynn held her breath, aware that something significant was happening and she had a front row seat.

"*This,*" Grandmama Lucia said, her voice oddly gentle. She stared at the golden bee resting on her fingertip. "I know this necklace. And I believe I know you, as well." She dropped the pendant and placed her hands on the girl's shoulders. "Your name isn't Larkin, is it? You're *not* the princess."

CHAPTER FIFTY-THREE

Alex

"Somehow, the stardust that you encountered, and the stardust that I encountered...I think it reacts when we're together," Tymbrelle explained to Alex. "It's the only thing that makes sense. Of course there's no way to test this theory. It was a rare phenomenon."

Alex considered it. "But you were permanently changed when you *encountered* it, as you say. Until recently, the only time my birthmark has glowed is when I was with you in Ireland. Even now, it doesn't glow all the time. And I'm not normally freakishly strong, either. That only happens when my birthmark illuminates. Both of those things seem to hinge on whether or not I'm angry. That's a lot of moving parts. You...you're not changing back and forth."

"I have a theory about that as well." She lifted her hand from his and tapped her temple. "I've been thinking a lot about these things since I've, uh, *encountered* you again."

"Yeah?"

"I swam right through that shower of stardust. It was still incandescent and, well, fresh—if that's a thing for stardust." She lifted a shoulder, uncertain. "My body came in contact with a lot of it. The water around me fizzing from the heat. You, on the other hand, probably had a good bit of actual dirt blow into your eye. Except you also had a touch of that star's dust from where it impacted the field. It no longer glowed or activated or whatever, when it hit you. Still, you absorbed enough of it that when we're together, there's uh..."

She trailed off. Was she blushing?

"Y'know," she said, circling her hand between them. "Like...chemistry. Or sparks. Between us. Or between our stardust, anyway."

Alex felt his cheeks grow warm at the unintentional play

on words. Great, now they were *both* blushing. "That seems farfetched, though it does fit. How does dust—from a hunk of star or otherwise—have the ability to do such a thing? I mean to transform us. Especially you. You were all fins and gills and breathing water and then, boom, you change in an instant?" He shook his head in wonder. "If so, what are stars really made of?"

"I actually have a theory about that too." She grinned, her scratched and swollen cheek making it a lopsided expression.

"Hmm, someone is quite the scientist."

"Not a scientist. More like a detective." She shifted onto both knees, so that she faced Alex, legs parallel. "Stars are unique. The Maker has something different to say about them than, say…the ocean. Have you noticed?"

Alex squinted in thought. "Not really."

"Stars aren't simply balls of gas and matter floating in space, Alex." Tymbrelle's eyes were bright and animated. Daybreak brought a warm glow to the girl's pale hair even as the mist began its dawn-dance, lending her an ethereal appearance. "Back in the Garden of Eden, what was Adam's first job?"

Oh, great. Bible lessons. Though Alex knew the answer, this really wasn't a conversation he cared to have. "He tended the garden. He named animals. What do those things have to do with stars?"

"It was the living, breathing things that were named, right? I mean, yeah, flowers and rocks and vegetation would all eventually be named by people out of necessity. You know, 'pass the eggplant' was a lot easier to say than, 'pass that oblong, shiny, purple thing.' But Adam and Eve were given personal names. God had Adam name each animal. Then, a bit later, we learn that God also calls the *stars* by name. The stars, Alex! That means they have individuality. They have *something* inherent to things here, on earth, that are alive. So much so that God has taken the time to name each of them. Think about it…there are billions of them, like there are billions of people."

Though Alex wasn't convinced, her idea intrigued him. "Interesting. I'll give ya that. Again, not something we can test to prove or disprove."

Tymbrelle nodded eagerly. "I know, I know. Trust me, I've had *years* to contemplate my situation in light of what I did that night in the Irish Atlantic. I'd heard tales about the rare

Mermaid or Merman who swam through the embers of a dying star, or meteorite. Then I actually had an opportunity to test that tale and find out it wasn't merely folklore. I'm proof of that. Something has happened to you too, because of it. You're proof of that as well."

"Sheesh. That's just so bizarre." Alex tossed his hands up. "Fine, yeah. Maybe that's what's happening. Frankly, I'm not crazy about my blasted birthmark having an 'on' button now. My whole life I've hated the attention it brought to me—that's without it literally glowing in the dark. I'm not sure I want to be part of some abnormal dynamic-duo, you know? It's not personal. I—I've actually grown to like having you around. Like, a *lot*. I know I told you guys not to follow me, but when I woke up and saw you were here...I was really glad. Still, if being together means I can't control things about myself, well..." He gave a helpless shrug, not sure where he was headed.

Tymbrelle scowled. "Well, what?"

He smiled at her stricken face, hoping to soften his words. "Listen...you've saved our sorry butts several times. We wouldn't have made it this far without you. Perhaps it's now best to get back on track with our original plan. You want to get home. I want to stay away from mine long enough to avoid marriage to a stranger." Alex felt a coil of conflicting emotions. This argument made sense in his head but, surprisingly, not his heart. "It might be best to part ways."

The girl's face was inscrutable. Her feature's flickered through a puzzle of emotions.

"What is it?" he asked.

Tymbrelle's lower lip slipped between her teeth and she closed her eyes, turning away.

"Tymbrelle. Hey..." Alex reached out, stopping short of touching her cheek to turn her to face him. They weren't that comfortable with each other. Unfortunately. "I don't want to hurt you. I'm only explaining—"

"Stop." She held up her hand and turned back, eyes glistening with unshed tears. "It's not what you said. I get it. I do. It's only...there's something else you should know."

Alex's brows shot up. "O-*kay*. Sounds serious."

"Yes it is, Brady Alexander Aviel Tuatha Dé," she said, leveling her gaze on him.

He stiffened and blinked at her. "How...how do you know my full name?"

"Your name, as long and cumbersome as it is to say, has been burned in my memory since the wedding proposal came from King Aviel to the courts of Éire House for Princess Larkin." A small, weary smile played at Tymbrelle's mouth and she sighed. "Alex...*I* am Princess Larkin. I ran away from you, and you ran away from me. We're supposed to marry each other."

CHAPTER FIFTY-FOUR

Ellynn

ELLYNN STARED AT HER GRANDMOTHER IN astonishment. Were those *tears* in her eyes? Why would Grandmama Lucia think that Larkin wasn't Larkin? Or, perhaps she meant to say that Larkin wasn't really a princess—though, hadn't they tackled that subject during brunch? And why was her grandmother looking so...so grandmotherly? The woman looked both sad and concerned, two words that Ellynn had never used to describe her before.

"Of—of course I'm Princess Larkin. I may be adopted, but I am still the daughter of King Odhran and Queen Clodagh." Larkin took a half step back, eyes wide.

Ellynn watched a tear slip down her grandmother's alabaster cheek. An authentic, salty tear. It was then that the rest of her grandmother's appearance registered in Ellynn's conscience. Though Lucia's hair was in its typical twist at the back of her head, it was not smoothed into place as usual. It was fuzzy and appeared slept in. In fact, her grandmother still wore yesterday's dress, all rumpled and twisted. Now Ellynn took a step back too, unsure of what might happen in this strange and unpredictable universe.

"No. No you're not," Grandmama Lucia reasserted, though not unkindly. "You are the daughter of Clarin White. You look so incredibly like her...but I didn't want to acknowledge that until I had all of the facts. Clarin was my dear friend. My very best friend." She swallowed. "My only friend, if I'm being honest. Before we were forced to part ways, I gave her that necklace."

Larkin stiffened and looked more regal and royal than Ellynn had seen before. Grandmama Lucia offered the young lady one of her rare, authentic smiles. The kind she once shared with Ellynn when Ellynn was younger and said something amusing. A bright smile that transformed the woman's cool, aloof face into a vision of warmth and beauty.

Her grandmother lifted her hands in a pleading gesture. "Please. Let's be honest with one another. If you are truly Clarin's daughter, as I believe, I owe her my very life. Forgive me for all of my harsh and rather unkind words yesterday. I...I am ashamed of how I spoke about you and how I spoke to you." Now her attention shifted back to Ellynn. "Ellynn can attest that I am not one to apologize."

Ellynn was dumbfounded by the entire diatribe and could only summon a nod.

"*Rather* unkind words, you say?" Larkin appeared to have found both her voice and her dignity. She crossed her arms, her features dark and distrustful. "If that's not the epitome of hyperbole. What makes you think I would want to discuss my personal life with you? How can I trust anything you say after yesterday's hateful speech and last night's midnight visit from your henchwoman?"

Ellynn caught the anger that sparked in her grandmother's eyes. Then it disappeared as fast as it had flared, as if she knew that this situation required a different approach from her usual queenly tantrum.

Grandmama Lucia pressed a hand to her mouth and took a steadying breath. "Again, let me reiterate my regret over my harsh and, yes, *very* unkind words. I'm afraid I've let the bad blood between my uncle and aunt and myself taint my view of you without giving you a chance. Truly, I am sorry."

Forget the proverbial olive branch, her grandmother was offering the entire tree. Larkin acknowledged it with a curt nod.

"There's more I'd like to tell you." Lucia gestured at the chairs near the hearth. "Might we sit? I'm dreadfully tired. Didn't sleep a wink last night, thinking about this situation. I knew I must speak to you today, and, of course, apologize."

"Fine." Larkin returned to the overstuffed chair.

Grandmama Lucia swept her arm toward the empty chair and said, "Ellynn, please. You may as well stay and hear what I have to say, since you'd likely find a way to overhear it anyway if I dismiss you." She quirked an eyebrow at her granddaughter, but her eyes held a playful glimmer. "Take this chair. I'll move that bench over for myself."

Ellynn was in a permanent state of bewilderment. Who was this queen who suddenly thought of others and took it upon herself to move furniture?

"Now then," her grandmother said, settling onto the needlepoint bench and looking entirely out of place. "As I said, there's more that I'd like to tell you about your *biological* mother. Surely you're curious to learn more about her. In return, I need you to be honest with me. I do not believe you are Princess Larkin. Well—Larkin may well be your name—but I don't believe you are the adopted princess."

Ellynn could read something beneath the surface of Larkin's cool gaze. Fear of the truth? Hunger for the truth?

"How can you be so sure?" Larkin finally asked. "Am I so far removed from *your* idea of a princess that I should have been rejected rather than adopted?"

Grandmama Lucia shook her head. "No, no that's not what I am mean to imply. Not at all." She slid from the bench so that she now kneeled in front of Larkin, who sat back, eyes round and unblinking. "I may have been away from Brihndle these past twenty years, but there are particular facts I know with certainty. One is that Odhran and Clodagh stole my kingdom from me. My father intended to pass an edict to the effect that the first born, male *or* female, inherits the throne. The palace was conveniently stormed and my father killed before that could be carried out, leaving the throne to the next male in line—Odhran, of course. Another is that my uncle does not wish for me to have any proximity to the throne, going so far as to arrange my marriage to Aviel, removing me from Brihndle. The King's Council knew of my father's plans and were considering enacting them posthumously. Unfortunately, Aviel's proposal came in time to relieve them of such an unprecedented fiat."

Larkin's gaze flitted to Ellynn, with whom she exchanged a mystified look.

"Which brings me to my last certainty." Ellynn's grandmother laid a hand on Larkin's knee and, to Larkin's credit, she didn't flinch. "You cannot be the adopted princess of Brihndle because, my dear, your mother was my step-sister, dearly loved by my father and myself. I cannot fathom my uncle adopting a child who had any connection to my father's family. They've worked too hard to erase his memory."

CHAPTER FIFTY-FIVE

Alex

ALEX PACED THE STRETCH OF GROUND between the cerulean pool of water and the birch tree where he'd left Tymbrelle to stare after him with an amused grin. She'd had a few days to process the irony. For his part, Alex couldn't grasp that his attempted escape from his forced nuptials had only gotten him as far as the stable.

Tymbrelle had explained how her royal parents had kept a close eye on their topside princess during the overland portion of their journey, but family dynamics returned to normal once they retreated below ground. Princess Larkin, whose true Mermaid name was Tymbrelle—a name she had not claimed since her fluke became feet—watched and waited until she found an opportunity to run one night.

Her running inadvertently brought her to the kingdom she had meant to avoid. Once she realized this, her plan had been to catch a wink of sleep hiding in the stables before hightailing it elsewhere before dawn. Alex and friends had shown up and changed everything.

Now, Alex felt more conflicted than ever. They couldn't simply part ways. She was no longer a mere Topsider running from a bad situation. Or a former Mermaid with whom he had an unusual connection. He knew her story now. He understood what had been taken from her, and—despite her insistence to the contrary—believed he was partially responsible for it. Reluctantly, Alex conceded that the Maker Himself must have had a hand in bringing them together again. Perhaps a second chance for Alex. Perhaps a way of escape for Tymbrelle.

Coloring all of these facts was one big, awkward reality— their engagement. It was laughable to Alex that in running away from his mysterious fiancé, he had all but eloped with her instead. Now, unable to trust his own judgment, he believed he had feelings for this Colin who was really Larkin who was actually a Mermaid named Tymbrelle.

He shook his head as if it might straighten out the jumbled facts.

"I know it's a lot to process," Tymbrelle said as he circled back toward her. "Unfortunately, there's something else I have to tell you. It's pretty important."

Alex stopped pacing and puffed his cheeks. He didn't know if he could handle another life-altering revelation, but Tymbrelle seemed to be on a roll.

"Don't you find it strange that, if Odhran and Clodagh could not have children of their own, they would adopt a girl? I don't know if you're aware that Brihndle's rights of inheritance are the same as yours—the throne goes to the next male in the family."

Alex crouched in front of Tymbrelle and gave her his full attention. "I hadn't cared enough about the situation to think it through, honestly."

"Of course." Tymbrelle gave him a timid smile. "Well, let me assure you that I was not their first choice when they were looking for a child of their own. They wanted a boy. That is, until they learned about my unique abilities with water. What they really adopted was a *weapon*. They saw my talents as an asset to their military arsenal. They snatched me up and eventually, miraculously, had a boy of their own. His name really is Colin, by the way."

Alex grinned. "I see. Though that answers a few questions, I'm not sure why this is so important to our situation."

Somehow his fingers had wandered over to hers. She didn't pull away.

"Because, Prince Brady Alexander, it's the *other* reason I ran away. My crazy parents were expecting me to help them take out Queen Lucia and, if possible, members of the royal family of Calamus."

Alex let that sink in. "I see."

"I wanted no part of it." Tymbrelle squeezed his fingers. "They had various scenarios worked out involving an unfortunate series of so-called accidents. Things like drowning in a bath, choking on wine. Lovely and uplifting ideas, obviously. So, I ran. I had to."

Alex was shocked. Once again, he was in this girl's debt.

This time he didn't mind. She didn't only have impressive skills, she also had impressive character. "I don't know what to say other than thank you. Makes me wonder what is happening in your absence."

Tymbrelle trailed her free hand through the morning mist that coalesced around them. "The plan relied heavily upon me, so it's doubtful they could carry out a different version of it. With the exception of Queen Lucia, that is. They *really* despise her. I think they'd get rid of her themselves if they thought they could get away with it."

"Wow." Alex wondered what they should do with this information. As awful as his Grandmama Lucia could be, he didn't want her dead. "I wonder how it's going since there's no bride and groom, no one to weaponize water, and no warm feelings between my grandmother and your parents."

"Good question," Tymbrelle said. She released his hand and stood. "We should share our situation with the others and collectively figure this out. Make a plan together. Or are you still insisting we split up?"

Alex glanced at his snoozing friends. These guys were better friends than Alex deserved, that was a fact. And Tymbrelle, well, there was too much to unpack where she was concerned. Still...she had been nothing but brave and loyal.

He stood and shoved his hands into his pockets, aware that she was waiting for an answer. "No way. You're officially stuck with me." He winked. "Like I've been saying all along, there's strength in numbers."

Tymbrelle rolled her eyes, and the two wandered to the bright blue pool of water. The mist seemed to part as they approached, allowing them an unobstructed view of the unusual pond. Tymbrelle kneeled, fingering the white rocks.

Alex recalled his vivid dream of wings and flight that had felt so authentic. Inside his left pocket, he rubbed his thumb across one of the pearly stones that he had squirreled away for Ellynn. Despite his tangled thoughts, he was struck anew by how out of place this pool of water appeared. Could it, perhaps, have some special property that might help his father's fever dreams?

A pang of guilt needled him as he realized how miserably he'd failed to get anywhere in *that* particular quest. No, not failed. Rather, downright forgotten to think about it—so wrapped up was he in worrying about life and limb and self-pity. Well, the least he could do was bring a canteen of this water back to his dad. *Worth a shot.*

He looked around, absentmindedly patting his sword belt for the canteen that normally hung opposite his sheath. *Duh.* Confiscated with everything else. It would be impossible to bring his father even one drop of this liquid.

Disappointed, he squatted down next to Tymbrelle.

"Everything okay?" she asked, looking at his mirror image in the water.

"Just thinking that this strange, out-of-place water might somehow help my father with his condition. Except I don't have"—he blinked and crouched closer—"Tymbrelle, do you see yourself? I mean, the way I'm seeing you?"

Tymbrelle focused on her own reflection and gave a little gasp. Her scratched and swollen face was back to its heart-shaped smoothness. Long, silver-blond hair framed her face in a tumble of waves. She lifted a hand to touch her tresses and pulled it back with another gasp of astonishment, looking from the water's reflection to her actual hand. The water mirrored every twist of wrist and wiggle of fingers but with a gossamer webbing of skin stretched between them.

"My hands!" Then, suddenly, she pointed at Alex's reflection. "Look! You—you have wings."

Alex stared, dumbfounded, at the pale feathers that arced above his shoulders like before, their pearlescent color a perfect match to the stones around the pool. "What is this...this thing? I don't understand." He gestured at the water and shook his head.

"What thing?" Another voice piped. Spock had wandered up to stand on the other side of Tymbrelle, beanie lopsided on his head and a leaf stuck to his cheek. "Roots and fruits. What in the name of Whitt Lake is this?" Hands on knees, the Gnome didn't have far to crouch to study his own reflection, which included chain mail and a metallic pointed traditional Gnome hat. "*Dude...*"

"Bizarre, isn't it?" Alex said. "Check out my wings. And Tymbrelle has...er, long hair." Alex noticed that she had fisted her hands. Perhaps she wasn't ready to reveal her Mermaid self to everyone else.

"*Wow.* You're almost pretty." Spock's eyebrows shot up. "No traces of Colin there."

"Uh, thanks?" Tymbrelle sputtered.

Spock hunched lower, rubbing his chin. "Look at all these whiskers I don't really have." His toothy grin reflected back, encircled by a dark swath of beard.

A flutter of wings startled the threesome as Parsifal, who must have been sleeping on a nearby branch, landed on Spock's back. Between being surprised and, it was later decided, tipped off balance, Spock suddenly plunged into the turquoise water, sending the Dragon squawking skyward.

"Spock!" Alex shouted.

Both Alex and Tymbrelle reached into the water for the Gnome, who, despite being a fine swimmer, seemed to be sinking. When his flailing fingers breached the swirling surface, Tymbrelle managed to grasp Spock's hand in hers. Somehow, instead of pulling the miniature man out, he seemed to effortlessly pull her into the pool after him.

As the water swallowed her, Alex clamped a hand on Tymbrelle's ankle, vaguely aware that Finn and Josiah and Dempsey had clambered up behind him. Alex only had time to register their presence before he, too, plunged headlong into the cool depths of the pool like a compass compelled to true north.

He heard someone shout his name as the water drew him down, still grasping Tymbrelle's leg. As his feet disappeared below the surface, he heard the unnatural sound of a door being slammed.

CHAPTER FIFTY-SIX

Ellynn

Larkin's name is Deborah.

Not Larkin. Deborah.

Not a princess. A lady's maid.

Not adopted by King Odhran and Queen Clodagh. Instead, an orphaned toddler and considered household property.

And most recently...forced to play the princess when the real Larkin ran away.

Once it all came out, Deborah looked relieved to finally drop the charade and admit the truth.

Now, she stood at the window of her guest room, looking out over the courtyard and shaking her head. "This is more than I can fathom. All these years, I've been told I came from the orphanage in Moored-below. That I was a misplaced Topsider. It was even implied that I may have been part of a Faery changeling event. You're saying my mother was raised in the palace and called the king 'Da'?" Deborah pivoted to look back at Grandmama Lucia, standing a few feet behind.

Ellynn remained tucked into the armchair, processing the tale her grandmother had revealed. She was shocked to learn of all the persecution the woman had endured. It went a long way in explaining why she was so harsh and unbending.

First, Grandmama Lucia's kingly father had fallen in love with and married Susan, a commoner. A commoner who was a widow left raising her step-daughter, Clarin. Within the first year of the king's controversial marriage to Susan, baby Lucia had come along.

Most labeled Lucia a half-breed and a mistake born of the king's poor judgment. But Clarin doted on her baby step-sister, and the two enjoyed a close relationship for many years, even after Susan's suspicious death when the girls were ten and eight respectively. Eventually Grandmama Lucia's father succumbed to the pressure of the elites to remove "that girl" from the palace, since Clarin had neither royal blood nor genteel breeding.

The king placed the then-fourteen-year-old with a nearby family, where she was forced to earn her keep on their farm as a milkmaid and housekeeper. Young Lucia sneaked off as often as possible to visit Clarin and often helped with chores so they could be together. When Lucia's comings and goings became the subject of gossip, she was forbidden from visiting any longer.

"But I continued," Grandmama Lucia explained. "Though I was careful to visit in secret to keep tongues from wagging. We adored each other and, in our minds, were as much each other's family as any two blood-related sisters could be."

"When did you give her this necklace?" Deborah asked, leaning in to reveal that she was invested in the story. She grasped the tiny bumblebee in her fingers.

"On her sixteenth birthday," Grandmama Lucia said. "I used to tell her that she was as busy as a bumblebee when she set about her work, quickly moving from one task to the next, always humming a tune. When I heard that my father had found her an honorable man to marry—a lord of some distant village—I wanted to give her something to remember me by. Something to show the love I felt, since I was less adept at expressing it."

"More arranged marriages," Ellynn groused.

Grandmama Lucia eyed the bumblebee as Deborah fingered it. "Honestly, I think my father felt guilty about how he had turned her out, which is why he went to the trouble of arranging a more suitable future for her. Though I was happy that her station would improve, I knew it unlikely that we'd see each other often. Travel is difficult in Moored-below. So I had that necklace commissioned with our smithy and presented it to her on her birthday. She loved it."

"How do you think Deborah ended up with Odhran and Clodagh?" Ellynn asked.

Grandmama Lucia shook her head. "This I can't say. We lost contact after a few letters sent by homing pigeons. Likely our correspondence was intercepted and thus discouraged. By the time Deborah came along, my father had been killed, and I'd been given in marriage to Aviel and started a family of my own. I'm sad to say I lost track of Clarin and can only assume she and her husband have passed away, since Deborah was brought to live in Castle Brihndle.”

“That’s what I’ve gathered.” Deborah said. “This necklace was given to me when I turned ten. ‘A gift from your birthmother’ was all I was told when the house mistress gave it to me. It’s my most precious possession. I rarely take it off. I have no memories of my parents, and I've always understood I should not ask questions about my biological family. Servants are to be seen and not heard.”

“Unless they’re being forced to imitate a princess.” Ellynn couldn’t resist pointing out.

Deborah gave a wry chuckle. “True. Lucky me, being brought up to be a lady’s maid so I know what’s expected of a princess—in theory anyway. I’ve felt completely inept since we arrived, as if everything I knew about Larkin’s life had run away with her.”

“I’ve no doubt that Clarin loved you fiercely, Deborah.” Grandmama Lucia took the girl’s hand in hers. “What little I know of love and kindness, I learned from my mother and from Clarin. Once our mother passed away, Clarin somehow increased her capacity to lavish me with love. As a child, I didn’t always appreciate it. I sometimes found it smothering. It wasn’t until she was forced to move to the farm that I understood what a gift her love and relationship had been to me. I have failed to carry on her example. Of this, I’m quite ashamed.”

At that, Grandmama Lucia broke down and cried.

The atmosphere between the three had shifted. Sharing such deep, intimate things had a way of doing that, Ellynn noticed. She found she almost *liked* her grandmother. She still couldn’t believe that Grandmama Lucia let her stay and take part in such a personal conversation, but she was glad for it. They were allies now, though the cause and purpose of the war remained foggy from Ellynn’s perspective. Was there some way these revelations could help her grandmother rid Brihndle of her Uncle Odhran and Aunt Clodagh? Did Deborah have any leverage over her own life, now that she knew the truth about her biological mother?

“There’s something else you should know,” Deborah said,

her voice hesitant. The girl stood and set to pacing between the hearth and the window. "I—I know why the real Princess Larkin ran away."

"Besides being forced to marry a stranger?" Ellynn quipped.

Deborah nodded. "Larkin and I were close. In fact, I'm still angry that she didn't warn me of her plans."

"Rude," Ellynn said. "She should've trusted you."

"Yeah, well, I'm sure she'd say it was for my own protection. Larkin knew I'd be thoroughly questioned, and this way I wasn't forced to lie to protect her. Except she also knew that I'd have asked to join her—I want out as much as she does. I guess she preferred to avoid telling me no."

Deborah stopped pacing and rubbed the back of her neck, plopping onto the stone window sill. "I should probably give some context to what I'm about to tell you, or it may not make sense." She grabbed an auburn curl and swirled it around her index finger. "Because of their infertility, King Odhran and Queen Clodagh had planned to adopt a boy who could carry on their name and all that. A *baby* boy. There was even talk about the queen faking a pregnancy so no one would know the boy was adopted."

"Oh, heavens!" Grandmama Lucia pressed her hand to her forehead. "Terrible idea."

"Yes, they decided that would be difficult to pull off. Stranger still, however, they adopted and brought home a scrawny seven-year-old girl. I'm talking about Larkin, of course. We were nearly the same age and naturally drawn together. They made me her playmate at first, and I helped her acclimate to life in the palace as well as work on her English. She had a stilted, clumsy accent, and I never could get a straight answer about where she'd come from. I secretly wondered if we were both part of a Faery conspiracy of changeling babies."

"There's no truth to those old wives' tales," Grandmama Lucia said with a dismissive wave.

Deborah stood and walked to the bedside table, grabbing a goblet of water that had been left there. "We live in a land full of creatures from old wives' tales, Queen Lucia. It isn't much of a stretch to include changelings within the realm of possibility."

"Point taken," Grandmama Lucia said.

"Anyway, Larkin and I grew close. Eventually I understood why the King and Queen chose her over a bouncing baby boy." Deborah swirled the goblet, watching the water inside. "The short version of a long story is that Larkin has some sort of power over water. She can manipulate it to her will."

Grandmama Lucia made a sputtering noise of disbelief. "I've never heard of such a thing."

Deborah raised her arms in a gesture of innocence, sloshing the contents of the goblet like some sort of visual aid. "Oops!" She set it back down. "I know, but trust me, I've seen it for myself on many occasions. The staff called her a water witch behind her back, though she was no witch. She didn't do anything to cultivate her abilities. They were simply a part who she was, like someone naturally good with arithmetic or singing. Larkin can turn water into ice or make it boil. She can make it jump up and move about. She admitted that she didn't entirely understand her power. It took her years to master her skills, but it wasn't some dark art that she sought out or desired."

"Bizarre," Ellynn mused, trying to imagine having such a superpower.

"The orphanage had noticed Larkin's unusual relationship to water, which is why the king and queen adopted a daughter rather than a son." Deborah mopped the spilled water droplets with her skirt, a gesture more lady's maid than princess. "The people who ran the orphanage thought the royal couple might find Larkin's powers intriguing. Which they did. And although Odhran and Clodagh lavished Larkin with all the bits and baubles of a princess, they also treated her as someone within their employ. She cultivated her talent under their watchful eye, and they trained her to become their secret weapon."

"Hmm." Grandmama Lucia pursed her lips thoughtfully.

Deborah returned to her seat by the fireplace. "You see, they planned for Larkin to be a weapon they could put to use once they arrived in Calamus. Larkin told me that they wanted to force her to arrange a series of believable tragedies, as they phrased it. Deadly accidents. They planned to, uh, remove you, Queen Lucia, first and foremost."

Grandmama Lucia's fists curled in her lap as her spine snapped straight. "You don't say."

"And if she saw a way to get anyone else out of the way, like King Aviel or Prince Xander, they expected Larkin to take those opportunities as well. Not all at once, mind you. They entertained some grandiose ideas about becoming the new king and queen of Calamus—eventually—if Larkin could use her marriage strategically."

"That's regicide," Ellynn sputtered. "Can't we lock them up, Grandmama?"

Lucia lifted a silencing finger in Ellynn's direction. "Let's hear Deborah out, Ellynn."

"Larkin wanted no part of such plans and, as you know, ran away. However, to save royal face, *I* was immediately pressed into becoming Larkin. A position which, you've probably noticed, doesn't quite fit—much like her clothes. King Odhran and Queen Clodagh have been scrambling to find a way to carry out their plans without Larkin, at least where you're concerned, Queen Lucia."

Ellynn could barely believe her ears. She guessed that none of the adult conversations she'd ever been excluded from could be half as interesting as this one.

"Well, well. I shouldn't be surprised. My father's regicide may have appeared to be an accident, but I know better." Grandmama Lucia looked like she could easily murder a certain uncle and aunt who had their own set of titles and crowns.

"What are we going to do?" Ellynn asked, suddenly fearful for her family. "Do you think Blaylock's murder had anything to do with all of this?"

Her grandmother shook her head. "Doubtful. That happened before Éire House arrived."

"I wouldn't dismiss it," Deborah said. "I've gotten the impression that there are people here who've been secretly corresponding with King Odhran and Queen Clodagh. Loyalty is often for sale to the highest bidder. I've no real proof, no names to offer, though."

A knock on the door made the threesome straighten and turn as one, an understood code of silence clamping their mouths closed.

Before the jowly faced soldier could finish opening the door, it was shoved wide by a man with unkempt hair and a cocky smile.

Magnum strode into the room and flung his arms wide. "Mother, dear. I'm back!"

CHAPTER FIFTY-SEVEN

Alex

ALEX FELT COCOONED, CARRIED ALONG BY the water. This was extraordinary. Somehow his lungs weren't desperate for oxygen. A muffled rushing sound thrummed around him. A sound that, he realized, came from the speed with which he, Tymbrelle, and Spock were propelled upward through the pool.

Wait. Hadn't they fallen headfirst—downward? Perhaps he was disoriented, but he would swear they were now rushing upward. Who would've guessed it could be this deep? Everyone had tumbled in so unexpectedly, they must have somersaulted and reversed course in the chaos. Above the bodily connection of Alex to Tymbrelle to Spock, Alex could see dappled golden light dancing on the water's surface.

A disorienting tingle buzzed in his bones in a way that reminded Alex of traveling by Faery cyclone. Almost like the water was working its way through his pores and into his very cells. As the threesome approached the surface—which lingered much farther away than Alex would have guessed— he became aware of something else. Something odd and unsettling.

He no longer held onto Tymbrelle's ankle. Instead, he grasped the fluke of a tail fin. The fin of a very large fish with iridescent scales. Alarmed, he withdrew his hand the same instant he understood that this was no fish. It was a Mermaid. *Tymbrelle* was a Mermaid!

Their connection lost, Alex's upward ascent slowed. Tymbrelle effortlessly propelled herself on, grasping Spock's wrist in one webbed hand as the other reached and stroked through the water so that she pulled the Gnome along like a doll. Alex pursued her retreating figure, mesmerized by her scales, which somehow shimmered with an internal light as her lithe body breached the surface.

Moments later, a stunned Alex found himself bobbing and treading water, half-convinced he must be dreaming. He blinked very real, very wet water from his eyes, astonished that he didn't feel out of breath. Beside him, Tymbrelle burst into a gleaming, ecstatic smile, and giggled. Inexplicably, the abrasions on her face had healed and her bird-nest hair had become platinum waves that undulated around her shoulders. She radiated beauty in a way that swept his heart and head into a tangle, making it hard to focus on anything but her.

"Surrender, infidels!"

Alex's stupor evaporated as he absorbed their current situation. A dozen or so Gnome warriors stood a few yards off, arrows nocked and ready to penetrate their floating, fleshy targets. If not for the intimidating weapons, Alex would have thought them comical with their chainmail and pointed metal hats. He once had plastic toy soldiers that looked more threatening.

"It's me! *Lucas*. Commander Reiko's son!" Spock shouted, using his proper name and waving his soaking wet beanie frantically. "Don't shoot! We can explain."

We can?

One diminutive soldier stepped forward and barked a word that Alex didn't catch. The others obviously had. As one, they lowered their weapons but kept their bowstrings taut. The commanding soldier gestured for Spock to swim to where he stood.

Alex took in the bright, opalescent floor that stretched as far and wide as a basketball court. Positioned high along the wall, balconies surrounded the area at intervals, each with a pair of Gnome guards who, he noticed, *hadn't* lowered their weapons. Above these balconies rose a ceiling that looked to be made of the identical, glowing crystal of the skydome itself. Alex didn't need to turn around and look at what was behind him to understand where they now found themselves.

Though he'd never been allowed inside this chamber before, he had read about it in his mother's books and heard her describe it many times. Mysteriously, he and his companions were in the Garden Dome of Vituvia. Protected home of the Flaming Sword of Cherubythe and the Tree of Life. Land of the Gnomes, ruled by High King Brock, Alex's autistic uncle.

"…and the next thing we knew, we were surfacing here, in the Garden Dome. It's unbelievable." Spock was saying. He heaved himself out of the lagoon and onto the gleaming floor at the water's edge, wringing out his beanie and giving his head a shake worthy of a wet dog.

The soldier shrank back from the flying flecks of water and retracted his arrow, sliding it into the quiver at his back. "At ease, men," he said. "Lavelle, make Commander Reiko aware that her son is here. Stanley, track down Lady Sophie and let her know about our visitors. She can decide whether to interrupt High King Brock."

Alex watched the two soldiers hurry off, then glanced at Tymbrelle beside him. Head tilted up, she appeared to be taking in the scenery as she effortlessly kept herself buoyed in the water. This only made Alex achingly aware of how tired his gangly limbs felt from treading his seven-foot frame. In a few strokes he reached the water's edge. He pulled himself up, turning so he sat on the ledge, facing the awe-inspiring sight of the Flaming Sword of Cherubythe.

Mentioned in the book of Genesis as wielded by an angel who guarded the way back to the Garden of Eden, the Sword was now anchored atop a pyramid of boulders, pierced into the rock and immersed in tongues of fire. Behind the pyramid stretched a polished granite wall that separated the Sword's space from a lush garden. Stretching the breadth of the Garden Dome, end to end, the wall was massive and unscalable.

Within the sequestered garden grew a tree sown from a seed that had come from the very Tree of Life that once graced the Garden of Eden. Alex could see the topmost branches of what he assumed to be said tree, stretching several feet above the height of the wall. The scene was an exquisitely stunning sight, enhanced by the delicate dance of Tymbrelle basking in the turquoise water. Sweet and citrusy smells kissed the air, hinting at the lush beauty that lay beyond the granite shield. It smelled so delicious, he thought he could taste the air.

Gazing at this ancient vista sparked a longing inside Alex he'd never known. He suddenly yearned to be a part of something bigger than himself. Though his parents had always tried to impress this truth on him, there was something about the scope and splendor of this place that gave clarity to their insistence that the Maker of all had a purpose for making *him*. It probably didn't hurt that he felt strangely lighter after sharing his dark and weighty secrets with his friends.

Somehow, the palpable joy of Tymbrelle swimming and

smiling before him only intensified his pang of longing. As if her newfound wholeness and freedom transmuted the water and infused him with an extrasensory dose of emotions. Alex liked it, though it scared him a little. The only intense emotions he knew were bitterness, regret, and anger.

"Strangest thing I ever did see," the soldier nearest Spock was saying. "Thought my eyes were playing tricks on me. Except everyone else was seeing the same thing."

Spock gave an enthusiastic nod. "I know, I know. I still don't believe , and I just experienced it. Boy, will Mum be *surprised.*" Spock gestured at Alex. "Oh, hey. You've probably recognized him by now, but this is Alex—er, better known to you as Prince Brady. He's King Xander's son."

The Gnome removed his hat and bowed, chainmail rattling. "Prince Brady. It is an honor."

"Thanks," Alex said, swiping dripping dreads off his forehead. "You may call me Alex, now, actually."

"And this is our new friend Tymbrelle," Spock went on, sweeping his hand her way. "She's come all the way from Brihndle and she...uh...she..." Spock rubbed his eyes with vigorous fists and blinked at Tymbrelle. He pointed. "Great yodeling yetis!" He whipped his head from Alex to the girl. "Tymbrelle! You—you've turned into a Mermaid."

Tymbrelle laughed and swept her arms up and over her head, arcing a spray of water off of her webbed fingers. Below her collarbone, her skin morphed into oil-slick scales of a grey-green hue. It was fascinating. No, *she* was fascinating.

"I feel so free!" she said, plunging backwards into the water, her fluke flinging droplets onto Alex and Spock before disappearing beneath the surface.

Alex watched as she twirled and twisted—a mesmerizing water ballet. It struck him that she would be confined to the water for good. Hang on...how would she ever get back to the Atlantic? Would the Gnomes let her stay here? Even worse, could Alex go on without her in his life? As happy as he was for her, today had turned into one of his happiest days *because* of her.

Uh oh...what about the giant sea creature that roamed the depths of this lagoon? Alex knew the eight-armed guardian had helped rid the Tethered World of at least two undesirables who had fallen into its watery lair. His grandmother Estancia, King Aviel's first wife, had been one of its victims.

Alex turned to the soldier who stood watching the

frolicking Mermaid in slack-jawed wonder. "Hey, w-what about the creature—the giant octopus that lives in the water? Is it still in there? How do we keep it from attacking Tymbrelle?"

"Goodness!" The soldier cast about, looking uncertain. "Yes. Leviathan—*er*, Levi—the guardian of the lagoon. Let's hope he's asleep."

That wasn't helpful. Alex leaned in and gave a shrill whistle when Tymbrelle popped her head out of the water and gave him another one of her heart-stopping smiles.

"You need to be on the lookout. There's a giant—and I mean *giant*—octopus that guards this body of water." Alex motioned her over. "Please, can you stay nearby? If we see him, I'll pull you out temporarily. Will you be okay if I do? Like, can you breathe?"

Tymbrelle's brows dipped together. "Is that a serious question? What am I doing right now? Gargling?"

Alex flushed. "Sorry, that was dumb. I don't know, I thought..." He trailed off and made a helpless gesture at her.

"You thought I'd react like a floppy, flailing fish if you pulled me out. *Uh huh*, thanks." Tymbrelle waved him off good-naturedly. "Trust me, it's not a problem. Mermaids and sea creatures are mostly compatible. Octopi are highly intelligent, and there's a certain understanding between us."

"All right. Cool."

Tymbrelle winked and slipped out of sight. Alex was dimly aware that Spock had gotten to his feet and stood chatting with several soldiers. But mostly, Alex knew that he both liked and feared the fascination he felt watching Tymbrelle in her element.

And that wink, just now. *Wow.*

It left him wishing he could sprout some fins and gills in order to be with her and understand her world. Who needed wings?

CHAPTER FIFTY-EIGHT

Sadie

"A wedding? You can't be serious. Magnum only came home hours ago." Sadie stared at Lucia, making no attempt to disguise her distaste.

Lucia wrung her hands and abruptly sat down on the divan as if her legs had given out. She, Xander, and Sadie were in the sitting room of Sadie's and Xander's bedchamber.

Hoping to catch a quick nap after her near-sleepless night, Sadie had stretched out on the velvet lounge, only to have Xander peek in with an apologetic "Sadie?" followed by an unusually flustered Lucia.

Now, Sadie stared with longing at the napping couch, resenting Lucia for interrupting the possibility of sleep *and* stealing the couch to boot. Xander shifted impatiently, filling the room with his bulk. They had dealt with Lucia's moods enough to know not to push the woman. But what was this nonsensical babbling—Magnum was now to marry Princess Larkin?

Sadie had heard that the Prodigal Son had returned, and on the back of a hippogriff no less. Whatever. She had other concerns. Like a nap.

"I know, I know." Lucia leaned back and put her feet up on the cushions. She pressed a hand to her forehead and shut her eyes. "Much has happened in the last few hours. I have plenty to tell, which is why I insisted I talk to you both."

A prick of alarm piqued Sadie's curiosity as she studied her stepmother-in-law. The well-known fashion diva sported rumpled feathers, no make-up, and clothes that were creased and unkempt, like they'd been slept in. In fact, wasn't that the same outfit from yesterday's brunch? Was there a blizzard in hades?

"Are you unwell?" Sadie asked, catching Xander's eye.

Had he noticed how out of sorts Lucia seemed?

"Ugh. Nothing that a week of sleep wouldn't cure. Sadly, there's no time for that." Lucia turned her head and looked from Xander to Sadie. "I know we've not been a particularly close family, the last few years. I—I take some responsibility for that."

"Some?" Xander arched a doubtful eyebrow.

Lucia pressed both of her palms to her face and spoke into her hands. "Very well, feel free to point your fingers. It's not as if you welcomed me with open arms."

Xander grimaced then opened his mouth to respond, but Lucia held up a silencing hand.

"We can place blame later." Lucia sat up and planted her heeled boots on the ground with an exaggerated thump. "I've learned some *very* disturbing things. They must be discussed. Immediately. It is time for our family to unite against a great evil."

Sadie shot Xander a dubious look and settled onto a carved stool that was more for decoration than utility.

Xander remained standing and leaned against the wall, arms crossed. "That sounds a little melodramatic."

Amazingly, Lucia neither scowled nor scoffed. Strange things were surely afoot.

"Please, hear me out," she said. Wringing her hands together, she leveled her gaze on Xander. "Larkin's name is actually Deborah. She's not the princess of Brihndle—she is the daughter of my stepsister."

Sadie's head was spinning by the time Lucia finished her tale. Flashbacks from childhood asserted themselves, replaying other instances of misplaced identities, royal treason, and double crossings. Xander stared into the mid-distance, obviously lost in his own jumbled thoughts.

"Magnum was crushed when he learned of his father's death and rushed home as soon as the news reached him." Lucia dabbed at her eyes with her sleeve. "You know there's nothing like the finality of death to bring a dose of sobriety into one's world."

"I bet," Xander said dryly.

"I know he's not been very loyal or reliable, Xander. But

it occurred to me that his marrying Princess Larkin—whom we know to be Deborah—would go a long way toward upsetting Uncle Odhran's and Aunt Clodagh's plans. After we discussed his father's death and funeral, I explained about Larkin arriving and how Alex ran off. Magnum offered to marry her, as a way to unite our families, since the two are not blood related as Aviel and I assumed when we planned this betrothal."

Sadie did not like the sound of this. Wasn't the whole premise of Aviel wanting Alex to marry Larkin based on the need to produce a male heir ASAP? What were the implications of Magnum being the one to accomplish this task, and why was he eager to do so? It didn't really matter, she realized, since the authentic Larkin had vacated her role like Alex had. Fake Larkin couldn't give birth to a genuine heir. Sadie had a mental giggle thinking that the two runaways may be better suited to each other than they knew.

"I'm not sure that this undermines Odhran's plans at all, since Deborah isn't really the princess of Brihndle." Xander seemed to be reading Sadie's thoughts.

"Except they don't know that we know," Lucia said.

"So what would be the point?" Xander asked. "We wait and bring it up later? You're willing to deceive Magnum and let him think he's marrying royalty? What happens to their marriage when the charade is exposed?"

Lucia groaned and shook her head. "Oh, I don't know. I don't know! We have no way to prove the things Deborah told me. They have no idea we are aware of it, however. All they have is their insatiable desire to get their claws in Calamus—and I admit, I want *my* kingdom back. If Magnum marries Deborah, it gets me, well..." she looked up, apparently thinking it through.

"It gets you nowhere," Xander supplied. "The fact that Deborah is not their adopted daughter means the wedding is of no benefit to either side, unless we continue to play along indefinitely. Which is not possible. I may not be able to *prove* these accusations, but I can most definitely send Éire House back to Moored-below empty handed and with no son-in-law."

Lucia gave a reluctant nod. "You're right. Ugh, you're right. I was so happy to see Magnum home and, really, so pleased to have discovered that Deborah is my niece—step or not, she's all I have from my once happy family. And I...well, I truly despise what my uncle has done to Brihndle."

Sadie felt for the woman yet didn't know what to say.

Lucia's expression darkened and she dropped her gaze. "I have a confession of my own, I'm afraid."

Sadie tensed, bracing herself. Xander moved to her side and reached a hand to massage her neck. Sadie leaned into him, appreciative of how well he could read her.

"Go on," Xander said.

"I may have encouraged this match between Brady Alexander and Larkin in order to lure my uncle and aunt here. I—I had some plans of my own." Lucia's voice was flat, reminding Sadie of a reluctant suspect confessing to a crime in some television drama.

Xander grunted. "Why doesn't that surprise me?"

Before Lucia could explain herself, someone rapped on the door.

It opened a few inches, to reveal Gage's freckled, weathered face. "Your Highness?"

"Yes?,"

Gage emerged with a stoic grimace. Sadie's heart clenched at the sight of the rugged warrior's expression. She felt the color drain from her own, expecting more bad news.

"What is it?" Xander stepped toward his commander.

Gage held the door and moved aside, a heavy wrought iron candlestick in his right hand. He gestured with his bronze prosthetic at Avalen, the maid, who entered after him.

The woman's round face was blotchy, eyes swollen from crying. A feather duster blossomed from a pocket in her apron, and she twisted a lace-trimmed handkerchief in her fingers.

Sadie rose and went to the tearful woman, putting an arm around her, catching the smell of lavender used in most of the household cleaning products. "Avalen, what happened?" Sadie hoped her voice sounded more soothing than anxious. The day had been brutal, and she didn't know how much more she could handle.

Lucia stood and smoothed her skirt absentmindedly.

Avalen sniffed and, when she noticed Lucia, stiffened beneath Sadie's supportive arm. "Maybe this isn't a good time, m'lady."

Xander rubbed at his stubble, and Sadie knew that listening to two hysterical women in one fell swoop was a challenge. As ever, he was gracious.

"Stepmama," he said, evidently hoping to appease Lucia

by using her preferred familial moniker. "Will you please excuse us?"

Lucia had slipped back into her austere countenance, chin lifted, shoulders square. "If you insist."

"We'll continue our conversation. *Soon*," Xander whispered as she swept past.

Avalen exhaled in apparent relief.

Gage gave Lucia a moment to retreat, then shut the door gently. He faced the others and gestured with the candlestick. "Avalen found this in the back of one of the other maid's closets."

Sadie looked at the simple black candlestick. It looked like one of hundreds of candlesticks used throughout the palace. There was a side table here in the parlor that held at least a half dozen. The height was the only variation in the twisted vine motif of the wrought iron. "Why is that unusual? Surely there are candlesticks in most closets to provide a source of light when needed."

"Oh, no," Avalen said between snuffles. "I mean, yes. Yes, there are. Except this…this particular candlestick." She tipped her head toward Gage. "It's the missing candlestick. I'm certain."

Sensing that her husband had no patience left for the frenzied woman, Sadie took the lead. "I wasn't aware that we kept a close count of the candlesticks. Surely it's not anything to worry about. If you misplaced it, I certainly didn't notice." She squeezed the woman's shoulders.

Avalen shook her head and swiped at her eyes.

"It's the candlestick missing from the grouping on your table, Your Grace," Gage offered, using the object to point at the nearby flaming collection that dripped with waxy frosting.

Sadie didn't want to be rude, but this seemed like much ado about nothing. "I wasn't aware we were missing a candlestick. I'd never dream of accusing you of stealing one."

Avalen shook her head again. "No, no. Sorry, m'am, I— I'm not making much sense. You see, we've been searching for a candlestick because we believe it was what…what killed…"

"Oh. *Blaylock*," Xander said, with an understanding nod.

"Yes. Him." Avalen hiccuped and wiped at her nose. "I dust your room every day, and I had already dusted the morning that Blaylock was…was found. There were nine candlesticks there." She gestured to the side table. "Sometimes there are more, sometimes less, but I always think it looks best to have an odd number. I remember feeling satisfied that there were nine. Silly, I know. When we tidied the room afterward, I noticed there were only eight candlesticks. *Eight.*"

She gave a nod of satisfaction, as if that fact alone proved her point.

"Avalen reported the discrepancy," Gage said. "And a candlestick certainly fit with the injury to Blaylock's head. A blunt object struck him. Hard."

"What makes you think it's this particular candlestick?" Sadie asked. "Surely it's been used to provide light in the closet."

"Oh, that's another story," Avalen said, waving her damp hanky as if in surrender. "Each maid has her own closet of supplies where we keep extra linens or dusters or whatnot. We all have our own systems, see. Don't have to chase someone else down if we need a broom or fresh towels. Anyway, with the extra company coming on the heels of the funeral guests, I'd run out of several things. I decided to go into Raechel's closet to grab a clean set of sheets after everyone's unfortunate stomach bug last night. Raechel's closet was nearly as low on supplies as mine. I got on all fours to procure sheets at the back of the bottom shelf. That's when I...when I found *that*, wrapped in a pillowcase."

With the flair of a magician, Avalen pulled a rumpled white cloth from the pocket of her apron and shook it out. A pillowcase, stained with rust-colored splotches, unfurled in her hand. The woman dropped the offensive fabric, stepping away as if it might strike.

Gage bent and skewered it with the end of the candlestick, placing the cloth beneath his left arm. "I've learned some alarming information while investigating Blaylock's death. There seems to be a network of servants passing information to Katheryn. Of course, we all know whose ear she bends. The investigation is still preliminary with the arrival of Éire House on the heels of the murder. It appears Blaylock was being pressured, and refusing, to spy on the two of you. I believe he threatened to expose the palace moles, and one of them retaliated." He lifted the candlestick between them.

"You believe Raechel—that shy and scrawny maid—had it in her to strike down a massive man like Blaylock with one swift blow?" Xander pressed his lips together and gave a quick shake of his head. "I don't buy it."

"Not impossible with the heft of the base of this candlestick." Gage flipped it over so the square-edged base was at eye level. "This would work as well as any sword."

Sadie could see something dark and crusty along the candlestick's edge. Was that blood?

Xander pulled a skeptical face. "Possible yet unlikely."

The candlestick joined the pillowcase beneath Gage's arm. "I agree. Though I'm not ruling her out, it's more likely that someone else did the deed and hid it in her closet. In hopes of either retrieving it at some point or, quite possibly, with designs on framing Raechel by planting it there."

"Oh, I don't know about that." Avalen straightened, chin lifted. "I know for certain that Raechel has been spying on you, ma'am. This I know as fact." She frowned. "I've kept my mouth shut long enough. Actually, I, uh...*oh.*"

The woman's face flushed pink, a fresh round of tears plummeting down her plump cheeks. Sadie didn't make a move to comfort her again, trying to imagine the limp-winged, mealy-mouthed Raechel spying on anyone.

Avalen shuffled to the stool that Sadie had vacated. "Oh, dear me. I am so ashamed." Her misty gaze lifted but didn't quite meet their eyes. "About two months ago Raechel approached me about passing on any information I might overhear in the course of tending to you two. Said that I would be rewarded with a better position and that my sister, Tilly—for whom I've been trying to find a position at the palace—would also be offered a job. She went on to promise the termination of *my* job if I refused."

Sadie shot Xander a look, shocked that such subterfuge was happening right under their noses.

"Well, I'm humiliated to say I agreed to it." More tears spattered her ample bosom. "I was absolutely miserable. Knew I was doing wrong. So, instead of sharing any information—not that I had anything to share, mind you—but whenever Raechel asked for something useful, I'd explain how you two are never around when I'm cleaning or whatnot. True enough because I've made a point of only coming when you're out, or popping in quick as a minute if you happen to be here."

Xander sat on the divan and said in a conciliatory tone, "You did the right thing, Avalen. Thank you for your loyalty. Do you know who Raechel is reporting to?"

She shook her head. "No. The way it works is that each spy has a handler. Raechel is my handler. I'm to report to her.

She reports to someone else. Eventually, I'm expected to be a handler to another person whom I would approach, without revealing their identity to Raechel. Not sure how many handlers it takes to make it to Katheryn's ears, but it certainly makes it hard for one to name names or point fingers."

"Shall I take Raechel into custody, Your Highness? Or Katheryn?" Gage asked.

Sadie gritted her teeth. *Yes, and leave me alone with them both—and, a candlestick.*

Xander shook his head. "No. Not at this time." He leaned toward Avalen in a way that pulled her attention from her fidgeting fingers to meet his gaze. "Avalen, do your best to carry on as if you're cooperating. If you hear of anything that may be relevant, tell Gage or me or Queen Sadie. In the meantime, it sounds like I should continue the little heart-to-heart conversation I was having with my dear old stepmother."

CHAPTER FIFTY-NINE

Alex

TYMBRELLE SAT AT THE WATER'S EDGE, fluke languidly rippling the water. Alex felt hyper-aware of her presence beside him as he gave a brief overview of the past few days to the family and friends who had trickled in as news of their arrival spread through the Vituvian palace. He only wanted to give the detailed version once.

After a round of dripping wet greetings and hugs and introductions, Alex checked in with Tymbrelle, asking how much of her story she felt comfortable with him sharing.

"All of it," she said. Gesturing at her lower body she laughed and added, "I can't exactly hide the real me from anyone, at this point."

Beginning with his nuptial news on the heels of King Aviel's funeral, and ending with their tumble into the water, Alex hit the important points in between. Spock and Tymbrelle chimed in here and there with additions of whatever they deemed important.

"So, I'm guessing we fell into some sort of well or, I don't know, a water tunnel that connects to this pool. It's not something I can explain. Actually, it felt a lot like Faery transport." Alex swept a hand to indicate their threesome. "And here we are."

He took in their astonished faces, feeling like a child who had attempted a whopper of a tale in hopes of weaseling out of being in trouble. Would they believe him?

It didn't help, he decided, that he sat on a towel beside Tymbrelle and Spock, forced to look up at Uncle Brock and Aunt Sophie, who sat in chairs that had been brought waterside. Like poolside children speaking to grown ups.

Commander Reiko sat on the ground with them, beside her son, Lucas—Spock's formal name. Reiko radiated pleasure at having her young man home again. She had never been enthusiastic about Spock living in Calamus as a glorified page, when she could train him to be part of the Vituvian special-ops and keep him close to home.

"It's an aqua-portal, actually," someone said.

Alex looked at the wizened Gnome, Sir Noblin. He rocked back on his heels, tiny fingers clasped across his round belly. The old Gnome had permanent crinkles at the corners of his bright blue eyes. His tunic was rumpled, and his conical green felt hat sat askew on his wiry grey hair. The Gnome was the former advisor to Queen Judith, King Brock's predecessor, and remained on staff as a consultant.

"A portal, you say?" Alex repeated. He had read of such phenomena in science fiction books.

Sir Noblin gave a ponderous nod. "Indeed, my boy. A unique and rare occurrence to be sure. Yet it has precedent. I've read about such things in Vituvian history."

Sophie lifted a finely arched brow. "You have? Where have such tales been hiding? I'd be all over something like that, and want to go find one for myself."

Alex knew his beautiful aunt had an extreme-sport sense of adventure as well as a reputation for playing hardball in diplomatic circles. He had always joked that when the apocalypse happened, he wanted to have Aunt Sophie at his back.

"Well, I'm afraid you'd be hard pressed to find one." Sir Noblin stepped closer to Sophie's chair and leaned on the edge with one hand, rubbing his lower back with the other. "You don't mind, do you dear? Thank you. As I was saying, one doesn't merely go searching for a an aqua-portal, or any kind of portal for that matter. No, indeed. If Alex here drew a detailed map of where he and his friends encountered their portal, you would arrive and be sorely disappointed. It would no longer be there."

Alex recalled the sound of a slamming door.

"Dude! What are you saying?" Spock blurted.

Reiko elbowed her son in his ribcage. "Show some respect, Lucas."

"Sorry," Spock mumbled. "Sir Noblin, sir..."

"No, no, it would not be there." Sir Noblin continued, as if no one had spoken. "Portals are offered out of necessity. What brought them here is a living extension of this here body of water." One stubby finger jabbed at the tranquil lagoon as he continued to lean on Sophie's chair. "Historically, aqua-portals have been used to translate someone to our Garden Dome who either needed the assistance of Vituvia or had a great role to play in turning the tide of Tethered World events. Last time, it was with the wise Hermit of the Hinterlands. He was brought to Vituvia quite suddenly in the wake of Queen Constance's illness. With no successor yet named and at death's door, it is said that Queen Constance prayed for help. The hermit found himself tumbling into a hitherto nonexistent body of water, only to surface here as you did today. Being well schooled in the art of herbal remedies, he nursed the queen to a full recovery. Queen Constance and the hermit, Clive, fell in love. The two married and, upon her death a few years later, he became the venerable King Clive. Also one of our most gifted prophets."

"I am a prophet," King Brock said matter-of-factly.

Everyone looked to Brock, who sat, palms resting on knees and face serene, staring at nothing in particular. He always had a quiet, understated way to him, but this was the first Alex had heard about him being some sort of prophet.

Sophie, who acted as Brock's mouthpiece to a degree, grinned at the group and dipped her head toward her older brother. "True story. He's had several dreams come to pass and has occasionally shared a piece of news with me before it happens."

A smile played on Brock's lips. "True story," he repeated. Then his gaze fell to Alex. It was so out of character for his uncle to make eye contact that Alex gave a small twitch of surprise.

"I dreamt of you," Brock said. "You fought to save your kingdom."

Alex felt his stomach drop. Could his uncle's portent be trusted? As a prince, Alex was destined to train for battle and likely participate in a few, which meant his uncle was merely making an educated guess. Even so, Alex had mostly exchanged monosyllabic conversations with Brock, so having him say such a thing—with such certainty—left Alex anxious about his future.

"Is there anything else, big brother?" Sophie asked, after catching Alex's distressed expression.

"Yes," he said, now focusing on the water as if it was sending him a message. "You must return to Calamus soon. You may use the lagoon. You have the tools."

On that cryptic note, with no "goodbye" or "see you at dinner," King Brock stood and walked out of the Garden Dome.

Sophie offered Alex a reassuring smile. "Never a dull moment in Brock's company." She got to her feet and offered Alex a hand to stand.

He grasped her forearm and got to his feet. "Care to interpret? What's this about having tools?"

Sophie glanced from Alex to Tymbrelle and twitched a shoulder. "No idea." She gave a bewildered shake of the head. "Maybe aqua-portals work in the opposite direction from the lagoon. I'll see if I can get Brock to elaborate. You might check with your girlfriend and see if she has any special knowledge about such things."

Alex's face flushed. "She's...not my girlfriend."

Sophie grinned and patted his shoulder. "You keep telling yourself that. Now then, I should let your parents know you're here. A few Calamus scouts came looking for you yesterday."

He nodded. "Of course." Alex hoped the wedding had been called off by now. If not, both bride and groom were currently too far away and, well, in two very *opposite* environments to plan any nuptials.

Aunt Sophie suddenly grabbed Alex in a bear hug. "Holy guacamole. This is absolutely crazy. Crazy good, of course, but still. I mean, a *portal*?" She released him and stepped back. "Whenever I think I've learned all the bizarre secrets of this place, something else surprises me. That's why I love it here."

"Hey, catch you at dinner, Alex," Spock said, giving his tall friend a salute. "Mum wants me to visit some of the fam." He shoved his damp beanie on his head.

The Gnome pointed at Tymbrelle, who was back in the lagoon treading water. "See you, uh, in *here*, I guess." He took a few steps and turned back to Alex with a low whistle. "Wonder what Josiah, Finn, and Dempsey thought when we disappeared? You think they're headed back to Calamus?"

Alex hadn't considered the aftermath from his friends' perspective. They likely assumed Spock, Tymbrelle, and he had drowned. "Probably. Poor blokes probably think the worst. Maybe the messenger from Vituvia will make it to Calamus before the three of them find their way home with an Ogre and Dragon in tow." Alex snatched the towel off the ground and pressed it against his dripping dreadlocks. "Later, shrimp."

Sir Noblin came over as several Gnomes busied themselves removing chairs and sopping up puddles.

"We're so honored to have you brought to us under such auspicious circumstances, Prince Alex." Sir Noblin's eyes twinkled with pride. "It will be interesting to see what develops, since aqua-portals are said to only present themselves to serve the Maker's purpose. Perhaps the two of us can comb through our collection of historical tomes and learn what brought others to us in this way. I can only recall the account of King Clive that I mentioned. Though it happened another time a few centuries prior, if my memory—"

"Sure. Thanks, Sir Noblin. Great idea." Alex cut him off to avoid another billowy speech. There was something Alex needed to do, and it couldn't wait.

"Listen." Alex took a knee and bent close to the elderly Gnome. "Would it be possible to speak to Tymbrelle privately? Of course, your soldiers must keep the Sword guarded and all. Maybe if the guards could, y'know, stand back a bit and give us some space. Tymbrelle is stuck in the water, so if we're going to talk, it's sort of here or nowhere."

Sir Noblin nodded and steepled his fingers. "Ah, yes, yes. Certainly. I'll speak to my men, and you'll have it mostly to yourself in a moment. Will I see you at dinner, or do you prefer to take yours in here?" He nodded at the rippling water.

Alex's stomach must have ears because it burbled at the mention of dinner. "In here, if you don't mind."

"Not at all. Not at all." Sir Noblin dipped his chin and circulated through the remaining Gnomes to give instructions.

Alex wandered to the edge, spread out the towel, and sat down with his feet dangling in the water. He realized that there had been no octopus sightings, just as a sudden tug at his ankles made him gasp.

CHAPTER SIXTY

Alex

Tymbrelle popped out of the water and shook her head, spattering Alex's legs. He felt too relieved to be annoyed. She couldn't know that he had been imagining death by tentacles moments before.

"You've got some big feet, landlubber." Tymbrelle reached for the ledge and hauled herself up, sitting beside him in all of her shimmery-scaled glory.

"At least I *have* feet," Alex said, laughing at his own joke.

Her silence made him look at her. Seeing her downcast, dewy lashes and her pouting mouth, Alex had an urge to wrap his arms around her and press a kiss to her forehead. He blinked several times as if to erase both the image and the urge. Blast it! This girl was doing a number on him.

"I'm sorry. I didn't mean to make fun...or insult," he said, settling for a touch on her arm. "Really." He looked back to ensure they had the privacy he had requested. Tiny guards stood like replicated soldiers along the back wall, far out of earshot.

Tymbrelle gave him a sidelong glance. "No, it's not what you said. It's—well, it *is* what you said, actually. Though I know you're joking. Fact is, it's the sudden, stark truth. I—I'm feeling really conflicted, Alex. I have a serious decision to make."

"I'm not following." Alex's gaze slipped to her neck where three hairline slash marks indicated her gills had returned along with her scales. They were sealed shut while she remained out of the water.

She let out a frustrated sigh and propped her chin on her elbows, leaning on what appeared to be a very tight and luminescent skirt. Her fluke gave a half-hearted flick. "I don't have any feet."

Oh, boy. How should he respond?

That's okay, I don't have wings?

Why are you stating the obvious?

Trade ya?

She fisted her hands in her lap and turned to Alex. "All this time stuck in the belly of the earth...all I ever wanted was to get home. Like *really* home. Back in the sea with my family. My pod. There's absolutely no joy or sense of freedom that compares with dancing in the ocean spray, diving deep and twirling through seaweed, or jumping out of the water with my friends. Playing tag with dolphins or racing a school of fish. It's amazing." Her shoulders drooped again, and she turned to stare back in the water.

"Sounds wonderful," Alex offered. "Sounds a lot like flying, actually. Not that I would know about *that* firsthand. Except when I was little and my dad carried me, which was way cool."

"Oh, Alex." Tymbrelle reached for his hand. "You of all people can relate to what I've been missing." She squeezed his fingers. "Here's the thing. As wonderful as it is to have my old, uh, body back. I, well, I miss my feet. I never realized how confining water is. I mean, not if you're in the ocean of course. Though, even that had its limits. Now that I've been living with legs and feet for over half of my life, I suddenly don't want to give them up. I want to feel grass under my toes and the rough bark of a tree I've climbed. I want to stretch my legs in freshly washed sheets and savor the ache in my limbs after a long run. I'm shocked by this. Shocked that this is what I feel. Returning to life as a Mermaid has been my focus for so long. And here I am, an hour into living my dream and I—I don't love it like I thought I would."

Alex nodded. "I'm sorry, Tymbrelle. I get it. I do. I've secretly wondered whether flying would be all I imagine it would, if I had wings. I wish I knew how to help you."

Tymbrelle went silent. Alex saw the track of a tear meander down her pale cheek.

The urge to wipe it away swept over him so powerfully that he sat on his hands to keep from acting on it. "Listen, I was wondering about this, uh...sudden change of circumstance. I really don't want to leave you here to hang out with a giant octopus indefinitely. What should I do? How can I best help you? I'm not sure what my Uncle Brock meant about the lagoon helping us get back to Calamus, but I can't run off and leave you here."

"Sheesh. *Alex*." Tymbrelle practically breathed his name as she exhaled, gazing at him from beneath heavy lids, lashes shading her fascinating eyes. "There *is* something you can do. You've already done it, actually."

"I have?" Alex searched her face, sensing she was implying something he wasn't quite catching. "What did I do?"

She gave him a sly half-grin. "Before I tell you, would you mind if I wrapped this towel around me? I'm, uh, cold-blooded, after all." She gave a nervous laugh.

"Sure." Alex scooted off the towel, and Tymbrelle wrapped it around her torso, tucking the end securely beneath her arm like she'd just come from the shower.

Alex settled down beside her and wondered how someone like him could help someone like her. He hoped he could. But if it involved carrying her topside to get her to the ocean...well, as much as he'd be willing, he didn't think he was able. Maybe he and the guys could rig something up to transport her. It would take some planning.

Mostly, he found his mind returning to how nice it felt when she reached for his hand. He looked at her. "So. How can I be of assistance?" Alex gave himself an imaginary smack in the head. This wasn't a business transaction.

"Remember when I told you I grew up listening to different Mermaid tales? Particularly about swimming through stardust and becoming fully human?"

He nodded. "Of course. It worked!"

"Indeed it did." She warmed him with a smile while brushing her hands up and down her arms like she felt chilled. "*Aaand* there's another way in which they say a Mermaid can become human. There are several, actually. I happen to be interested in testing one in particular."

Alex's heart did a weird clenching thing in response, and he shouted mental commands at his body to keep it together. "I guess this is the part where I ask what that entails."

Her enigmatic eyes traveled his face. "Indeed it is."

"That was actually my way of asking." He nudged her fluke with his foot.

"It's a two-part process, see." Now her eyes dropped to the space between them, and a flush tinged her cheeks. "Part one—a Mermaid must"—she gulped—"she must fall in love with a Land-folk."

"A Land-folk. Uh-huh..." He found he needed to clear his

throat. Did she use the word love? "I guess I qualify as a Land-folk type of guy."

She nodded, still averting her eyes. "And, though you may have infuriated me, like, *tremendously* since we met...another conflicting emotion has emerged. Seems that, as we've fought and run and spilled our guts with each other, I've actually begun to love you, Brady Alexander."

He started to speak, but she raised her hand to silence him, meeting his gaze. "You're not obligated to say anything—even if, by some miracle, you feel the same way. This is not the moment for that. This moment is my shot at getting back what I've recently lost, and that's the *possibility* of a life with you. Being confined to this water, I don't have a remote chance of furthering our friendship, not really. Certainly nothing *beyond* that."

Alex nodded, aware that his mental commands were falling on deaf nerve endings. It felt like his skin and his heart and, possibly, his hair follicles were only tuned to the frequency of the sound waves in Tymbrelle's voice. They were responding in ways that left his scalp tingly and his tongue suddenly too big for his mouth.

"So, regardless of how you may feel," she went on, "what matters for now is how *I* feel. *Love* is how I feel, Alex. Love."

He offered a goofy grin, the best he could muster with his current rebellious body. "Very well." His voice quavered. "What does the second part of this legend require?"

"This..."

Tymbrelle leaned in and brushed her cool, slightly salty lips across his. It was sweet. And savory. And feather light. It made Alex want to melt into the water and die a happy man.

She pulled away, and their eyes met. They shared a shy smile, and Alex cupped her cheeks with his hands. "Anything for science. Experiments were always the best part of—whoa!"

Alex pulled his hands away as Tymbrelle shuddered violently. Her eyes rolled back, and Alex caught her as she fell against him. "Tymbrelle?" he said. "Hey! *Tymbrelle.*"

Alex scooped her up, clambering awkwardly to his feet, mindful of the wet, slick floor. Unsure what to do, he cast about in panic, about to cry out for help when he caught sight of her legs.

Her. *Legs.*

It had worked! A small part of his brain suddenly registered exactly why she had needed that towel.

"*Tymbrelle*. Your legs are back. It worked!" He hugged her bundled body against his chest. She felt limp. Had he lost her to the transformation process? He shifted her, hoping to feel her breath against his cheek. Oh, yes! Thank the Maker, she was breathing. He felt a strong pulse when he slid his fingers to her neck, to the place where gill-slits had marked her only moments before.

"Thank you, God!" He kissed her forehead. "Thank you!"

The lone door at the back of the Garden Dome opened, and several Gnomes scurried inside. One of the guards must have sent for help. A stretcher appeared, carried on the shoulders of a half-dozen miniature Gnome men and women.

Tymbrelle stirred and opened her eyes, looking up at Alex. "Hey..." Her voice was weak. "Are you my guardian angel?" She gave him a sleepy grin, eyelids at half-mast, like her energy was spent.

"If guardian angels can have big feet and no wings," he said with a chuckle. "I'm available."

Her own feet fluttered, and she gave a weak squeal. "Speaking of feet." She hugged his neck. "I guess that little experiment turned out as predictably as my first one."

"Mad scientist Tymbrelle," he said. "Looks like we've got company." He jerked his chin toward the miniature medical team. "Dramatic fainting spell and all."

Tymbrelle gave the Gnomes a weak wave. "I'm fine, really." She glanced up at Alex, then back at the Gnomes, who had sputtered to a stop and looked uncertainly between the two of them.

"We are prepared to take the Mermaid to the—the..." a Latino-looking Gnome sputtered to a stop at the sight of Tymbrelle's feet.

"Thank you for your concern." Tymbrelle smiled at the stunned little guy. "The real problem is that we're both weak with hunger and in need of a good night's rest."

A sweet-faced female offered a bow. "I happen to have two guest rooms available and a hot meal being prepared as we speak. You feel up to walking, m'lady?"

"That's an understatement," Tymbrelle said, turning her eyes on Alex. "You mind setting me down, Mr. Landlubber?"

"That's 'Land-folk' to you." Alex tipped Tymbrelle upright and watched as she bounced on the balls of her feet, then morphed into a happy dance, one hand gripping the towel.

"Amazing! Twice in a lifetime amazing."

Alex took her hand as they followed the Gnomes from the Garden Dome, both sets of bare feet splatting the floor with the sound of all sorts of possibilities moving forward.

At the door, Tymbrelle glanced back at the placid water.

Alex hoped she had no regrets. "You okay?"

"Absolutely."

He lifted their clasped hands to see that she now had neither webbing nor scars between her fingers. "Look at that!"

She released his hands and spread her fingers wide. "This is crazy! What a bonus. I don't have to explain my webbing or hide the scars any longer. Thank you for making this possible, Alex. Looks like loving a human has made me more *completely* human." She gave him a dimpled smirk. "Brady Alexander, you're more powerful than stardust."

Alex tried not to scoff. "Trust me. Whatever good things have happened to you have happened in spite of me."

"Alex, this is the last time I want to hear you say such a thing." Tymbrelle blinked back tears and lifted her chin. "Don't you see that together we are more than the sum of our parts? *Together.* That's how we are walking, yes—*walking*—out of this room. On our own two feet with a purpose neither of us yet understands. We've been brought here for a reason, haven't we? I'm learning that every failure is an opportunity to see what the Maker can do with us, and often despite us. Quit blaming, making excuses, and setting your sights so low."

Alex felt slapped. In a good way. "Okay." He lifted his hands in surrender. "I'll try. I'm admittedly tired of letting my past define me." He looked to where the Gnomes stood clustered in the narrow hallway, trying to act as if they hadn't heard every impassioned word.

"I'm holding you to that," she warned.

"You know what?" Alex looked at her wistfully. "Aunt Jules sure would have liked you. She often gave me the same speech. Too bad you two never met."

CHAPTER SIXTY-ONE

Aunt Jules
Then

Aunt Jules watches Brady Alexander devour a slice of homemade brown bread with butter. Lowering herself onto the chair across from him at the breakfast table, she sips her tea and anticipates hearing his story from the night before. Though she tried to wait up for him last night, she wasn't terribly surprised to wake in her favorite rocking chair with a sore neck beside a spent peat fire. These days, she only needs to be still for a moment and her eyelids seem to close of their own accord.

Brady must've been knackered, sleeping as he did until nearly ten this morning. Despite being eager to hear about his night, it was *her* errand that kept him up late, so she felt obliged to let him sleep in.

The steam from her tea briefly fogs her eyeglasses. Brady, who has thus far avoided eye contact, stops mid-chew to quirk an amused grin. Encouraged by any sign of life, she lifts the cup again and puffs her cheeks out.

"You're goofy," he says, in a way that tells her he's only responding because she is trying so hard.

"Yer a sleepy head," Aunt Jules replies. "What time did ya make it back last night?"

Brady shrugs and studies his plate again. His birthmark looks puffy and irritated, as if he's been rubbing it.

"Sorry I fell asleep before ya got back, love. I'd meant to wait up, but old age and late nights are no longer compatible." Aunt Jules waits for some sign of acknowledgment.

Brady chases crumbs around his plate until Aunt Jules slides the platter of bread across the table. He reaches for another slice and mumbles, "Thanks."

"Yer welcome, doodlebug. Ya make me feel like the queen

of the kitchen, scarfin' me food as ya do." Aunt Jules butters a slice for herself and tries not to let her impatience show. Why isn't the boy bursting with either news or disappointment? Had she misread the entire night and sent Brady on a fool's errand?

He guzzles the rest of his milk, leaving a frothy mustache across his olive skin that's too cute to point out. Stuffing the rest of the bread into his mouth, he hooks a thumb at the back door, raising his eyebrows in question.

"What's the hurry, pet?"

Another shoulder shrug.

Aunt Jules grasps her teacup and levels her green-eyed gaze on the boy. "Perhaps I'm bein' too subtle fer yer cotton-stuffed head. How about a bit o' news about what happened when ya went traipsin' across the island in search of a strayin' star?"

Brady wipes his mouth on a napkin, removing his milk mustache, keeping his eyes averted. "Just...not much to tell." His grimace turns upward a bit, and he glances at her. "You were right about it landing near the standing stones. Mr. MacAndre and others were there. I stayed out of the way, like you told me."

"Good, good." She offers an encouraging nod.

The boy drums his fingers lightly on the table and scans the stone-walled kitchen as if he has exhausted his side of the conversation.

Aunt Jules feels disappointment settle like a chill in summertime. She's been trying so hard to reach this boy with wonder and beauty and the Maker's goodness. She can all but see the shadows growing long over his soul and the weight of guilt that clouds his mind. It's somehow worse today, heavier, which is not what last night was supposed to do for him.

Had she completely misread the reason the Mer-folk came back to the island yesterday?

It's been fifty years since she last saw them frolicking in the bay. Back then, she was a heartbroken newlywed with a husband who was MIA. Though everyone believed her Daniel to be dead, a casualty of war in Vietnam, Jules felt certain he was alive and that she would see him again. At a very low point, ten years after his disappearance, she returned to the family home here in *Inis Chléire* to find some peace for her conflicted soul.

She either needed to accept his death, as everyone urged,

and get on with life as a widow. Or, she needed some sort of assurance that this gut-deep conviction—that Daniel was alive and would come back to her—was worth clinging to.

She'd brought a picnic lunch to one of her favorite bluffs overlooking a secluded cove on the south side of the island. The grassy patch was sunk into the surrounding cliffside, protecting it from the buffeting wind that rarely stilled on this wild isle.

Morning clouds were beginning to thin, allowing for glimpses of blue sky. She gave herself over to tears and memories and anger and questions, while the cleansing tang of salt slowly settled her insides into something resembling peace.

Still, she had prayed for a *wee* something more. Something to cling to, one way or another.

"How can it be that after ten years, and against everyone's advice to the contrary, I feel like I still know better? Is this me, givin' meself over to wishful thinkin', God? Or is it Yer way of tellin' me to keep faith?"

That's when she saw them. At first she thought they were playful sea lions, a common sight in these parts. But as heads bobbed up and disappeared, drifting closer as minutes passed, Jules realized these sea lions had hair. And shoulders. Occasionally one would risk lifting a hand out of the water to point at something.

Seeing the Merrows was not the "something more" Jules had prayed for, though it may have been enough for some people. However, Julie—*Jules*—McGriffin had grown up with Faery visits, occasionally traveled by Dragon, and heard all manner of tales from her twin sister who was High Queen of Vituvia, land of the Gnomes.

No. It was what the Mer-folk were looking at that brought Jules her much-needed peace.

The dozen or so Merrows were intently looking at something off to the west, pointing and turning to stare. Jules slipped behind a gorse bush—not wanting to frighten the shy Mer-folk away if they noticed her—and crawled up the small embankment sheltering her picnic spot. She peeked her head above clumps of heather and looked west.

A *triple* rainbow stretched across the wide expanse of the Atlantic, bright and beautiful and promising. Two widely arced ribbons of color blazed bright, and a third, more tightly curved bow sprouted from the middle of the two and rose above the height of the double bow. Jules stared and wept and wished she'd brought her Polaroid. But camera or no, she'd kept the image of that miraculous bow vividly in her mind until the day, decades later, that she'd found her Daniel once again.

A Trinity Rainbow was how she'd always thought of it. A sure promise from the One Who was Three-in-One. She'd never seen such a sight before or since.

That incident was also why she had expected something to happen last night. Earlier in the day, the two had made their way into town to grab a few supplies. Aunt Jules leaned heavily on the boy's arm, thankful he was tall and strong like his father. Her slow hobble surely tested his patience and youthful energy, but he never complained.

Aunt Jules insisted Brady leave her to rest and feed the fish on a large rock beside the water at one of the more secluded coves. Brady could pick up the groceries and post her letters while she enjoyed a few minutes of solitude beside the water.

Armed with a bag of grapes she'd brought for fish food, she tossed one into the water.

The grape had sunk a foot or so when something—a pale colored eel perhaps—grabbed the fruit and disappeared. Two more times Jules released a grape and watched it get snatched by something unidentifiable. She waited, staring into the depths in hopes of seeing what was swimming there. When a blinking, grinning face appeared below the surface, Jules jumped in shock.

Silver blond hair swirled around the face of a shy, curious child. A girl, Jules assumed, though Mer-boys likely had long hair too. Somehow this child's heart-shaped face seemed too pretty to belong to a boy. Jules held a grape over the water, hoping to entice the girl to come up. Instead, the Mermaid gave an eager, underwater nod and poked one webbed hand out of the water. With a laugh of delight, Aunt Jules dropped the grape into the girl's palm. Or she tried, anyway. It rolled off into the water where the girl snatched it up and disappeared.

Aunt Jules held her breath, hoping the Merrow would return. She did, this time coming nearer the surface. Close enough that Aunt Jules could see that the girl's eyes were two different colors. So charming! When, at last, the girl peeked her head out of the water, her face a mixture of awe and terror, Aunt Jules made the mistake of speaking to her. "*Dia duit,*" a simple hello in Irish, sent the girl diving down, not to return.

Though she regretted her impulse to speak, Aunt Jules savored the interaction, wishing Brady had been with her. There was nothing as fortifying as keeping a sense of wonder about God's wide, mysterious world. She decided not to tell him about it. The disappointment of missing the Merrow might add to how down he seemed to be, fairly convinced that the world, and the Maker Himself, was against him.

Later that day, right before dusk, Aunt Jules looked through her birdwatching binoculars, spotting a *caróg liath,* or grey crow, hopping along the stone wall. The marbled reflection of the butterscotch sunset drew her focus to the bay. Aunt Jules sucked in her breath with a start. There they were, a whole clan of Mer-folk looking skyward.

That's how Jules knew the Maker was up to something for her boy. Aunt Jules called Brady outside to watch the sunset. Tempted as she was to show him the Merrows, she didn't want him to miss whatever might happen in the sky. It might be fleeting.

Then, after a routine sunset, she couldn't constrain him to remain outside. Though it was too dark to see the distant Mer-folk, they were surely gathered for a reason. She tuned into her staticky transistor radio to learn if she should anticipate anything unusual—weather related or otherwise.

Indeed! A spectacular meteor shower was expected later that evening. "Possibly the best celestial display of the decade," gushed the woman on the radio.

And, so...

Had her encounter with the Mermaid, the appearance of the Merrows in the bay, and last night's close encounters with a shooting star been for naught?

Jules McGriffin did not believe in coincidences.

Now she studies Brady's pinched and impatient face, wondering if she should've attempted to accompany him. Maybe she would've discovered something that his young, inexperienced eyes missed. Or maybe the blinding, stray star was what the Maker had sent to shake up Brady's world.

Something inside her is convinced there was more to it. She trusted that still, small voice when it spoke to her.

"Is there nothin' else that stands out, chipmunk?" Aunt Jules asks, knowing from his grimace he has nothing to add. Or nothing he's *willing* to add, anyway.

Sadness touches his eyes for an instant. Brady shakes his head. "I don't want to talk about it."

"You don't want to talk about it because there's nothin' to talk about, or because somethin' happened that you don't wish to discuss?" she says, praying he'll change his mind.

"I don't want to talk about it because I don't. The only interesting thing to report is that the star plowed up part of the field before skidding into the sea."

"Wow, sounds pretty cool," Aunt Jules says, knowing she's trying too hard to keep the boy engaged by employing words she'd never use in everyday conversation.

At this, Brady gives her a look that reveals he's a bit embarrassed by her choice of vocabulary. He nods, gaze drifting away. "I've gotta...make my bed."

With that, he leaves the kitchen.

Aunt Jules sits there for a long time, tea untouched. Finally, she breathes a tired prayer, weary of life being fraught with pain no matter how young or old a person might be.

Did I mishear Ya, Lord? I had such certainty that Ye were up to somethin' in this boy's life. That Ye were givin' him a measure of hope for his future.

A quiet knowing, familiar and comforting, settles on her. Bone deep. She doesn't have answers, but she has faith—and that, ultimately, is going to be enough. With a sigh of acceptance, her gaze roams to her kitchen window.

Across the meadow, where a pair of Kerry Bog ponies nibble on clover, Aunt Jules spies a rainbow stretching heavenward, full of promise.

Oh yes...there are plenty of reasons to hope.

CHAPTER SIXTY-TWO

Ellynn

ELLYNN GNAWED HER THUMBNAIL AND SETTLED onto her window seat. She had a bird's-eye view of the vineyards, the old well that provided water for the grapevines, and the two figures slowly strolling between rows of vintage grapes. What Ellynn wouldn't give to be an actual bird who could swoop down and trail innocently behind these two and overhear their conversation. Even from this distance, Ellynn could see the coy way in which Deborah looked at Magnum. She cocked her head flirtatiously and trailed her fingers down his feathery wings.

Ellynn decided her birdcall would be "Barf! Barf! Barf!" instead of "Chirp! Chirp! Chirp!"

Since Magnum's return two days prior, he'd spent an inordinate amount of time in the company of Deborah, whom he still believed to be Princess Larkin. Ellynn tried to warn the girl away from him, but she appeared dazzled by the tall, dark, and handsome son of the woman whom Deborah now privately referred to as Auntie Lucia. All of these double identities were sure to catch up with someone somewhere, Ellynn feared.

Once again, Ellynn had been delegated to the fringes of palace life and the goings on between Éire House and Pacific House. The two families seemed to have called a truce. Once it was discovered that the stomach bug experienced by some in King Odhran's company was due to a spoiled sleeping tincture that they themselves had brought, suspicions mellowed and the two families were genial once again.

Ellynn's parents were no longer fooled by their guests' affable manner, of course. Despite Lucia and Deborah divulging their linked past to Xander and Sadie, everyone continued to refer to Deborah as 'Princess Larkin' to play along with King Odhran's charade. Ellynn knew her uncle Magnum wouldn't be so taken with the girl if he knew the truth. He always preferred whatever benefited himself.

Meanwhile, the confessions her parents had heard from both Grandmama Lucia and Deborah created a lot of tense back-and-forth, especially between her grandmother and her parents.

For Ellynn, time spent with Deborah now depended on whether or not Magnum had made plans with the girl first. Though Deborah claimed to dislike playing the role of princess, she didn't seem bothered putting on airs for Magnum's sake. This left Ellynn unoccupied and sorely tempted to resort to her old, sneaky habits. She knew she shouldn't consider it, after getting into so much trouble, but how could everyone dare shove her out of the way again and ignore her?

She huffed and hopped off the window sill, stealing one last glance at the vineyard. She stiffened to find Deborah sprawled on the ground. Magnum stood over her, arms crossed. Ellynn could easily imagine her uncle's condescending smirk.

Magnum finally stooped and extended a hand toward Deborah, who slapped it away and struggled to her feet, stepping on the ruffled fabric of her dress and nearly toppling forward again. Magnum merely watched her efforts. Ellynn felt a little worried for her friend. Her uncle always had a way of making others feel small and less than.

Finally, Deborah stood and faced Magnum. He leaned close. Was he *kissing* her?

Ellynn made a noise of disgust.

Then Deborah slapped his cheek and took a step back. This wasn't going to end well. Magnum had Deborah by both shoulders now, shaking her. Deborah screamed, and Ellynn knew she must do something.

Pulse escalating, Ellynn leaned through the widow opening and shouted, "Hey! Get your hands off her."

Magnum paused, still gripping Deborah's shoulders. His dark eyes roamed the stone structure of the palace until his gaze alighted on Ellynn.

"That's right. I see you!" Ellynn screeched. "Let her go." She sounded more in command than she felt, aware of incurring his wrath.

Deborah twisted from his grip and ran toward the palace. Magnum didn't give chase but turned his contempt on Ellynn. She could make out his sneer despite the distance.

"And *I* see *you*, my nosey little niece!" he shouted back. Like a great, sinister bird of prey, Magnum took flight, straight toward Ellynn's window.

She quickly slipped from the windowsill, closing and latching the shutters. Running to her bedroom door, she paused, hand on latch. Her first instinct was to insulate herself within one of the secret passageways. She'd promised her parents that her spying days were over, however, and Ellynn needed to find a new way to cope with her fear or boredom or curiosity.

Ellynn's actions had given Deborah a chance to escape from Magnum—that's what was important. Thankfully, the palace was enormous. Surely Ellynn could avoid being alone with him.

Crack! The thick, wooden shutters convulsed beneath a blow from outside. Ellynn froze, watching as the shadow of her maniacal uncle hovered for a moment then disappeared.

She took a steadying breath and pulled her door open, stepping into the wide stone corridor of the family wing. During the day only one guard was employed to watch the mostly empty and uneventful sleeping quarters of the palace, so no one stood on duty at her door.

Ellynn headed toward the guest wing, hoping to catch up with Deborah and make sure she was okay. Maybe her friend would finally understand why Ellynn had warned her about Magnum.

Ellynn's stomach growled, and she realized she'd been too caught up in the turmoil of her thoughts to think about food. Maybe she could bring a snack to share.

Since the kitchens were on the ground floor and a long way from the family wing, there was a small pantry of snacks kept in one of the nearby storage rooms. Ellynn made a beeline for the slender door, removing the torch beside it to illuminate the inside. The door swung silently open—something her brother had seen to over the years. He was diligent to oil the hinges so no one would detect his midnight raids.

The space was narrow but deep. Shelves lined one side stocked with sealed boxes and canisters to keep out the vermin. Ellynn had never been terribly enamored with the usual selection of biscuits and crackers—things that had a long shelf life—though she did love to stuff a few strips of jerky in her pocket to snack on during the day...particularly days spent in the labyrinth of the palace walls.

She placed the torch in a sconce, illuminating the paltry selection. No doubt the staff had been kept too busy with a funeral and the present company to bother with refilling the shelves. Two stale scones sat in a pipe tobacco box and felt sturdy enough to skip across a pond. Greasy crumbs from homemade potato chips littered another metal box, leaving Ellynn to grab a handful of dried brandyberries from the only other container with a trace of edibles.

She decided to make a quick dip into the kitchen to get a tray of something—anything—more presentable to bring to Deborah's room. Ellynn would use the servant's stairs to shave off a few minutes. With a shrug, she tossed the chewy berries into her mouth. A deep, phlegmy cough brought her up short. She cast about for a source of the noise.

"Keep it down, Gouldor," said a hushed female voice. "Someone's bound to hear you coughing up a lung. Why don't you cure that awful cough yourself? You're supposed to be a doctor."

Ellynn recognized Katheryn's cold, choppy intonation but couldn't figure out where the conversation was coming from.

"You think I haven't tried?" the physician rasped, sputtering into another cough.

"Oh, good grief." Katheryn often sounded like she was biting into whomever she spoke to.

Oh-good-grief. Chomp-chomp-chomp.

Finally, Ellyn found the source of the sound. One long slit at the top of the rear wall vented into the room on the other side. But what was next door? She pictured the corridor and the narrow, carved door of the storage room where she stood. The hallway wall made a right-hand turn and then…and then there was another, regular-sized door. A larger storage closet was there. Raechel's closet, if Ellynn remembered correctly. The one stocked with linens for the rooms in her charge. The two spaces apparently shared a vent to help regulate the temperature, or maybe to keep the little pantry from becoming stuffy.

"To the point," said Gouldor. "That annoying Gnome is poking around my laboratory, claiming she wants to learn from me. I think she suspects something amiss with King Aviel's death. To my knowledge, King Xander shows no symptoms yet, so I'm not sure why Queen Sadie sent for the healer. Perhaps Sadie is not satisfied with our explanation of the king's death. Whatever the reason, the little nuisance is in the way. I want her gone."

Ellynn leaned against the stone wall, needing its coolness to calm her ratcheting emotions. What did Gouldor mean about her father not showing any symptoms *yet*?

"It's probably premature," Katheryn said, "but one of the guards reported to his handler that he witnessed a disturbing incident with Xander, though it may have merely been a nightmare. Still, if that Gnome goes poking around where she doesn't belong...well, I trust you've gone to great pains to conceal any evidence of foul play?"

Ellynn concentrated on keeping her breathing slow and steady. Evidence? Foul play? What sort of incident did this guard witness involving her father?

"Of course I have. I've been in the poisoning business since before you were born." Gouldor made a *tsk-ing* sound. "And you—you and your *handlers*. This isn't one of those moving picture shows about spies that Queen Sadie arranges for a palace movie night. Call me old-fashioned, but *you* should take care to use the title of *King* Xander when you speak of him. That is proper palace etiquette, after all."

"Which makes you the palace hypocrite, Gouldor," Katheryn hissed. "Or should I refer to you as *Doctor* Gouldor, or the Royal Physician? Why do you care what I call Xander and his lot? It's not as if either of us are loyal to him. And, yes, I did indeed get the idea of a handler from one of those topside films. It's a fitting moniker for a specialized position."

Ellynn couldn't believe what she was hearing—and all this quite by accident. Would she get in trouble for unintentionally eavesdropping? If so, she would accept whatever her punishment might be. This conversation seemed immensely important.

"I'm beginning to wonder if Lucia—excuse me, *Dowager Queen* Lucia—may suspect me in some way," Katheryn said. "She's been very aloof and preoccupied of late."

"Surely, that's due to the complications surrounding Éire House and her own vengeful plans for King Odhran. She's distracted."

"Perhaps. But she's spending an inordinate amount of time with Xander and Sadie and seems to be avoiding me. Interestingly, she no longer speaks disparagingly of Larkin. I have to wonder if she may have figured out the girl is an imposter. If so, that makes biding our time more difficult. If only that blasted water witch hadn't absconded. She's ruined everything. Without her powers in our employ, it's going to be nearly impossible to pull off this coup. There's only a measly contingent of soldiers from Éire House and a handful of loyal supporters here in Calamus. Even if we *do* get the benefit of Magnum's ragamuffin army showing up for the cause, I have grave doubts. Too many moving parts to coordinate. The water witch was our key to success, despite Odhran's insistence that she was only a small part of the puzzle."

"I've seen how the man practically salivates as he looks around Calamus and imagines himself its monarch." Gouldor grated through another phlegmy throat-clearing. "I say we pull our support for King Odhran if Magnum's army doesn't come through—if we can even trust the likes of Trolls and Ogres and disgruntled Nephilim to fight shoulder-to-shoulder. It's a gamble that *may* pay off, due to the element of surprise. Without their numbers, however, it will be impossible."

Katheryn hummed her agreement. "I spoke with Magnum briefly last night. He claims the army is mustered and waiting. Like us, he would like to know the chance of success is in our favor before showing his traitorous hand."

"It feels as if the entire palace is holding its breath," Gouldor said.

Ellynn heard three quick, muffled knocks. Katheryn gave an impatient huff before hissing, "Get in here. Don't stand there attracting attention, foolish girl. What took you so long?" *Chomp-chomp-chomp.*

"Beg your pardon. Brady Alexander's companions have just turned up outside. Prince Brady—er—that is, Prince Alex is not with them, however."

Ellynn recognized the timid, breathy voice of the maid Raechel.

"My word. It's always something. Fine, fine," Katheryn said dismissively. "They're the least of our worries."

"There's one more thing, m'am," said the mousey maid.

"*What.*" It didn't sound like a question.

"Prince Alexander's friends are quite distraught. They bring news that you may find, uh, helpful? They...they believe his highness the prince to have drowned."

Ellynn's hands flew to her mouth. She did her best to suppress the gasp of alarm that threatened to expose her. After a few deep breaths, she thought better of the urge to run away in an emotional tangent, determined to learn all that she could from these three dreadful people.

A sardonic trickle of laughter oozed from Katheryn. "Well, well. Sometimes fate, or God, or *somebody* up there does us a big, fat, juicy favor."

Ellynn's stomach propelled her out the silent door and into the bathroom, where she lost the mouthful of brandyberries she'd eaten.

CHAPTER SIXTY-THREE

Sadie

"POISON? ARE YOU CERTAIN?" SADIE ASKED Prilla, the Healer who had arrived from Vituvia to assess Xander.

The elderly Gnome clutched her hands and nodded. "I'm certain, Your Majesty. It *is* shocking. Though there's no way to prove it now, I'd bet my Lion's Mane mushrooms that King Aviel was slowly poisoned to death. I only wish he had called for me at some point. He might still be with us."

Stunned by this news, Sadie dropped onto the chair beside the unlit hearth. "Who would poison him? Who should I suspect?" Even as she asked the question, Sadie had a few faces parading through her mind.

"Oh, now, that I couldn't say. Obviously, someone with regular access to His Highness." Prilla grasped her khaki tunic and sat down on the stone hearth. "It wasn't until I noticed the faint blue tinge beneath some of his toenails that the pieces fell into place. With Xander's dark skin—and Aviel's was darker still—that characteristic doesn't present itself clearly. It's very faint. Probably helps that I know what to look for and have exceptional eyesight. I take an herbal tincture every day to keep my vision strong. My patients depend on my accurate assessments."

Sadie nodded, thinking about Avalen's confession and the spies infesting their home. Maybe they needed to fire everyone and start over. "So, is this something that Xander has been drinking or eating? He randomly uses a taste-tester, though he thinks the practice a bit medieval. He certainly doesn't employ his services with every meal or snack."

Prilla drummed her tiny digits on her knees. "Might be spiked in his water or wine. It could be a substance placed on the bottom of his plate that slowly dissolves into his food—in which case the royal taster would likely be fine. It could also be something he comes into contact with regularly, placed on a latch or his saddle horn, for instance. Some substances can take on multiple embodiments. Powder. Liquid. Vapor. I would need to stay here and observe the household for some time if you wish for me to try and identify it."

"Oh, would you?" Sadie's heart soared to have Prilla's insight working for them. "That would be a huge blessing. You've already given me a great sense of relief. Learning this is the cause of his fever dreams means he isn't diagnosed with a death sentence. If we can find the cause, we can stop its deadly effects. That alone is a source of solace. Thank you, Prilla." She grasped the Gnome's diminutive hand.

"If you would, please send word to the staff that I shall be here for an extended period and need some leeway to nose about. It will help to have access to certain areas where I normally may not be welcomed." Prilla frowned. "I already had a run-in with the physician when I stopped by his laboratory."

"Certainly. I'll convey that point personally."

A frantic pounding at the parlor door brought Sadie to her feet. Before she could call out, the door flung wide and Avalen catapulted inside.

Sadie tamped down her impatience when she caught sight of Avalen's stricken, tear-stained face.

"Beggin' yer pardon, ma'am." Avalen pulled up short and offered a clumsy curtsy as Sadie approached.

"What is it? What's wrong?" Sadie asked, casting an apologetic glance over her shoulder at Prilla.

Avalen adjusted the lace kerchief on her head and stood up straight, swallowing loudly before speaking. "Your Grace, King Xander has sent me to fetch you. Brady Alexander's friends have returned. His majesty asks that you come to the courtyard straightaway."

Sadie's insides contorted at the maid's choice of words. "Only my son's *friends* have returned?" Perhaps the overwrought maid had misspoken.

A stilted nod plunged another round of tears down Avalen's blotchy cheeks. Sadie dashed from the room with a cry.

CHAPTER SIXTY-FOUR

Alex

"ARE YOU OKAY?" TYMBRELLE EYED ALEX like a cat studying a mouse. "You seem...different."

Alex and Tymbrelle had been escorted from their individual guest quarters to the double doors of the dining hall for breakfast, but Tymbrelle pulled Alex aside before they entered. He could almost see her sly smile twitching with whiskers.

Was his drama-filled night that obvious? In fact, Alex had the worst nightmare of his life, which morphed into some sort of supernatural encounter. The nightmare felt so authentic that to recall it now made him queasy.

He had been trapped in a deep trench somewhere topside. Despite it being nighttime, the moon's glow illuminated his surroundings in monochrome shades of grey.

Alex's mother loomed above him, standing at the edge of the trench, looking down. She handed him a wrapped bundle. He took it from her, then lifted the corner of the cloth to see what was inside. His stillborn brother Benjamin stared back with empty, accusing eyes, his ghostly pale skin contrasting with dark lips. Recoiling in shock, Alex looked at his mother for an explanation, but she was gone.

He hurried to lay the shrouded baby on the ground, only to find his dead uncle Baron, gazing up with similarly unseeing eyes. Alex gasped and nearly dropped his tiny bundle. Baron's small frame sprawled between Alex's feet and the other end of the trench.

That's when Alex understood that he was inside a grave. A grave meant for himself. One dug with his own hands—his self-loathing as good as any shovel to get the job done. Alex had cried out, convinced he could either bury himself in condemnation or make the effort to climb out of this pit of misery and live.

And Alex wanted to *live.*

He'd barely acknowledged this truth when a blinding light sliced the night sky. A shooting star was about to make a crash landing. The meteor would strike him then and there, the grave ready to receive him.

His change of heart had come too late.

The dying star shot past him, skimming treetops, as Alex braced for impact. He felt the thunderstruck earth reverberate, bringing to mind the meteorite collision on *Inis Chléire.* The force of it flung him against the dirt wall, briefly drenching the darkness in a blaze of light. It lasted just long enough for Alex to see that the bodies of Benjamin and Baron were no longer there. Where did they go?

He squinted as light suddenly streamed from his pores, tiny rays emanating from his body like micro-sunbursts. He gasped at the warmth that surged through him, riding the wave of his pulse and radiating from all the pinpricks in his skin. A gleaming red luster illuminated his birthmark and, for the first time since this phenomenon had begun, Alex felt happy about it. This brilliance pouring forth from inside him had something to do with the stardust—precisely as Tymbrelle had predicted—and his stardust was reaching out like an answer to the meteor that had brightened his world and, somehow, obliterated his hurt.

In the strange way of dreams, Alex understood that the falling star had come to burn away his self-condemnation and finally allow him to forgive himself, enabling him to put these tragedies in the past and move forward. To give himself the grace that God and his family had been offering him all along.

Alex had awakened with a jolt of relief mingled with joy. Could he really be free from the heavy guilt of his past? For the first time, Alex dared to believe his life had purpose beyond basketball and royal inadequacy. Though nothing had changed on the outside, he knew it to be true with the certainty that he knew the color of his own eyes.

Could Tymbrelle see it too? She studied Alex as his mind meandered through his nightmare-turned-miracle. He didn't feel a need to explain. Not yet. Instead he offered a shy smile, thinking they might be able to make their relationship work.

Explanation or not, the way Tymbrelle was sizing him up was proof enough that his inward changes were making themselves known. She circled him, appraisingly.

"So how am I different?" he teased, turning to keep pace

as she orbited him. "You're the one who suddenly has two legs, long hair, and perfect fingers."

She stopped walking and looked at her hands, front and back. "Perfect? You think so?"

"Like the rest of you," he whispered. And he meant it. These arranged marriages might not be so bad, he laughed to himself. Not that he planned to say "I do" anytime soon.

Tymbrelle's cheeks warmed, but she gave Alex a pleased grin. "Thank you."

Alex made an awkward gulping noise that, he guessed, yanked his coolness status back to ground level. He might feel more confident and optimistic, but really, change took time. He was still the runaway prince who needed to decode a cryptic message from his uncle Brock and find a way back to Calamus—with Tymbrelle at his side, of course.

"Oh my goodness, Alex!" Tymbrelle's chirp of surprise brought Alex out of his reverie. She had managed to shift behind him while his thoughts raced ahead.

He spun to face her. "What?"

"Wait, turn back." She made a shooing motion. "Turn around and let me look at you."

Alex gave her a side-eye glance and turned obediently. A touch on his shoulder blades made him flinch away. "*Ouch.*"

"Sorry." Tymbrelle said. "So...your back hurts?"

"Yes," he replied, drawing the word out like a hiss. "I, uh, had a rough night." Another explanation occurred to him, and he looked over his shoulder. "I may have hurt my back when I fell into that water-portal. We all tumbled in pretty hard."

Tymbrelle sidestepped so that she stood perpendicular to him. "I don't think that's what happened." She shook her head slowly.

"What then?" Alex attempted another glance over his shoulder. "Have I turned into a hunchback or something?"

She gave an amused chuckle. "No, silly. Something much better than that." She grasped his arm in a way that made him focus on her face.

"What could be better—nay, more attractive—than a hump on my back?" he joked, though his mind flashed to Gouldor, the physician, and his disturbingly stooped spine. His heart gave a little stab of panic. Surely not!

Tymbrelle trailed her hand up his arm and around to his shoulder blade with the softest touch. "I've lived among the Nephilim long enough to make an educated guess. I do believe your wings are beginning to sprout, Mr. Landlubber."

Alex couldn't have been more stunned if she told him he had a tail. "No way." He tried to touch his shoulder blade with his opposite hand. "There's no way! I mean, how?"

She lifted her palms. "I...I think it must've been the water. Your reflection had wings, remember? The water must contain, I don't know, some sort of restorative properties."

Alex stared at her, slack-jawed. "Maybe. I mean, you had once been a Mermaid, after all. But I've *never* had wings. Just two wingbuds that have always been wing-*duds*."

"You've always had the wingbuds though, haven't you? Which means you were probably *supposed* to have wings, same as I am supposed to have a fluke and gills. Perhaps the water restores things to the way they are meant to be."

Alex nodded, thinking it through. "Right. You have been a Mermaid before, whereas I've never had wings. Only the wingbuds. So, you were fully restored and I...well, maybe my wingbuds have been restored so they can function and develop into wings."

Tymbrelle grabbed his hand. "That's it! Alex, I think you're right." She jumped. "Oh, Alex, I'm so excited for you. This means you're going to *fly*. Can you believe it?"

It was over the top. The whole of it...Tymbrelle, the portal, the dream. And now, *wings*? He was afraid to get his hopes up—it was beyond what he deserved.

He scooped Tymbrelle up and spun her around. "I didn't know a person could feel like they might explode from happiness. You are a huge part of it, Tymbrelle. Thank you."

She giggled and beamed up at him as he set her down.

He returned her smile and wondered how he had missed the two dimples that punctured her cheeks when she smiled with abandon. "I'm also glad we figured out why my back aches. It's been subtly getting worse all morning."

Alex glanced at the two chainmail-clad Gnomes flanking the doors to the dining hall. They were making a valiant attempt to act disinterested by the romance unfolding a few yards away. "

Let's eat," he said, grabbing her hand and twining his fingers in hers. "I *am* a growing Nephilim, after all."

CHAPTER SIXTY-FIVE

Sadie

SADIE SWAYED AGAINST XANDER, WRECKED BY the news of Alex's disappearance. Finnegan, Josiah, and Dempsey—along with a chattering miniature Dragon and an enormous, aromatic Ogre—stood in a loose cluster, shuffling their feet, heads bowed.

Unfortunately, the news had also been delivered in front of Queen Clodagh, King Odhran, and Deborah, who had been strolling with King Xander in the garden when word came about the returning entourage. Assuming a reunion of sorts, the visitors and a handful of others had gathered around the forlorn-looking runaways in the courtyard. Alex was not among them. A stilted tale unfolded between the crestfallen friends, as more people gathered to listen.

Once Sadie joined Xander, he insisted they explain it again in greater detail. Josiah had taken a step forward and launched into their misadventures—including some unflattering details about Magnum and his Dregs that would undoubtedly reach Lucia's ears within the hour. No one interrupted to tell Josiah that Magnum had beat their group home two days prior with no mention of having seen the others.

"We can only assume that Alex and Spock and our new friend Tymbrelle were...you know." Josiah had swallowed and taken a deep breath. "The—the thing is. The small pool of water quite literally devoured the three of them. They tumbled in, and the pool instantly dried up with them inside of it. The water and the rocks that rimmed it were sucked down. Like quicksand. The only thing left was a barren circle of dirt. Strangest thing we've ever seen."

Sadie had dropped to her knees, face in hands, and sobbed.

"Evidence of dark magic at work," King Odhran had

bellowed, oblivious to her pain. "It's best our daughter avoid such a union."

"Not now, Odhran," Xander said through gritted teeth.

Sadie's anger had sparked, compelling her to stand, with Xander's help. It took all of her willpower to refrain from screaming that she knew the truth about his so-called daughter. *Odhran, you are a self-righteous liar!*

She swiped at her tear-slicked face, wondering if this was the proverbial straw that might break her back. Could she handle losing another son? Had she truly lost him, or was something else afoot? This was not an unequivocal drowning, which left room for hope. Shoving down her despondency, Sadie determined to get through this public moment as best she could.

It occurred to her that Odhran and Clodagh had just been delivered the news that their secret weapon—the *real* Larkin— was gone as well. Sadie flicked her gaze to them, curious. Their faces remained stoic, though Deborah's cheeks flamed as red as her hair. No doubt they were forging ahead with their farce. But if this Tymbrelle—who *had* to be Larkin, based on Josiah's explanation of her skill with water—if she was really the adopted daughter of Éire House, wouldn't there be a trace of grief in Clodagh's face?

If anything, the set of the woman's bulldog mouth made her look annoyed by the news. Or inconvenienced. Not a trace of sadness to be found.

"What did I miss?" Ever the star of his own show, Magnum strolled up beside Xander and took in the disconsolate mood.

When he caught sight of Josiah and Finn and their companions—and as they stared back with tangible loathing— Sadie sensed his cockiness deflate.

"King Xander," Finn said, stepping forward, pointing at Magnum. "You need to take Magnum into custody. Josiah didn't exaggerate, he's a yellow-bellied traitor."

A rumble of disgust trickled through the crowd. Gage stepped up behind Magnum, and Sadie wondered when the commander had appeared on the scene. She hadn't paid much attention to who all had been present and now cast about hoping Ellynn had been spared the sickening news. It seemed she had, thank the Maker.

"Sheesh! Finnegan. *Relax.*" Magnum put his hands in the air to show his glowing guilelessness. "I'm a man without a country, so to speak. I've no place of prominence in Pacific House, nor could I hope to one day reclaim my maternal grandfather's throne in Éire House." He turned to the wide-eyed scowls of Odhran and Clodagh, giving them an exaggerated bow. "Your throne is under no threat from me, dear uncle."

The king and queen kept their matching default expressions on 'glower'..

"Who can blame a prince for wanting his own little corner of the world over which to rule and reign?" Magnum gave Xander an imploring stare. "My friends here are misrepresenting what happened. I can explain."

"Yous no fwend." The mountain of muscle stepped toward Magnum, pointing a meaty, accusing finger at him. "Yous a bully. Yous a meany and wanna make war."

Magnum gave a nervous chuckle. "Big Ogre here can barely speak. He's blathering nonsense."

Xander looked at Commander Gage and gave a slight twitch of his head.

"Let's go," Gage ordered, grabbing Magnum's upper arm.

Merrik stepped up to flank his other side.

"Stash his sorry behind in the dungeon," Xander called after them. "We're going to have a friendly chat in a bit." He turned and slipped an arm around Sadie's waist and said in an authoritative voice to everyone present, "Time to go about our business and duties. Until we confirm these speculations, Prince Brady Alexander remains *missing*. That is the only fact we have in hand. If anyone spreads rumors to the contrary, you will keep my brother company in the dungeon. Am I clear?"

Heads bobbed in agreement, and onlookers began to disperse.

Odhran and Clodagh approached Xander. "Pacific House is a fractured mess since King Aviel died," Odhran said. "I don't know that we have any further interest in pursuing a wedding that would join our houses."

Xander swept his hand toward the stables. "Fine. We will gladly send you back to Brihndle posthaste. Say the word, and we shall ready your horses."

"M'lady! Queen Sadie!"

Sadie turned to find Joanie charging down the palace steps, waving something overhead. The stout Dwarf clutched her skirt and apron with her other hand, her feet churning up dust as she approached.

"Carrier pigeon came from Vituvia, m'lady," Joanie huffed, holding out a tiny, tightly rolled scroll tied with a silver thread indicating the missive was urgent. "Master Willoughby sent me to deliver it straightaway."

"Thank you." Sadie plucked the scroll from Joanie's hand. It was no bigger than a french fry.

"You all right, m'lady? Yer awfully pale. May I bring ya some tea?"

"No thank you, Joanie," Sadie said, praying there wouldn't be more sad tidings within the slip of paper. She drifted to a bench, not trusting her legs.

Odhran and Clodagh turned in a huff toward the palace. Xander slipped onto the bench beside Sadie as she tugged the thread off the scroll. Heads together, they read the brief note in Sophie's handwriting.

"Oh!" Sadie gasped as she and Xander rapturously embraced.

They pulled far enough apart to smile into each other's faces and laugh.

"Thank the Maker, Sadie." Xander leaned in and kissed Sadie's cheeks. "Alex is fine. Our boy is *alive*."

CHAPTER SIXTY-SIX

Alex

"SOMETHING IS *DEFINITELY* HAPPENING WITH YOUR wingbuds," Sophie exclaimed, inspecting her nephew's back with the help of a step stool. "Simply amazing."

Alex had asked his aunt if he and Tymbrelle could have a word in private after breakfast. The three now stood in Aunt Sophie's office, which looked more like a library with its floor-to-ceiling bookshelves and cozy reading nook.

The pain in his shoulder blades had steadily increased throughout the morning meal. Despite the jocular conversation shared with friends and family—which included a happy reunion with Grandmother Amy and Aunt Nicole, whom he had recently seen at King Aviel's funeral—he could no longer pretend to be okay. At this point, it literally hurt to breathe.

He had gingerly removed his shirt, cool air providing a new sensation of pain. Tymbrelle had gasped at the sight of his pink, swollen wingbuds before clamping a hand over her mouth when he turned to look at her.

"How am I supposed to go back to Calamus right away when I can barely breathe, let alone move or ride a horse?" He walked to where an oval mirror hung on a gilt frame beside the office door. He had to squat a good bit to view his shoulder blades, and the sight made him wince. His wingbuds had swollen to three or four times their previous size. They looked disgusting, like a couple of sweltering boils ready to split his skin.

His aunt shook her head. She looked a little pale. "Let's ask my mother to take a look since she's a nurse."

"It's not as if anything's wrong. This is normal. The pain is part of the process." Alex moved to the polished mahogany desk and perched on its corner, still clutching his shirt. He'd been given a clean white tunic that belonged to Brock, though it was too short on Alex to be considered a tunic. He still wore his trousers, which had dried out overnight. "It's only going to get worse—plus it lasts a couple of weeks. Uncle Brock said I should go home right away. I *want* to go home. There's a lot at stake, and I should be there. I'm wondering how I can manage the trip, though, let alone be of any help once I arrive."

"Your uncle also said you should use the lagoon," Tymbrelle reminded him. "And that strange thing about your having the tools. Maybe the water will help in someway."

Alex nodded, recalling his uncle's cryptic words. "You know him better than anyone, Aunt Soph. Do you know what kind of tools he thinks I have? There's no way I can swim with this pain level—operating tools is out of the question. I don't even want to lift my hand to scratch my chin. Sir Noblin claims the portal is gone, so maybe the lagoon isn't the answer."

Aunt Sophie paced the length of her desk, tapping a finger against her lip. "I've been trying to make sense of it myself."

"Maybe it recreates itself with those mysterious tools," Tymbrelle offered, taking a seat on the nearest wingback chair.

Evidently, Aunt Sophie had loaned Tymbrelle a pair of olive-colored breeches and a black, topside T-shirt. Both of which hung loosely on the girl's small frame. A simple pair of black flip-flops completed her casual ensemble.

Alex marveled that only yesterday Tymbrelle had gills and scales and a fluke—a vision straight out of a fairytale. Today she could slip into any Portland coffee shop and blend right in. Well, her tumble of silver-blond tresses and heart-shaped face would still be turning heads, just not in quite the same way as a Mermaid.

"Let me have a word with Brock," Sophie said. She looked from Tymbrelle to Alex. "And a word with your grandmother, too. She may have something for your pain. Too bad Prilla isn't here—she probably has some experience with Nephilim transformations. We've had our share of Nephilim guests through the years. Anyway...hang tight."

Alex watched her leave. It even hurt to move his eyeballs.

"Who's Prilla?" Tymbrelle asked, coming over to Alex.

"The Vituvian Healer. A Gnome, obviously. My mom summoned her to help with my father's, you know, situation." Alex's face fell, and he managed a small shake of his head. "Man, I've barely thought about my father's fever-dreams this whole time, even though I tried to tell myself that looking for a cure was one reason for running away. I wish there was a way to get him some of the water from the lagoon. Look what it did for both of us."

Tymbrelle swished a lock of hair behind her ear. "Maybe your aunt can give you a container to take back to him."

"Good idea." He grinned at Tymbrelle, hoping she couldn't see the prickly beads of sweat on his upper lip. Talking was becoming an effort. The pain seemed to be oozing from his very pores. How had Finn and Josiah dealt with this when they were scrawny twelve or thirteen-year-old boys?

His limbs were beginning to tremble, and he slowly slipped his hands in his pockets to hide them. The white rocks from the portal were still nestled inside, and he wondered how he hadn't noticed them knocking about in his pocket whenever he moved. He supposed that the pain had distracted him for longer than he realized.

"You okay?" Tymbrelle was looking at him funny.

He attempted a nod but found he couldn't stop himself from slumping over as he wondered who had snuffed out the torches.

CHAPTER SIXTY-SEVEN

Ellynn

ALEX. DROWNED. ALEX. DROWNED. ALEX. DROWNED.

Ellynn couldn't stop repeating the two devastating words as she aimlessly tromped within the castle's maze-like walls. Her footsteps matched the tempo of the chant as she tried in vain to shut off her mental metronome. In her grief, she didn't remember slipping into the familiar space, so she steered herself to the older, deserted parts of the palace. At least no one would find her and she could avoid eavesdropping on anyone—accidentally or otherwise.

By now the tears had dried into itchy trails on her cheeks and neck, and her heart was rattling around in pieces inside her chest. Meanwhile, her mind refused to accept it.

Alex was an excellent swimmer. His lack of flight drove him to be the best at everything else. Drowning sounded wrong.

Drowned. Alex. Drowned. Alex. Drowned. Alex.

The two words drummed on a continuous loop until they switched emphasis in the rhythm. The shift in meaning brought her up short. Of course! The *real* Princess Larkin had a special ability with water. If Alex had run away, and Larkin had run away...maybe their paths had crossed and things did not end well.

That was the only way to reconcile the inconceivable loss of her brother. Larkin better watch her back if she ever decided to show her face in Calamus.

Ellynn suddenly needed fresh air and made quick work of finding an exit from this stuffy, uncharted portion of the castle. She didn't travel far before spotting an opening in the wall that had been boarded over—one wide slat of wood conveniently missing. How had she never noticed this point of interest? She must have wandered deeper and further than she realized, since she normally haunted the lived-in areas.

The musty smell of dirt and tobacco piqued her interest. An old larder? Mindful not to set the wall on fire, she shined the torch inside the space, wishing she would have brought a flashlight instead.

Something scuttled away, but her furtive habits meant she'd learned not to be squeamish. She spied a busted, empty barrel. The iron bands encircling it were rusty. Cobwebs danced on the air she disturbed, festooning the walls and corners. Shelves lined the perpendicular wall, contents coated with so much ashy dust as to be unrecognizable, though her nose told her that cigars or pipe tobacco must be among the items. The space fed into a bigger room through an open doorway.

She carefully threaded her limbs through the deteriorating wall and tiptoed through the larder and into the next room. A swipe of her torch revealed a larger and equally dusty and forgotten space. A roughhewn table was shoved into one corner with a busted chair lying dejectedly nearby. A faint ribbon of light along the floor indicated a door on the opposite wall. Where was she?

Ellynn crossed to it, pausing to listen. By the flickering flame, she noticed something hanging on a hook beside the door. A grimy serpentine shape revealed itself as a leather whip—and not the kind a horse trainer would use. *Weird*. Also on the hook hung a ring of brass keys.

She grinned. These might come in handy for future expeditions—that is, if she ever, per chance, found herself wandering the labyrinth of spaces between the walls again. One day. Maybe.

Ellynn clasped her fingers around the dangling skeleton keys to muffle sound and stuff them into her pocket.

Again she waited, ear to the doorjamb, and heard nothing. With care, she grasped the lever. It groaned from disuse, but she managed to open the door a few inches. She placed one eye against the crack, straining to focus in the paltry light. A nondescript passage greeted her. She slipped from the room and stood there, listening. The faintest noise came from her right, along with the hint of distant torchlight. Placing her own torch in an empty sconce, she headed that direction.

The corridor curved out of sight, and Ellynn kept to the wall as she followed it around. Her ears focused on an indistinct, rhythmic scraping noise. Then she spied a barred door standing wide.

She was in the dungeon! A place strictly forbidden by her parents. The largest of the castle's turrets housed the prisoners. There was no way she could sneak out the dungeon doors unnoticed. She should turn and go back the way she came.

The scraping noise continued. Ellynn recognized it as a soft snore. Beyond that solitary sound, the space felt deserted. Though she'd never given any thought to how many prisoners were kept in the dungeon, she didn't expect it to be nearly vacant. Of course, there was a prison within the town of Calamus, so perhaps there was little need to hold criminals in this archaic place.

Emboldened by her conclusions, Ellynn decided to take a peek at the unlucky sap who was stuck here. Plus, when would she get another opportunity to observe this area? It wasn't as if she planned on being a regular visitor.

Cell doors stood ajar on either side of the wide, curving passageway. Keeping to the wall, Ellynn spotted a pair of filthy black boots. The crescendo of sound meant this person must be the source of the snoring. Who was he guarding?

Ellynn's insatiable curiosity pushed her on. If the guard woke, she would warn him to keep his mouth shut unless he wanted Commander Gage to know about his sleeping habits while on duty. She would simply take a peek at the prisoner and go back to where she began.

Her moccasins were quiet as a whisper, and she took care to press her hand against the keys in her pocket. With more boldness than she felt, she walked as normally as she could manage—in case the guard woke up—while keeping her eyes glued to his noisy nose.

Tilted back so that his head rested against the wall, an explosion of black whiskers made it hard to see much beyond the beacon of his sniffer. His wings were the color of the rock and dust surrounding him, and they drooped in a way that told Ellynn he was sleeping deeply, though it seemed an odd time of day to be so tired. Perhaps he was drunk, which would only give her more leverage.

He sat a good five feet from the only cell door that was closed. Maybe he'd purposely moved away in order to nap out of arm's reach. Ellynn stopped in front of the barred door, her heart bumping wildly behind its own cell of its ribcage. She stepped closer, squinting at the murky gloom inside.

A single candle dripped wax onto the base of a candleholder and cast its limp pool of light on the filthy floor. Someone sat with their back against the wall, revealing part of a wing and arm and hip, while the rest of the person remained in shadow.

"Ellynn, what are you doing here?"

Ellynn jumped at the sound of her name, realizing she hadn't thought past being caught by the guard. A prisoner could tattle too. Although it was no surprise to be recognized, she was stricken by the unpleasant familiarity of the voice.

The figure stood and moved toward the door. Torchlight in the passage revealed the quizzical, scowling face of Uncle Magnum. What in the name of Whitt Lake was he doing in the dungeon?

She opened her mouth, but he pressed a finger to his lips and shook his head. Ellynn stole a glance at the snoozing soldier and nodded at Magnum to show her understanding.

He came close and she took a step back, her mind flashing to the scene in the vineyard with Deborah.

His face fell as he registered her fear. "*Please.* You have to help me, Ellynn." Magnum's voice was as hushed as an exhale, though his eyes were pleading loudly. He spoke with slow deliberation.

She shot an uneasy look at the guard, then shook her head *no.*

"*Lis*-ten." He swiped a hand across his mouth then leaned his forearm against one of the bars. "You have every reason to distrust me. I get it. I deserve it. Please, hear me out," he said between the guard's snores.

Ellynn swallowed at the desperation she saw in his face. It couldn't hurt to listen, could it? She gave a nod.

"Thanks," he mouthed.

Ellynn held up her palm before he could get started. "Why are you here?" She mimicked his careful, quiet way of speaking.

He pressed his lips before answering. "I've made some choices that are being misconstrued. That's what I want to talk to you about. There's a way for me to make it right. It will reveal the truth. It's just, well, I can't do it from in here. I need your help."

This guy was so full of himself. Ellynn narrowed her eyes. Could this have anything to do with the news about Alex? Had

Magnum been responsible? He had motive.

"You've never needed my help before." She hissed the words more loudly than she intended, and Magnum's eyes flashed.

He made an impatient gesture. "Yeah. I get it. Like I said, I deserve it." He shifted so both hands gripped the bars on either side of his face, which made him look like a very authentic prisoner. "Please. I'm begging you. Help me."

"I'm listening."

"Thank you." He may have attempted a smile, but it looked more like a grimace. "I need you to sneak into the stables and set the hippogriff free. That's it. She will fly away and that will be that."

That's all? Ellynn couldn't see why a tethered hippogriff would matter to a man who pulled the wings off ladybugs as a child. "Why?"

"I can't explain that right now. Please, you have to do this for me." His grip tightened on the bars. "I was about to set her free when"—he gestured impatiently at the cell—"when this happened. Believe me, it's essential for the protection of Calamus. You won't regret it."

"Does this have anything to do with your army of Dregs?"

Magnum blinked and gave a little gasp. "How...who told you *that*?"

The guard snorted loudly and folded his dangling arms. Ellynn instantly pressed herself against the wall until she was certain the guard was back in dreamland.

"Is it true?" she repeated, stepping back to the door.

"It's not what it sounds like." Magnum shook his head, mouth set, jaw flexing. "Ellynn, I promise that what I'm trying to do is *protect* Calamus. I know I've been a jerk. But part of it has been...like a charade. I've been playing a part."

"Your entire life?"

He grinned at that. "It may seem that way. Maybe it wasn't a stretch for me to step into this particular role. Only it is just *that*. A role. A façade. I've had to make it believable. I can't explain right now, but hopefully, if everything I've worked for goes as planned...then you'll see. Everyone will see."

Ellynn felt conflicted. Magnum's impassioned speech was quite convincing. How hard could it be to set the hippogriff free? It didn't belong here anyway. She nodded. "Fine. I'll do it."

Magnum released a noisy breath. "Thank you, thank you,

thank you. I promise I'll never be a jerk to you again."

"Yeah, well what about Princess Larkin? In fact, unless you promise to apologize to her, I'm backing out."

Magnum's nostrils flared at this. "Trust me. She's no princess."

It was Ellynn's turn to react. "What makes you so sure?"

"Doesn't matter. I know. I can tell by your reaction that you do too."

His voice had steadily grown louder, and the guard smacked his lips together. Ellynn couldn't risk his catnap coming to an end. She needed to leave.

"You still owe her an apology." She gave Magnum her best smug thirteen-year-old smile.

"Fine. I will. Still, it wasn't what it looked like."

"Whatever. Just make sure you apologize." She flashed him that smirk again. "*If* you ever get out of here."

He only glared.

"So, should I walk out the main dungeon door or what? How many guards are out there?"

"What? How did you get in—never mind. Obviously, you've been flitting about in the dark with the bats again."

She gave an innocent shrug.

"Go back the way you came, if you can manage it. There are several guards between here and freedom. Plus, your dad is heading here any minute to *chat* with me, as he put it."

Well, that was a no-brainer. Time to go. She took a step back and leveled her gaze on her uncle. "I better not regret this."

"You won't."

She made to turn away when he said, "Ellynn."

"*What?*" Her thumping heart was like a clock ticking down to zero. She didn't want her father to catch her here.

"It might be hard to believe but...I was actually sitting here asking the Maker for help. And suddenly, you were standing in front of my cell."

CHAPTER SIXTY-EIGHT

Alex

ALEX GROANED AT THE EFFORT IT took to lift his eyelids. They felt weighted down and, possibly, glued shut. Maybe he was in that ultra groggy state of deep sleep. What Finn called "sleep drunk." By sheer will, he opened his eyes—only to blink them closed against the glaring white sand.

Hold on. Sand? That couldn't be right.

He peeked again. The gleaming floor of the Garden Dome stretched before him like a pearly desert. Further away, the cerulean water of the lagoon rippled beneath the arch of the footbridge and disappeared under the ebony granite wall that separated the Flaming Sword of Cherubythe from the garden beyond. His gaze shifted to the pyramid of boulders and the blueish flame of fire enveloping the ancient sword.

How did he end up here? Alex lay on his stomach on some sort of pallet. His head felt as stuffed as a feather mattress, and he closed his eyes again, rummaging in his brain for the last thing he could remember.

Ah, yes...Aunt Sophie, in the library, with the revolver. He grinned into his pillow, amused by his own sense of humor. Drool slipped from his mouth, and he made an indelicate slurping sound.

Then the rest of his memories slowly stitched themselves together. Sophie had left him and Tymbrelle to speak with Uncle Brock and his grandmother Amy. He had been in a supreme amount of pain. Perhaps he'd blacked out?

Alex couldn't currently detect any sort of back pain—and, based on the fuzzy filter holding his brain captive—guessed his grandmother had come through.

So why had he been placed in the near-sacred space of the Garden Dome and left on his own? As if in answer to his question, several people headed his way from the floor-level door.

As his vision cleared, he noticed the usual contingent of guards stationed along the back wall and upon the balustrades of the raised platforms. They really are such cute little guys and gals, he thought. And giggled.

The next thing he knew, Tymbrelle was leaning over him, her knees near his nose.

"You okay, Alex?" She touched his arm.

Several sets of feet surrounded him, and he reluctantly shifted his gaze from Tymbrelle's sweet smile to Spock's grinning face.

"Dude!" he said, giving Alex a thumbs-up. "You okay? I hear you're going to be flying solo soon. That's awesome."

Alex hoped he wasn't drooling in front of Tymbrelle.

In quick succession, he recognized his grandmother, Uncle Brock, and both Aunt Sophie and Aunt Nicole as they took turns peering at him, inspecting his back, feeling his forehead, and making a fuss. Well, except for his aloof uncle, who stood nearby to watch their ministrations.

Alex tuned in and out like a faulty radio signal. Slowly the words and movements began to make sense. Unfortunately, this meant he also grew aware of the searing pain in his wingbuds again.

"Hello, Mimi," he whispered when his grandmother placed a cool cloth on his head. "*Mm.* Thanks."

"Shh. You're doing great, hon. I know this is rough." She stroked his hair. "Good news. We've contacted the Garden Dweller. He's working on an herbal concoction to get you through the next twenty-four hours. Something that will help you deal with the pain without knocking you into tomorrow like the medicine I gave you. Brock says you need to return home as soon as possible, but you're not going to make it in this condition."

Garden Dweller...

Alex squinted up at his grandmother. "Enoch?" He remembered his family's encounter with the man who "walked with God and was no more" from their shared experiences and his mother's books. Enoch tended the garden on the other side of the wall. Specifically, the Tree of Life. His public appearances were rarer than Bigfoot sightings.

Mimi's chocolatey eyes crinkled into a smile, and she nodded. "The one and only. Straight out of Genesis."

Goosebumps raced up his arm at the thought of meeting a man who famously never died.

"That's why we placed you here, dear," she went on. "He's a bit of a recluse. Plus, as soon as the medicine does its thing, you and Tymbrelle can be on your way." She removed the damp cloth, dipping it back into a small bucket of water that Alex hadn't noticed before, and wrung it out again before placing it back on his forehead.

"Thanks, Mimi," he murmured. "Where's Bops? I haven't seen him since I arrived."

"I hope you never get too old to call us Mimi and Bops," she said, patting his cheek. "Bops and your Uncle Nate went hunting in Berganstroud with some of the Dwarves. Scarce father-son bonding time lately. They'll be sorry to've missed you."

"Enoch is coming!" Sophie announced.

Alex felt a strange thrill and wished he was meeting this legend under different circumstances. One without blossoming pain and leftover brain-numbing medicine.

Enoch was a man of small stature and a large yet serene demeanor. Alex recalled some snippets surrounding the things he had done to help the Larcen family back in the day. It had been several years since Alex last read his mother's trilogy, but he remembered that this bronze-skinned, barefoot, bald man had been there that fateful day when Brady—the original Brady—heroically saved the Flaming Sword and his twin brother Brock.

Now, that very wizened and wise man crouched beside Alex, his rough burlap tunic brushing Alex's knuckles. Shame washed over Alex in the presence of such a famously devout legend. Maybe if he lay still and didn't interact with the man, Enoch wouldn't know what kind of person Alex really was—so different from his namesake. Maybe he wouldn't sense the gaping chasm that separated Brady Alexander of Calamus from Brady Larcen of Orchards, Washington.

That's the old me, he reminded himself, flashing back to his strange dream. *Today is a new day.*

No one spoke as Enoch worked. Alex sensed that everyone was a bit in awe of the man. He rarely left his garden, so every interaction was like a celebrity sighting in Hollywood. Except Hollywood was full of darkness while Enoch was full of light.

The man hummed softly as he set down his pouch and withdrew some plant cuttings–two fern-like stems about six inches long. Alex watched by lazily opening his eyes every few seconds. Sort of a reverse way of blinking.

A stone mortar and pestle and small bottle with a cork were removed, followed by tiny, twin crockery bowls wrapped protectively in rough cloth similar to Enoch's tunic. In under a minute, Enoch had sprinkled a pinch of this and that from the crockery bowls into the stone mortar, then drizzled what appeared to be oil from the small, corked bottle, giving the contents a stir with his knobby fingers. Finally, he tore the bright fern-like plant into bits and set about crushing it into the mixture with the pestle. A tangy, bitter scent enveloped Alex, though it wasn't unpleasant.

Enoch scooted closer to Alex's ribcage, making it harder for Alex to see the man hovering over his shoulder. No matter, focusing was difficult with the burgeoning pain at his back. It felt to Alex as if his skin might burst like a hot sausage splitting its casing.

The sticky sound of Enoch scooping out his homemade concoction was followed by the sting of the man's palms placed over each of Alex's wingbuds. Alex sucked in a pained breath before releasing an agonized growl through gritted teeth. When the pain abated somewhat, Alex managed to open his eyes and look at his audience.

Everyone had stepped back. King Brock stood halfway to the door with his hands over his ears, sensitive as ever to sound.

With each application, Alex felt as if Enoch was branding his wingbuds with a hot iron, searing them to his palms. Tears leaked from Alex's eyes and a buzzing sort of headache took flight.

Then, as suddenly as the pain had obliterated his senses, it went away. Not exactly gone but miraculously dull. Enoch mixed more salve, then repeated the process again, each round causing less of a reaction.

Finally, Alex felt nothing. He felt normal. It was bliss! A sluggish smile rippled his lips, and Tymbrelle, Mimi, and the others slowly crept back to their spots.

Enoch wasn't finished. The next time he glazed his hands and placed them on Alex's back, he leaned over so that his mouth was beside Alex's ear.

"I have been waiting for you, my son," Enoch whispered. His accent was faintly Middle Eastern, his herbal breath warm against Alex's cheek.

Waiting...for me? Alex didn't believe the man knew of his

existence before yesterday.

"He who created and named each star in the heavens also created you and knows your name and the pain of your losses here in the belly of the earth. You have not escaped His notice, my son. Quite the opposite." And here, Enoch gave a quiet chuckle. "He who created and named each star reminds you that He turns broken things into beautiful things, be they stars or people. Nothing is wasted when sifted through the Maker's hand."

Alex's swollen wingbuds were no match for the swelling of his heart. Joy, rather than pain, blossomed inside with each word Enoch spoke. They were a salve of truth, and Alex marveled that he had not seen it for himself. Alex always thought his soul had been crushed by the tragedies in his life. Yet, somehow, he was really undergoing the pain of transformation that would, one day, allow him to soar. His wings growing and his soul awakening were intrinsically, mysteriously connected, much like last night's dream and today's encounter with Enoch.

"Do not shun the tears, my son. They are very cleansing." Enoch touched Alex's cheek, then sat back and wiped his hands clean with a scrap of cloth from his pouch.

Alex hadn't known he was crying.

CHAPTER SIXTY-NINE

Alex

ALEX FELT LIKE A NEW NEPHILIM, inside and out. He stood at the water's edge, amazed by the twin miracles of hope and healing he had experienced. The reprieve from the pain might be temporary, but at least he could handle the journey home.

He turned to his Vituvian family and friends with a sheepish grin. "As much as I would love for us to stay, I feel a bit like Cinderella. If I don't get home before this medicine wears off, I'm going to turn into a pumpkin. Or a rat. Choose your insult."

"I would say you're going to turn into a handsome prince, but you are already that and more," Mimi said. "I'm so glad Enoch was able to help."

"Me too." Alex glanced to where the lithe, ancient man had climbed up a rope ladder that soon disappeared with him over the other side. "Though at first it felt like he was trying to kill me."

"Don't suppose you'd tell us what sort of secrets he was whispering to you?" Sophie gave him her best innocently pleading look.

"Yeah, c'mon," Spock chimed from the vicinity of Alex's feet. "Share the old guy's words of wisdom."

"Hey, there's a reason whispering is a thing." He winked at Aunt Sophie, then turned his attention to Aunt Nicole, grabbing her in a hug. "Good to see you, Auntie Nic. I hope to come stay with you soon." He didn't mention that, if plans had carried on as he'd intended, he would've turned up on her doorstep.

"My house is your house, Brady—uh, Alex. You know we'd love to have you for as long as you can stay."

Alex plunged his hands in his pockets and scrunched his shoulders together. "Thanks. You know I'll take you up on that. We're long overdue for a Trailblazers game."

"Speak for yourself, I have season tickets," his aunt taunted.

"So..." Alex clenched and unclenched the trio of rocks in his pocket. "Any genius ideas about how I'm supposed use the lagoon to get home?"

"We," Tymbrelle stage-whispered beside him. "How do *we* use the lagoon."

"Right," Alex said. "*We*. Tymbrelle, Spock, and me. How do we get home?"

Spock made a slicing motion with his hands. "Nope. Sorry, dude. Mom's insisting I stay. You know how she can be..."

"Yeah. Concerned and loving and all that annoying stuff." Alex nudged his tiny friend with his knee. "Hope you can put up with it."

The Gnome stepped close and waved Alex down to whispering level. "I'll be back sooner than you think. Mom keeps talking about some girl she wants to introduce me to. Can you believe it?"

Alex had to laugh. "Take it from me, you might be surprised. Keep an open mind." He straightened and gave Tymbrelle an appreciative glance.

"Oh, speaking of Reiko," Aunt Sophie said. "After you mentioned Magnum's army of Dregs and how Éire House had nefarious plans for Calamus. Well, she thought it prudent to dispatch a company of soldiers to provide back-up."

"Excellent! Thank you," Alex said. "I've no clue what we might find when we get there." He looked at Tymbrelle. "You ready?"

She slipped her hand in his. "Lead the way."

"Uncle Brock?"

Brock hung back a few feet in his usual aloof manner. He wore a long, white linen shirt and brown breeches that made from supple leather. Alex always thought his uncle looked very regal with his spun-gold hair, square jaw, and the confident way he carried himself. He had the posture of someone born for greatness.

"Alex, you have your tools," King Brock said.

Alex and Tymbrelle exchanged an uncertain glance.

"I was hoping you might have some tools to share, Uncle Brock," Alex said. "All I've got are the clothes on my back."

Sophie stepped beside her brother. "Care to elaborate, big

brother? Is there something special about what Alex is wearing?"

"Clothing and rocks, actually." Alex fished two of the rocks from his pocket and held them in his palm. "They're from the water portal. I forgot they were in my pocket until a little while ago."

"Yes." Brock shifted closer to Alex and picked up one of the rocks, turning it over in his palm. "These are your tools." He squatted down and held one of the oval stones inches above the pearly floor. "The rock and the floor are one and the same."

Alex was thrilled by how accidentally easy it was to be equipped with these 'tools'. Maybe the rest of the journey would unfold with as little effort. *Ha.* "I have three of the rocks, actually."

Brock handed him the rock. "You each need your own rock, unless you hold onto each other."

Alex wiggled his eyebrows at Tymbrelle. "I promise to hold on to you if you promise to hold on to me." He slipped one of the rocks back into his pocket.

Tymbrelle laughed.

Brock gestured at the turquoise water. "It is time."

Curious to learn how these rocks, or *tools*, might get them to Calamus, Alex trailed after Tymbrelle toward the lagoon. Everyone followed along.

Alex looked at the rock, then down at the water. "I'm sorry, Uncle Brock. I really don't understand how this rock can get us back." He had visions of tapping the rock against his forehead and repeating, "There's no place like home, there's no place like home."

"The rock knows where to take you," Brock said. "Hold onto it. And hold Tymbrelle's hand. If you are separated, I do not know if you will make it to the same place together. A sending out is unlike a gathering in."

"Where did you learn this, Brock?" Sophie asked. "It's not as if any of us have firsthand experience with this portal business."

"Sometimes, you just know," he said and gave a little shrug.

Sophie, Nicole, and Mimi shared a knowing smile.

"Classic Brock-ism right there." Nicole said, applauding. "I sure miss you when I'm away."

Brock only grinned.

Alex retrieved another rock and gave it to Tymbrelle. "In

case something happens and we get separated."

She nodded and took the rock but didn't meet his eyes. Alex sensed a sudden reluctance.

"You okay?" he asked.

Tymbrelle gave a little shrug. "Guess we'll see. Fact is, I've no idea if jumping back into this pool will change me back into a Mermaid again. Worked that way yesterday."

Alex wondered why he hadn't considered that himself. "Tymbrelle, I—I don't know what to say." Then he had a flash of brilliance. "But if you *do* change back, I'll let you kiss me again. I'm happy to help. Repeatedly."

She gave him a playful slap. "You'll let me? Generous of you. Let's see what happens then."

The family wished them well and stepped back, giving them space to get in on their own terms.

"Count to three and jump?" Tymbrelle asked.

"Can Mermaids count that high?"

"*Ooh*, ouch. I don't know. Can hairless Yetis swim?"

They stepped to the edge, and Alex did a quick scan for the enormous blob of an octopus that might be lurking nearby. "Ready?"

"As ever."

They grasped their rocks, clasped their hands, and counted in unison.

CHAPTER SEVENTY

Ellynn

IT HADN'T BEEN HARD TO SET the hippogriff free. The difficulty came from second guessing her uncle, herself, and what the repercussions might be. Her tumultuous thoughts left her queasy with anxiety.

Once Ellynn had retraced her steps from the dungeon and found a safe place to slip back into the palace, she'd strode into the stable yard like she belonged there. The imposing eagle-horse hybrid had been eating from a trough, dragging a length of chain that shackled her right hind leg to a metal hitching post.

Ellynn found two stable hands cleaning horse stalls and tried using her princess privilege. "My father, King Xander, says that there's no reason to keep the hippogriff here. Magnum will not be permitted to leave. He's in the dungeon." She relished throwing that in for authenticity and could tell by their reactions that gossip of his arrest had made the rounds.

They nodded deferentially, and the freckled stable hand started toward the door, taking a set of keys out of a pouch at his waist. The other man followed, bowlegged and limping slightly.

Ellynn watched them leave, paralyzed by a sudden wave of doubt. Why was she trusting her lying, traitorous uncle—especially after what she'd overheard from Katheryn and Gouldor? Magnum was a master manipulator, after all. And what would her father say when he learned of Ellynn's lie to manipulate his stable hands? Recalling Magnum's pleading, however, made her doubt her doubts.

But not enough.

Panicked, Ellynn ran after the stable hands. "Wait!" she called, flinging wide the half-door of the barn.

Before she could say more, the magnificent creature was

airborne, wings outstretched, talons and hooves neatly tucked beneath her belly. She circled once as if to say goodbye, then flew away.

Ellynn watched the creature grow smaller as the sick feeling in her stomach expanded. Ugh! She was going to be in some deep doo-doo if Magnum was playing her.

She took her time getting back to the palace. It wasn't as if anyone would notice she'd been gone for hours. They were too busy with their grown-up business, after all. This stunt would only reinforce everyone's childish notions of her. *Great.*

With no further diversions, Alex's drowning came back in full force. She felt the strangest mixture of sadness and numbness, like her emotions didn't quite belong to her. Ellynn only knew that she could not conceive of a future without her big brother.

Lost in thought, she hadn't noticed her mother pounding down the steps of the portico, running toward her.

"Ellynn! Honey. Where have you been?"

Ellynn looked up right as her mother enveloped her in a hug.

"Oh, *Mom.*" At least her mother had noticed she'd been gone. "I can't believe it. I can't!" It felt so good to cry about it with someone else.

"Oh, no. Ellynn, dear. I'm sorry. *So* sorry." Her mother said into Ellynn's curls. "It's not what you think. It's not what you've heard."

Ellynn pulled back and looked at her mother through blurry eyes. "What do you mean?"

Sadie grasped her daughter's face in gentle hands and wiped at Ellynn's tears with her thumbs. "I've been looking for you everywhere. I hoped to prevent you from hearing any nasty rumors about your brother, but I see I'm too late. Honey, Alex is fine. He's turned up in Vituvia."

Ellynn gasped. "Are you serious?"

Sadie nodded, shedding a few happy tears of her own.

"I can't believe it!" Ellynn squealed. "Thank God! I'm so relieved. I'm so relieved."

Mother and daughter exchanged a good, long hug and headed inside.

Ellynn was very happy and suddenly *very* hungry.

Dinner was a strange affair. As per usual, Éire House felt insulted about something and took their meal in their quarters. Ellynn had barely seen Deborah the last few days and planned to pay her a visit later. She hoped the girl had recovered from her run-in with Magnum in the vineyard.

Ellynn, Mom, and Grandmama took their meal in the family dining room, but the whole evening felt off. Her mother was evasive when Ellynn asked why her dad wasn't eating with them. Grandmama Lucia spoke only when spoken to. Despite the stilted conversation, Ellynn did manage to get a rehash of the difficulty that Alex and his friends had faced on their journey.

When her mother explained about Magnum's little kingdom in the mountains, Ellynn remembered the things she overheard from the pantry. That info would have to wait for a private revelation, however. Thoughts of Magnum and the hippogriff continued to make her insides squeamish so she pushed them aside as best she could.

The best news was learning that Aunt Sophie had sent word that Alex—and Spock, too—was *alive*. Alive and well and with this girl whom Josiah and Finn called Tymbrelle who was, Ellynn knew, the real Princess Larkin.

Apparently King Odhran had threatened to leave and take their "princess" with them. Ellynn considered that option the simplest and safest for all. Calamus could find some semblance of normalcy again, and it would save Deborah from Magnum's clutches as well. A 'two-fer'.

"What did Deborah mean when she mentioned a midnight visit from my *henchwoman*? If that is even a word," Grandmama Lucia asked, breaking her silence and completely off-topic.

Ellynn looked from her grandmother to her mother. "Sorry, did I miss something?"

Her grandmother placed her fork on the plate with a metallic clank. It looked like she'd only pushed her food around and hadn't eaten a bite. "I've been thinking about our conversation with Deborah the other day. She said something that I brushed off at the time because it was beside the point. But it's been bothering me. She said something about a midnight visit from your—meaning *my*—hench-woman." She pronounced the last word in two distinct parts.

Oh yes, Ellynn knew all about that. Since Katheryn was her grandmother's lady's maid, surely *she* knew as well.

Grandmama Lucia was the one who had warned them that she had eyes and ears all over the palace, after all.

Her mother looked at Ellynn and froze with her fork halfway to its target. "Ellynn Jules, I can tell you know something about this. Answer your grandmother."

"Yes, ma'am." Ellynn wasn't trying to hide anything, but she was surprised that Grandmama wanted to have this conversation in front of Mom. "I...guess I figured you knew about it."

"About what?" Grandmama Lucia asked.

Did she really need Ellynn to spell it out? "I figured you had, well, authorized it. Lady Katheryn came into our rooms while we were asleep. As a—a warning."

"What?" Her mother smacked her fork onto the tablecloth and looked from Ellynn to Grandmama Lucia. "Exactly why would my daughter think you had *authorized* such behavior, Lucia? Please, explain."

All the spiciness seemed to be missing from her salty grandmother. In fact, it had been missing the entire meal, which was one reason things felt so weird. Like a thermometer rapidly rising, a flush of crimson swept up her grandmother's neck and blushed her cheeks. She pressed her fingertips to her temples and slowly shook her head.

Ellynn exchanged a look of shock with her mother. Something must be terribly wrong for Grandmama to be in such a state.

Her mom offered no sympathy. "Is that you shaking your head 'no' that you *cannot* explain Ellynn's comment, or do you have something you wish to tell us?"

Grandmama Lucia folded her hands in her lap and sat up straighter—the woman never entirely slumped—and took a long inhale through her pinched nose. "I may have insinuated as much with Ellynn and Deborah, whom I thought was Larkin." Another deep breath. "Look, I realize I have a lot to explain. Perhaps 'confess' is a better term for it, I don't know. This whole thing has gotten way out of control, and if I don't have some help reining it in..." She shuddered. "Things could go really bad really fast, Sadie. I'm truly sorry to involve you and, of course, my granddaughter in this—this *situation*." She looked at Ellynn and reached for her hand. "I owe you a most sincere apology, my dear."

Ellynn was flummoxed once again. She felt the sting of tears.

"Lucia." Her mother's voice still had an edge. "I've no doubt that you mean what you've said, and your honesty is appreciated. You and I will be speaking with Xander, *straightaway*. However, I demand an explanation of how this involves my daughter."

Grandmama Lucia's poise deflated slightly with another heavy sigh. She squeezed Ellynn's hand. "You tell her, dear. Start with our conversation after our brunch. Yes, yes, I remember my warning, but if I'm going to come clean then I'm going all out. Isn't that one of those Topsider clichés? Don't forget to explain what happened with Kat—that double-crossing witch. I want to hear it too."

Ellynn sputtered at that last statement, and Grandmama Lucia laughed. She clapped her hands together lightly. "Gracious, it feels good to finally say that out loud. Now then." With a sweep of her hand, she encouraged Ellynn to tell all.

Ellynn didn't hold back, doing her best to quote the insults and share the terror of waking up with someone's hand pressed over her mouth. Grandmama Lucia slowly withered against her chair as the story exposed her ugliness, especially her threat to *kill* their families if they breathed a word of what they heard.

Ellynn's mom, on the other hand, seemed to fill the space with righteous indignation. Ellynn sensed her mother holding back from a good tongue lashing and, perhaps, a bit of bodily harm.

In the end, Grandmama Lucia was crying, clearly ashamed. She also assured Ellynn and her mother that—for the sake of guaranteeing that the girls wouldn't talk—she had greatly exaggerated her network of listening ears. She swore she would never have asked Katheryn to threaten them in that way. Things were coming to light that revealed Kat and a few others as double-crossers.

"Well still, Grandmama Lucia," Ellynn said, not entirely convinced. "You threatened to *kill* our families if we breathed a word of it. Actually, you said as long as we kept our mouths shut you would *allow* our families to live. Same idea. How is that an excusable exaggeration?"

"Indeed, how?" her mother hissed. "Those are treasonous words, Lucia, and they will have to be addressed."

"Yes, yes. I know." She looked at them through red-rimmed eyes and dabbed at her runny nose. "I will fully cooperate, Sadie. You have my word. But can we first combine our family's strengths and get Katheryn and her miscreants rounded up before something truly dreadful happens? I don't have a good grasp on what is going on. I only believe they're working with Éire House to attack us."

"They're planning a *coup*," Ellynn blurted.

"What makes you say that?" Her mother looked at her sharply, scooting her chair back like she might jump up and take down everyone singlehandedly.

Would she be in trouble for accidentally overhearing the plans discussed in the pantry earlier? Ellynn's mother had never asked Ellynn where she'd learned the news about Alex. Ellynn decided it would be best to follow her grandmother's example and lay it all out. Perhaps the many bits and parts each of them knew would paint a more complete picture of the threat. Maybe it would help protect Calamus.

And what about her trip into the dungeon and setting the hippogriff free for Magnum?

Yes. Yes she should explain *everything*. Ellynn knew that if she wanted to be truly clean, she needed to get all the dirt exposed.

CHAPTER SEVENTY-ONE

Alex

ROCK IN ONE HAND, TYMBRELLE IN the other, Alex jumped feet first into the lagoon. For a moment, they looked at one another suspended in the crystal blue depths, enjoying the gradual, sinking sensation. Their clothes fluttered in slow-motion contortions, and tiny bubbles burst from their mouths and noses, racing to the surface.

So far so good with Tymbrelle, too, Alex observed. No fluke. No scales.

They smiled at each other.

They clinked rocks in a gesture of "cheers."

They continued to hold hands and sink.

The lagoon was far deeper than Alex would have guessed. Tymbrelle's eyes flew open at something over his shoulder and he twisted around, alarmed. An orange and gracefully gelatinous creature floated toward them.

Leviathan!

This wasn't working out as Uncle Brock had predicted. Alex decided to swim back to the surface at warp speed. His lungs were starting to burn, and panic ebbed at his faith that this lagoon could somehow transport them to Calamus.

Alex pointed at the surface but was violently jerked backwards, stripped from Tymbrelle's hand. He was about to become octopus sushi.

Except Alex rushed right past the sea creature as if he was being sucked through a giant straw. Though his lungs no longer felt desperate for oxygen, his wingbuds suddenly blazed with pain. Alex somersaulted through the powerful current even as he writhed and struggled helplessly against it.

Screams tore from his throat and yet his lungs did not protest. Was he morphing into a Merman? Could that be the cause of his pain? No, he glimpsed his legs thrashing about and the pain remained concentrated in his back.

Why had Enoch's medicine stopped working so instantaneously? Not to mention so soon. If the water didn't kill him, the agony might.

His vision narrowed, and a distant part of his mind was thankful he had given Tymbrelle her own rock. Hopefully she would make it through alive and be able to warn Calamus.

CHAPTER SEVENTY-TWO

Sadie

SADIE HAD NEVER SEEN XANDER THIS angry. Though she knew it wasn't directed at her, Sadie flinched at his outbursts while she explained the revelations of her earlier conversation with Ellynn and Lucia.

Xander was livid, and rightly so. His kingdom was decomposing from the inside out and he hadn't smelled the rot. Sadie and Lucia—to her credit—had cornered Xander in his study and verbally vomited up the details.

Now, Commander Gage, General Merrik, and Tassitus had been summoned and Xander went through a brief version of events and set about cleaning up his kingdom. "Gage, you and Merrik are to find Katheryn and Gouldor and place them in immediate custody," Xander ordered. "Take a couple of extra men to make sure you have the unquestionable upper hand."

"Yes, Sire," Gage said. He and Merrik saluted and left.

Sadie could almost see Xander's brain shuffling through possible next steps. She skimmed her gaze to Lucia, who sat looking down at her hands. With her greasy hair, the dark circles under her eyes, and her disheveled wings, she almost looked pitiable. Except Sadie knew the woman had actively created problems for herself and others. Consequences were inevitable.

"Tassitus, I think it's time we had a little chat with the maid Raechel. And Avalen too, actually. Fetch them and bring them here. I don't imagine either of them will put up a fuss."

Tassitus wasn't a soldier, though he always carried a small dagger on his belt. Now he gave the sheathed weapon a pat and bowed to Xander. "Right away, Your Highness."

Once the door closed, Xander stormed over to Lucia. She gave him a startled look, as if she'd forgotten where she was and why she was there.

"And you!" Xander towered above her, pointing a finger in her face as if scolding a naughty child. "I am so disgusted with you I can't even see straight. My father would be devastated to know that you used him like this. That you used your station here and the people who trusted you for such selfish personal gain. I"—he broke off. His pointing finger curled inward and he made a fist. He punched the palm of his other hand. "You've dishonored our family and our country. No wonder your son is an absolute disaster!"

Lucia reached toward Xander. "But he—"

"Don't make excuses, Lucia. I heard enough of his lies and pretexts earlier today." Xander was a coil of energy. He stalked the room like a bird of prey with silvery wings billowing behind. "You two make a fine pair. When one of my men returns, he'll be taking you to the dungeon to join your son."

Lucia burst into tears at this, and Sadie handed her a handkerchief if only for the sake of something to do.

"And Ellynn!" Xander boomed. He grasped the back of his chair and slammed it into the floor, making both women jump. "That girl..." He shook his head. "You're going to have to keep a better eye on our daughter, Sadie."

Now his finger pointed at her.

"Me? This is somehow my fault?" Sadie knew this was his anger talking, but she couldn't help feeling defensive. "I've been a bit busy planning a funeral and a wedding with a host of guests coming in and out who have certain expectations of my time."

"That doesn't mean—"

The door flew open, cutting off whatever Xander was about to say.

Tassitus stood beside a blubbering Avalen. His grim face revealed more bad news.

"That was quick." Xander strangled the back of the chair like he was practicing for the real thing.

Tassitus stepped inside with the maid and closed the door. "Avalen said Gouldor asked for Raechel's help with something late this afternoon. No one has seen her since. Raechel never came to dinner and Avalen fears the worst. She was on her way here to report her missing."

Avalen held a hanky to her nose and nodded. "Oh, I do fear the worst. I do. It's not like her to miss her chores and her victuals. Something isn't right. 'Tain't right at all."

Xander didn't look convinced since Avalen sobbed with

little provocation. "Fine. Tassitus can grab a couple of men and do a search. Any idea where Gouldor wanted her to accompany him? His laboratory perhaps?"

"He—he mentioned something about the dungeon, Your Highness."

CHAPTER SEVENTY-THREE

Alex

Someone slapped Alex's cheek. And then slapped the other one. Sensing a pattern, he waited for another slap, prepared to snatch the person's wrist. When nothing happened, he opened his eyes, curious. It wasn't as if the slaps hurt, but it was terribly rude.

"Oh, thank the Maker! Alex, c'mon, focus. Can you see me?"

Alex blinked at the indistinct figure above him. "Tym...brelle?" he wheezed.

"Yes, yes. C'mon now. We need to get you somewhere less visible. Up with you now. That's right, lean on my shoulders."

Alex could only sort of help her help him. He wasn't sure he was helping at all, actually, as he shambled along beside her, wondering why he was dripping wet.

Tymbrelle propped him against a wall, and he coughed spastically until he spewed water from his mouth and nose. His chest hurt from the effort, although he felt a little better. He raked his sleeve across his face and remembered the girl of his dreams was sitting nearby.

He lolled his head to look at her. "I'm hard to resist right now, aren't I?"

Her eyes twinkled with amusement, but she shook her head. "I don't think we've got time to flirt, mister."

"Oh." His brain was still foggy—waterlogged, he guessed—so he would take her word for it. "Where are we?"

"I was hoping you could tell me."

Alex made an effort to concentrate on more than her pretty face. They were *both* sopping wet. He looked down at his shirt, which clung to his narrow torso, his wet, clumpy feathers, and his black trousers with one pant leg twisted and the other shoved up to his knee. Why was he wearing only one boot?

A shot of adrenaline tingled through his senses. Those were *his* clumpy feathers! Alex blinked and stared at the silvery wings framing his body.

"I...have wings." He spoke it at the same time he understood it. "Tymbrelle, do you see this? I have *wings.*"

He made to stand but couldn't rise past trembling hands and knees, his wings draped limply on either side. Exhaustion claimed him as he dropped onto his belly.

Tymbrelle had been watching with an amused expression. Almost as if she expected him to face plant.

"Take it easy, Landlubber." Though her voice revealed her own fatigue, she scooted across the scrubby grass and lay on her side facing him, their feet pointing in opposite directions. "I don't think you're particularly clearheaded, and we both need to recover from what just happened. You especially. Congratulations on your new wings, by the way." She reached a hand to his downy feathers and stroked them, using her fingers like a comb to straighten them out. "They're lovely."

Fractured images began to coalesce, and he remembered the lagoon, the rock, the jump...and oh, wow, the pain. The searing, sizzling, off the scale and out of the galaxy pain. He was astonished that he had survived.

"Roots and fruits. I remember everything," he said quietly, enjoying watching her fascination with his silken plumage. "No wonder I can't move. I've gone through a two-week process in the course of, well, however long it took for us to travel through that aqua-portal. I've watched others endure this agony. I'm not sure if I got it over with, or if I got two weeks worth of pain all at once."

"I'm so sorry." She grasped his hand and they both lay looking at each other without speaking for a moment.

"You sound as tired as me. You okay?"

She gave him a lazy grin. "I'm great, considering I had to pull your huge, limp body from the portal while you were unconscious. Also fun trying to flip you over to expel the water. It wore me out."

"Wow. Thank you. That couldn't have been easy." He quirked his eyebrow. "You know, you could've used your water wielding skills to make the water lift me out or something."

Her eyes grew round. "Oh, goodness! I can't believe I didn't think of that." She sat up on her elbow, her brows in a deep V. "I...I don't know whether I still have any skill. I haven't had a reason to try it since I got my legs back. Guess we'll see.

What matters at the moment is getting you back on your two big feet. We need to figure out where the portal brought us and what we do next. I'm guessing you won't be flying anytime soon."

"Normally, the wings have to dry out for a few hours." He chuckled. "Then I should be good for some practice flights. Short ones." He glanced over his shoulder, awestruck that these silvery wings—a perfect match to his father's—belonged to *him*. "It's a skill that comes with practice and strengthening particular muscles."

"It would be helpful to know where we've landed. Looks like a pasture. I think this is a shed for maybe tools or feed." She gestured at the weathered brown building where she had propped him up.

"How far are we from the portal?"

"It's on the other side of the shed. Or it was, anyway. As soon as I dragged you out, it disappeared."

Alex considered this. "Whoa. Weird."

"Right? There's a town in the distance and I didn't want anyone to spot us. So that's why I made you move."

"Good plan." Alex was feeling stronger by the minute and raised himself onto his elbows for a better view of the landscape. The shed took up a large swath of the scenery to one side while the other revealed distant foothills with larger, purplish mountains in the distance. "We're in Calamus."

"How can you be certain?"

"Those hills and the mountains behind them"—he pointed—"I can see them from my bedroom. That one peak that curves over on top, I recognize that. Liberty Peak."

"Perfect. That makes it easy. Guess those rocks, or the lagoon, maybe…they knew where to send us."

He leaned his cheek on his fist. "I'm so glad you had your own rock. Who knows what would've happened."

Tymbrelle shuddered. "Not something I want to consider." She stiffened and squinted at the mountains.

"What is it?" Alex followed her line of sight and gasped. "Get down! Get down!" He pulled Tymbrelle's sleeve and she flattened. A steady stream of Dregs were emerging from the base of the foothills and weaving just inside the tree line as they headed toward Calamus. Alex caught the glint of weapons now and again.

Tymbrelle shimmied her body around to face the same

direction as Alex. "*What* is going on?" she hissed. "Are those Dregs?"

"Yep. Looks like we arrived just in time for an invasion. I can't believe Magnum is literally making a move on my father's kingdom." Though Alex felt weak and spent, he couldn't waste another minute on recovering. They had returned to Calamus for a reason.

Alex grabbed Tymbrelle's hand and pressed his lips against her knuckles. "I've never been a praying person, Tymbrelle. I've largely ignored God and hoped He would do the same. Well, I cannot gamble my father's kingdom—*my* kingdom—on some impulsive, selfish decision. We've been brought here for a reason. Let's find out what it is."

CHAPTER SEVENTY-FOUR

Sadie

SADIE FELT LIKE A SALMON SWIMMING upstream as she dodged the current of soldiers and servants who heard the horn blast signifying an impending attack. The men and women of the guard hurried through the corridors even as they strapped armor and swords in place. They were headed to their stations, familiar with the procedure after many drills.

Of course, the royal family had procedures to follow as well, but Sadie wouldn't do anything until she located her daughter. Ellynn had gone to her room after supper, and Sadie desperately hoped that's where she'd find her.

"Queen Sadie! Wait," someone called amidst the hubbub. Begrudgingly, Sadie stopped and looked for the source of the sound.

Hartwell jogged up behind her, his bronze skin gleaming from the exertion. "Your Highness, Commander Gage said I'm to stay with you." The deep baritone of his voice always managed to surprise her.

"Aren't you needed out there?" Sadie made a vague motion. She didn't have time for this.

"My orders are to stay with you, ma'am."

"Fine." It was easier to play along than argue. "I'm looking for Princess Ellynn."

He grunted his assent, easily keeping up. The two fought their way through the controlled chaos and found themselves in the relative quiet of the family wing.

"I forget how many people it takes to run this place," Sadie commented, a bit bewildered.

"Indeed."

Sadie knew that Hartwell was a man of few words who would probably agree with anything for the sake of simplicity. They passed Lucia's room, where a female guard stood by, looking hacked about missing all the action. Xander had ordered Lucia and Avalen to be locked in Lucia's quarters until he had time to deal with them. Sort of a house arrest since so much had unfolded so quickly.

Arriving at Ellynn's door, Sadie burst in without knocking. "Ellynn! Ellynn! Are you in here?" Though the girl's room wasn't overly large and didn't have a parlor, Sadie well knew that Ellynn could be hiding in plain sight or inside some secret passage—though she better not be doing that after their candid chat today.

Still, Sadie called out and opened the wardrobe and looked under the bed. Hartwell eyed her with an expression that said it was obvious the girl wasn't here.

"I'm sorry. She often hides," Sadie explained.

He nodded.

The bedroom door creaked open and Sadie turned, relieved, but it wasn't Ellynn.

Trinny came scuttling in, wide skirt and apron swishing around her short legs, mopping her face with a handkerchief. "Ellynn! El—oh my!" She saw the two visitors. "Pardon me, Your Grace." She curtsied.

"I take it you don't know where Ellynn is either. We must find her. She's too curious for her own good. I heard there are hundreds of troops surrounding us."

"Good heavens." Trinny waved the handkerchief at her face. "It's awful. Absolutely awful and unprovoked."

"Any idea where I should look? Favorite hideaways and the like?"

Trinny narrowed her eyes. "That sneaky little lady could be anywhere. She knows the innards of this castle better than most of us know the populated parts. I've no idea." The Dwarf threw her hands up.

Sadie tapped a fingernail against her teeth, thinking. "Yes, except I don't think she'd dare go back into the passageways because Xander gave her quite the scathing lecture about her behavior. Regardless, she's the most curious kid I know. If there's a way to be in the middle of something, she'll find it." Sadie couldn't keep a tear from barreling down her cheek. "Sorry. I'm finding it hard to process the amount of heavy news that has hit us today."

"Of course, m'lady. I've shed me own tears—some of them happy. Good news about Master Alexander."

"Yes," Sadie agreed. She sensed Hartwell's impatience

and placed a reassuring hand on Trinny's shoulder. "Well, I must keep searching. Please do the same."

They parted and Sadie made a quick stop to check Xander's and her room. Sometimes when Ellynn wanted to talk, she would wait for them in there.

Sadie went through the same rigamarole in her quarters, calling Ellynn and poking about. Though she didn't believe her daughter capable of hiding and ignoring her, Sadie had heard tales of kids hiding and then falling asleep, so she wanted to be thorough. Hartwell only anchored the center of the room with his bulk, hand on his sword hilt, eyes scanning as if he expected a mob of miscreants to materialize and attack.

"Quick check out here." Sadie crossed to the double doors, which opened onto the large balcony.

Hartwell stepped into her path. "Sorry, Your Majesty. It's too exposed. Allow me."

Sadie didn't protest because it never did much good when the guards had their orders.

He opened the doors and followed the curve of the balcony, which stretched the length of the the turreted wall. Sadie stepped out anyway, keeping close to the door, eager to know what was happening. Distant shouts and another long blast on the horn made her shiver.

"M'lady, please..." Hartwell grimaced at Sadie's defiance.

Sadie surprised them both by squatting down and doing a military crawl on her belly to the edge of the balcony, where she peeked between the stone balusters.

"You *can't* do that, Queen Sadie."

"Hartwell, you don't sound very tough when you whine. I'm safe as can be. No one can see me, even if they were looking for me. I want to know what's going on. This is beyond the pale."

"The pale what?"

"Never mind." Sadie focused on the numerous, large figures that stretched in a roughly circular formation around the palace's perimeter. Why hadn't King Aviel put in that moat?

Even from here she could tell they were a hodgepodge army, though that didn't make them any less of a threat. Trolls and Ogres—and were those *Nephilim*?—were incredibly powerful creatures. What could they want? What was their objective? Well, they certainly had the element of surprise on their side. Apparently Calamus needed to step up its military intelligence.

Closer to the castle, Sadie watched Xander's troops taking positions behind fences or walls, crouching down, bolting quickly, sending hand signals. A look at the skydome told her that dusktime was descending. She wondered if the dimness would be an advantage or a hinderance, as military strategy had never been her particular interest.

Sadie had seen enough for now. It appeared a standoff was the inevitable first step as both sides flexed their muscles. Ellynn's safety was her priority.

Right as Sadie made to scoot away, a handful of horses and riders exploded from the end doorway of the horse stable sporting full battle regalia. The spirited, statuesque drafts paraded their riders between the buffer zone of Calamus and the front line of Dregs.

King Odhran led the charge, followed by Izaiah and his men. They wheeled between two surly Sasquatch soldiers and joined their ranks. The emerald and black flag of Éire House followed, held aloft by none other than Magnum who glowered down at the troops of Calamus from the back of a hippogriff.

CHAPTER SEVENTY-FIVE

Alex

ALEX AND TYMBRELLE CROUCHED BEHIND AN angular boulder, one of several colossal chunks of granite that flecked the land beyond Alex's basketball court. Behind them stretched the length of wall that encircled the palace property along the back boundary, broken only by one lone gate.

The two had trailed the Dregs from the pasture to the rear of the palace. They watched hundreds of troops filter through the gate, which someone had *conveniently* left unguarded and unlocked.

In Alex's compromised—though steadily improving—condition, he'd taken his time closing in. As they sidled past the shed to where the water-portal had been, Alex was pleased to find his missing boot. Properly shod, he and Tymbrelle scrambled to the outside of the stone wall. They slowly migrated its length to the unsupervised gate and dashed over to the boulder.

The exertion revealed that Tymbrelle was back to her spunky self, while Alex still had some fine-tuning ahead. His balance was off, for one. The newly sprouted feathered appendages were substantial and challenged his balance. His scapula ached and his skin felt raw. What he wouldn't give for more of Enoch's salve.

Thankfully, the condition of his wings, much like his metamorphosis, was progressing quickly. His feathers were almost dry and they'd settled into their smooth and silky pattern of longer primary and secondary feathers with their shorter coverts. Despite the lingering pain, Alex had managed to flap and flutter his prodigious plumage several times, though any test flights would need to wait. He marveled that he, Brady Alexander—the flightless royal—was now the proud owner of this stunning set of pinions. Of course, he'd kept these observations to himself while they percolated in the back of his mind.

"Nothing happening over here. You see anything?" Tymbrelle asked from her side of the boulder.

They were on opposite ends of the hunk of rock, trying to gauge what was happening near the palace. Before Alex could answer, the sonorous sound of horns called Calamus to battle. His scalp tingled and his stomach dropped in response. Though he'd experienced his share of drills in the past, the call to arms aroused a grave urgency.

"What does that signify?" Tymbrelle asked, appearing beside him.

"A single, long blast like that means we must prepare to defend Calamus," Alex said, hoping he sounded more fearless than he felt. "Looks like the Dregs have spread out, attempting to encircle the palace—this side of it, anyway. I don't believe there are enough troops to completely surround it."

"Unless more invaded from the other side."

Alex pulled back and looked at Tymbrelle. "True. I hadn't thought of that."

"So...what now?" She touched his arm. "How are you feeling? You sound more energetic and look like you're moving easier by the minute."

He crinkled his eyes at her appreciatively. "I am. It's as if the warp speed transformation caused by the water has lingered and given me warp speed recovery, thank the Maker." He gave his wings a flutter and grimaced. "*Yikes.* That still smarts. Won't attempt an airstrike anytime soon." He winked at her. "Best bet is to see if we can sneak up from behind. We'll have to make it up as we go. There's a well and horse troughs closer to the palace that you might be able to utilize. Assuming you're still skilled."

"Let's hope. I feel pretty confident that if I had that ability the last time I had legs, there's no reason why I shouldn't have it this time around."

On impulse, he leaned in and gave her a short, sweet kiss. "I don't know what's about to happen, Tymbrelle, but I'd hate to miss an opportunity to have kissed you one more time."

And with that, he grabbed her hand and crept to the edge of the rock, preparing to sprint.

CHAPTER SEVENTY-SIX

Sadie

"PACIFIC HOUSE!" KING ODHRAN CALLED TO Calamus. "You are surrounded and ill prepared to mount a defense. Submit to Éire House and there will be no unnecessary shedding of blood." Outfitted with shield and helmet and the enormous spear with which he had paraded into Calamus less than a week earlier, the king sat erect and imposing. Even his horse sported elaborate, protective barding.

King Odhran's fear factor was somewhat diminished beside the towering and powerful hippogriff with Magnum seated at her helm. The intense bird-of-prey stare from the eagle was matched only by the imperious sneer of its rider.

Sadie wondered who helped Magnum escape from the dungeon.

As if to keep the attention on himself, King Odhran lifted his spear overhead. "Your kingdom is in disarray, cousin Xander. Your father's correspondence disclosed his hesitancy to place the kingdom in your hands."

Sadie stifled a gasp behind her hand. What a liar. No one in Calamus would believe such a fabrication. Surely it *was* a fabrication...

Despite her shock, Sadie's mom-radar reminded her that Ellynn was still unaccounted for. Yet, something demanded she stay and bear witness to what was unfolding. These ungrateful people had been guests of Pacific House. How had they arranged this dramatic exhibition of evil from across the globe? Obviously, they'd arrived with an ambitious agenda and extravagant confidence in their insiders' help. Confidence that was not misplaced, it would seem.

"Odhran, you are a snake!" Xander called from somewhere out of Sadie's line of sight. "And Magnum, you are a disgrace to our father. Neither of you are worthy to bear the name of Tuatha Dé."

"It's time for new leadership, big brother," shouted Magnum. "King Odhran is a visionary who has outgrown the borders of Moored-below. The Tethered World will benefit from his strength and acumen." At this, Magnum's mythological mount strutted forward a few paces. "And I will be given my rightful due as king of Astra, realm of those disillusioned with the perpetually archaic ways of the Tethered World and beyond. King Odhran has granted me land and title as his ally."

At this pronouncement, the Dregs behind Magnum cheered, while the army of Calamus exclaimed their collective disapproval.

Sadie was flabbergasted. She knew Magnum had few redeeming qualities, but she would never have guessed he'd declare himself an enemy to his father. Behind her, continuing his post as her personal guard, Hartwell swore under his breath. Sadie heard him kick the wall.

The protestations and cheers died down as Queen Clodagh rode out of the open end of the barn on the back of her enormous draft.

She wasn't riding solo.

Gasps of incredulity rippled through the troops of Calamus at the sight of Queen Clodagh holding a dagger to Princess Ellynn's throat.

CHAPTER SEVENTY-SEVEN

Alex

ALEX AND TYMBRELLE CROUCHED AGAINST THE stable wall farthest from the evolving drama, thankful for the adjacent haystack that also hid them from view of the cobbled road. He was thoroughly undone. But his trembling limbs and glowing birthmark were not due to the start-and-stop sprint across the pasture.

No. Alex's condition was fueled by rage and indignation at the blasphemous pronouncements broadcast by the likes of King Odhran and Magnum. How did these two traitors manage to coordinate this coup?

What was his father waiting for? They must be taken out and their vile plans demolished. Diplomacy had surely left the premises.

At the sound of Odhran's voice, Tymbrelle's eyes had smoldered to life. Alex could tell she was itching to be Odhran's secret weapon all right—one who would backfire and destroy Éire House.

Alex gave his wings another fluttery evaluation. The movement only registered as a dull ache and managed to produce a respectable breeze. "We need to find a better position. I want to see what's going on in case there's an opportunity to distract Magnum and your dear old dad. It might give my father and his men a chance to get the upper hand."

"You can't take them on by yourself. Don't be ridiculous! Your existence is a threat to both of their thrones. They would as soon kill you as look at you." Tymbrelle grabbed his arm for emphasis.

Alex shook his head, aware of the heat radiating from his birthmark. "The Maker didn't send me back here to watch my country be destroyed. Watching from the sidelines is not an option."

Exclamations of alarm suddenly erupted from the frontlines, and Alex knew he had to act.

Tymbrelle worried her lip but gave a nod. "All right. Yes. We've got work to do."

He nodded at the same time a woman's throaty voice called out in a heavy Irish brogue.

"That would be dear old mum," Tymbrelle said, narrowing her eyes. "Did you catch what she said?"

Alex shook his head. Maybe it was the accent. "Are you okay with this, Tymbrelle? These are the parents you've had most of your life."

The woman said something else, which was drowned by another wave of protest from Calamus.

"I'm fine. They are *not* my parents." She jerked her chin toward the pasture. "I'm going to the horse trough that we ran past." She waggled her fingers beside her face. "Time for a little water wielding."

Together they peeked out from the back corner of the stable—the stable where their two worlds had literally collided, Alex realized. That seemed like ages ago.

An Ogre stood beside the open barn door with his back turned, obviously watching the drama unfold. Tymbrelle bolted for the large metal trough at the fence line between paddock and pasture.

Then, Alex stiffened at the sound of his sister's name.

"…we can start with her if you really want to find out how serious we are about this," King Odhran was saying. "Or we can do this peaceably. Surely, cousin Xander…your life in exchange for your daughter's life is an easy decision."

No!

Alex had barely formed the thought that he needed to get on the roof of the stable than his wings had carried him up there in a wobbly liftoff. For a moment, he was too shocked to register anything except amazement. It hadn't been very smooth or steady, but it *had* been successful. Not bad for his first flight.

He crouched low and then shimmied on his belly to the ridge of the roof, where he peered over to assess the state of affairs below. It wasn't pretty.

Straight ahead, the throng of Dregs stretched around the perimeter of the palace, agitated and ready for a fight. Alex would not have guessed there had been this many miscreants tunneled into the mountains where he and his friends had been imprisoned. King Odhran—or so he guessed the heavily mustached man to be—jabbed a lengthy spear above his head as his enormous steed stamped and jostled beneath the king's bulk.

Alex glanced in the direction of the horse trough below and to his right and watched as Tymbrelle silently climbed into its murky depths. She crouched so that the only thing visible was her shock of platinum hair as she peeked over its rim.

His father's troops were gathered on Alex's left, awkwardly crowded onto steps and under the eaves and portico, extending onto the main thoroughfare, which curved around this side of the palace. They maintained only a small buffer zone with the enemy. Calamus had been taken by surprise and was completely on the defensive.

"Ellynn! Be brave, sweetheart. I won't let them hurt you."

That was the devastated voice of King Xander. Alex couldn't see his father from his vantage point, but his heart hurt for him. Nor could he see his sister or the others making their ridiculous demands, but the sound of sobbing told Alex that Ellynn must be right below the roofline on the other side.

He was about to risk climbing over the peak when an enormous eagle's head strutted into Alex's line of sight. It took a moment for him to work out that Magnum sat on its back and the two were parading along the column of Dregs.

"I only want what's naturally in my blood—I want a kingdom," Magnum said, and spread his arms wide. "Trust me, big brother...I've no desire to rule the status quo here at home. These motley creatures are loads more fun than the stuffy masses populating this place." An odd assortment of feral jeers and grunts filtered through the ranks.

King Xander came into view, sitting regally atop Ansyn. Yes! The horses had found their way back. Or at least Ansyn had. The war horse pranced restlessly, ready for his master's slightest command.

"Enough discussion!" Odhran thundered. "Will you spare your daughter and countless others, Xander of Calamus? Bow your knee, cousin, or prepare to watch the blood flow, beginning with your own flesh and blood."

His father was made of steel and never backed down from a bully, but this was the first bully to threaten Ellynn's life. Alex could only imagine the internal battle raging inside their dad. Would he choose the country he was sworn to protect until death, or the daughter he would die for? It was a choice his father shouldn't have to make alone.

Calamus was Alex's country too—one he was destined to protect and rule, in the footsteps of his father and grandfather. Alex may have been unable to protect his twin brother Benjamin, his Uncle Barron, or even Tymbrelle when they first met, but he could protect his sister now. Brady Larcen's heroic blood flowed in his veins, did it not?

For the first time in his life, Brady Alexander *wanted* to be like his namesake.

Another scream from his sister and a distant cry of "No!" galvanized Alex's thoughts into action.

That distant cry came from his mother.

Leaping to his feet with a guttural yell, Alex planted himself on the crest of the roof with his birthmark blazing and his silvery wings unfurled.

CHAPTER SEVENTY-EIGHT

Ellynn

QUEEN CLODAGH HAD ONE HERCULEAN ARM beneath Ellynn's chin, dagger held high in her other hand to underscore her nefarious intention. Ellynn writhed and tried to bite her captor when an unidentifiable roar collided with the din and chaos. Blurred by tears and choking on mucus, Ellynn was unsure of what was happening but sensed everyone's attention shift.

She couldn't turn her head to see what or who made the sound. From the height of Clodagh's horse, she perceived mixed reactions. Fear? Incredulity? One or two soldiers staggered backwards.

Nearby, Magnum made a strangled sound of surprise and cried out, "Impossible!"

Several of the Calamus troops unfurled their wings, ready to leap at the source of the sound. A flash of metal suddenly collided with the queen's dagger and cast it away—taking Clodagh's entire fist with it.

Hot blood splattered Ellynn's face as Clodagh screeched loudly in her ear. The horse spooked and reared, throwing Ellynn onto the cushioned landing pad of Clodagh's bosomy body.

Ellynn rolled off, gasping, trying to parse out what was happening. The queen lay there groaning like a farm animal giving birth, the wind knocked from her lungs. She clenched her bleeding stump with her other hand, everything slick with blood.

Ellynn recoiled and managed to stand. She needed to flee, but her trembling legs were uncooperative. Then someone's strong, protective arms encircled her waist and she was airborne. Despite her panic-stricken defiance, Ellynn's rescuer managed to deposit her onto her parent's balcony, where she was instantly smothered by her mother's welcoming arms.

"Oh, my precious girl!" Mom crushed Ellynn in an embrace, kissing her cheek, her ear, and her hair between tearful words of comfort. "Oh, baby. It's okay. You're okay, you're safe."

The rush of relief Ellynn felt came in a flood of wrenching sobs and quivering legs that could no longer hold her up.

CHAPTER SEVENTY-NINE

Alex

ALEX HAD LEAPT FROM THE ROOFTOP, relishing the recognition he saw flash across Magnum's face. Clodagh's sword was strapped to her back, one arm busy choking Ellynn, the other threatening her with a dagger. In a surprisingly well-aimed dive—his first ever—Alex swiped the sword from its sheath between her wings and parried it against her dagger, inadvertently flinging hand and dagger to the ground.

Ellynn and the queen tumbled from the frightened horse and he prayed he'd done enough to give his sister a chance to escape.

Alex had the sense that neither side knew who he was, what with his brightly glowing facial anomaly and his unsteady wings. Of course, Magnum had a front row seat and wasted no time charging at Alex from the back of his freakish bird. "Look at you, bratty Brady! Congrats on the wings, though I'm dying to know what kind of magic you're into to conjure them up so suddenly."

"*Dying* is right, traitor." Alex flew at his uncle, guided by Clodagh's bloody sword.

But Magnum didn't draw his weapon. Rather, he hoisted his hands overhead and said, "Take it easy. It's not what it looks like."

Alex scoffed, aware that Ellynn had been scooped up and out of harm's way by one of his father's men. *Yes!*

On the ground and in the air, skirmishes erupted. An emboldened Calamus army pressed their advantage with Clodagh's defeat.

"Believe it or not, I'm on your side, Alex."

Did his uncle notice how lies poured from his mouth as effortlessly as breathing? The man still had his arms raised, gaze latched onto Alex, who hovered just beyond the sharply curved beak of the hippogriff now eyeing him hungrily.

Magnum slowly lowered his right hand and gripped a polished curve of antler that hung from a strap around his neck. He gingerly set it to his lips while his left hand continued to stretch heavenward. It was such an odd sight. Time seemed to fracture into slow motion snatches as Alex understood this to be some sort of signal.

Alex veered into his uncle the same moment a burst of high-pitched harmonics buzzed through the antler horn as Magnum blew. Alex managed to smack the heavy hilt of Clodagh's sword into Magnum's mouth, catapulting the horn away as Magnum's teeth scraped the skin off Alex's knuckles. Magnum toppled from the hippogriff and onto the ground.

Still, his signal had been broadcast.

Though Alex was hyper-focused on subduing his lifelong tormentor, he sensed a change in atmosphere. He hesitated for a split second, questioning the sensation. No matter...he had to deal with Magnum first, aware that his newfound wings might give out soon.

His uncle pressed up to a sitting position, smiling at Alex from swollen and bloodied lips.

Smiling.

A ghastly smile at that—his top tooth dangling onto his crimson coated lower lip. Alex landed beside Magnum with a simultaneous kick to the chest to lay him out. He was convinced that Magnum was some sort of maniacal sociopath. The full-on kick left his uncle gasping for breath and clutching his chest.

Alex pressed the sword's tip against Magnum's exposed throat. Not to kill him—that would be too easy on the man—but to force his submission. Alex relieved his nemesis of sword and dagger. Magnum seemed in a world of pain and oblivious to being disarmed.

Was he faking injuries so Alex would back off, or had Alex kicked him harder than he realized? The reddish glow around Alex's eye reminded him of the crazy strength that came whenever his birthmark blazed. He guessed his uncle had gotten much more of a blow than Alex intended.

Now Magnum coughed and sputtered and swore, stealing fearful glances at Alex looming above. Still, Alex kept the sword trained on his uncle's fraught figure while surveying the restlessness he sensed around him. Something was happening that he didn't understand.

Magnum's Dregs were surrounding King Odhran and the handful of soldiers from Éire House. Not ten yards away sprawled a fierce-looking warrior with a tattooed star blackening one side of his eye. He was pinned to the ground by a mangy Troll with bald patches in his black fur. The Troll's leathery fingers were wrapped around the soldier's neck while the muscular soldier fought back, attempting to dig his fingers into the creature's eyes.

Alex's gaze swept across the melee, unable to see far in the dusktime light. The nearby, familiar faces from Calamus were a mixture of confusion and reticence, surely a reflection of his own. Best he could tell, the Dregs had turned on Éire House. They had effectively shifted their allegiance at the blast of Magnum's horn. Odhran's soldiers, maybe a dozen in all, were being pulled off their mounts. A few—including the king himself—were being pursued into the pastures and vineyards.

It's not what you think.

Believe it or not, I'm on your side.

Alex remembered Magnum's bizarre assertions. He looked down at his uncle, beaten and bloody. The man still lay obediently beneath the point of Alex's sword but looked somewhat recovered from the blow. Magnum blinked up with an odd combination of fear, admiration, and I-told-you-so. Regardless, Alex couldn't bring himself to trust the man.

"Wipe that look off your face," Alex ordered, bending down and clutching Magnum by his collar, hauling him upright.

The jolting movement caused his uncle to cry out in pain. "Please. It hurts! It hurts to breathe. I can't..." He took shallow breaths revealing how much the simple movement pained him.

"Deal with it," Alex said, twisting one of Magnum's arms behind his back, rumpling the man's feathers even more than they already were.

"*Ahhh.* Oh, please. That"—Magnum huffed—"that pulls my chest. I can't breathe."

"Don't currently care."

Alex scanned the unbelievable scene. The Dregs who weren't attacking the party from Éire House had surrendered. There was a long line of troops on their knees, weapons tossed to the ground, hands in the air.

"What's happening here, Magnum? Explain it," Alex ordered.

"It's like—like I said," Magnum wheezed out with effort. "I'm on y—your side."

Alex barked a sardonic laugh. "You've never been on my side, dear uncle."

Commotion in the vineyard caught Alex's attention. Despite the distance and lowlight, the emerald green regalia of Éire House was unmistakable, not to mention the pale-grey steed that Odhran rode.

A larger than average Ogre stood beside the mounted king, his immense hand on top of Odhran's head. The Ogre's silhouette led Alex to guess that this giant must be Babel, the outcast from Magnum's fortress. His heart leapt with hope that his friends had made it back safely. In fact, those surrounding Odhran could easily be construed to look like Finn, Josiah, and Dempsey.

The clustered group appeared to be waiting for something, holding the protesting king hostage. What Alex wouldn't give for a bird's-eye view.

That's when he realized he was—in a way—a bird. He could be there in seconds!

Magnum was obviously in a bad way, whimpering and breathing with quick, shallow breaths. Alex whistled at a couple of guards who were disarming a Stygian. Their formal uniforms revealed they worked inside the palace in some capacity. One of them looked up at the shrill sound, and Alex indicated that he wanted the soldier to take his uncle into custody.

As soon as Alex handed Magnum off, he turned and leapt into the air, unfurling his wings. As they undulated above him, Alex knew he would never take his newfound ability for granted. A blackbird all but dive-bombed him, then circled back, chattering obnoxiously. Except that was no bird—it was Parsifal the Dragon! Alex grinned and saluted, thrilled to see the faithful companion that had guided them on their journey.

Parsifal hovered close as Alex glided toward the group surrounding King Odhran. Gliding, he realized was a restful sensation for his tired flight muscles. Alex's friends were gathered at the horse trough, Tymbrelle standing knee-deep in the water, a bucket in hand.

King Odhran was blubbering, "I could not have loved you more if you were my own daughter, born of my flesh. Please! Let's be reasonable."

"You only loved what I could do for you," Tymbrelle called. "And now you're going to learn what that's like in a very personal way."

She dredged the bucket through the trough. As she

followed through with the motion, water careened from the container, splashing into Odhran's chest. Alex alighted on a limb of a nearby tree to watch the show.

The once-imposing king bawled like a baby, his eyes squeezed shut. The water froze his arms to his torso, essentially restraining him like a length of rope. Tymbrelle repeated the drenching several times, encasing Odhran in a thick layer of ice.

Everyone chortled with laughter. The gesture was surely meant to mock and humiliate the king because Alex knew that Tymbrelle could do a lot more damage if she wished. It was also good to know that she did, indeed, keep her special ability with water.

Tymbrelle climbed out of the trough and stood in front of the pitiable, shivering king on his horse. A puddle quickly formed around her dripping body. "I took it easy on you, *Da*, because, frankly, it'll be fun to watch you squirm in court. Let's hope King Xander is kinder to you than you had planned on being to him."

Odhran only glared from beneath his bushy, icicle-laden brows, teeth chattering.

Tymbrelle twisted her tangled blond hair, squeezing to rid it of excess water. "'*Go n-éirí an t-ádh leis na Gaeil leat*'. May the luck of the Irish be with you." She gave an exaggerated curtsy and added, "Your Royal Highness."

Though the ice was beginning to melt, the king made no attempt to free his arms or move. He was defeated—droopy mustache and all.

"Babel, would you please remove this man from his horse and escort him to King Xander?" Tymbrelle asked.

The humungous hunk of muscle grinned like a child given the entire cookie jar. "Babel es a gunna take cares of this meanie. Yous can counts on mees."

He wrapped a bulky arm around Odhran's middle and plucked him off his horse, cradling the squirming monarch beneath his arm like a sack of grain. "Cold!" Babel remarked, as his perspiring body melted the rest of the ice.

Alex slipped out of the tree, hovering under its leafy bough, ready to assist if Odhran caused any trouble.

Turning toward the palace, the Ogre caught sight of Alex and pulled up short. "Hey, fwend." He lifted his free hand and waved.

The others looked up at Alex, their faces bursting into smiles like celebratory fireworks.

CHAPTER EIGHTY

Sadie

ONCE ÉIRE HOUSE HAD BEEN TAKEN into custody, Sadie released Ellynn to the capable ministrations of Trinny—who was herself in an emotional tizzy from the events of the night. Sadie excused herself to hear Alex's and Tymbrelle's testimonies, though a more formal inquest would take place a few days hence. The two had been whisked aside to give statements to Xander and Gage.

After the pertinent facts were shared, Sadie itched to get back to Ellynn and reassure herself that her daughter was none the worse for wear. She located Ellynn—cleaned up and wearing her favorite topside T-shirt—gathered with Alex's friends in the family parlor. A pang of sadness clenched Sadie's heart as she realized Ellynn really hadn't any friends of her own. No wonder the girl had taken up stealth and secretive activities to pass the time.

Alex hadn't been far behind, anxious to reunite with his faithful friends. After a round of handshakes and back slapping, Sadie had pulled her beautiful boy—her *winged* beautiful boy—down on the couch beside her. With Ellynn safely flanking her other side, Sadie felt indescribably whole.

Big Babel sat in a corner, petting one of the barn cats that had been brought to the family quarters for a bit of critter control. Having visited to the Isle of Skellerwad, home of the Ogres, Sadie had seen hundreds of the behemoth-sized giants in her day—but Babel was the most massive Ogre she'd met.

Alex, Josiah, Finn, and Dempsey recounted their adventures—and Sadie tried to keep her opinions to herself. They took turns giving their perspectives and stitching together the events. Even the diminutive Dragon, whom Sadie learned was named Parsifal Plinderpuff, appeared to be chiming in, in some unintelligible way. Everyone was disappointed that Spock hadn't been able to come back to Calamus, especially since he could help interpret the creature's chatter.

Sadie's arms looped through the arms of her children as if she could keep them from venturing out into the cruel world ever again. Though she sensed their growing embarrassment at her demonstrative affection, she knew they wouldn't dare ask her to let them be. After all, she had watched them both practically *die* only hours before.

The Dwarves Joanie and Trinny wheeled two laden carts inside. One cart was heaped with food while the other held stacks of damp and dry towels, which Joanie distributed with orders to "wash and dry yer filthy hands before ya put them all over me food."

Trinny was the crowd favorite when she set platters of fruit and vegetables on the sideboard, along with a pyramid of Joanie's heavenly homemade biscuits. Pitchers of water and a kettle of tea rounded out the casual fare.

In the midst of frenetic food energy, Xander joined them, accompanied by Tymbrelle. The petite girl appeared comfortable beside the imposing king of Calamus. Sadie recognized Tymbrelle's topside T-shirt and jeans as belonging to Sophie.

Alex was on his feet and threading his way to greet her with a hug.

A rather long hug, Sadie noted.

She shifted in her seat and caught Xander's eye. He quirked an eyebrow at his wife in a way that said, "Well, what did you expect?"

Finn and Josiah applauded, and Dempsey stuck two stubby fingers in his mouth and whistled. Babel's delayed clap was so loud it scared the cat away and made Alex and Tymbrelle jump apart before laughing nervously.

Tymbrelle's face was red as a radish as Alex took her hand and made a surprisingly formal introduction.

"Dad, Mom"—he looked at Ellynn and winked—"and brave little sister, I want you to meet Tymbrelle. She saved our sorry behinds several times after the guys and I met her." He cleared his throat. "Or, met *him*, I should say."

Everyone chuckled, and Tymbrelle's face flushed again.

Alex looked at her and his Adam's apple bobbed in a nervous swallow. "I want you guys to know that, crazy as it sounds, things are, well, *serious* between us. We aren't exactly making wedding plans—despite Grandmama Lucia's best efforts—but Tymbrelle has changed my life and, truly, made me a better person. I don't think the Maker deals in coincidences."

Sadie laughed and clapped her hands together. "Aunt Jules would be thrilled to hear you quoting her with such conviction."

Alex's face grew serious. "I hope so. She poured so much into me that I never, y'know, *got* until this past week. It's like I've learned all the lessons she tried to teach me at once."

Tears smarted Sadie's eyes as she fought the urge to jump up and scream hallelujah. She settled on a pleased and understanding smile, standing to wrap Alex and Tymbrelle in a grateful embrace.

CHAPTER EIGHTY-ONE

Ellynn

ELLYNN LEANED INTO HER FATHER'S PROTECTIVE arms. He had come round to where she sat as soon as her mother got up to hug Alex and Tymbrelle.

Would Tymbrelle be considered Alex's girlfriend? She mused over this strange development even as her dad enveloped her in his salty scent. The last time she was near her father, she thought one of the two of them was about to die.

Her father kissed her springy curls and she heard him sniff, pressing Ellynn to his chest. It made her snuggle into him so he would know that she was okay.

Her mom busied herself pouring drinks and encouraging everyone to grab a plate and put some food on it—after they washed their hands per Joanie's instructions. Joanie and Trinny were hovering nearby in case they were needed. Ellynn could tell they were intensely curious about everything that had happened.

Her dad pulled away and looked down at Ellynn. "Mind telling me how you ended up in Clodagh's clutches, young lady?"

Ellynn frowned. "You say that like it was my fault."

"No, dear. Though I am a bit concerned that you may have forgotten the drills we've rehearsed for emergency situations."

She slid an arm around his waist, knuckles brushing his warm, silky feathers. Her dad's heavy arm draped across her shoulders, which made her wingbuds complain a bit. A reminder that big changes were on her horizon, and she would have her own beautiful wings soon enough.

"It began when I went to check on Deborah."

Since everyone was busy eating, they naturally turned to listen to Ellynn's tale.

It would be best, she thought, to tell this once and get it over with. She cleared her throat and began again. "Like I said, I went to check on Deborah because I hadn't seen her all day. She wasn't in her room or the guest area, so I thought I'd try the kitchens. On my way there, the warning horns sounded. I knew Deborah wouldn't know what to do and figured I would grab her and bring her with me to our designated safe place."

"Ah, you didn't forget our drills. Good girl." Her father squeezed her shoulder.

"Of course not. It was really chaotic though and everyone was running about, so I took the lower passageways that connect to the back staircase, near the kitchen. That took me right by Gouldor's laboratory. The corridor was deserted, and I heard something as I passed the lab door. A muffled sort of scream. So I looked in to see what was happening."

"Of course you did." Her mother placed a hand to her forehead like she might faint.

Trinny hummed her agreement from where she stood near the door.

"I thought someone needed help. And I was right." Ellynn felt vindicated, though her father emitted a little groan. "Katheryn and Gouldor were inside. They were trying to hold Deborah down and force her to drink something. She had her mouth squeezed shut and was trying hard to turn her head away. Behind her, I saw a Gnome lying there, lifeless—or so it seemed. I shouted, hoping it might give Deborah a chance to escape. And it did!"

"Way to go, little sister," Alex cheered.

"Alex, don't encourage her, please." Mom gave Ellynn a reluctant grin.

Ellynn could feel her heart revving again as she relived what happened. "Deborah shot past me, out the door. I still held the door open and noticed that the key was sticking out of the lock. So I slammed the door shut and locked them inside."

Finn and Josiah clapped.

"Quick thinking, Ellynn," her father said. "*That* explains how they came to be locked in that room. We found them while doing a room-by-room search, and they've refused to talk to us so far."

Ellynn glowed from his praise, though the next part would be less impressive for sure. "Yes, thanks. I locked them in and turned to run. That's when I smacked right into Queen

Clodagh. She's so...so huge—and strong. I saw Deborah struggling in Izaiah's grasp. 'We don't need our fake princess after all, Izaiah,' that foul woman said. 'We've got the real princess of Calamus. The Maker must be smiling down upon our plans.' Yeah, can you believe she said that?" Ellynn looked around questioningly but didn't wait for an answer. "I'm kicking and telling her she's definitely listening to the devil if she thinks what she's doing is a good idea."

Her audience broke into laughter and spontaneous applause.

Ellynn stood, absorbed in the retelling. "Anyway, they start carrying us out one of the doors that the servants use, and I'm fighting and making it as difficult as possible. That queen is so freakishly big, and Deborah's not even trying, she's getting carried along like a limp fish. Maybe she thought they'd go easy if she didn't put up a fight." Ellynn covered her mouth and coughed.

"Slow down, honey," her mom said. "Here, have a drink."

She came around the table with a goblet of water, which Ellynn gulped down, refueling.

"I don't know where Izaiah took Deborah. The next thing I know, he's shoving me on top of Clodagh's big, white horse and she's climbing up behind me and sticking a knife in my face."

Her dad stood and reached for her again. "We know what happened after that. No need to relive it." He hugged her. "Thank the Maker you're okay."

Ellynn reveled in his reassurance, then pulled away and looked at Alex. "I'll never forget how you saved me, Alex. One minute I'm staring down the blade of this dagger and the next minute, *swoosh*. Blood is splattering. Fingers are flying. The blade has gone bye-bye, and I've been saved."

A stupefied silence followed, and Alex shot his mom an apologetic look.

"What?" Ellynn said, looking from her brother to her parents. "*That's* what happened. It's kinda creepy but, well, this was life or death. What are a few fingers or whatever when it could've been Daddy or me bleeding out, costing us the entire kingdom?"

CHAPTER EIGHTY-TWO

Alex
One month later

THE FESTIVITIES WERE IN FULL SWING by the time Alex joined the party in the courtyard. His father's coronation had been long and formal and stuffy, but at least it had finally taken place. After the ceremony, Alex and Ellynn were conscripted to pose with their parents while the family portraitist worked out a preliminary sketch for a commissioned painting.

Alex then dashed to his room and changed from his stiff, uncomfortable suit into his best pair of supple, black calfskin trousers with a white linen shirt and black vest. Still dressy, but less fussy. Oh, and his favorite kicks, though he couldn't convince his mother that tennis shoes matched everything.

Though he'd never cared a lick for fashion, his new plumage required a wardrobe overhaul, and he rather enjoyed the makeover. All of his shirts and vests were either altered or replaced, and a custom-made cape accommodated his broadened back.

Now, he stood in the shadow of one of the columns flanking the stairway into the courtyard. He leaned against the stone pillar, hands in his pockets, relaxed and lighthearted...and aware of how novel *both* of those sensations were to him.

The finality of his father's coronation felt like a line of demarkation, as much for Alex's life as his father's. The turmoil and shadows he had always struggled against no longer defining him. Oh, he had his low moments, especially through the past month of political and familial turmoil.

But then he would remember the stardust.

He would remember the vision and the words of Enoch. Those were the truths he was choosing to believe. Then, of course, there was Tymbrelle. Her smile as bright and illuminating as any star.

Alex watched her dance with Uncle Brock, who had a flair for making stilted dancing look good. The two barely touched their hands together as they rocked from foot to foot to the tunes being pounded out by a band of Dwarves from Berganstroud. Every so often, Brock would spin Tymbrelle or pull her into a backwards dip, and Alex saw her laugh with delighted surprise.

His parents were out there too, looking younger and more in love than Alex remembered. He guessed they were reliving their courtship days—the ones Alex had sort of glossed over when he read his mother's books. In fact, his mother had mentioned that she hoped to recreate the feel and atmosphere of her brother Brock's coronation as High King of Vituvia. It had been an enchanting event, according to his mom.

Alex believed she had recaptured that magic. It was a night filled with the sparkle of luminescent Faeries, a banquet table heavily laden with food and flowers and candlelight, and the soulful sounds of good music with plenty of space to dance. Normally it was the Dwarves and Gnomes who knew how to throw a party.

Speaking of Gnomes, where was Spock? Poor guy had been stuck in Vituvia since he had tumbled through the water with Alex and Tymbrelle. During the coronation, Alex caught sight of his friend from his position on the dais. He was amused to find Spock looking a lot more *Lucas-like* than Spock in his conical metal hat.

Alex spotted him sitting on the lowest step of the fountain, a saucer of food precariously balanced on his micro-sized lap and his slouchy beanie back in place. Like Alex, the little guy had wasted no time changing out of his formalwear.

Alex headed over but was intercepted by Aunt Sophie.

"Hey now, who's this handsome young man with such stunning plumage?" She laughed and wrapped him in a hug. "How ya doing, kiddo? I heard that Enoch's herbal remedy didn't exactly do the trick."

He pulled a face. "Understatement of the universe. Still...I'm pretty pleased with the end result." Taking a step back, he turned and ruffled his feathers. "Whatcha think?"

"I think...I think I'm beyond proud of my amazing nephew."

Alex glanced back to find his aunt looking serious, drilling him with her eyes.

"Sadie told me everything that happened. Longest letter

I've ever received. It read like one of her books. Sounds like you were brilliant. You and your sister...just so brave! Our Vituvian troops missed all the fun because you took care of it yourself before they arrived."

Alex scuffed his tennis shoe against the pebbly ground. "I don't know about that, Aunt Sophie. This adventure didn't start off brave. Exactly the opposite. I'd planned on running all the way to Aunt Nic's house in Portland. Then things sort of took on a life of their own."

"Hey, now." She gave his arm a playful punch. "I'd probably have done the same if I suddenly learned I was expected to wed a total stranger—especially at your age. Don't be so hard on yourself. What counts is where you ended up. You've had to face things most people never have to deal with and, by God's grace, you learned how."

He felt his cheeks grow warm and decided to change the subject. "Hey, I'm really sorry about what happened to Prilla the Healer. She was always so helpful to us. Especially my mom."

"Thank you. It was such a shock. We're still mourning her loss. At least she didn't die in vain. So thankful she found the poison. Your dad, he's better, isn't he?"

Alex nodded, conflicted by the sadness of her loss and the relief of his father's healing. "Much better. We're really grateful. I only hope she didn't suffer. I swear, Katheryn and Gouldor must be the spawn of Satan. Poisoning King Aviel. Poisoning my father. Then forcing it on Prilla when she discovered it. She was so tiny, I'm sure it didn't take much."

"Maybe once those two are convicted, your father can recommend the death penalty—by poison. Literally give them a taste of their own medicine." She gave Alex a lopsided grin. "I don't see why Odhran and Clodagh couldn't benefit from the same. They were all working together, right? Punishment should fit the crime and all that."

"Yeah, maybe so. I think there've been a lot of suggestions by a lot of angry people. Death by candlestick for Katheryn since she took out Blaylock. Death by injection for the doc since that's how he killed Raechel, one of our maids. Plus, there's been, like, two dozen arrests. From guards to stablehands."

"Wow! And Lucia knew nothing about these things? I mean, Katheryn was her lady's maid."

Alex gave an uncertain shrug. "She claims limited

involvement—seems Katheryn had taken things to the extreme behind her back. Grandmama Lucia's focus was getting Éire House here. She used the wedding as a way to lure them to Calamus. She wanted her father's kingdom back and knew it would be easier if they were on her turf, so to speak, than for her to attempt something in their realm. Of course, she didn't know about Princess Larkin being adopted, which meant *I* drew the short straw to avoid marriage between close cousins."

Sophie's eyes slid to the dance floor, where Tymbrelle was now getting flung about by Finn in some sort of fast-paced polka. "Turns out your grandmother is a pretty good matchmaker, after all." She wiggled her eyebrows.

Alex flushed. "Yeah. I guess it accidentally worked in our favor."

"You guys are so cute together."

"Thanks, but cute's never really been my thing," he said with mock solemnity.

She laughed. "Too bad. Cuteness is all over you two. In fact, here comes your cute girlfriend now."

Tymbrelle was indeed weaving her way to where they stood, breathless and red-faced from all of her footwork. "Hey, you." She reached for his hand. "Hello, Lady Sophie. Lovely to see you again."

Sophie gave Tymbrelle a quick sideways embrace. "You too, dear. What a special day. And, please, call me Aunt Sophie. I have a feeling it'll be more appropriate." She winked at the girl's surprised expression. "Catch you lovebirds later. I'm starved."

"Uh, wow. She's subtle," Tymbrelle said, laughing.

"Right. So very subtle."

"Your mother sure knows how to throw a party." Tymbrelle turned to watch the dancers work through a series of steps belonging to an earlier time when everything was complicated and choreographed.

"Oh, yes. I'd say the staff has learned a lot from her and her topside ways. From pizza night to scavenger hunts, she's always made a big deal of every little event. She's the best."

"I love that your grandparents are out there dancing with everyone, too." Tymbrelle pointed at Grandmother Amy and Grandpa Liam, who were smiling at each other as they turned in promenade. "They've been nonstop."

"They've got a ton of energy. I guess my mom gets it from them. Mimi and Bops are all about having a good time."

"Mimi and Bops…I guess you'd have to be fun to live up to those quirky names—especially Bops.Wouldn't sound quite right to say, 'Bops is such a hard-nosed grouch.'"

Alex chuckled. "True. When I was a toddler, I apparently mispronounced 'Pops' as 'Bops' and it stuck. First grandkid gets to pick the name, y'know."

The band morphed into a new song, slow and melodic. Alex led Tymbrelle to the makeshift dance floor and wrapped his arms around her. "This is more my speed."

"I'll get you out here for some faster tunes before the night is over, Brady Alexander." Tymbrelle arched a brow, daring him to contradict. "You can get your uncle Brock to give you some pointers."

Alex held her right hand in his left and attempted to match the tempo of the song. "There's something very incompatible between my seven-foot frame and my skinny, sapling-sized body—they only coordinate when speeding down the basketball court."

Alex checked to see if Spock was still sitting on the fountain steps and was taken aback to find his friend wasn't alone. A pretty, strawberry blond Gnome sat beside him. She wore her hair in two plaits beneath a—wait—was that a baseball cap? Alex couldn't believe what he was seeing and made a note to get an introduction as soon as he finished dancing.

"*Ugh,*" Tymbrelle sounded disgusted.

Alex looked down at her questioningly. "What's wrong?"

"I didn't expect to see *him* here. Plus, I can-*not* believe Deborah is willing to entertain him as a potential significant other."

Alex followed Tymbrelle's line of sight to where Magnum and Deborah danced on the fringes of the crowd. "Yeah, not sure how I feel about that either. Magnum claims that his plan all along was to expose Odhran. Claims he played along to protect Calamus. Keeping our enemies close, as they say. Says if he hadn't cooperated with Odhran, the man would've eventually come for Calamus and that we would not have had the benefit of Magnum working on the inside to help. Of course, there's really no way to prove otherwise. Most of us believe that Magnum's actual plan was to go along with whomever had the upper hand—Odhran or my father. It was a win-win for him, and he could be hailed a hero either way."

"What a convenient scapegoat of a scheme." Tymbrelle

made an exaggerated eye roll. "He expects everyone to thank him, I suppose, and welcome him back home. He's got a lot of nerve."

"Well, it's not been a friendly welcome, if that's what he was hoping for. No one truly trusts him, but he's tolerated. After all, King Aviel's dying request was for my father to look after him and give him mercy. Thankfully, Magnum seems to be behaving himself—for now anyway." Alex studied his uncle and Deborah. "No doubt Deborah has told you that he hopes to get his little kingdom of Astra recognized. My dad is actually considering it. Says it's better to have a known neighbor than a secret society."

Tymbrelle stopped swaying and stared up at Alex. "No, she hasn't mentioned it, but things aren't the same between us. She's no longer my lady-in-waiting, and everyone knows she was pretending to be a princess. I can tell she feels awkward, which is one reason she's drawn to Magnum. They've probably played on each other's sympathies—two outsiders that can relate to each other."

Alex lifted his arm and twirled Tymbrelle beneath it before catching her up again. "And they both have Lucia in common, too, With grandmother under house arrest, Deborah's found a pretty good fit as her new lady-in-waiting. Especially since she and her 'Auntie Lucia' are practically family."

"Really, I'm happy that's worked out for them both."

The band finished their song and announced a short break. Alex pulled Tymbrelle across the dance floor to where Spock was perched at the fountain, still chatting up the gal in the ball cap.

"Dude and Mrs. Dude!" Spock shouted when he spotted them. He stood and offered Alex a fist bump, then turned to his sweet-faced companion. "Estrella, meet Prince Alexander and Tymbrelle. Guys, this is Estrella."

They exchanged polite hellos.

"I'm not *Mrs.* Dude, just to clarify," Tymbrelle remarked, flushing.

"Not yet anyway," Spock said, giving Estrella a little nudge.

Estrella waved him off. "Oh, Lucas, you shouldn't tease them about something as serious as marriage."

"Who's teasing? These two are made for each other."

"Glad you approve, despite your being an avowed

bachelor," Alex said, chuckling. "Should I, uh, call you Lucas now?"

Spock shook his head vehemently. "No way. Estrella here is the only one besides my mother who can call me that. We grew up together." He slid his arm around her shoulder. "She knew me before the nickname."

Alex offered her a little bow. "Well, you must be quite a special young lady to be given that privilege."

Estrella blushed and adjusted her baseball cap. "Maybe so."

"Special indeed." Tymbrelle gestured at the girl's hat. "I'm guessing *Lucas* shared some of his valuable topside accessories with you." Tymbrelle crouched down and squinted at the cursive insignia, which looked to be hand-embroidered. "What does it say?"

Alex kneeled beside Tymbrelle as Estrella giggled shyly behind her fingers.

Spock went uncharacteristically still and quiet.

Alex did a double take at the baseball cap. He and Tymbrelle looked at each other, wide-eyed.

"Fiancé?"

Acknowledgments

It's hard to wrap my mind around the fact that *The Tethered World*, *The Flaming Sword*, and *The Genesis Tree* have grown into six and seven-year-old book babies! They're little kids, at this point, riding bikes without training wheels and climbing trees. *Sniff* time flies, doesn't it?

Although *The Secret of Stardust* was a planned family member (I mean, a book doesn't show up fully formed on my Mac, unfortunately) it was also a baby whose beginnings were vague ("I want to write a story about Xander's and Sadie's kids"). When my publisher and editor extraordinaire, Miralee Ferrell, asked me to consider writing another story in the Tethered World Chronicles, I had the *barest* idea about where to begin (see quote above). Yeah, not a lot to work with there, right? And yet...so many possibilities! Thankfully, Miralee had faith in me. And patience (which I would put to the test).

Let me tell you a true story about the beginnings of this book you're holding.

About the same time that Miralee requested another TW novel, I was putting gas in my Jeep. There were some sketchy characters in the downtown area, so I sat inside the Jeep while it pumped. I noticed a cluster of people hanging out against the wall of the 7-Eleven, one of whom had a T-shirt that read: "Y'all Need Jesus" which made me chuckle.

Suddenly, that particular man was standing at my passenger door, leaning in toward the window that was rolled down a few inches. He was smiling and friendly and we exchanged a brief greeting. Then, he said something that I'll never forget.

"I bet you're a writer."

Say what? *I must have misheard.* Of the millions of possible jobs, there was no way he correctly guessed something that obscure. "What did you say?" I asked.

"I said, I bet you're a writer."

I blinked. "Actually, I am! What made you say that?" Heart pounding, I was shocked.

The man shrugged. "I don't know. I guess you just look like a writer." He smiled again. "So, you just keep writing, ya hear?"

I thanked the man—an angel?—and watched him walk

away. My mind was blown and my spirit rejoiced at this divine appointment. I believe the Lord sent this messenger my way because I was about to embark on a novel in the midst of many trials. My heavenly Father knew I would need this encouraging encounter to keep pressing through.

It wouldn't be long before my mother spent months in the hospital recovering from falls and a stroke (she is so strong!), and the Corona Virus would rear its ugly, all-encompassing head and drag the whole world into a fearful lockdown. My own health began to suffer, and other trials would join the fray.

But through it all, when I wanted to give up and my creativity felt as desolate as a Texas summer, I was able to return to that day in October when the Lord called me out as a "writer".

So, here's to the man in the Jesus T-shirt—angel or emissary—whoever you may be...this book owes much of its existence to your seemingly offhanded remark back in October of 2019.

I also want to thank my family for believing in me. My husband Billy—engineer, businessman, and far removed from fantasy books—supports my endeavors and tells others about these novels that he doesn't quite understand, just because he loves me. (I love you too!) My kids, and now my GRANDKIDS, are the juice that keeps me writing books. Thank you for your ongoing prayers and support. You bring me joy every day. Mom, thank you for being an example of faith and fight. I know the last few years have been a challenge, but your love of the Lord has only grown fiercer.

To my Ladies of Spec Fic Facebook family...I always appreciate your weekly check-ins. I'm not great at communicating some weeks, but knowing you guys are there, always ready to pray and encourage, has been fortifying.

Finally, thank you to my publishing house, Mountain Brook Fire. I'm so proud of the continued growth and professionalism you offer. Thank you for giving us small-time authors a voice, and for giving readers clean fiction that enriches their faith. You guys are an amazing team with a growing reputation. I especially wish to thank Jenny Mertes and Miralee Ferrell for spit-shining and cheering on *The Secret of Stardust*. Can you believe we finally got the word count to a manageable number?!

As always, it's incredibly humbling that something coherent and entertaining comes out of this crazy brain of mine...and gets turned into a real live book with pages and a beautiful cover and a plot. I feel like it's a miracle every time. Not even kidding. So, thank you Jesus, for giving me this opportunity to use my gifts and a platform to share my faith. I pray it brings you glory and makes you proud of your daughter.

Readers...what's the point of a book without *you*? Thank you for sharing your valuable time with my characters. And if you are one of my ARC readers—wow! You've invested in this story in a deeper way than ever, and I am grateful.

If you made it to this point and you actually *read* acknowledgments, you're hardcore and I have only one thing left to say..."Y'all need Jesus!"

More Ways to Connect with Heather and The Tethered World

Hey, it's Heather :-)

I *love* to hear from my readers.
Thoughts? Questions? Fandom?
Text me (yep, seriously!)
(503) 470-1639

Instagram:
@heatherllfitzgerald

Website/Newsletter:
HeatherLLFitzGerald.com

Facebook Group:
Heather L.L. FitzGerald~Author

Please consider leaving a review on Amazon, Goodreads,
Barnes & Noble, or ChristianBook.com.
Don't make me beg...
but, truly, reviews are an author's life blood.

Thanks! You're the best.